GEPT Classroom—Intermediate

全民英檢中級教室

閱讀&寫作
Reading & Writing

陳明華◎著

作者序

本書的目的是幫助學習者建構英文閱讀與寫作的基本技巧。除了做有效閱讀及基本寫作的培養外，也提供參加中級英檢考試的解題技巧。全書共有七大主題，如下所述，涵蓋了中級英檢考試的主要大題。

1. 詞彙和結構－字彙篇

探討如何從上下文意，猜測字詞。分為八個主要的線索(context clues)。包括：同義或重述、對比和反義、舉證、因果關係、上位詞、類比、陳述句的名詞化，及外在經驗等。有效率的讀者能善加利用這些線索猜測不認識的字，以回答字彙測驗題。另外，依據每一線索，皆附有相關的轉折語，讓讀者知道如何尋找上下文的線索。

2. 詞彙和結構－片語篇

除了要具備至少一定數量的單字外，學習者也要記上幾百個片語，尤其是片語動詞(phrasal verbs)。英文片語動詞是由動詞和介系詞或副詞組成的。這些介系詞或副詞大都有固定的意義，如能熟知這些介系詞或副詞的特殊意義，在閱讀或考試時，即使沒看過某個片語，根據它所接的介系詞或副詞，也能粗略猜出該片語的意思。在這方面，本書針對每個介系詞和副詞列出常用意思，並輔以常用片語動詞作例證。

3. 詞彙和結構－文法結構篇

熟知英文文法基本概念就能很快解構文意並寫出正確的英文。本書這部分講述了英文核心文法的主要重點，也把閱讀及考試經常出現的文法要點做條列式解說，包括：時式、助動詞、比較級、假設語氣、被動式、關係代名詞、動狀詞、主詞與動詞的一致。

4. **段落填空**

這部分也有人稱作「克漏字填空」，就是在文章中挖掉幾個字，然後要求學習者或考生還原該遺漏的字，在本書除了說明這種題型如何作答外，還將文章分為單一段落及包括兩段以上的行文，讓學習者練習如何應付這兩種形式的文章。

5. **閱讀理解**

在這一部分是闡述段落文章的基本組織：主題句及支持句的關係。並且將閱讀理解常考的題型歸為四類：主題、主旨、重要細節、推論及修辭結構，並詳述如何在文章中找主旨、主要細節，以及如何做合理的推論。

6. **中譯英**

分為兩小部分，首先概述英文的九個基本句型，再列舉各種不同功能的連接詞，以及所形成的複雜句或複合句，包括：類化及對比、因果關係時序、舉例、過程、增減等。

7. **英文作文**

分析段落組織，逐步教導學習者，從構思、寫主題句、增補細節、作結論到發展兩段落以上的文章。由認知到實作，完整的寫作訓練盡在其中。

以上每一主題包含二個 Units，所述的技巧說明皆有實作練習。每一主題的第一個 Unit 之後有「課後作業」，複習該單元內容；而第二個 Unit 後的「課後作業」則練習該主題下的兩個 Units 的全部內容。除此之外，最後還有一回完整的中級英檢模擬測驗。書末並附有解析及譯文以供參考。

使用方法

To Teachers

　　本書為一應付全民英檢測驗的密集課程，針對各種考試題型，介紹各種應考技巧與考試重點，共有十五單元共一學期使用。每一單元需一節授課時數。這只是原則性，老師可以依實際教學狀況調整。教學過程依據每一單元內容的次序實施。大約如下：

1. 老師重點提示：重點提示皆詳述在每一小節，老師可依此講述。

2. 學生實際演練：每一小節皆提供練習題。

3. 老師講解：老師針對每一題目做重點講解。

4. 學生做課後作業：每一單元後有一綜合練習以供複習演練。

5. 學生提問題討論：第二節課上新單元前先花十分鐘讓學生提課後練習不懂的問題。

To Students

　　本書為一應付全民英檢測驗的密集課程，針對各種考試題型，介紹各種應考技巧與考試重點。全書共有十五單元，學習者可按每一單元內容依序研習大約如下：

1. 細讀重點提示

2. 實際演練每一小節所提供的練習題

3. 核對答案

4. 做錯的題目再重新思考

5. 文義有疑惑者參考書末的譯文

全民英檢簡介

　　通過全民英語能力分級檢定測驗（General English Proficiency Test）中級測驗者，英語能力相當於高中畢業的程度，具有使用簡單英語進行日常生活溝通的能力。需要具備這項語言能力者為一般行政、業務、技術、銷售人員、接待人員和旅遊從業人員等。

一、全民英檢各級能力說明

級　數	綜合能力說明
初　級	具有基礎英語能力，能理解和使用淺易日常用語，英語能力相當於國中畢業者。
中　級	具有使用簡單英語進行日常生活溝通的能力，英語能力相當於高中畢業者。
中高級	英語能力逐漸成熟，應用領域擴大，雖有錯誤，但無礙溝通，英語能力相當於大學非英語主修系所畢業者。
高　級	英語流利順暢，僅有少許錯誤，應用能力擴及學術或專業領域，英語能力相當於國內大學英語主修系所或曾赴英語系國家大學或研究所進修並取得學位者。
優　級	英語能力接近受過高等教育之母語人士，各種場合均能使用適當策略作最有效的溝通。

二、全民英檢各級測驗項目說明

級　數	初　試	通過標準／滿分	複　試	通過標準／滿分
初　級	聽力測驗	80／120 分	口說能力測驗	80／100 分
	閱讀能力測驗	80／120 分		
	寫作能力測驗	70／120 分		
中　級	聽力測驗	80／120 分	寫作能力測驗	80／100 分
	閱讀能力測驗	80／120 分	口說能力測驗	80／100 分
中高級	聽力測驗	80／120 分	寫作能力測驗	80／100 分
	閱讀能力測驗	80／120 分	口說能力測驗	80／100 分

三、全民英檢中級測驗時間說明

測驗項目		題　型		題　數	時　間	說　明
初	聽力測驗	第一部分	看圖辨義	15 題	45 題	約 30 分鐘	在日常生活情境中，能聽懂一般的會話；能大致聽懂公共場所廣播、氣象報告及廣告等。在工作情境中，能聽懂簡易的產品介紹與操作說明。能大致聽懂外籍人士的談話及詢問。
		第二部分	問答	15 題			
		第三部分	簡短對話	15 題			
	閱讀能力測驗	第一部分	詞彙和結構	15 題	40 題	45 分鐘	在日常生活情境能閱讀短文、故事、私人信件、廣告、傳單、簡介及使用說明等。在工作情境中，能閱讀工作須知、公告、操作手冊、例行的文件、傳真、電報等。
		第二部分	段落填空	10 題			
試		第三部分	閱讀理解	15 題			
複	寫作能力測驗	第一部分	中譯英	1 段		40 分鐘	能寫簡單的書信、故事及心得等。對於熟悉且與個人經驗相關的主題，能以簡易的文字表達。
		第二部分	英文作文	1 篇			
	口說能力測驗	第一部分	朗讀短文	2~3 篇		約 15 分鐘	在日常生活情境中，能以簡易英語交談或描述一般事物，能介紹自己的生活作息、工作、家庭、經歷等，並可對一般話題陳述看法。在工作情境中，能進行簡單的詢答，並與外籍人士交談溝通。
		第二部分	回答問題	10 題			
試		第三部分	看圖敘述	1 圖			

測驗分數換算

　　全民英檢中級聽力及閱讀能力測驗成績採標準計分方式，60 分為平均數，滿分 120 分。初試各項成績均達 80 分以上者始可參加複試。如以傳統粗分計分概念來說，聽力測驗每題 2.67 分，閱讀測驗每題 3 分，各項得分為答對題數乘以每題分數。實際計分方式會視當次考生程度與試題難易作等化，因此每題分數及最高分與粗分計分方式可能會略有差異。寫作及口說能力測驗成績採整體式評分，使用級分制，分為 0-5 級分，再轉換成百分制（如附表）。

　　初試通過，複試未通過或未參加複試，必須於下兩次之中級複試擇一報名參加。初試成績自測驗日起一年內有效，兩次複試皆未通過或未報名者須重考。初、複試四項成績都達到 80 分才算通過測驗，可獲得合格證書。

一、口說能力測驗分數換算

級　數	分　數	說　　　　明
5	100	發音清晰、正確，語調正確、自然；對應內容切題，表達流暢；語法、字彙使用自如，雖仍偶有錯誤，但無礙溝通。
4	80	發音大致清晰、正確，語調大致正確、自然；對應內容切題；語法、字彙之使用雖有錯誤，但無礙溝通。
3	60	發音、語調時有錯誤，因而影響聽者對其語意的了解。已能掌握基本句型結構，語法仍有錯誤；且因字彙、片語有限，阻礙表達。
2	40	發音、語調錯誤均多，朗讀時常因缺乏辨識能力而略過不讀，因語法、字彙常有錯誤，而無法進行有效的溝通。
1	20	發音、語調錯誤多且嚴重，又因語法錯誤甚多，認識之單字片語有限，無法清楚表達，幾乎無溝通能力。
0	0	未答 / 等同未答

二、寫作能力測驗分數換算

第一部分：中譯英

級　數	分　數	說　明
5	40	內容能充分表達題意，結構及連貫性甚佳。用字遣詞、文法、拼字、標點及大小寫無誤。
4	32	內容適切表達題意，句子結構及連貫性大致良好。用字遣詞、文法、拼字、標點及大小寫偶有錯誤，但不妨礙題意的表達。
3	24	內容未能完全表達題意，句子結構鬆散，連貫性不足。用字遣詞及文法有誤，但不妨礙題意的表達，且拼字、標點及大小寫也有錯誤。
2	16	僅能局部表達原文題意，句子結構不良、有誤，且大多難以理解並缺乏連貫性。字彙有限，文法、拼字、標點及大小寫有許多錯誤。
1	8	內容無法表達題意，語句沒有結構概念及連貫性，無法理解。字彙極有限，文法、拼字、標點及大小寫之錯誤多且嚴重。
0	0	未答／等同未答

第二部分：英文作文

級　數	分　數	說　明
5	60	內容適切表達題目要求，組織甚佳，靈活運用字彙及句型，句型有變化，文法、拼字或標點符號無重大錯誤。
4	48	內容符合題目要求，組織大致良好，正確運用字彙及句型、文法、拼字或標點符號鮮有重大錯誤。
3	36	內容大致符合題目要求，但未完全達意，組織尚可，能夠運用的字彙有限，文法、拼字、標點符號有誤。
2	24	內容未能符合題目要求，大多難以理解，組織不良，能夠運用的字彙有限，文法、拼字、標點符號有許多錯誤。
1	12	內容未能符合題目要求，完全無法理解，沒有組織，能夠運用的字彙有限，文法、拼字、標點符號有過多錯誤。
0	0	未答／等同未答

目 錄

Part 1 閱讀能力測驗篇 Reading

Contents 目錄

Part

閱讀能力測驗篇 Reading

Unit **1**

詞彙和結構－字彙 (一)

　　考試要得心應手除了勤背單字、大量閱讀之外，還要多做題目磨練答題技巧。解答字彙題目的要訣是能從上下文的線索 (context clues) 猜出遺漏的地方要用什麼字。事實上這也是閱讀技巧之一。語言學習家告訴我們，聰明的讀者往往是最會猜的人。這些上下文線索包括：定義、重述、同義字、反義字、對比、因果關係、上位詞、舉證或語言外的生活經驗。以下將按這些線索分類提供大量的練習。

Strategy I 同義字、定義或重述關係

同義字

言談行文大都是以具體來說明抽象，以已知比喻未知，以簡字解釋難字，以事實輔助看法，以冗長敘述闡明模糊概念。最常用方式是用同義字，以較熟悉的字來指涉前述較難的字。這兩字在意義上必須是相同的。如下面題幹的第二句中 violent (兇暴的) 與選項 (D) fierce 同義字。第二句的定冠詞 the 是用來指涉前面第一次提及的人物，這裡指的是 a fierce dog。

例 The house is guarded by a _____ dog. The violent dog will attack any stranger who enters the house.

A. stray B. mad C. wild D. fierce

定義字

另外一個方式是用定義來說明某一個詞，通常這個定義放在要被定義的字的直接後面，以同位語、破折號、括弧、引號、that is、namely、in other words 或 or 的模式呈現。如下面題幹的第二句中的 Sons of Heaven (天子) 就是答案 emperor (皇帝) 的定義。第二句中的 were called (被稱為) 很明顯就是告訴讀者其後的字群就是 emperor 的定義。

例 In the past Chinese _____ had absolute power. They were called "Sons of Heaven."

A. intellectuals B. monks C. civilians D. emperors

重述關係

第三種是用較具體的文字重述前面提及的概念。如下面題幹的第二句就是用較具體的言語來重述第一句較抽象的概念。「連六歲大的小孩都知道他的大名，也讀過他的劇本。」來重述「莎士比亞是個著名的劇作家」。此題的答案爲 (C)。

例 Shakespeare is a ＿＿＿＿ playwright. Even six-year-old children know his name and have read his plays.

    A. smart   B. mean   C. famous   D. mysterious

✎ 練習一

請依此解析做以下題目，並找出解題的上下文的線索，將此線索劃底線。

1.   It takes time and effort to learn a foreign language, and it is still more difficult to be good at it. And only a few native speakers can ＿＿＿＿ it.

    A. abuse   B. master   C. interpret   D. purify

2.   I like to put my cards on the table so that no misunderstandings will arise. Similarly, I expect ＿＿＿＿ answers when I put questions to you.

    A. wise   B. brief   C. immediate   D. direct

3.   I work as a(n) ＿＿＿＿. I find it great fun to show people around.

    A. athlete   B. guide   C. pilot   D. director

4.   We all agree that we need to boost our sales. It is this ＿＿＿＿ goal that helps us to put aside our differences.

    A. common   B. distant   C. immediate   D. ultimate

5.   We have agreed to have a college class reunion, but the date has not yet been ＿＿＿＿. Once the date is set, we will begin to prepare for it.

    A. canceled   B. extended   C. determined   D. changed

6.   Share prices fell sharply, and many factories were shut down. Unemployment shot up to a previously unheard-of 5%. The prime minister's popularity was hit by the economic ＿＿＿＿.

    A. miracle   B. climate   C. crisis   D. growth

7. Some countries in the world are still very _____. For example, they still do not have running water, and they live on handouts from developed countries.

   A. aggressive   B. prosperous   C. backward   D. democratic

8. Professor Lee _____ that I become his assistant. But I rejected his offer.

   A. proposed   B. insisted   C. ordered   D. demanded

9. Illness and age had changed her beyond _____. Had she not noticed me first, I would have mistaken her for a total stranger and passed her by.

   A. recognition   B. criticism   C. control   D. compare

10. Mr. Church has had a heart attack and his doctor is operating on him. The _____ will take six hours.

   A. checkup   B. surgery   C. recovery   D. treatment

Strategy II 對比關係和反義字

對比關係

除了用同義相似關係，我們也常用對比來呈現兩句關係。所謂對比就是意義相反，用得恰當在行文言談之中可形成很好的效果。上窮碧落下黃泉，兩處茫茫皆不見。生當隕首，死當結草。黃鐘毀棄、瓦斧雷鳴。這些都是利用反義字來形成對比關係。在英文中常用轉折語來預示對比關係。這些轉折語包括：

連接詞	but, while, whereas, yet, though, even though, even if, rather than
副詞	nevertheless, nonetheless, however, still, on the other hand, by contrast, even so, on the contrary
介系詞	despite, in spite of, with all, for all, unlike, compared with, in contrast with, regardless of, instead of

如下面題幹的 but 就是預示前後句為對比關係。前半句是說被關在牢裡，而後半句是說他被誤會，因此答案應為 "release (釋放)"。關在監獄 (put in jail) 與釋放 (release) 是相反意思。

例 Bob was put in jail, but later on, he was _____ because the police had mistaken him for the man who robbed the bank.

A. detained　　　B. released　　　C. indicted　　　D. pardoned

反義字

又如以下題目的 on the other hand 也是告訴我們前後句為對比關係。在這句 mother tongue (母語) 的相對詞是 foreign language (外國語)，因為後面的 English 和 French 提供了另一上下文線索，即「舉證」線索 (請參閱 Strategy III 舉證)。

例 My mother tongue is Taiwanese, but on the other hand I can speak two _____ languages. One is English, and the other is French.

A. artificial　　　B. formal　　　C. foreign　　　D. official

✎ 練習二

請依此解析做以下題目，並找出解題的上下文的線索，將此線索劃底線。如果有轉折語，請將該轉折語圈起來。

1. Work began on the temple in 1858, and was _____ in 1862. Since then, it has become a tourist attraction.

A. designed　　　B. completed　　　C. destroyed　　　D. repaired

2. An increase in the crime rate comes as a shock to _____ people. Unlike high-ranking officials, they go around without bodyguards to protect them.

A. lucky　　　B. ordinary　　　C. stubborn　　　D. innocent

3. Clothes made of _____ fibers such as wool and cotton are more expensive than those made of synthetic fibers such as nylon.

A. artificial　　　B. natural　　　C. coarse　　　D. fine

4. No one can prove that ghosts do _____, but some people believe in ghosts all the same.

   A. survive   B. exist   C. vanish   D. mate

5. I had an intense desire to own that beautiful dress; however, I had to _____ the desire because I was low on cash.

   A. express   B. realize   C. yield to   D. suppress

6 Mr. Rush is thought of as a born orator now, but when he was a student, he was _____ of giving even a casual talk in public.

   A. tired   B. capable   C. confident   D. terrified

7. Your report is too lengthy; you should _____ it. A condensed report is more readable.

   A. shorten   B. confirm   C. present   D. issue

8. The bill seems, on the _____, to be genuine; but on closer inspection, it is clear that it is counterfeit money. At first glance, you may be tricked into believing it is real.

   A. surface   B. whole   C. average   D. contrary

9. Anita arrived just as I was leaving, but whether this was by accident or by _____, I'm not sure. But I feel that she is unwilling to come into contact with me.

   A. guess   B. instinct   C. design   D. mistake

10. The USA is a wealthy nation, but some people are still living in _____. The homeless are often seen sleeping on street corners.

   A. fear   B. comfort   C. misery   D. peace

Strategy III 舉證

　　有些概念難以定義，這時用實例則較能讓別人理解。「水果」一詞就是一例。《國語日報辭典》解釋為：鮮果，含有漿液的果實。這個定義比水果本身更難理解。什麼叫做鮮果？什麼叫做漿液？什麼叫做果實？愈解釋愈令人迷糊。如果這時用舉例的則較明白易懂。什麼叫「水果」？諸如柳丁、西瓜、葡萄。在英文中常用轉折語來預示例舉。這些轉折語包括：

類型 1	for example, for instance
類型 2	such as, like
類型 3	and so on
類型 4	to name just a few, among other things

下面題目的 such as 就是例舉的轉折語。其後的實例用來具體化前述的意念。這裡 America, Japan, and France 都是指 nations (國家)的實證。

例 Rich _____ such as America, Japan, and France are being asked to write off the debts which poor African countries owe them.
　　A. companies　　B. nations　　　　C. organizations　D. families

✎ 練習三

請依此解析做以下題目，並找出解題的上下文的線索，將此線索劃底線。如果有轉折語，也請將該轉折語圈起來。

1.　I find a bicycle is a(n) _____ way to get around town. For one thing, a cyclist doesn't get stuck in traffic jams. For another, it is easy to park a bicycle, even in small spaces.
　　A. legal　　　　　B. enjoyable　　　C. expensive　　D. convenient

2.　I am not interested in _____ affairs such as who goes to bed with whom.
　　A. foreign　　　　B. domestic　　　C. private　　　D. public

3. The appeal for _____ supplies to help the refugees met with a positive response. People from all over the world hurried to donate food, clothing and money.

    A. relief   B. military   C. medical   D. fuel

4. There was _____ evidence that the car had been in an accident. The headlight was broken, and there were scratches on the finish.

    A. concrete   B. insufficient   C. statistical   D. inconclusive

5. He is a man of great _____. The young and old, and males and females are all attracted to him.

    A. vision   B. wealth   C. magnetism   D. potential

6. When the fireworks went off, they presented/created a _____ sight. They produced loud noises, colorful sparks and beautiful designs.

    A. pitiful   B. horrible   C. disturbing   D. spectacular

7. The decision to offer English classes in elementary schools raised some _____, one of which was that few of the classes would be taught by qualified teachers. Even teaching materials were called into question.

    A. hopes   B. doubts   C. protests   D. fears

8. Her three sons have pursued different _____: the eldest son is a jeweler, the second one a butcher, and the youngest one a college professor.

    A. fashions   B. careers   C. customs   D. policies

9. While reading, you should be able to _____ opinions from facts. For example, "Mr. X was born in 1951" is a fact whereas "Mr. X is handsome" is an opinion.

    A. derive   B. choose   C. isolate   D. separate

10. The best way to help teenagers develop a sense of responsibility is to involve them in decision making. They should be encouraged to _____ their ideas.

    A. revise   B. contribute   C. clarify   D. gather

Strategy IV 因果關係

事出皆有因，所以探索兩句的因果關係也是猜測字詞意義的重要線索。物腐蟲生，人去樓空，樹大招風。都是利用因果關係造出來的成語。英文表示因果關係的轉折語有：

連接詞	because, as, since, so, such...that..., so...that..., so that
副 詞	therefore, thus, hence, consequently, as a result, in consequence
介系詞	because of, thanks to, owing to, due to, on account of, on grounds of
不定詞	too...to, so...as to, only to, never to, enough to

下面的題目就是用了 so...that...(如此...以至於) 的句型來表示前、後半句的因果關係。過去學校的生活猶如昨天的記憶，那麼學校的生活一定很"生動 (vivid)"才能記憶猶新。答案應選 (D)。

例 Parts of her school days are so _____ to her that they could be memories of yesterday.
　　A. invaluable　　B. bitter-sweet　　C. tedious　　D. vivid

✏ 練習四

請依此解析做以下題目，並找出解題的上下文的線索，將此線索劃底線。如果有轉折語，也請將該轉折語圈起來。

1. I am _____ of snakes because I was once bitten by a snake when I was a child.
　　A. scared　　B. fond　　C. tired　　D. jealous

2. The children made such a _____ in the living room that I had to spend a lot of time clearing it up.
　　A. fuss　　B. mess　　C. scene　　D. display

3. Their arrival was delayed because of heavy _____. They were caught in a long line of cars for three hours.

   A. irony   B. perfume   C. traffic   D. consumption

4. Jean lives beyond her means; no wonder she has gotten into _____.

   A. debt   B. politics   C. a panic   D. a fury

5. Helen has a good figure. She is also nice-looking, athletic, and outgoing. She is expected to win the beauty contest and be _____ the Queen of Beauty.

   A. appointed   B. nicknamed   C. crowned   D. designated

6. The air in the desert is very dry; it contains hardly any _____.

   A. oxygen   B. hydrogen   C. moisture   D. dust

7. With the outbreak of SARS, people are advised to take their temperature twice a day to see if they have a(n) _____.

   A. headache   B. shock   C. fever   D. injury

8. Before taking any medicine, you should be sure to read and follow all the directions. Some chemical _____ might result from the misuse of medicine.

   A. poisoning   B. composition   C. substances   D. elements

9. The workers weren't satisfied with their low wages and long work hours; therefore, they walked out and staged a(n) _____.

   A. comeback   B. demonstration

   C. exhibition   D. opera

10. A bomb exploded, sending shockwaves throughout the building. In an instant, the building fell into _____.

    A. decay   B. disuse   C. disrepair   D. ruin

課後作業

請從下面四個選項中選出最適合題意的字或詞。

1. Keep your camera _____ while you're taking a picture. Otherwise, the photo might be blurred.
   A. afloat   B. steady   C. apart   D. aflame

2. I am in _____ with my wife over money management. I prefer saving money in a bank, but she likes to invest in the stock market.
   A. partnership   B. sympathy   C. conflict   D. contact

3. People used to be _____ about sex, but now even women are more open about discussing it.
   A. mad   B. bitter   C. frank   D. shy

4. The crowd picked up sticks and bottles and threw them at the police. The police used shields to guard themselves against the _____.
   A. punishment   B. reward   C. attack   D. signal

5. Jack tripped over a chair and fell. His ankles were injured and started to _____. His mother put an ice pack on them.
   A. bleed   B. shake   C. bend   D. swell

6. The twins look so much alike that I often _____ one with the other.
   A. associate   B. compare   C. replace   D. confuse

7. The balloons are available in _____ colors—red, white, green, and so on.
   A. various   B. brilliant   C. natural   D. somber

8. It is impolite to _____ when someone is speaking. Instead, you should wait until he finishes.
   A. nap   B. interrupt   C. sigh   D. shrug

9. Make sure the soil is _____ before planting the seeds. If it is dry, spray water on it.

    A. fertile   B. barren   C. moist   D. sandy

10. The child put a coin in his mouth and almost _____ to death. His face was twisted in pain and he turned pale.

    A. starved   B. froze   C. choked   D. bled

11. I was almost out of breath after walking up the _____ hillside. Because the path rose up so quickly, I sweated heavily all the way.

    A. steep   B. rocky   C. slippery   D. sloping

12 I have poor _____, so I cannot see things clearly without glasses.

    A. hearing   B. judgment   C. records   D. vision

13. I finally climbed the _____, but it nearly wore me out. I was gasping for breath. It took me two hours to reach the summit.

    A. peak   B. valley   C. cliff   D. cave

14. When water is cooled below 0 degrees, it freezes and becomes ice. If the temperature goes up again, the ice _____.

    A. melts   B. shines   C. vanishes   D. drifts

15. Male teachers are generally in the _____ at school. One in ten teachers is male. That could have a certain influence on students.

    A. minority   B. majority   C. limelight   D. dock

Unit 2
詞彙和結構—字彙 (二)

Strategy V 上位詞關係

　　所謂的「上位詞」就是某一字詞的包容量能涵蓋另一詞。譬如說 relatives (親戚)，這個字能包括 uncles, aunts, cousins 等。relatives 就是 uncles, aunts, cousins 等的「上位詞」。同樣，wander (漫步)、stride (大步行走)、strut (大搖大擺地走)、wade (跋涉) 等字都是走路 (walk) 的樣式，因此 walk 就是這些動詞的「上位詞」。我們經常用這種上位詞的指涉關係來達成文義的連貫 (cohesion)。在行文中提及某人物或行為時我們用它的上位詞，一來避免重複，二來有指涉效果。如下面題目 stew (燜) 是煮食的一種方式，因此答案為 cook。cook 是 stew 的上位詞。

例 Let the meat stew slowly in its own juices. We must _____ it until it becomes tender.

　　A. cook　　　　B. grind　　　　C. dissolve　　　　D. freeze

✎ 練習五

請依此解析做以下題目，並找出解題的上下文的線索，將此線索劃底線。如果有轉折語，也請將該轉折語圈起來。

1. Mr. White has retired as sales manager and his _____ will be taken over by Mr. Church.

　　A. position　　　B. business　　　C. leadership　　　D. firm

2. Jane gave up her _____. She was a nurse. She felt she couldn't get ahead at the job.

　　A. habit　　　　B. career　　　　C. property　　　　D. project

3. I bought a flute for my daughter. The _____ cost me $NT4,000.

　　A. tool　　　　B. weapon　　　　C. instrument　　　D. metal

4. When the company got into financial trouble, the bank came to its rescue with a huge loan. The financial _____ prevented the company from going bankrupt.

　　A. crisis　　　　B. condition　　　C. support　　　　D. independence

5. The age of _____ maturity varies from person to person. Some people attain intellectuality sooner than others.

    A. sexual   B. emotional   C. mental   D. physical

6. The president had a(n) _____ with a pop singer. The scandal led to the fall of his government.

    A. chat   B. interview   C. affair   D. appointment

7. A car speeding down the street at night created a(n) _____. Many people were aroused from sleep by the noise.

    A. crisis   B. illusion   C. sensation   D. disturbance

8. With _____ supplies running short, few people in this country can survive the harsh winter. Many factories will shut down for lack of oil.

    A. fuel   B. arms   C. food   D. medical

9. A nutritious meal is important to children. It must contain numerous vitamins and minerals, and the ____ must be high in protein.

    A. medicine   B. beverage   C. diet   D. material

10. Linda was nibbling a piece of bread. Her mother shouted at her, " _____ your breakfast quickly, or you will be late for class."

    A. Cook   B. Eat   C. Serve   D. Purchase

Strategy VI 類比

　　類比就是用熟悉的來比喻不熟悉的，用具體的來比喻抽象的，用已知的來比喻未知的，用近的來比喻遠的。中文的「像」、「似」和「如」是常用的類比轉折語。大絃嘈嘈如急雨，小絃切切如私語。就是一例。英文常用的類比轉折語有：

連接詞	like, as
副　詞	similarly, likewise
介系詞	like

下面一題就是利用 "as...so..." 的句型把運動與讀書互相做類比。與前半句的動詞 strengthen 能成類比的只有選項 (D) 的 sharpen。

例　As exercise can strengthen the heart, so reading can _____ the mind.

　　A. corrupt　　　B. ease　　　C. distract　　　D. sharpen

✎ 練習六

請依此解析做以下題目，並找出解題的上下文的線索，將此線索劃底線。如果有轉折語，也請將該轉折語圈起來。

1. Jack cannot _____ good music. If you play him a sonata, it is just like casting pearls before swine.

　　A. appreciate　　B. compose　　C. perform　　D. record

2. Having a low-salt and fat-free diet can _____ the risk of heart disease. Similarly, the possibility of getting heart disease can be lowered if we exercise regularly.

　　A. involve　　B. increase　　C. court　　D. lessen

3. In a co-educational school, boy and girl students can _____ together freely just as they do in society.

　　A. labor　　B. mingle　　C. migrate　　D. stutter

4. The clams were delicious. Likewise, the smoked salmon was _____.
   A. excellent   B. nutritious   C. poisonous   D. rotten

5. There were no more than two hundred words in her first composition and her second composition was similarly _____.
   A. perfect   B. wordy   C. brief   D. boring

6. Wine is best when it is preserved over a long time, and as with fine wine, France likes its politicians to _____ over time.
   A. age   B. mature   C. vanish   D. wither

7. A ship is to the sea as _____ is to the desert.
   A. a wagon   B. an oasis   C. a cactus   D. a camel

8. James is as busy as a _____, but he is still as poor as a church mouse.
   A. bee   B. dragonfly   C. butterfly   D. grasshopper

9. Our life span is short, so life is often compared to _____.
   A. a paradise   B. an abyss   C. a candle   D. a stage

10. Japan's economy is dependent primarily on exports. Like Japan, Taiwan has also enjoyed _____ by exporting its products all over the world.
    A. prosperity   B. security   C. stability   D. credibility

Strategy VII 陳述句的名詞化

　　用一個字概括一個句字的涵意，可能是一意念，可能是一行為，也可能是一事件。要用何字來總結端看原句的意思。如下面題幹第一句的 make noise (製造噪音) 是一種 "行為 (behavior)"。因此 behavior 是 make such noises 經名詞化後的濃縮語。

例 That boy often makes noise in the office. I cannot tolerate such _____.
   A. pain   B. heat   C. opposition   D. behavior

練習七

請依此解析做以下題目，並找出解題的上下文的線索，將此線索劃底線。

1. We have been told that global warming might cause a lot of damage to the earth and the life on it. These _____ sound reasonable but are actually overblown.

    A. doubts　　　B. incidents　　　C. rumors　　　D. alarms

2. Two cars collided with each other on the highway. The _____ resulted in a traffic jam. Fortunately, no one was injured.

    A. rehearsal　　B. feat　　　C. accident　　　D. tragedy

3. The political party's chairman firmly believed that he could seize power by continuing the mass demonstration, but some of its younger members didn't sympathize with his _____.

    A. hypothesis　　B. view　　　C. threat　　　D. order

4. Three bombs exploded in the London subway, killing 56 people. All political leaders condemned this barbaric _____.

    A. act　　　B. custom　　　C. treatment　　　D. penalty

5. The tax burden is mostly on salary men while rich people enjoy tax cuts and street vendors do not need to pay any tax. This _____ must be corrected.

    A. impression　　B. deficiency　　C. injustice　　　D. pronunciation

6. China exports a lot more to America than it imports from it. This trade _____ has strained relations between the two countries.

    A. agreement　　B. surplus　　　C. barrier　　　D. policy

7. Two Palestinian gunmen opened fire on a car at Kissufim, a key entry point into Gaza's Israeli settlements, and killed an Israeli man and his wife. Israeli troops chased the two gunmen and killed them. This _____ has endangered a peace agreement between the two sides.

    A. negotiation　　B. trade　　　C. quarrel　　　D. conflict

8. Hundreds of gays marched down the street, demanding their civil rights, but their _____ was disrupted by anti-gay activists.
   A. parade   B. carnival   C. demonstration D. celebration

9. Police ran after a suspect in the London subway. The _____ lasted for a few minutes, and then suddenly gunshots rang out in the subway. The man was killed on the spot.
   A. chase   B. march   C. argument   D. battle

10. The mayor said that a new baseball stadium would be built in three years, but his _____ was never fulfilled.
   A. role   B. promise   C. duty   D. prophesy

Strategy VIII 語言外的生活經驗

　　有些遺失的字無法由語言本身的上下文猜測出來，這時只有訴諸語言外的生活經驗。像下面的題目，就沒有任何上下文的語言線索讓我們來猜測空格裡應該用那個字較恰當。但我們可以用生活經驗去判斷。當看見一頭公牛衝過來時，我們會如何反應？我們會集合在一起？各自散開逃命？抗議？還是瞪著眼睛看？依常理我們的本能反應該是逃。因此較好的答案應是 "scatter (散開)"。

例 On seeing a bull rushing towards us, we _____ in all directions.
   A. assembled   B. scattered   C. protested   D. stared

✎ 練習八

請依此解析做以下題目。

1. A(n) _____ fire broke out, and hundreds of fire fighters went up to the mountain to put it out. Many trees burned down.
   A. forest   B. electrical   C. coal   D. gas

2. Mr. Church's new book has come out. It is _____ in every bookstore.
   A. visible   B. valuable   C. available   D. durable

3. A bus crashed into a tree. Fortunately, neither the driver nor the _____ were hurt.

   A. passengers   B. engineers   C. crew   D. staff

4. It hadn't rained for a long time. The mayor held an incense stick and knelt down in _____ to God.

   A. response   B. prayer   C. obedience   D. opposition

5. I was seized with _____ at the sight of the amazing waterfall. It ran over a cliff and poured down into a large pool.

   A. wonder   B. melancholy   C. terror   D. loneliness

6. Whenever a player breaks the rules, the referee will blow _____. By doing so, he hopes to stop unfair play.

   A. his nose   B. his trumpet   C. a fuse   D. the whistle

7. The President laid _____ at the war memorial in honor of the unknown heroes who gave their lives during the war.

   A. bricks   B. wreaths   C. carpets   D. mines

8. _____ is emitted from the spout of the teakettle when the water is boiling.

   A. Steam   B. Light   C. Smoke   D. Fragrance

9. That bunch of idiots chatted nonstop in a corner of the classroom while I was delivering a speech. In the end, my _____ was exhausted, and I blew up at them.

   A. strength   B. patience   C. topic   D. resources

10. Recently, many workers were laid off. With no economic recovery in sight, they can't earn a living. They are on _____ .

    A. strike   B. trial   C. welfare   D. leave

課後作業

請從下面四個選項中選出最適合題意的字或詞。

1. Cindy slammed the door in a(n) _____ and burst into tears. No one in the office knew why she was so angry.
    A. hurry   B. panic   C. temper   D. instant

2. The doctor examined Janet carefully and _____ her illness as a rare bone disease. To date, no cure for the disease has been found.
    A. dismissed   B. described   C. diagnosed   D. accepted

3. When you have a headache, take two aspirin. The pills will ease your _____.
    A. anxiety   B. pain   C. crisis   D. mind

4. In English "envious" and "jealous" are synonyms. There are _____ differences in their meanings.
    A. significant   B. considerable   C. subtle   D. noticeable

5. After 40 minutes of keen competition, the game ended in a ____. Neither team got the better of the other.
    A. tie   B. victory   C. fight   D. tragedy

6. Fruit picking is _____ work; that is, certain fruit is picked during a particular time of the year.
    A. routine   B. manual   C. seasonal   D. intellectual

7. The custom of forcing a woman to marry is only _____ to some tribes. Not all aborigines have this kind of custom.
    A. harmful   B. peculiar   C. familiar   D. advantageous

8. To his teacher's surprise, John got all the answers right. Later on, he confessed to cheating on the test. He was quite _____ -stricken.
    A. panic   B. conscience   C. poverty   D. terror

9. On summer nights, we can see numerous stars _____ in the sky. The brightest one in the north is called the North Star.
    A. vanish　　　　B. twinkle　　　C. dim　　　　　　D. revolve

10. Under the glare of the sun, the ice _____ until it turned into water.
    A. drifted　　　　B. gleamed　　　C. melted　　　　D. cracked

11. There was a flash of _____ a moment ago. The sound of the thunder will come soon after.
    A. pity　　　　　B. excitement　　C. lightning　　　D. inspiration

12. The general manager presented a _____ report, warning that the company might not be able to balance its budget.
    A. technical　　　B. financial　　　C. environmental　D. medical

13. You'd better choose good comic books for your son to read. Some evil thoughts in bad ones may _____ his mind. He's still too young to tell right from wrong.
    A. ease　　　　　B. broaden　　　C. sharpen　　　　D. poison

14. His speech barely stimulated my interest. I was _____ to death.
    A. worried　　　　B. sentenced　　C. bored　　　　　D. frightened

15. Mr. White is very strict with his children. He demands total obedience and requires them to meet his _____.
    A. obligations　　B. deadline　　　C. expectations　　D. expense

16. I didn't go to the karaoke bar with them because I had to make some _____. I was running out of food, and the supermarket was about to close.
    A. purchases　　　B. choices　　　C. requests　　　　D. decisions

17. After the downfall of the Soviet Union, some of its republics separated from it and declared their _____.
    A. loyalty　　　　B. independence　C. intention　　　D. innocence

18. A cold front swept the whole island with pouring rain and freezing winds. Our plan to hold an outdoor party was completely _____.
    A. devised   B. spoiled   C. fulfilled   D. disclosed

19. You should learn to _____ your rights. No one can stand up for your own rights.
    A. abuse   B. exercise   C. defend   D. surrender

20. We pitched our camp by the lake and began to _____ some chicken over a fire. As we did, we added sauce for flavor.
    A. stir-fry   B. roast   C. steam   D. stew

21. I asked my mother if I could go to the movies, but she rejected my _____. She wanted to punish me for my poor grades.
    A. request   B. offer   C. application   D. suggestion

22. Two boy students put on girls' school uniforms and went dancing downtown. It is surprising that they should choose to adopt this _____ to draw the public's attention.
    A. custom   B. method   C. attitude   D. suggestion

23. Singapore's _____ achievements are extraordinary. Their standard of living reflects their prosperity.
    A. academic   B. economic   C. technological   D. diplomatic

24. The newly built 54-story skyscraper near the Taipei Train Station has formed a _____ in Taipei. It can be seen from many miles away.
    A. square   B. shelter   C. landmark   D. background

25. We all _____ at the vastness of Lake Michigan. We could only see the horizon in the distance.
    A. blushed   B. marveled   C. grieved   D. trembled

26. Many Chinese people still live in the same house with their parents as well as their children; however, the _____ family is becoming more and more popular today, especially in the city.
    A. royal   B. adoptive   C. nuclear   D. extended

27. The city government has banned citizens from setting off _____ in residential areas. For one thing, it produces noise pollution. For another, it may start a fire.

    A. firecrackers   B. bombs   C. the alarm   D. the fire bell

28. Ancient Egyptians knew how to _____ dead bodies. They rubbed a dead body with salt and resin and then wrapped it in hundreds of yards of linen.

    A. preserve   B. bury   C. expose   D. identify

29. When driving, make sure to _____ your seat belt. By doing so you can avoid being seriously hurt if you have an accident.

    A. fasten   B. undo   C. loosen   D. design

30. Whenever bus drivers stage a strike, the mayor yields to their demands. This soft stance has weakened the city government's _____.

    A. forces   B. confidence   C. economy   D. authority

31. Mind your _____ at the party. Don't devour the snacks as if you were starving to death.

    A. tongue   D. step   C. manners   D. business

32. That black people are inferior to white people is a deep-rooted _____; it is hard to remove.

    A. suspicion   B. prejudice   C. dislike   D. faith

33. In order to improve efficiency, many factory owners have _____ old machines with new ones. The new machines are computerized and user-friendly.

    A. identified   B. combined   C. integrated   D. replaced

34. Boys like toys such as guns, cars, and so on. By _____, most girls prefer dolls and stickers.

    A. contrast   B. profession   C. definition   D. tradition

35. Mrs. Jones couldn't bear _____. So after her husband died, she got a dog to keep her company.

    A. noise   B. pain   C. hardships   D. loneliness

36. Our boss is in a _____ mood today because he has just signed a new sales contract which will bring in record profits.

    A. thoughtful   B. sorrowful   C. melancholy   D. cheerful

37. The newlyweds are renting a house because they cannot _____ to buy a house of their own.

    A. resolve   B. afford   C. promise   D. refuse

38. Whenever Jill goes out on a date, she likes to put on make-up so that her _____ will be enhanced.

    A. beauty   B. tension   C. value   D. awareness

39. You must assert your _____; otherwise, people might think you are guilty of stealing the money.

    A. innocence   B. independence C. authority   D. superiority

40. The gap between the rich and the poor has become even wider. We should try hard to narrow the _____ gap.

    A. income   B. trade   C. generation   D. gender

41. Dick had a sense of _____ after realizing that he had made an error. He was ashamed of himself.

    A. guilt   B. justice   C. security   D. pride

42. You are always _____ with others but you lose your temper easily with your own brothers.

    A. furious   B. strict   C. patient   D. frank

43. Chris often acts on _____; she just follows her heart without thinking carefully.

    A. impulse   B. information   C. advice   D. orders

44. Peter left the school in _____ because the train was about to leave in five minutes.

    A. despair   B. shock   C. joy   D. haste

45. Mr. Hall has made no secret of his wish to dominate the fast-growing broadcasting industry. His _____ ambition poses a threat to his rivals.

    A. humble   B. sensible   C. political   D. intense

46. Gary's _____ deepened when he heard the news that his son was lost in the mountains.

    A. crisis   B. anxiety   C. hatred   D. voice

47. There was an air of _____ at the meeting. The people in attendance observed a three-minute silence in honor of the dead.

    A. mystery   B. excitement   C. dignity   D. grief

48. In _____, the project sounds practicable. In practice, you'll find a lot of problems with it.

    A. reality   B. general   C. brief   D. theory

49. Nowadays it is very common for women to have their hair _____. Blonde hair is their favorite.

    A. dyed   B. combed   C. trimmed   D. shampooed

50. I am staying here for only one month. I would like to rent a(n) _____ house because I cannot afford to stay in a hotel for that long.

    A. imaginary   B. luxurious   C. furnished   D. deserted

Unit 3

詞彙和結構—片語 (一)

✪ Type I 動詞 + 介系詞 + (代)名詞

✪ Type II 動詞 + 副詞

✪ 課後作業

最常考的片語是片語動詞。片語動詞是一個動詞和一副詞或介系詞形成的片語。可分為四類型：

1. **動詞 + 介系詞 + (代)名詞**

   例 I called on my uncle yesterday.

   我昨天拜訪我叔叔。

2. **動詞 + 副詞**

   例 John dropped off in class.

   約翰上課時打瞌睡。

3. **動詞 + (代)名詞 + 副詞**

   例 Mary called me up last night.

   瑪莉昨晚打電話給我。

   Note

   如果受詞是名詞也可放在副詞之後。但受詞是代名詞則只能放在動詞與副詞之間：

   A. Mary called John up last night.

   B. Mary called up John last night.

4. **動詞 + 副詞 + 介系詞 + (代)名詞**

   例 I cannot catch up with Tom.

   我趕不上湯姆。

雖然片語動詞很多，但其後所接的副詞或介系詞通常具有特定的意義。如果能了解這些特定的意義，即使某片語動詞沒學過還是可以藉著這些副詞或介系詞猜出大約意思。

Type I 動詞 + 介系詞 + (代)名詞

以下是第一類型「動詞＋介系詞＋(代)名詞」中常見的介系詞，以及這些介系詞所代表的意義。

1. **about** 關於：care about sth (在乎), wonder about sth (感到疑惑)

2. **across** 無意中發現：come/run across sb/sth (偶然發現)

3. **after**

    a. 追求：go after sb/sth (追求)

    b. 問安：ask/inquire after sb (問起某人健康或狀況), see/look after sb (照顧)

    c. 模仿：take after sb (像)

4. **against** 對抗：run against sb (競選中與某人競爭), rise (up) against sb (反抗), go against sth (違反)

5. **around** 避免某個主題：get around sth (規避)

6. **at**

    a. 目標：look at sb/sth (注視), laugh at sb/sth (譏笑), grasp/grab/catch at sb/sth (拼命要抓住)

    b. 原因：blush/pale at sth (因...而臉紅/蒼白), wonder/marvel at sth (因...而感到好奇)

7. **by**

    a. 堅持：abide by sth (遵守), stand by sb (支持), stand by sth (信守)

    b. 經過：stop by sth (順道到), pass by sb/sth (經過)

練習一

請依上下文選出適當答案。

1. All players must _____ the rules of the game; otherwise, they will not be allowed to take part in the game.

A. laugh at B. abide by C. get around D. go against

2. Walking along the street, I _____ an old friend of mine. It never occurred to me that I would meet him again ten years after I left school.

A. passed by B. looked at C. took after D. came across

3. Since you have promised your son a gift, you should _____ what you said.

A. stand by B. laugh at C. marvel at D. blush at

4. Paul got into financial trouble, but his wife _____ him as always. Finally he made a comeback.

A. ran against B. asked after C. stood by D. grabbed at

5. What Paul _____ is money. He will even sacrifice his health for it.

A. wonders at B. cares about C. pales at D. wonders about

8. **for**

a. 尋找：look for sb/sth (尋找), reach for sth (伸手拿某物)

b. 渴望：long for sth (渴望), want for sth (缺乏)

c. 贊成、支持：go for sb/sth (支持), care for sb/sth (喜歡 [用於否定句]、照顧), feel for sb (同情)

d. 前往：leave for sth (前往), head for sth (向某地行進)

e. 替代、交換：stand for sth (代表), substitute for sb/sth (替代)

9. **from**

a. 停止、避免：refrain from sth (忍住、抑制), shrink from V-ing (不願做某事)

b. 分開：part from sb (與某人分手、斷絕關係), wander from sth (偏離主題), differ from sb/sth 不同

c. 原因：arise/spring/result from sth (起因於), suffer from sth (患病), die from sth (因...而死)

10. **in**

a. 在某方面：specialize in sth (專門研究), believe in sth (相信), persist in V-ing (堅持), lie/consist in sth (在於)

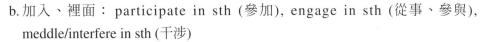

b. 加入、裡面： participate in sth (參加), engage in sth (從事、參與), meddle/interfere in sth (干涉)

c. 結果： result in sth (結果造成), end in sth (結果)

11. **into**

a. 轉變： turn/change into sth (轉變成), get/fall/go into sth (陷入某狀態)

b. 分裂： fall into sth (分為), split into sth (分裂成)

c. 遭遇： run/bump into sb (不期而遇)

d. 調查： look/see/inquire/go into sth (調查)

12. **of**

a. 感官： think of sth (想到), dream of sth/V-ing (夢到), hear of sth (聽說), learn of sth (獲悉、得知), speak of sth (談及), smell of sth (有點兒...味), beware of sb/sth (當心), become of sb/sth (發生)

b. 其他： die of sth (死於), consist of sth (由...組成), dispose of sth (處理掉)

13. **off**

a. 斷絕： break off sth (斷絕關係), swear off sth (發誓戒掉)

b. 光或聲音的反射： give off sth (發出味道), bounced off sth (彈開)

c. 靠...維生： live off sth (以某物為食物)

d. 避開： keep off sth (遠離), fight off sth (抗拒)

✎ **練習二**

請依上下文選出適當答案。

1. We began to _____ our homeland after traveling overseas for twenty days.
   A. long for   B. hear of   C. look for   D. stand for

2. I know what it is like to be looked down upon, so I _____ Mark when he was laughed at by his classmates.
   A. looked for   B. bumped into   C. parted from   D. felt for

3. The bank was robbed, and the police are _____ the robbery. They are watching the videotapes in order to find out who robbed the bank.

   A. meddling in　　B. looking into　　C. swearing off　　D. shrinking from

4. The strength of the grammar book _____ the fact that its example sentences are quoted directly from newspapers and magazines.

   A. becomes of　　B. results in　　C. lies in　　　　D. differs from

5. _____ the dog! It will bite.

   A. Live off　　　B. Dispose of　　C. Beware of　　D. Reach for

14. **on**

   a. 依靠：rest/depend/rely/count on sb/sth (依靠)

   b. 思索：dwell/reflect on sth (細想)

   c. 吃食：live on sth (以某物為食), feed on sth (吃飼料)

   d. 專注：focus/concentrate on sth (精神集中於), turn on sb/sth (把某物對準某人物、攻擊某人物), work on sth (忙於某事), wait on sb (伺候)

   e. 決定：decide/settle on sth (決定), insist on sth (堅持)

   f. 利用：play on sth (利用某人的恐懼、不信任、弱點、偏好等)

   g. 侵略：prey on sb/sth (捕食、掠奪), step on sth (藐視某人的情感/權利)

   h. 告密、監視：tell/inform on sb (告密、告發), spy on sb/sth (監視某人/行為)

   i. 賭博：gamble/bet on sth/V-ing (孤注一擲、冒險)

   j. 關於某方面：expand/enlarge on sth (詳述), touch on sth (論及), deliver on sth (履行諾言)

   k. 喜惡：smile on sb/sth (讚許某人或事), frown on sth (不贊成)

   l. 突然想出或發現：strike/hit on sth (突然想出), happen/chance on sb/sth (偶然發現)

   m. 拜訪：call on sb (拜訪)

15. **out of**

   a. 不做某事：drop out of sth (退出), stay out of sth (避開), grow out of sth (長大戒掉)

b. 失去： run out of sth (沒某物了)

c. 從某處離開： check out of sth (辦理退房), pull out of + 地方 (撤離開)

16. **over**

a. 原因： weep/cry over sb/sth (因...而哭泣), mourn over sb/sth (哀悼)

b. 沉思： go over sth (仔細考慮), puzzle over sth (猜測)

c. 略過： skip over sth (略過), gloss over sth (避開思考不愉快的細節), brush over sth (輕描淡寫)

d. 勝過、控制： triumph over sb/sth (戰勝), get over sth (生病好了)

e. 注意： watch over sb/sth (留心注意、看管), fuss over sb (過分操心)

f. 重複、各處： look/go/run over sth (溫習), go over sth (檢查)

17. **through**

a. 經歷─應付： get/go through sth (過日子), come through sth (歷經)

b. 仔細閱讀或尋找： skim/thumb/leaf through sth (瀏覽), go through sth (細讀)

c. 完成： rush through sth (倉促寫完), go through sth (用/喝完)

d. 突破： break through sth(突破), see/look through sth (識破)

18. **to**

a. 反應： awake to sth (意識到), answer to sb (for sth) (向某人負責)

b. 遵守、符合、有關係： cling/stick to sth (堅持、執著), correspond to sth (一致、符合、相配稱), appeal to sb (使某人感興趣), apply to sb/sth (適用於), conform to sth (遵守)

c. 導致某種結果： lead/contribute to sth (造成), come/amount to sth (總共)

d. 指涉： refer to sth (指涉)

e. 屈服： bow/yield to sth (順從接受), surrender to sb/sth (屈服)

f. 改變： adapt/adjust to sth (適應), convert to sth (轉變成)

g. 同意、承認、證實： agree/consent to sth(贊同), object to sth (反對), admit/confess to sth/V-ing (承認)

h. 致力於： warm to sth (熱衷於), warm to sb (對某人產生了好感), attend to sb/sth (專心致力於、照顧處理), see to sth (照顧處理)

i. 對某人物表心意： appeal to sb (要求), propose to sb (向女人求婚)

19. **with**

a. 某種情緒的原因： quiver/shake/tremble with sth (因恐懼、寒忍等顫抖),
pale/blush with sth (因...而臉紅/蒼白)

b. 連接關係： correspond/agree with sth (符合), comply with sth (遵守), sympathize with sb (同情), sympathize with sth (贊同)

c. 應付處理： deal/cope with sth (應付處理), interfere/meddle with sth (未經允許
擺弄某物)

d. 棄絕： break with sth (棄絕), part with sth (丟棄)

✎ 練習三

請依上下文選出適當答案。

1. The police are _____ the victim's apartment in search for clues about
the murder.
A. dealing with B. watching over C. interfering with D. going over

2. Peter _____ Jack and screamed, "I'll give you a good beating!"
A. turned on B. appealed to C. told on D. counted on

3. The ad _____ our fears, showing a man suffering from AIDS. Its purpose is to warn us against casual sex.
A. copes with B. settles on C. plays on D. dwells on

4. You need to _____ the details of the contract before you sign it.
A. skip over B. go through C. comply with D. adjust to

5. When we were in trouble and didn't know what to do, John _____ a
good idea.
A. worked on B. hit on C. stuck to D. warmed to

Type II 動詞 + 副詞

以下是第二類型「動詞＋副詞」中常見的副詞，以及這些副詞所代表的意義。

1. **around** 無目標的活動： mess/fool around (鬼混), hang around (遊手好閒)

2. **ahead**
   a. 進步： get ahead (出人頭地)
   b. 在前： get ahead (of sb/sth) (超過[人/物])
   c. 繼續： go ahead (with sth) (繼續做[某事]、放手去做)

3. **along** 進步或進行： scrape along (on sth) ([靠某物]勉強過日子), get along (with sth) (進展), muddle along (敷衍過去)

4. **apart** 破裂： fall/come apart (破裂), fall apart ([事業、交易或婚姻]破產、破裂)

5. **around** 恢復意識或痊癒： come around = come to (甦醒)【<=> pass out (暈倒)】

6. **away**
   a. 繼續： chat/talk/sing/dance/gamble away (不停地閒聊/說話/唱歌/跳舞/賭)
   b. 消失： fade away ([燈、聲音、記憶、影像]逐漸消失), die away ([聲音、風、燈]逐漸消失), waste/fade away ([人]逐漸衰弱), pass away ([人]逝去), wear away (磨損掉)
   c. 離開： go/get/step away (走開)

7. **back**
   a. 回復或重複一行為： talk/answer back (回嘴)
   b. 往後移動，可引申為不繼續做： draw/fall/pull back (撤/後退)

8. **behind** 進展落後： lag/fall/get/drop/trail behind (落在別人後面、不如人)

9. **by**
   a. 袖手旁觀，此時 by 可用 back 取代： sit by (坐視、無動於衷), stand by (袖手旁觀)
   b. 經過： pass by (經過), tick by (時間滴答滴答過去)

　　c. 生存下來： get/scrape by= scrape along (勉強餬口)

　　d. 短暫的非正式拜訪： drop/stop/come/go by (順道訪問)

✎ 練習四

請依上下文選出適當答案。

1.　Bob works very hard, but he doesn't seem to be able to _____ in school. He still gets low grades.
　　A. fool around　　B. get ahead　　C. talk back　　D. get away

2.　Could anybody, seeing a person drowning, feel comfortable _____ and doing nothing?
　　A. pulling back　　B. dancing away C. falling behind　　D. standing by

3.　Jane earns only twenty thousand dollars a month, but she manages to _____ on such little money. She is very frugal with her money.
　　A. get by　　　　B. pass by　　　　C. pass away　　D. go ahead

4.　Jane fainted from the heat, but she _____ after we put her in the shade of a large oak tree.
　　A. faded away　　B. hung around　　C. came around　D. sat back

5.　I live on Main Street. _____ anytime for coffee. You are always welcome.
　　A. Drop by　　　　B. Muddle along　C. Go away　　　　D. Scrape by

10. **down**

　　a. 向下： pour down ([雨]傾盆而下), lie/kneel/sit/bend down (躺下/跪下/坐下/彎下)

　　b. 停止運作： break down ([機器]故障、[身體]衰弱、[會談]失敗)

　　c. 減少、減弱： prices go/come down　(價格下降), slow down (減速), die/burn down ([火]漸漸熄滅), calm/cool down (冷靜下來), die down ([風]逐漸平息)

11. **in**

a. 進入或到達某處：check/book in (在旅館登記住宿/在機場辦理登記手續), clock/punch/ring in (打卡上班), sign in (簽到)

b. 投降、崩潰：give/cave in (屈服), cave/fall in (坍塌)

12. **off**

a. 離開：rockets blast/lift off ([火箭]發射), planes take off ([飛機]起飛), clear off (滾開), set/start off (for) ([地方]出發前往某地)

b. 關掉電源、瓦斯、水龍頭：lights go off ([燈]熄了)

c. 引爆：(a bomb/alarm) go off ([炸彈]爆炸、[警鈴]響起)

d. 成功：pay off ([計畫、事業]成功), go/come off ([事]成功)

e. 睡覺：doze/nod/drop off (打瞌睡)

f. 減少：cool off ([興趣]降低、[人]變冷淡、[物]變涼), die off (相繼死亡), ease off ([危險、痛苦]減輕、[人]輕鬆下來), pass off ([暴風雨、痛苦]停止), drop off ([數量、興趣]減少)

13. **on**

a. 開電源、瓦斯、水龍頭：lights (machines) go/come on (燈[機器]開動)

b. 繼續或進步：linger/drag/wear on ([味道或音調]繚繞、[事情]拖延下去、[時間或事件]慢慢過去), hold/hang on (抓住不放、不掛斷電話、堅持下去)

14. **out**

a. 消滅：sth run out ([物]用光了), sth sell out (售完), die out (死光、滅絕), (fires) burn out ([火]因燃料用盡而熄滅)

b. 離開：set/head out (for a destination) (動身前往[地]), start out (on a journey) (啟程), check out (of a hotel) (結帳離開[旅館])

c. 打破寧靜：(epidemics/fires/wars) break out ([傳染病/火災/戰爭]爆發)

d. 失去意識：pass/black out ([人]昏倒)

15. **through** 完成或成功：sb get through ([人]考試通過、做完工作), scrape/squeeze through (勉強及格), muddle through (勉強混過去)

16. **up**

    a. 起床： get up (起床), sit/stay up (熬夜), wake up (醒來)

    b. 毀滅或破壞： blow up ([炸彈等]爆炸)

    c. 發生： sb show/turn up ([人]突然出現), sth pop/crop up ([事]突然發生), sth spring up ([風、反對、城鎮]突然出現)

    d. 增加： sb grow up (長大), prices go up (物價上揚), interest picks up (利息上升), traffic builds up (車子增多), hurry up (趕快), sth heat up ([物]變熱), sb cheer up (振作起來)

    e. 乾淨、整齊： dress up (盛裝), make up (化妝)

✎ 練習五

請依上下文選出適當答案。

1. It was so hot in there that I nearly _____ from the heat.
   A. cheered up   B. bent down   C. dressed up   D. passed out

2. Peace talks _____, and the two sides took up arms again.
   A. came off   B. broke down   C. dragged on   D. paid off

3. Mr. Lee's speech was so boring that some students began to yawn and _____.
   A. calm down   B. cave in   C. doze off   D. die off

4. Jane fell asleep in class today. She must have _____ studying for the exam until long past midnight.
   A. stayed up   B. made up   C. cooled off   D. signed in

5. You have to learn to deal with difficult situations when they _____.
   A. break out   B. blast off   C. crop up   D. blow up

課後作業

請選出與劃線片語意思相同的字詞。

1. Comic books really <u>appeal to</u> young people.
   A. surprise　　　B. attract　　　C. disappoint　　D. anger

2. We must <u>awake to</u> the dangers facing our country.
   A. realize　　　B. ignore　　　C. avoid　　　D. create

3. It seems that my explanation only <u>adds to</u> your bewilderment.
   A. causes　　　B. eases　　　C. increases　　　D. highlights

4. Chris <u>blacked out</u> in the scorching sun. We used ice-water to bring her around.
   A. died　　　B. fainted　　　C. vomited　　　D. fell

5. The judge <u>called on</u> both sides to settle their dispute out of court, but they persisted in bringing it to court.
   A. forbade　　　B. challenged　　C. expected　　　D. asked

6. With entry to the WTO, farmers <u>call for</u> government subsidies. They claim that they can not eke out a decent living without subsidies.
   A. refuse　　　B. demand　　　C. grant　　　D. provide

7. Nowadays, one of the major concerns is how to <u>dispose of</u> nuclear waste. It will not go away as time passes.
   A. examine　　　B. conceal　　　C. store　　　D. discard

8. The meeting <u>dragged on</u> even though many teachers in attendance had dozed off.
   A. continued　　B. ended　　　C. began　　　D. occurred

9. It is rumored that someone bought votes in the last election. The police are looking into the case, trying to <u>get at</u> the truth, but seem to be getting nowhere so far.
   A. distort　　　B. tell　　　C. discover　　　D. reveal

10. The line was busy, and the operator asked me if I would like to <u>hang on</u>. I told her that I would hang up and call back later.

    A. leave　　　　B. talk　　　　C. sleep　　　　D. wait

11. A bomb exploded at the railroad station, injuring several people. The police are <u>inquiring into</u> this case. They are determined to find out who is responsible for the explosion.

    A. hearing　　　B. investigating　C. solving　　　D. citing

12. After work, married women have to hurry home to <u>see about</u> dinner while single women go see movies or spend time in karaoke pubs.

    A. eat　　　　　B. prepare　　　C. buy　　　　　D. enjoy

13. He only earns fifty thousand dollars a month; therefore, a donation of one hundred thousand dollars is not to be <u>sneezed at</u>.

    A. wasted　　　B. shared　　　C. ignored　　　D. exaggerated

14. The letter "V" <u>stands for</u> victory.

    A. represents　B. causes　　　C. matches　　　D. prevents

15. It is unfair of you to <u>trade on</u> Ted's generosity. You act like a parasite.

    A. despise　　　B. praise　　　C. exploit　　　D. criticize

Unit 4

詞彙和結構─片語 (二)

⭐ Type III 動詞 + (代)名詞 + 副詞

⭐ Type IV 動詞 + 副詞 + 介系詞 + (代)名詞

⭐ 課後作業

Type III 動詞 + (代)名詞 + 副詞

以下是第三類型「動詞＋(代)名詞＋副詞」中常見的副詞，以及這些副詞所代表的意義。

1. **around/about** 粗暴的對待： boss/push/kick sb about/around (任意驅使人、頤指氣使地對待人), kick sb/sth about/around (踢打人/物)

2. **across** 表達或了解： get/put ideas across to sb (讓別人了解你的想法)

3. **apart** 區別： tell people/things apart (區別)

4. **around** 改變看法： talk/win sb around = win/talk sb over (說服某人)

5. **aside**

   a. 忽視、丟棄： put/set the plan aside (未考慮計畫), brush/sweep the protest aside (漠視抗議), shrug criticisms aside (漠視所有批評)

   b. 保留： put/lay/leave/set sth aside (保留某物作他用)

6. **away**

   a. 貯存或藏起來： lock/hide/put/store sth away (把物鎖/藏/收拾/貯藏起來)

   b. 消失： wear/eat/rub/drain sth away (磨損/腐蝕/磨掉/耗盡掉), laugh sth away (對某事一笑置之), explain sth away (把[事]搪塞過)

   c. 趕/帶走： scare/send/clear/turn sb away (嚇/攆/趕走/打發走某人)

7. **back**

   a. 歸還或取回： give/hand/send/pay sth back (歸還/交還/退還/償還某物)

   b. 抑制： keep sth back (抑制情感、話語、事情的發展), hold back tears/laughter (抑制住眼淚/笑), hold sb/sth back (抑制)

   c. 往後移動可引申為不繼續做： pull back our forces (撤走兵力)

8. **down**

   a. 拆毀： pull/tear/knock/take/bring a building down (拆毀建築物)

   b. 停止運作： shut/close down a factory (關閉工廠)

   c. 規模、價值、速度、溫度的減少： put/bring/keep/hold prices down (降低價格), play sth down (降低重要性), slow sb/sth down (減速), cool sth down (使溫

度下降), calm sb down ([使]冷靜下來), settle sb down (使安靜下來), water sth down (削弱某事物的效果), turn sth down (調低聲音)

d. 記錄：write/take sth down (記下來)

e. 快吞：wash sth down (with a drink) ([喝飲料]把食物吞下去)

f. 鎮壓、擊潰：bring a government down (使政府倒台), put a riot down (鎮壓暴動), turn sb/sth down (拒絕)

g. 找到：hunt/track sb/sth down (追捕、捕捉)

✎ 練習六

請依上下文選出適當答案。

1. You are not my superior. I don't think you have the right to _____ me _____.

   A. scare ...away　B. settle ... down　C. boss...around　D. win...around

2. They _____ some houses in the center of the city to make room for a new luxury hotel.

   A. tore down　　B. shut down　　C. gave back　　D. hid away

3. The robbers are still at large, but the police are determined to _____ them _____ and bring them to justice.

   A. calm...down　B. turn...away　　C. kick...about　D. track...down

4. The customers often complain about the low quality of the bread, but the baker always _____ their complaints _____, saying they are too fussy.

   A. takes...down　B. shrugs...aside　C. tells...apart　　D. waters...down

5. A riot broke out and the police were called in to _____ it _____. Two hours later, everything returned to normal.

   A. play...down　　B. put...down　　C. laugh...away　D. put ...aside

9. **forth**

a. 表達：put sth forth (提出[計畫、建議])

b. 出現或產生：give sth forth (發出[聲音、氣味、煙])

10. **forward**

a. 時間或位置向前：bring/put sth forward (提前)【<=> put sth back(延後)】

b. 表達或提出：bring/put sth forward (提出[建議或想法])

11. **in**

a. 插入、滲透、吸收了解：drink sth in (吸收[水等]、專心聆聽、陶醉於[美景等])

b. 混合或加入：count sb/sth in (某人/物計算在內)

c. 收集或取得：send/hand/turn sth in (呈送/繳交)

d. 開始：phase sth in (逐步採用)

12. **off**

a. 離開：let/get/drop sb off (讓人下車), see/send sb off (送行), wave sb off (揮手叫人離開)

b. 脫下，相反字為 on：take/throw/cast clothes off (脫掉衣服)

c. 關掉電源、瓦斯、水龍頭，相反字為 on：turn/switch/shut sth off (關掉[電源、瓦斯、水龍頭等]), leave sth off (讓燈、瓦斯等關著)

d. 停止或取消某計畫：put sth off (將某事延期), call sth off (取消某計畫)

e. 中斷：cut sth off (切斷[供應]), cut sb off (打斷說話、切斷電話)

f. 引爆：let/set fireworks off (放[鞭炮])

g. 消除：write sth off (註銷[債務等]), cross sth off/out (劃掉[名字、文字等]), pay sth off (還清欠債), buy sb off (收買某人), swear sth off (發誓戒掉某事物)

h. 厭惡：put/turn sb off (使[人]倒胃口)

i. 開釋：let/get sb off (with a warning) (僅以警告使某人脫罪)

j. 成功：pull/bring/carry sth off (做成某困難的事)

k. 休假：take/have/get a day off (休一天假), lay sb off (裁員), pay sb off (發清工資解雇某人)

l. 從整體中去除一部分： shave sth off (剃鬍子、用刀刮去表面薄薄一層)，
cream sth off (抽取[奶油、精華])

m. 展示： show (sth) off (炫耀)

n. 責備： tell sb off (責備某人)

o. 釋放： let off a sound/energy/steam (釋放聲音或能源或蒸汽), give off a
smell/a sound/light/heat (放出味道/聲音/光/熱)

p. 阻止或保護： hold/keep sb/sth off (擋住[敵人或攻擊]), warn sb off (警告某人
避開)

q. 忽視： laugh sth off (對某事一笑置之), write sb/sth off (認為某人/事是失敗
的), brush sth/sb off (對某人/事充耳不聞)

r. 開始： sth spark/trigger/set/touch sth off ([事]引起/觸發某事)

✏️ 練習七

請依上下文選出適當答案。

1. I went to the airport to _____ Tina _____. She was departing for
France.
    A. tell...off   B. see...off   C. let...off   D. buy...off

2. Jane bought a new dress and _____ it _____. She said that it cost
ten thousand dollars and eagerly expected her colleagues to admire her.
    A. counted...in   B. turned...in   C. took...off   D. showed ...off

3. We had to _____ our plan for a picnic because of the typhoon.
    A. call off   B. put forward   C. water down   D. phase in

4. The factory is going to shut down, and the workers will be _____.
    A. let off   B. turned off   C. laid off   D. cut off

5. Bob ran into debt and had to _____ it _____ by selling his car.
    A. write...off   B. brush...off   C. pay...off   D. bring...down

13. **on**

   a. 穿衣物，相反字為 off ： put /have sth on (穿上/穿著衣服), try sth on (試穿[衣服])

   b. 開電源、瓦斯、水龍頭，相反字為 off ： keep (leave)/turn (switch) the radio/light/tap/gas/engine on (使收音機[燈/水龍頭/瓦斯/引擎]繼續開著/打開收音機等)

   c. 安排： put sth on (安排[表演、音樂會、話劇]的演出), lay sth on (安裝[水、電、瓦斯])

   d. 鼓勵： cheer sb on (給某人加油)

14. **out**

   a. 排除： count sb out (of a plan) (排除[人]在[計畫]之外), cross sth out (劃掉[物]), leave/miss sb/sth out (忽略[人/物]), rule sth out (排除)

   b. 消滅： wear shoes/tires out (穿/用壞鞋子/輪胎), wear shoes/tires out (穿/用壞鞋子/輪胎), put a fire out (撲滅火), wipe sb/sth out (鏟除)

   c. 疲憊： wear/tire/knock sb out (使人筋疲力竭)

   d. 解決： work/think/figure out a problem/calculation (解決問題/計算), sort out a mess/problem (處理雜亂事情/問題), find sth out (經研究或探詢獲知[事]), make sth out (瞭解), puzzle sth out (動腦筋解答), carry a plan out (執行[計畫]), ride out a storm/crisis (安然渡過暴風雨/危機)

   e. 打破寧靜： pour one's heart/grief out (宣洩情緒/哀傷), let out a scream (發出叫喊)

   f. 失去意識： knock/put sb out (將[人]擊昏/使[人]失去意識)

   g. 公諸於世： share food/money out (平均分配食物/錢), pass things out (分發東西), bring sth out (出版、發表、顯示[才能或氣質]), let news out (洩漏消息)

   h. 分散： lay things out (on a table) (陳列東西在桌子上) , spin sth out (拖延[討論、談判])

   i. 選擇： point sb/sth out (指出[人/物]), single/pick sb/sth out (挑選出來), seek/search sb/sth out (找出來)

j. 使完整、清楚、整齊： write out a prescription/a letter of application (填寫藥單/申請書), make out a check/a bill (開[支票/帳單]), fill a form out (填寫[表格、文件])

15. **over**

a. 轉換： turn/hand sb/sth over to sb (將某人物轉讓給某人), take sth over from sb (從某人手中接管某事物), win/buy sb over (把某人爭取/買通過來)

b. 重複： do/read/work sth over (重做/讀/做)

c. 熟思： talk sth over(討論), look/check sth over (仔細查看), think sth over (考慮)

d. 越過： run sb/sth over ([用車]輾過某人/物)

練習八

請依上下文選出適當答案。

1. I had _____ several pairs of shoes before I found any that suited me.
   A. tried on   B. threw off   C. singled out   D. passed out

2. The crowd _____ the runners _____ as they ran the last lap. The shouts of "Go! Go!" hurried them on.
   A. knocked...out   B. counted...out   C. cheered...on   D. ran...over

3. I'll have to _____ Jack _____ because he has dual citizenship. Under the law, he can't run for office.
   A. search...out   B. rule...out   C. point...out   D. win...over

4. What did you say? I couldn't quite _____ it _____. In fact, I'm completely clueless.
   A. look...over   B. spin...out   C. leave...out   D. make...out

5. You should _____ her generous offer for a day or so before you accept it. You have to make sure that she has no ulterior motives.
   A. turn over   B. turn down   C. think over   D. puzzle out

16. **through**

a. 完成或成功：carry a plan through (完成計畫), put/push/rush a law/proposal through (推動[法案、提議]通過)

b. 溝通：get sth through/across/over (to sb) (使[訊息]被人理解), put a call/sb through (to sb) (接通電話)

c. 從頭到尾：think sth through (反覆考慮某事), look sth through (仔細查看某事), follow sth through (徹底執行)

17. **up**

a. 建設：set up a school/committee (設立學校/委員會), fix up a meeting/an agreement/details (安排會議/合同/細節)

b. 迅速結束或完成：wrap sth up (成交[買賣]、商定[協議]、結束[事情]、做總結), pay sth up (付清[債務]), use/burn/buy sth up (用完/燒毀/全部買下)

c. 釘牢或關緊：wrap sth up (把物包起來), pack sth up (打包[行李]), button sth up (把扣子扣起來), zip sth up (拉起拉鍊), do sth up (把扣子扣起來、拉起拉鍊), cover sth up (蓋住某物、掩飾不良行為)

d. 毀滅或破壞：blow sth up (把某物炸掉), smash/bash sth up (摧毀), beat sb up (痛毆某人), mess sth up (把某物弄髒亂、破壞計畫好的事)

e. 發掘：look a word up (查單字), pick sth up ([用無線電]接收到[信號]、聽/聞/看到]

f. 發生：bring sth up (提出[議題、建議])

g. 尺寸、價值、速度、溫度、音量、活力的增加：blow sth up (誇大事物), play sth up (大肆渲染) 【<=>play sth down (輕描淡寫)】, speed (sth) up (加快速度), step up production (加速生產), heat/warm sth up (把物加熱/煮沸), cheer sb up ([人/事]使人振作起來), turn sth up (把[收音機、電視等]開大聲) 【<=> turn sth down】, shore sth up (支持某物)

h. 乾淨、整齊：clean/clear/wipe a mess up (清除雜亂物), patch sth up (補衣服), patch/stitch/make a quarrel up (言歸於好)

i. 聚集或混合：store sth up (儲存某物), round people/animals up (把人或動物聚集在一起), mix things up (把東西混合在一起)

j. 密集學習： brush/polish/rub sth up (溫習)

k. 想像或創作： think/dream sth up (憑空想像), cook/make sth up (捏造某事物), draw sth up (草擬)

l. 嘔吐： throw food up (把食物嘔吐出來)

m. 變成碎片： break/split/divide sth up (分開某物), carve sth up (瓜分某物)

練習九

請依上下文選出適當答案。

1. They dropped a bomb on the bridge and _____ it _____.
   A. blew...up   B. cleaned...up   C. broke...up   D. shored...up

2. Tina's parents died when she was only two years old. Therefore, her grandparents _____ her _____.
   A. cheered...up   B. brought...up   C. beat...up   D. picked...out

3. The story is not true. I _____ it _____.
   A. brushed...up   B. thought...through C. picked...up   D. made...up

4. I am going to _____ this project _____ this week. I'll call you when I finish it.
   A. push...through B. wrap...up   C. play...up   D. bring...up

5. I put my answers in the wrong blanks. Thus, I _____ the test and flunked out.
   A. drew up   B. looked over   C. messed up   D. rode out

Type IV 動詞 + 副詞 + 介系詞 + (代)名詞

以下是第四類型「動詞＋副詞＋介系詞＋(代)名詞」中常見的副詞或介系詞，以及它們所代表的意義。

1. **along**

   a. 進步或進行：get along with sb/sth (進展)

   b. 同意：go along with sb/sth (同意某人/觀點)

2. **apart** 區別：stand apart from sb (與某人有所區別)

3. **away** 不介入：shy away from sth (避免), stay/keep away from sb/sth (避開、不要接近[某人/物]), back away from sth (不願考慮)

4. **back**

   a. 過去時間：look back on sth (回顧), go/date back to sth (追溯到某時侯)

   b. 抑制：cut/scale back on sth (減少[費用])

   c. 往後移動，可引申為不繼續做：pull/draw back from sth (撤回諾言或協議)

5. **down**

   a. 向下：look down on sb (輕視)

   b. 基本要素：sth come/boil down to sth (事情終究)

   c. 停止運作：come/go down with a disease (生病)

   d. 規模、價值的減少：cut down on sth (減少[開支])

6. **forth** 表達：come forth/forward with sth (提出[計畫、建議])

7. **forward**

   a. 時間或位置向前：look forward to sth (盼望)

   b. 表達或提出：come forward/forth with sth (提出[建議或想法])

8. **in**

   a. 進入或到達某處：zero/home in on a target (槍砲瞄準某一目標), close in on sb/sth ([人]逼近某人/物), drop in on sb (拜訪)

b. 插入、滲透或吸收了解： tune/listen in to sth (聽廣播)

c. 混合或加入： go in for sth (參加[比賽、考試]、嗜好某事物)

d. 收集、取得： cash in on sth (不正當利用)

9. **off**

a. 離開： walk/go/make off with sth (順手偷走東西), walk off/away with a prize (輕易贏得[獎品等])

b. 開釋： get off with a light punishment (僅受輕罰而脫罪)

10. **on** 附著： hold/hang on to sth (緊抓住)

11. **up**

a. 發生： come up with an idea/an answer/a plan (提出想法/答案/計畫)

b. 接近： face up to sth (毅然面對[責任、困難]), live up to sth (達到[標準、要求或期望])

c. 密集學習： bone/brush up on sth (鑽研/溫習/攻讀某科目)

d. 向上方向： look up to sb (尊重某人), rise up against sb/sth (站起來反抗), stand up for sth (爭取)

e. 補償： make up for sth (彌補)

練習十

請依上下文選出適當答案。

1. Linda is easy-going, so he can _____ everyone.
   A. look up to　　　　　B. stand apart from
   C. get along well with　D. look down upon

2. I keep coughing and have a sore throat. I am afraid that I must have _____ a cold.
   A. come down with　　B. risen up against
   C. shied away from　　D. looked forward to

3. I went to Taipei yesterday and _____ an old friend of mine. We were happy to see each other again thirty years after graduating from university.

   A. closed in on
              B. dropped in on

   C. went along with
           D. stayed away from

4. Someone broke into the office and _____ the notebook computer. I wonder who the thief could be.

   A. made up for   B. cashed in on   C. held on to   D. made off with

5. John isn't rich enough. He should _____ his expenses.

   A. cut down on
              B. come forward with

   C. live up to
               D. stand up for

課後作業

請選出與劃線片語意義相同的字詞。

1. You have to <u>account for</u> the sudden change in your thinking.

   A. make   B. explain   C. oppose   D. experience

2. All players must <u>abide by</u> the rules of the game.

   A. pass   B. break   C. bend   D. obey

3. Sales <u>added up to</u> $2 million last year.

   A. totaled   B. exceeded   C. included   D. excluded

4. Even when <u>allowing for</u> delays, we should finish the work early.

   A. making   B. avoiding   C. considering   D. causing

5. All attempts to <u>bring about</u> a change in Jack's condition have failed.

   A. cause   B. explain   C. avoid   D. understand

6. Most members were against Bob, who would have lost his position if I hadn't <u>backed</u> him <u>up</u>.

   A. deserted   B. known   C. introduced   D. supported

7. Sorry to <u>break in on</u> you, but someone is asking for you at the door.
   A. awaken   B. leave   C. interrupt   D. frighten

8. How did it <u>come about</u> that humans can speak so many languages?
   A. happen   B. continue   C. end   D. last

9. How on earth did you <u>come by</u> these tickets for the concert?
   A. sell   B. lose   C. steal   D. obtain

10. Since I have promised to take my daughter to the zoo, I must <u>carry</u> my promise <u>out</u>.
    A. break   B. fulfill   C. make   D. ignore

11. The attempt to save the victims from the fire <u>came off</u>, and the fire fighters were hailed as heroes.
    A. succeeded   B. failed   C. was justified   D. was interrupted

12. He <u>popped up</u> on television in army fatigues and with an AK-47, calling himself a freedom fighter.
    A. fainted   B. appeared   C. exclaimed   D. admitted

13. Old newspapers and magazines are piling up; I am afraid that you will have to <u>do away with</u> some of them.
    A. collect   B. calculate   C. discard   D. study

14. Tina <u>fell out</u> with her boyfriend yesterday, but now they have made up.
    A. quarreled   B. consulted   C. agreed   D. competed

15. Chris has been given a leave of absence to attend a computer course. Can you <u>fill in for</u> her for a few days?
    A. contact   B. replace   C. teach   D. leave

16. You promised to return my money today, but now you want to <u>go back on</u> your promise. How can I trust you?
    A. make   B. fulfill   C. break   D. honor

17. The pickpocket <u>broke away</u> from the crowd and ran off down the street.
    A. separated   B. disappeared   C. came   D. escaped

18. Politicians tend to make more promises than they can deliver in order to be voted into office. Once they are in power, they find ways to <u>get around</u> their credibility problem.

    A. solve   B. avoid   C. create   D. understand

19. You had better <u>hold off</u> making any decision until you talk it over with your wife. After all, it is you two that are going to live in the house.

    A. deny   B. risk   C. delay   D. admit

20. A man wearing a helmet tried to <u>hold up</u> a bank on Nan Hai Road, but he was subdued by a guard. The gun used in the robbery turned out to be a toy gun.

    A. rob   B. surround   C. manage   D. establish

21. Before we use this computer, we have to <u>iron out</u> some operating problems first; otherwise, it might crash.

    A. solve   B. identify   C. create   D. raise

22. I wish the rain would <u>let up</u> before I set out on my trip, but it seems that it will go on.

    A. continue   B. fell   C. stop   D. pour

23. It sounds like someone is <u>listening in</u> on our conversation. I suspect that my telephone has been bugged.

    A. insisting   B. eavesdropping C. expanding   D. reflecting

24. I managed to <u>set aside</u> some money each month from my salary and now it adds up to one million dollars. I have decided to use it as a down payment for a new apartment.

    A. spend   B. borrow   C. save   D. withdraw

25. That woman <u>owned up</u> to shoplifting after the shopkeeper found a lipstick in her purse.

    A. objected   B. admitted   C. witnessed   D. stuck

26. Mark has a keen interest in jigsaw puzzles. He must be able to <u>match up</u> all the pieces.

    A. collect   B. recognize   C. assemble   D. separate

27. Clear this mess up immediately; I can't <u>put up with</u> it anymore.

    A. endure   B. forget   C. remember   D. understand

28. Henry got into an argument with me yesterday, but we have <u>patched up</u> our differences and are friends again.

    A. stressed   B. resolved   C. ignored   D. told

29. That saleswoman tried to <u>pass</u> the paintings <u>off</u> as originals, but I saw through her. I showed other customers that they were nothing more than replicas.

    A. disguised   B. dismissed   C. hailed   D. described

30. Dining with a woman like Mrs. Wang really <u>puts</u> me <u>off</u>. She is always showing off her jewelry, telling how much her husband loves her, and saying how smart her son is. Hearing her talk turns my stomach.

    A. frightens   B. amuses   C. embarrasses   D. disgusts

31. The house was an awful mess after the party. We <u>set about</u> cleaning up as soon as the guests left.

    A. began   B. continued   C. finished   D. avoided

32. After he retired from the school, Tim <u>set up</u> his own business. He ran a publishing company. Many of his colleagues wished him well in his new career.

    A. quitted   B. increased   C. started   D. restricted

33. I hung around the hotel lobby for half an hour, but Tina didn't <u>show up</u>. Finally, I left. I hate those who are never on time.

    A. leave   B. wait   C. apologize   D. appear

34. The owner wants $8 million for his house and won't <u>settle for</u> anything less.

    A. pay   B. return   C. raise   D. accept

35. Bob tried to <u>strike up</u> a conversation with the girl sitting opposite him. He cleared his throat and said, "Hi. Do you also like to travel by train?"

    A. end   B. continue   C. start   D. change

36. We usually <u>sum up</u> our main points in the last paragraph.

    A. present   B. discuss   C. omit   D. summarize

37. Jack is seriously ill, so I will <u>stand in for</u> him in tonight's performance of the play.

    A. comfort   B. replace   C. defend   D. accompany

38. Rick <u>takes after</u> his father not only in appearance but also in personality. His father is very proud that Rick's behavior mirrors his own.

    A. imitates   B. remembers   C. disappoints   D. resembles

39. Rick's boss tends to overwork his staff mercilessly. He often forces Rick to <u>take on</u> several tasks at the same time. Worse still, the tasks Rick is entrusted with are quite challenging.

    A. complicate   B. shirk   C. glorify   D. undertake

40. I was <u>tied up</u> all morning. I did not even have time to go to the bathroom.

    A. busy   B. tired   C. sick   D. sad

Unit 5

詞彙和結構—文法結構 (一)

　　較常考的文法重點包括：時式、助動詞、比較結構、假設語氣、被動式、關係子句、動狀詞、主詞與動詞的一致、轉折語、句子種類。轉折語已在 Unit 1 和 Unit 2 談過。句子種類將在 Unit 11 和 Unit 12 討論。其餘的就是本單元及下一單元的內容。這兩單元僅點出要特別注意的文法重點。

Focus 1　時式

1.　靜態動詞描述狀態，不可用於進行式。靜態動詞包含以下幾類：

意　義	動　詞
1. 情意	love, like, hate
2. 感覺	feel, smell, taste, look (= seem), sound, hear (聽見), see (看見), perceive, appear, seem
3. 認知	know, understand, realize, remember, remind, believe, doubt, imagine
4. 異同	differ, resemble
5. 適合	fit, suit
6. 存在、具有、歸屬、包含	be, exist; have (有), lack, belong to

> 例　The coffee **tastes** bitter, and the bread **looks** stale.
> 這咖啡嚐起來很苦，而麵包看起來不新鮮。

2.　過去簡單式與過去進行式經常併用在同一句子中。過去進行式描述較長久的動作在進行中，而過去簡單式描述較短的動作穿插在其中。

> 例　Sam **was reading** in bed when he **heard** footsteps in the hall.
> 聽見走廊腳步聲時，山姆正躺在床上看書。

3.　在時間副詞子句 (when, as, before, after, as, until, once, as soon as) 和條件子句 (if, even if, unless, as long as) 中，用簡單式代替未來式。但主要子句裡的動詞還是要用未來式。

> 例　If it **rains** tomorrow, the game **will be** put off.
> 要是明天下雨，比賽將延期。

4. 行為發生在過去某時，而與現在無關，用過去簡單式。如與現在有關，用現在完成式。

    例 a. I **read** three articles this morning.

    我早上讀了三篇文章→ 說話時間在午後。

    b. I **have** already **read** three articles this morning.

    我早上已經讀了三篇文章→說話時間在早上

5. 瞬間動詞如：die, buy, graduate, begin, appear, arrive, depart, leave, vanish 等動作的履行在瞬間就完成。沒有這種持續性的完成式用法，因此下面第 (a) 句是錯的，應改為第 (b) 句或第 (c) 句。但這些動詞可用於表完成性的完成式裡，如 (d) 句。

    例 a. My father has died for three years. (誤)

    我父親已經死了三年。

    b. It is three years since my father died.

    自從我父親去世已經有三年了。

    c. My father has been dead for three years.

    我父親已經死三年了。

    d. My father has already died.

    我父親已過世了。

6. 行為發生在過去某時的較早之前而與過去某時有關。通常指過去有兩個動作，一個先發生，另一個後發生。先發生的用過去完成式，後發生的用過去式。

    例 By the time Sam **stopped** by to get Amy, she **had** already **finished** her work.

    在山姆來帶艾美走時，她已完成她的工作。

✎ **練習一**

請從下面四個選項中選出最適合題意的字或詞。

1. Mom, something _____ good! What are you cooking?
   A. is smelling   B. smells   C. smelled   D. was smelling

2. An old man _____ the street at that moment. I stopped my car just in time.
   A. crossed   B. had crossed   C. was crossing   D. would cross

3. As long as I _____ enough money, I will buy a new car.
   A. have   B. will have   C. am having   D. have had

4. I _____ in Taipei since I was born.
   A. live   B. will have   C. am living   D. have lived

5. I _____ English for six years before I went to college.
   A. had learned   B. learned   C. have learned   D. will learn

Focus II 助動詞

　　助動詞包括： do, may/might, can/could, shall/should, will/would, must, have to, ought to, needn't, dare not 等，可表示不同的情意。要特別注意的是如指的是現在或未來則助動詞後用原形動詞，如指的是過去，則助動詞後用完成式。

例 a. Hurry up! Linda **must be** waiting at the airport.
　　快一點！琳達一定在機場等著我們。

　b. Sam dropped off to sleep in class. He **must have stayed** up all night.
　　山姆上課睡著了。他整晚一定沒睡覺。

助動詞所代表的意義，請看下表：

助動詞	功　用
will/would	承諾、威脅、決心、邀請或提議、請求、命令、可能性、未來、意圖、意願、傾向、習慣
can/could	能力、可能性、許可、建議、請求
may/might	可能性、許可、請求、建議、願望
must	義務需要、可能性、許可、命令
shall	承諾、威脅、建議、許可
should	可能性、義務需要、建議、驚訝、命令
have to	義務需要
ought to	義務需要
need	義務需要
dare	勇氣
be to	義務需要、命令、計劃安排
be going to	可能性、計劃安排、決心
had better	建議
would like	願望
would rather/sooner	願望
might as well	建議

✎ **練習二**

請從下面四個選項中選出最適合題意的字或詞。

1. Jane _____ play tennis very well. I'm no match for her.

    A. will   B. should   C. can   D. must

2. You _____ the boy from drowning, but you just stood by.

    A. could save   B. could have saved

    C. must save   D. must have saved

3. Sue: The telephone is ringing.

    Helen: That _____ Sam. He said he would phone at this time.

    A. might be   B. might have been

    C. will be   D. would have been

4.　Mike: I saw Rice having a drink with Tony at a pub last night.

　　Amy: The girl you saw _____ Rice. She was staying at my home last night.

　　A. might not be　　　　　　B. might not have been

　　C. could not be　　　　　　D. could not have been

5.　Husband: I was locked out last night.

　　Wife: You _____ the key with you when you were out of the house.

　　A. should take　　　　　　B. should have taken

　　C. must take　　　　　　　D. must have taken

6.　It is surprising that you _____ down her invitation yesterday.

　　A. should have turned　　　B. would have turned

　　C. should turn　　　　　　D. would turn

Focus III　比較結構

　　形容詞與副詞的比較句型是經常考的題型，必須多加練習以期熟練。主要的比較結構有以下幾種：

1.　**as + adj/adv + as**　和...一樣

　　例　a. All of us are just as busy as bees (are).

　　　　　　我們忙得猶如蜜蜂。

　　　　b. The band is playing as loudly as (it did) yesterday.

　　　　　　這樂隊演奏跟昨天一樣大聲。

2.　**no less + adj/adv + than**　不亞於

　　例　Helen is no less beautiful than her sister.

　　　　= Helen is as beautiful as her sister.

　　　　海倫的美麗不輸給她姊姊。

3. **no + 比較級 + than**　和...一樣不

   例 They are no better off economically than they were.

   　　= They are not any better off economically than they were.

   　　= They are just as poor as they were.

   　　經濟上他們和以前一樣不好。

4. **倍數 + as + adj/adv + as**　是...的幾倍

   例 Sam is twice as old as his wife.

   　　= Sam is twice his wife's age.

   　　山姆的年齡是他老婆的兩倍。

5. **~er + than 或 more + adj/adv + than**　比...還 (優等比較)

   例 Jack speaks English more fluently than Mark.

   　　捷克英文說得比馬克流利。

   Note

   比較級後如果是 of the two，則比較級前要加 the。

   John is the taller of the two brothers.
   約翰是兩兄弟中較高者。

6. **less + adj/adv + than**　比...還不 (劣等比較)

   例 Linda was now less anxious about her future than she had once been.

   　　琳達現在比以前較不擔心她的未來。

7. **the + 比較級 , the + 比較級**　越 ... 越 ...

   例 The further you get in politics, the fewer real friends you have.

   　　你愈涉入政治，你真正的朋友就愈少。

8. **less...than...或 not as/so...as...**　與其說...不如說

   例 I was less alive than dead.

   　　= I was not as alive as dead.

   　　= I was more dead than alive.

   　　與其說我生，不如說我死了。

9. **the/所有格 + 最高級　最...**

    例　John is the tallest boy in this class.

    = John is taller than any other boy in this class.

    = No other boy in this class is taller than John.

    約翰是這班最高的男孩。

10. **the/所有格 + least + adj/adv　最不...**

    例　Fried chicken would be my least favorite choice.

    炸雞是我最不喜歡的選擇。

11. **(just) as 子句, so 子句　正如**

    例　As you make your bed, so you must lie upon it.

    自作自受。

12. **A is to B what/as C is to D　A 之於 B 正如 C 之於 D**

    例　A camel is to the desert as a boat is to the sea.

    駱駝之於沙漠正如船隻之於海洋。

練習三

請從下面四個選項中選出最適合題意的字或詞。

1. Just as jade must be carved or polished, _____ the mind should be cultivated. The best way to develop the mind is to read great books.

    A. as   B. similarly

    C. so   D. likewise

2. A desk made of iron is _____ one made of wood. It can last for several decades, but a wooden desk will wear out in ten years.

    A. more durable than   B. less durable than

    C. as durable as   D. no more durable than

3. Objectively, Poland is _____ at any time since the 16th century. Yet the mood is gloomy.
    A. as badly off as
    B. as well off as
    C. worse off than
    D. better off than

4. Demand for steel has never been _____; therefore, its prices have reached a record high.
    A. high
    B. higher
    C. the highest
    D. the least high

5. A car bombing killed two Israeli soldiers yesterday. Among the security officials on the new front line, the mood was _____. They didn't feel a lot of anger towards the Palestinians; instead, they expressed their deepest sorrow at the deaths of the soldiers.
    A. sadder than angry
    B. more sad than angry
    C. as sad as angry
    D. less sad than angry

6. Jane is _____ of the two sisters. She is 160 centimeters tall while her sister is 155.
    A. very the taller
    B. very taller
    C. much the taller
    D. much taller

7. Sales of PCs amounted to $3 billion in Taiwan, _____ what they were two years earlier.
    A. twice as much as
    B. twice as many as
    C. twice more than
    D. twice less than

8. The death toll from the September 21 earthquake has risen still _____ in the _____ disaster since 1900.
    A. farther, worse
    B. farther, worst
    C. further, worse
    D. further, worst

Focus IV 假設語氣

有三種假設語氣你一定要熟記，相關用法與說明如下。

1. **未來可能發生的假設**

   ◆ If NP + V(現在簡單式)..., NP + (will/can/must/may) + V

   例 a. If I **drink** too much coffee, I **will be** unable to fall asleep.
   我如果喝太多咖啡，我會睡不著。

   b. If water **freezes**, it **becomes** hard and solid.
   水如果結凍，就變硬成固體。

2. **與現在或未來事實相反的假設**

   ◆ If NP + 過去簡單式/were ..., NP + would/could/might + V

   例 a. If I **were** a bird, I **would fly** to you.
   如果我是一隻鳥，我就飛到你身邊。

   b. If I **had** wings, I **would be** able to fly.
   如果我有翅膀，我就能飛。

   ◆ If NP + were to + V..., NP + would/could/might + V

   例 If the sea **were to** dry up, a lot of creatures **would become** extinct.
   要是海水枯乾，很多生物將會消失。

   ◆ If NP + should + V..., (NP + will/would) + V (萬一...)

   例 If you **should** run into trouble, don't hesitate to ask for my help.
   萬一你遇到麻煩，不要猶豫來找我幫忙。

3. **與過去事實相反的假設**

   ◆ If NP + had + -ed..., NP + would/could/might have + -ed

   例 If Billy **hadn't sprained** his ankle, he **would have won** the race.
   要是比利沒有扭傷腳踝，他會贏得競賽的。

Note

以下是衍生的句型：

1. wish (但願), as if/though (好像) 後的子句中用過去式動詞或 were，表示與現在或未來事實相反。其後的子句中用過去完成式表示與過去事實相反。但 as if 後的子句也可用現在式，表示事情可能發生。

2. it is (high/about) time (that) + S + V 的句型，句中的動詞用過去式。

3. but for + sb/sth (若非)，其後的主要子句，也是用與事實相反的句子。

練習四

請從下面四個選項中選出最適合題意的字或詞。

1. If I _____ my life to live over again, I _____ in love with Vivian.
   A. have, will still fall
   B. will have, will still fall
   C. had, would still fall
   D. would had, would still fall

2. If Helen _____ the meeting last week, she _____ David. Unfortunately, she was sick.
   A. had attended, would have met
   B. attended, would have met
   C. had attended, would meet
   D. attended, would meet

3. Dark clouds are building up. It looks as if it _____ going to rain.
   A. was
   B. is
   C. were
   D. had been

4. My clothes were wet—I may have looked as if I _____ sitting in a steam bath.
   A. am
   B. was
   C. have been
   D. had been

5. I wish I _____ young again.
   A. am
   B. have been
   C. had been
   D. were

6. But for your help, I _____ bankrupt last year.
   A. would have gone
   B. would go
   C. went
   D. had gone

課後作業

請從下面四個選項中選出最適合題意的字或詞。

1. The bill amounts to $550, including a 10% tip. If the 5% tax is also added, the bill _____ $575.

   A. was
   B. will be
   C. is going to be
   D. is about to be

2. I was relieved when I learned that all the children _____ back safe and sound.

   A. had come
   B. has come
   C. came
   D. come

3. The wind was so strong that, when Peter _____ the wall, he lost his balance and fell off the ladder.

   A. was painting
   B. painted
   C. had painted
   D. would paint

4. Look at the way the couple _____ to each other. They must have been in love for a long time.

   A. are talking
   B. talked
   C. will talk
   D. have talked

5. You have always had poor digestion. I am afraid that there _____ something wrong with your stomach.

   A. must be
   B. shall be
   C. must have been
   D. might have been

6. Paul: _____ you _____ go for a drink after work?
   Billy: Well, yes, I guess that would be okay.

   A. Do...have to
   B. Are...to
   C. Ought...to
   D. Would...like to

7. Jane: Oops. I spilled my juice.
   Paul: Don't worry. I _____ go get a paper towel.

   A. am going to
   B. am to
   C. should
   D. will

8. Chris: Let's go for a walk after dinner, _____?
   Sam: O.K.

   A. will you
   B. shall we
   C. will we
   D. shall you

9. He spoke with an air of importance as if he _____ the president of the company.
   A. were   B. is   C. had been   D. has been

10. It irritates me to have to listen to those women's idle gossip. I wish my boss _____ in the office every day so that they would shut their big mouths.
    A. will be   B. will have been
    C. would be   D. would have been

11. If the sun _____ in the west, I would lend money to you.
    A. had risen   B. should rise
    C. were to rise   D. should have risen

12. When driving, make sure to fasten your seat belt. By doing so, you can avoid being seriously hurt if a car crash _____.
    A. should happen   B. would happen
    C. happened   D. has happened

13. If I _____ in the stock market last year, I _____ spare cash for new furniture now.
    A. didn't invest; will have   B. hadn't invested; would have
    C. should invest; will have   D. hadn't invested; would have had

14. Cindy is thirty years old, but if she wears makeup, she will look _____ she really is.
    A. as young as   B. less young than
    C. as old as   D. younger than

15. Taipei is Taiwan's capital, so it is _____ in Taiwan.
    A. most prosperous   B. as prosperous as any city
    C. more prosperous than any other city D. more prosperous than any city

Unit **6**

詞彙和結構—文法結構 (二)

✪ Focus V 被動式

✪ Focus VI 關係子句

✪ Focus VII 動狀詞

✪ Focus VIII 主詞與動詞的一致

✪ 課後作業

Focus V 被動式

1. 要特別注意報導式動詞的被動式有以下兩種。 that 子句中的動詞如果比主要子句中的動詞還早發生，則用完成式的不定詞，如 (b) 句。

   例 a. People say that Alice is rich.

   = It is said that Alice is rich.

   = Alice is said to be rich.

   據說愛麗絲很有錢。

   b. People say that Alice was rich.

   = It is said that Alice was rich.

   = Alice is said to have been rich.

   據說愛麗絲以前很有錢。

2. 有少數主動式動詞如： read, sell, wash, clean, feel, smell, taste, sound, look, show, print, cook ，以及在 need, want, require, be worth 之後的動詞，有時可有被動語意。

   例 a. The knife cuts well.

   這把刀很好切。

   b. Freedom may indeed need fighting for.

   = Freedom may indeed need to be fought for.

   確實，自由可能要用爭取的。

3. 不及物動詞或不及物片語動詞和狀態動詞，不可有被動式。

✎ 練習五

請從下面四個選項中選出最適合題意的字或詞。

1. The book is worth _____.

   A. being read   B. to be read   C. read   D. reading

2. Something strange _____ last night.

 A. had happened   B. happened

 C. was happened   D. had been happened

3. The man is believed to _____ by a falling rock.

 A. be killed   B. kill   C. have been killed   D. have killed

Focus VI 關係子句

 關係子句具有形容詞的功用，放在被修飾名詞組的後面。關係代名詞的使用要特別注意以下幾點。

1. 限制型的關係子句指其先行詞在上下文不知何指，需有一形容詞子句來限定，使讀者能明白所指何人何物。前後不用逗點隔開。關係代名詞可用 that 來代替 who, whom, which (除非之前有介系詞)。受詞的 that, which 和 whom 可省略 (除非之前有介系詞)。

 例 a. Do you know the girl **who/that** is sitting in the corner?

    你認識坐在角落的那個女孩嗎？

   b. Lisa has no one (**who/whom/that**) she can talk to.

    莉莎沒有人可以跟她談話。

2. 非限制型的關係子句，指其先行詞在上下文已經很明顯，讀者也知其所指。前後要逗點隔開(有時也可用破折號或括弧)。關係代名詞不可用 that 來代替 who, whom, which。受詞的 which 和 whom 不可省略。

 例 a. Sam, **who** usually doesn't eat beef, had a steak today.

    山姆通常不吃牛肉，今天卻吃了一客牛排。

   b. Yesterday I called Alice, **whom** I hadn't spoken to for five years.

    昨天我打電話給愛麗絲，我有五年沒跟她通話了。

3. 先行詞為整個句子時，關係代名詞用 which。這時 which 之前須打逗點。

 例 John rolled towards Lily, **which** took her by surprise.

   約翰朝莉莉滾過去，這讓她嚇一跳。

4. 指事物的先行詞之前有最高級形容詞或 the only, the very, all, much, none, any, little, a few, something, everything, anything 。此時關係代名詞用 that 。

    例 a. All **that** matters is happiness and hope.

    　　最重要的事是快樂和希望。

    　　b. The grass on the beach was the shortest and softest (**that**) I had ever seen.

    　　這海灘上的草是我看過最短而柔軟的。

5. 在關係代名詞與動詞之間可插入一短語 "sb + think (認為) / know (知道) / say (說) / hope (希望) / be sure (確定) / believe (相信) / remember (記得) / admit (承認) / agree (同意)"。

    例 a. Folk songs, which **some musicians reckon** are undervalued, must be rediscovered.

    　　我們必須重新去探索民謠，因為一些音樂家認為民謠不受重視。

    　　b. My mother, whom **I'm sure** you remember, passed away last year.

    　　我媽媽，我確信你記得她，去年過世了。

練習六

請從下面四個選項中選出最適合題意的字或詞。

1. Columbus, _____ discovered America in 1492, believed the people there were Indians.

    A. that　　　　B. which　　　　C. who　　　　D. whom

2. The young people, the majority of _____ parents are poor and barely-educated, see little hope in their life.

    A. whose　　　　B. that　　　　C. who　　　　D. whom

3. Jack got married to a woman 20 years his senior, _____ surprised all of us.

    A. that　　　　B. who　　　　C. it　　　　D. which

4. Violence is the very thing _____ the police are trying to avoid.

   A. which   B. that   C. who   D. whom

5. You must be able to beat that guy, _____ I don't expect to be so strong.

   A. that   B. whom   C. who   D. which

6. He has not been tough enough in making reforms, _____ everyone agrees are needed.

   A. that   B. who   C. whom   D. which

Focus VII 動狀詞

動狀詞具有形容詞、副詞和名詞的功用。以下分別簡述。

1. 具有形容詞性質的動狀詞是由一關係代名詞所引領的形容詞子句縮減而來。不定詞具有用途或允許或必須的意義，現在分詞是由進行式變來，而過去分詞的前身是被動式。

例 a. I need someone who **can** help me with my homework.

    = I need someone **to help** me with my homework.

    我需要有人能幫我看家庭作業。

b. I have a lot of things that I **must** do.

    = I have a lot of things **to do**.

    我有很多事要做。

c. The girl **who is playing** the piano is Tina.

    = The girl **playing** the piano is Tina.

    正在彈鋼琴的女孩是緹納。

d. The picture **that was painted** by Jack was hung on the wall.

    =The picture **painted** by Jack was hung on the wall.

    傑克畫的圖被掛在牆上。

2. 具有副詞性質的動狀詞是由一從屬子句所引領的副詞子句縮減而來。不定詞表示目的或結果，而分詞表示時間、原因、條件、讓步。現在分詞表主動，而過去分詞表被動。另外 and 連接的兩句如表示兩事件同時發生，則第二句可改爲分詞片語。

例 a. We eat **to** live.

= We eat **in order to** live.

= We eat **so as to** live.

= We eat **so that** we can live.

我們吃飯是為了活下去。

b. The news is **too** good **to** be true.

= The news is **so** good **that** it cannot be true.

這消息太好了，不可能是真的。

c. Last night I awoke **to find** Jane sobbing.

昨天晚上我醒來發現珍在啜泣。

d. After Jack leapt out of bed, he rushed to the station.

= **Leaping** out of bed, he rushed to the station.

從床上跳起來之後，傑克就衝向車站。

e. Since Mark was faced with mounting debts, he shut down his factory.

= **Faced** with mounting debts, Mark shut down his factory.

因為負債，馬克關閉工廠。

f. If health permits, I will go on working until I am 65.

= Health **permitting**, I will go on working until I am 65.

假如健康許可，我將做到六十五歲。

g. Since this is Singapore, English is often spoken.

= This **being** Singapore, English is often spoken.

因為這是新加坡，人們時常說英文。

h. Mary lay in bed and meanwhile she was reading a novel.

= Mary lay in bed, **reading** a novel.

瑪麗躺在床上看小說。

i. He stopped in front of me, and his arms were loosely folded.

= He stopped in front of me, arms loosely **folded**.

他在我面前停下來，手臂交叉著。

3.　具有名詞性質的動狀詞，須記住哪些動詞之後要接不定詞 (to + V)，哪些動詞之後要接動名詞 (V-ing)。又有些動詞之後接不定詞和動名詞皆可，但義意不同。請看以下對照表：

動　詞	例　句
1. stop+ V-ing 停止做 V-ing 之動作 stop to + V 停下原來動作開始做 to + V 之動作	a. You look tired. You had better stop **working**. 你看起來很累。你最好停止工作。 b. He stopped **to have** a talk with me. 他停下來跟我談話。
2. forget + V-ing 忘記已做了 V-ing 之動作 (事已做) forget to + V 忘記要做 to + V 之動作 (事未做)	a. I will never forget **seeing** Jane on the stage like that with light shining on her face. 我永遠無法忘記看見珍在舞台上時所有燈光照在她身上。 b. Don't forget **to turn** off the lights before you leave. 離開時不要忘記關燈。
3. remember + V-ing 記起已做了 V-ing 之動作 (事已做) remember to + V 記住要做 to + V 之動作 (事未做)	a. I remember **awakening** with somebody shouting. 我記得有人在呼叫時我醒來。 b. Remember **to turn** off the lights before you leave. 離開前記住關掉電燈。

動 詞	例 句
4. regret + V-ing 後悔已做了 V-ing 之動作 (事已做) regret to + V 遺憾要做 to + V 之動作 (事 未做)	a. I don't regret for a single moment **having** lived for pleasure. 我絲毫不後悔為享樂過活。 b. I deeply regret **to have** to announce to you the death of your father. 我深深遺憾要向你宣佈你父親的死亡。
5. mean + V-ing 表意義 mean to + V 表意圖	a. Love means never **having** to say you are sorry. 愛到深處無怨尤。 b. I don't mean **to hurt** your feelings. 我沒有意圖要傷你的情感。
6. try + V-ing 表實驗 try to + V 表設法	a. Try **adding** acid to water and see what will happen. 把酸加在水裡，實驗看看會怎樣。 b. He tried **to open** the door, but it was in vain. 他設法打開門，但徒勞無功。

4. 使役動詞 have 和 make 的受詞之後用原形表主動，而用過去分詞表被動。感官動詞 (如：see, hear, feel, notice, watch) 的受詞之後用原形或現在分詞表主動，原形表完整的事件，而現在分詞強調事件正在進行。另外用過去分詞表被動。但這兩類動詞如變成被動式，則原來用原形的動詞要改成不定詞，如 (f) 句。

例 a. Money can **make** the devil **push** the mill-stone.
錢能使鬼推磨。

b. John had his bike **stolen**.
約翰腳踏車被偷了。

c. I heard him **cough**.
我聽到他咳了一聲。

d. I heard him **coughing**.
我聽到他咳得不停。

e. I finally saw my wishes **translated** into reality.
我終於看到我的願望實現了。

f. They **saw** three boys **jump** over the wall.

= Three boys **were seen to jump** over the wall.

三個男孩被看見跳牆。

✏️ 練習七

請從下面四個選項中選出最適合題意的字或詞。

1. Lily is said to have seen that man _____ on the street. He died a violent death.

    A. killed   B. killing   C. to kill   D. kill

2. I felt the house _____ and rushed out on impulse.

    A. shake   B. shaken   C. shaking   D. to shake

3. I was made _____ for one hour before I was examined by a doctor.

    A. waiting   B. to wait   C. waited   D. wait

4. Don't forget _____ in your paper. The deadline is March 1st.

    A. handing   B. handed   C. hand   D. to hand

5. I still remember _____ for help when the house was shaking violently.

    A. to cry   B. crying   C. cry   D. cried

6. He put his hand into his pocket, _____ as if _____ for something.

    A. and looked, reached   B. looked, he was reaching

    C. who looked, to reach   D. looking, reaching

7. _____ up in the countryside, Mike is _____ wood. He can cut a piece of wood in two with a single blow.

    A. Bringing, good to chop   B. Bringing, good at chopping

    C. Brought, good to chop   D. Brought, good at chopping

8. The main character in "The Old Man And The Sea", a novel _____ by Earnest Hemmingway, was an old man who sailed the sea alone, _____ for sharks.

    A. which is written, to fish   B. which is written, and fishing

    C. written, fishing   D. written, fished

9. Workers _____ the strike risked _____ when they left the factory.

    A. broke, being attacked   B. who broke, being attacked

    C. breaking, attacking   D. to break, attacking

10. On hearing his dog had been kicked to death, Gary sprang to his feet, _____.

    A. and his face trembling with rage   B. and his face was trembled with rage

    C. his face trembled with rage   D. his face trembling with rage

Focus VIII 主詞與動詞的一致

英文的主詞決定動詞的形式。單數主詞(包括單數名詞、第三人稱單數代名詞、不定詞、動名詞、名詞子句)接單數形動詞;複數主詞接複數形動詞。但有些較特別的須要牢記。

1. 有些名詞是 s 結尾,但實際是單數,爲不可數名詞 (U),因此其後接單數形動詞。這些名詞如下表:

名　稱	實　例
學科	physics (物理學), electronics (電子學), athletics (體育), gymnastics (體操), mathematics (數學)。
遊戲	billiards (撞球) , dominoes (骨牌遊戲) , aerobics (有氧運動)。
疾病	measles (麻疹), herpes (疹), rabies (狂犬病), diabetes (糖尿病)。
國名、書名、名字、引言等	the United States (美國), Ali Baba and the Forty Thieves (《阿里巴巴與四十大盜》), The Stars and Stripes (《星條旗—美國國旗》), Athens (雅典)。
其他	debris (瓦礫), news (消息)。

2. 不同意義的 s 結尾名詞如 politics 作「政治」解爲單數;作「政治觀點 (political opinions)」解爲複數。 statistics 作「統計學」解爲單數;作「統計數字」解爲複數。

3. 有些名詞的單複數形相同。接單或複數形動詞視上下文決定。這些名詞包括：series (系列事物), species (物種), sheep (綿羊), deer (鹿), fish (魚), salmon (鮭魚), trout (鱒魚), aircraft (飛機), offspring (子女), spacecraft (太空船), means (手段), works (工廠)。但 fish, salmon, trout 等和 chicken 如當作食物則為不可數名詞與單數形動詞共用。

4. 時間、金錢、距離、重量、速度等，如指一整體單位用單數形動詞。如指個別用複數形動詞。下面例句 (a) 用 have 是因為動態的十年是一天天的經過，強調個別性。而例句 (b) 是以十年作一單位。

> 例 a. Ten years **have** passed since I graduated from this school.
> 自從畢業後十年已經過去了。

> b. Ten years **is** a long time.
> 十年是一段很長的時間。

5. 用 and 連接的名詞片語，如為一體用單數形動詞。如為分開的兩物，用複數形動詞。

> 例 a. The king's son and the heir to the throne **was** there.
> 國王的兒子也是他的王位繼承人在那裡。

> b. The king's son and the heir to the throne **were** there.
> 國王的兒子與他的王位繼承人兩人在那裡。

6. 兩人或事物為 or, either...or, neither...nor, not only...but also 所連接，動詞與最靠近的主詞一致。

> 例 a. (Either) Jack or **you are** to blame for the accident.
> 傑克和我其中有一人要為意外事故受責備。

> b. Neither you nor **I am** supposed to pay the bill.
> 既非你也非我該付賬。

7. 兩人或事物為 not 或介系詞片語 together with, along with, coupled with, as well as, in addition to, plus, but, except, no less than, like, unlike, rather than 等所連接，動詞與最前面的主詞一致。

例 Paul, together with some of his classmates, **has** decided to go swimming after school.

保羅和一些同學已經決定放學後去游泳。

8. 形容詞或分詞前加 the 表示全部的人。其後接複數形動詞，如：the rich (有錢人), the poor (窮人), the unemployed (失業者), the disabled (殘廢者), the French (法國人), the Taiwanese (台灣人)。

9. 代名詞 all (三個以上全部), some, any, most, the rest, the remainder, the bulk, a lot of, lots of, plenty of, part of, 分數 (如：one half, one third, two thirds, a/one quarter, two fifths)等，如果指的是不可數名詞則接單數形動詞；如果指的是可數名詞則接複數形動詞。

10. 其他易混淆的狀況條例如下：

a. a (small/large) number/total of + 複數名詞 + 複數動詞

b. the number of + 複數名詞 + 單數動詞

c. a large/small percentage/proportion of + 複數名詞 + 複數動詞

d. a large/small percentage/proportion of + 不可數名詞 + 單數動詞

✏️ 練習八

閱讀下面的句子，圈選出正確的動詞形式。

1. A large percentage of women (is, are) choosing not to get married.
2. A small percentage of my salary (is, are) spent on repaying my loan.
3. The number of babies born in Taiwan (is, are) expected to fall this year.
4. A small number of students (comes, come) from the city.
5. When Linda was dancing to the disco music, the rest of the girls (was, were) watching in admiration.
6. The unemployed (is, are) found to be very prone to depression.
7. Nobody except his relatives (is, are) willing to come to his aid.
8. All work and no play (makes, make) Jack a dull boy.
9. Dozens of miles of railway track (was, were) torn up by the 1999 earthquake.

10. Salmon (lives, live) in the sea but (swims, swim) up rivers to lay eggs.

11. Smoked salmon (is, are) delicious.

12. Official statistics (indicates, indicate) that house prices have fallen by 10 percent.

課後作業

請從下面四個選項中選出最適合題意的字或詞。

1. A huge wind rose for a moment, whipping the four palm trees that _____ near his house.

   A. was standing
   B. stood
   C. had been standing
   D. has been standing

2. Don't interrupt me when I _____ on the telephone. Can't you wait until I _____?

   A. talk, finish
   B. talk, will finish
   C. am talking, finish
   D. am talking, will finish

3. A large amount of money _____ into the state-owned companies, but they still cannot thrive.

   A. is injected
   B. was injected
   C. has been injected
   D. will have been injected

4. Jane took the first train, so she _____ there now. I will get there to pick her up. She is eager to be home.

   A. might have been
   B. might be
   C. should have been
   D. should be

5. I waited for more than one hour. You _____ me you were going to be late, but you didn't give me a ring at all.

   A. should tell
   B. must have told
   C. could tell
   D. could have told

6. The streets are humming with life even during the night. You _____ used to the hustle and bustle as soon as possible. This is the only advice that I can give you.

   A. had better get　　B. can get　　C. might get　　D. will get

7. Sales of PCs amounted to $3 billion in Taiwan, _____ what they were two years earlier.

   A. twice as much as　　　　　　B. twice as many as

   C. twice more than　　　　　　D. twice less than

8. This is a war. AIDS has killed _____ the case in all previous wars. We must not continue to be debating or arguing when people are dying.

   A. fewer people than have been　　B. fewer people than they have been

   C. more people than has been　　　D. more people than it has been

9. Our eyebrows serve a useful purpose. Without eyebrows, drops of sweat _____ down into our eyes. We _____ very well.

   A. would run, could not see　　　B. will run, will not see

   C. run, do not see　　　　　　　D. ran, did not see

10. Sometimes I feel life is not worth living and wish I _____ born.

    A. were never　　　　　　　　B. had never been

    C. was never　　　　　　　　　D. have never been

11. Mr. Smith garnered 51 percent of the vote, so _____.

    A. the winner was declared him　　B. the winner declared him

    C. he was declared the winner　　D. he declared the winner

12. The door _____ all the day. No wonder the burglar could sneak in and out at will.

    A. was opened　　　　　　　　B. was open

    C. had opened　　　　　　　　　D. had been opened

13. On the way up to the peak of the mountain, I found a stone _____ someone had carved the Chinese character "忍", meaning "perseverance."

    A. that　　　　B. , where　　　　C. on which　　　D. , on which

14. If you say someone has a round face, people can understand. Anything _____ is round looks like a circle. But if you say someone is beautiful, it will be difficult to imagine _____ she looks like. Beauty itself is abstract.

    A. that; what   B. which; what   C. that; how   D. which; how

15. After all the votes had been counted, the judge announced the outcome of the election. The winner was David _____ would become the next chairman of the Amateur Athletic Association.

    A. who   B. that   C. , who   D. , he

16. Susan emerged from the pool, _____.

    A. and blue with cold   B. blue with cold.

    C. she was blue with cold   D. which was blue with cold

17. Human waste, like nuclear waste, can cause serious damage to the environment _____.

    A. if not disposing of properly   B. it not to dispose of properly

    C. if not disposed of properly   D. if we are not disposed of properly

18. Sherry blushed with embarrassment when she was found _____ her nose.

    A. to pick   B. picking   C. pick   D. picked

19. There is a girl _____ leaflets to passers-by at the gate.

    A. who distributes   B. to distribute

    C. distributing   D. distributed

20. Mary stroked the young man's cheek tenderly with her delicate hands. The soft touch made him _____ with happiness.

    A. drink   B. drunk   C. drinking   D. to drink

21. I need _____ me of some of the administrative work.

    A. to hire someone to relieve   B. to hire someone relieving

    C. hiring someone to relieve   D. hiring someone relieving

22. Thirty percent of well-educated women _____ to marry. The high percentage _____ the government very much.
    A. refuse, alarms
    B. refuse, alarm
    C. refuses, alarms
    D. refuses, alarm

23. Statistics _____ too difficult a subject to study. Moreover, the figures are often open to dispute. Among them, government economic statistics _____ the most confusing.
    A. are, is
    B. are, are
    C. is, is
    D. is, are

24. If all _____ smoothly, we will arrive at the lake as scheduled. Then all except the driver _____ going to have a picnic by the lake.
    A. goes, is
    B. goes, are
    C. go, is
    D. go, are

25. Thirty years _____ passed since I began to teach. Thirty years _____ really a long time.
    A. have, is
    B. have are
    C. has, is
    D. has, are

Unit **7**

段落填空 (一)

✪ Focus I 單段落的短文

✪ 課後作業

Focus I 單段落的短文

　　傳統上段落填空是將一篇選文有系統的挖去其中的一些字，通常是每隔五到七字就有一字故意拿掉。原因是如果每隔三到四字就挖洞，則受試者會很難猜測什麼字遺漏了。如果每隔十到十二字挖洞，則又常要較長的文章。原先的段落填空是用來衡量選文的難易度，以瞭解是否適合某一群學習者的學習程度，後來被拿來檢測學習者的閱讀能力，受試者必須依文法觀念和上下文來還原遺漏的字。

　　傳統上段落填空是用填空方式，目前的考試為了易於閱卷而改為四選一的方式。但是如依上述原則，以下的文章至少要空二十格，受試者有無耐心去做是個問題。另外，這二十個空格中有很多可能是虛字，對閱讀能力的評估並無意義，因為遺漏一個冠詞或介系詞並 不會太干擾整體理解。

　　閱讀能力的強弱是與單字、片語、句子結構、句與句的關係、轉折語的運用、上下文意的連貫、主題句與支持句的安排、對某一主題的預先瞭解等較有直接關係。因此後來的段落填空著重考**文句與語意的連貫性** (cohesion and coherence)、**整體的認知**，而非只是句子內的文法要點。題目強調可恢復性，也就是說遺漏的字可很清楚地從上下文的語意線索和句與句的結構關係猜測出來。

　　以下各練習即是依此概念所出的段落填空範例。

✎ 練習一

請從下面四個選項中選出最適合題意的字或詞。

　　Recently, a purity test on honey set off an uproar among bee farmers. According to the Consumers' Foundation, most honey consumed in Taiwan is not ___1___. The Foundation says that bee farmers add cane sugar to their honey. They make a huge profit on their ___2___ mixture. Bee farmers threaten to take the foundation to court if it is not willing to admit to having wrongly tested the purity of honey. They will demand compensation for their great losses. Their ___3___ of honey have since slumped. One bee farmer estimates his daily losses at between NT$100,000 and NT$200,000 because fewer orders have been received. To the bee farmers' __**4**__, the foundation uses a toothpick to test the purity of honey. They claim that the method is totally wrong. The best way to test whether honey is pure, they say, is to add water to real honey and shake it. __**5**__ the honey is pure, the liquid will be dirty and muddy and there will be a lot of bubbles. They doubt that those eggheads in air-conditioned rooms, __**6**__ have never made any honey in their lives but have only eaten it, have the ability to tell pure honey from fake honey.

1.   A. pure   B. cheap   C. sweet   D. sticky

2.   A. odd   B. complex   C. inferior   D. peculiar

3.   A. shares   B. imports   C. prices   D. sales

4.   A. surprise   B. fury   C. relief   D. delight

5.   A. Though   B. If   C. Since   D. Unless

6.   A. and   B. that   C. they   D. who

✏️ 練習二

請從下面四個選項中選出最適合題意的字或詞。

    Since the ban on cross-strait travel was lifted, intermarriage between older Taiwanese men and younger Chinese women has been increasing and some social problems have arisen. With a pension for life at his disposal, an elderly veteran buys a rural woman in China to be his wife. The Chinese woman is __**1**__ to get married to the older man who is twice her age, with the expectation that, after her husband dies, she will be paid half of his pension, __**2**__ can amount to NT$30,000 a month—a large sum of money for a rural Chinese woman. But once married, the Chinese woman begins to mistreat her Taiwanese husband. More often than not, she __**3**__ his savings and enjoys her life back in her own country. One old veteran showed multiple __**4**__ on his body to a social worker. He says that, since they got married, his Chinese wife has never slept with him in the same bed. She hits him often and he constantly lives in ___**5**___. There are at least 150,000 Chinese—mostly women—married to Taiwanese. Such ___**6**___ violence is only the tip of the iceberg. Now the government has proposed that a government worker's pension cannot be transferred to his spouse if he marries in the last two years of service or after he retires.

1. A. willing   B. fortunate   C. forced   D. ashamed

2. A. that   B. it   C. which   D. this

3. A. stores away   B. makes off with   C. gambles away   D. goes through

4. A. wrinkles   B. tattoos   C. stings   D. injuries

5. A. fear   B. poverty   C. peace   D. silence

6. A. racial   B. sexual   C. political   D. domestic

練習三

請從下面四個選項中選出最適合題意的字或詞。

    Taiwan's top fashion model, Lin Chih-ling, suffered a serious injury in China when she was thrown from a horse. The accident grabbed headlines immediately, but it has also brought to light the ___**1**___ national insurance system. According to local news reports, Lin needs to pay only NT$604 in health insurance premiums per month ___**2**___ her annual income of more than NT$43 million. A similar ___**3**___ came to light when Chan His-ming, one of the most notorious wanted kidnappers in Taiwan, was gunned down and rushed to hospital. The hospital found that he had never taken out any insurance, but health officials applied for the national health insurance ___**4**___ him. It is ridiculous that he should not need to pay any insurance premiums under the current national health insurance system. That is, all ___**5**___ people have to pay his medical bills which are estimated to be more than NT$200,000. High-paid entertainers are charged lower premiums than people with low incomes and a violent fugitive enjoys free health insurance. It causes us to doubt the ___**6**___ of the original designers of the system.

1. A. unfair   B. complex   C. flexible   D. perfect

2. A. unlike   B. except   C. despite   D. besides

3. A. rumor   B. absurdity   C. theory   D. scandal

4. A. in support of   B. at the sight of   C. by courtesy of   D. on behalf of

5. A. innocent   B. rich   C. poor   D. business

6. A. morality   B. health   C. intelligence   D. strength

✏️ 練習四

請從下面四個選項中選出最適合題意的字或詞。

Some customs are quite amusing, but none is more amusing than building one's own grave when one is still __1__. No small number of people do so in Yuli township, Hualien county. Some even build their graves in their own yards. There are several reasons why they build their own graves. __2__, some people think they will not see what their graves look like after they die, so they build their own graves before departing this life to do so. They invite their relatives and good friends to a ceremony when their graves are completed. They even __3__ at their graves on Tomb-sweeping Day. For another, other people do not have male off-spring. They are afraid that, when they die, no one will lay them to rest, and that their afterlife will be __4__. For a third, others entertain a __5__ idea. One rich businessman has one wife and two concubines. He has built a __6__ grave, where he hopes he, together with his three women, can still live together happily in the next world. He is now 86 years old and still very healthy. It has been more than 30 years since his magnificent grave was built.

1. A. awake   B. alive   C. young   D. rich

2. A. For one thing   B. To sum up   C. In addition   D. In consequence

3. A. laugh   B. murmur   C. talk   D. weep

4.　A. lonely　　　B. busy　　　C. miserable　　D. ordinary

5.　A. romantic　　B. odd　　　C. absurd　　　D. valuable

6.　A. cozy　　　　B. spacious　　C. modern　　　D. splendid

✎ 練習五

請從下面四個選項中選出最適合題意的字或詞。

　　The Bush administration rejected the 1997 Kyoto Protocol, which is intended to save the planet from global warming by reducing industrialized countries' emissions of greenhouse gases by 2012. __1__ the U.S., Australia also refused to sign the agreement. For one thing, they complain that big __2__ countries such as India and China were let off the hook. However, __3__ their rapid economic growth, India and China are responsible for very high emissions of greenhouse gases. For another, the protocol will gravely damage the economies of America and Australia and destroy their __4__. A lot of factories might be shut down, and the American and Australian __5__ will lose out to emerging countries like India and China.

1.　A. Except for　　B. Owing to　　C. Like　　　D. Despite

2.　A. developed　　B. developing　　C. foreign　　D. communist

3.　A. in　　　　　B. from　　　　C. on　　　　D. with

4.　A. jobs　　　　B. systems　　　C. faith　　　D. land

5.　A. governments　B. arms　　　　C. populations　D. industries

✎ 練習六

請從下面四個選項中選出最適合題意的字或詞。

　　For Japan, whaling is part of its culture. But, the commercial whaling moratorium has driven Japan's whaling industry into decline and Japan has been trying hard to preserve this industry. It has been increasing the scale of its catches in the name of ____1____. If not stopped, Japanese research vessels will take more than 1,000 whales each year in Antarctic waters. ____2____ the research is conducted by Japanese scientists, whale meat is sold to wholesalers and served to patrons in restaurants. Moreover Japan is often accused of buying the votes of some small countries for ____3____ to commercial whaling. The ____4____ has been strongly denied by the Japanese government. However, Dominica, a tiny Caribbean nation, lost its environmental minister in 2000 after news broke ____5____ Japan bought his government's vote by offering aid.

1. A. trade   B. culture   C. nature   D. science

2. A. As   B. While   C. Unless   D. When

3. A. a return   B. an end   C. a clue   D. an obstacle

4. A. news   B. rumor   C. charge   D. promise

5. A. because   B. that   C. which   D. when

✏️ 練習七

請從下面四個選項中選出最適合題意的字或詞。

A heat wave is sweeping much of Europe and temperatures are continuing to rise. Europeans are searching for ways to cool off, and nothing is more ____1____ than wandering around naked and viewing erotic paintings at the same time. Is there any such place which offers such a relaxed atmosphere? Yes. Vienna's prestigious Leopold Museum is currently staging a new exhibition of early 1990s erotic art, "The Naked Truth". In order to ____2____ more people to the exhibition, the museum is offering free entry to anyone who is willing to show up with only a swimsuit ____3____ or even naked. Scores of naked or scantily-clad people—both male and female—wandered around the museum in front of a phalanx of TV cameras. Many tourists from overseas left the museum amused, but for Roman Catholic clergymen, it was not an ____4____ thing. Their outcry was, however, brushed aside by museum officials, who said that they wanted to give people a chance to ___5___ off and bring nakedness into the open. As for the naked visitors, they also shrugged off the uproar. One of them said, "What's the big deal? We're born naked into this world. Why can't we walk around in it without ___6___ from time to time?"

1.　A. shameful　　B. appropriate　　C. comfortable　　D. somber

2.　A. lure　　B. herd　　C. usher　　D. pull

3.　A. off　　B. on　　C. in　　D. over

4.　A. incredible　　B. probable　　C. amazing　　D. amusing

5.　A. clear　　B. cool　　C. doze　　D. show

6.　A. care　　B. effort　　C. clothes　　D. masks

✎ 練習八

請從下面四個選項中選出最適合題意的字或詞。

　　Bill Frist, Senate Majority leader, declared that stem cell research should be encouraged and funded by public money. Like other supporters, he argues that stem cells offer the prospect of a cure ___1___ cancer and Alzheimer's disease. His view puts him on a collision course with President Bush, who vehemently ___2___ such a kind of research. Like other pro-life activists, President Bush thinks that the process of extracting the stem cells destroys the embryo and so ___3___ a life. Mr. Frist is said to have plans to seek the Republican nomination for President when Mr. Bush serves out his second term. ___4___, Mr. Frist's decision to back the stem cell bill might ruin his chance to be voted into the White House. However, Mr. Frist, who is a surgeon, insists that he is still pro-life and that stem cell research is a matter of science, not a matter of ___5___.

1.　A. for　　B. to　　C. in　　D. from

2.　A. funds　　B. approves　　C. opposes　　D. conducts

3.   A. sustains   B. terminates   C. recreates   D. weakens

4.   A. Even so   B. By contrast   C. In the end   D. As a result

5.   A. faith   B. business   C. education   D. art

課後作業

請從下面四個選項中選出最適合題意的字或詞。

Questions 1-5

According to a recent report, the birth rate in Taiwan has fallen to a new low. Having fewer babies means that fewer young people will work in the future and that elderly people will not be well looked after. __1__, the country's economy will be weakened, and the government will have to spend an astronomical sum of money to take care of the __2__. Another effect is that a low birth rate will cause some people to lose their __3__. Recently, many schools have become overstaffed because there are fewer pupils now. The __4__ of teachers has posed a big problem for education officials. Finally, to make up for the labor shortage, a lot of foreign workers have to be hired to build houses or bridges, to work as nannies, and so on. Many __5__ have arisen, as witnessed by the recent Thai workers' riot in Kaohsiung.

1.   A. At any rate   B. As a result   C. On the whole   D. In other words

2.   A. babies   B. young   C. disabled   D. aged

3.   A. jobs   B. chances   C. temper   D. balance

4.   A. qualification B. health   C. oversupply   D. overwork

5.   A. opportunities B. conflicts   C. obligations   D. needs

Questions 6-11

Though the death penalty cannot completely curb crime (as human rights activists claim), it should not be abolished, at least until a more effective way can be devised to replace it. First of all, the death penalty saves hundreds of millions of tax dollars that would normally be spent to keep criminals in prison for life. __**6**__ a rough estimate, meals and lodging alone cost taxpayers at least NT$12,000 for each convict per month. Compared with a homeless person, a convicted criminal lives __**7**__ he were a king. In addition, imprisonment doesn't act as a deterrent to other criminals. If a criminal need not worry about being put to death, he will be __**8**__ to kill. Under these circumstances, can innocent people expect to feel safe from harm? Most importantly, death is an appropriate punishment for someone who commits a terrible crime. A victim's family is desperate to see __**9**__ being done. For a killer, death is not only the best way to redeem himself but also the most honorable way to __**10**__ his conscience. For example, a notorious death-row inmate in America constantly appealed to the courts to execute him immediately after he had been in jail for twenty years. He preferred to die a __**11**__ death rather than languish in prison.

6.　A. In　　　　B. By　　　　　　C. With　　　　D. For

7.　A. just as　　B. simply because　C. even if　　　D. as if

8.　A. free　　　B. careful　　　　C. reluctant　　D. afraid

9.　A. wonders　B. tricks　　　　　C. justice　　　D. harm

10. A. ease　　　B. examine　　　　C. trouble　　　D. arouse

11. A. violent　　B. accidental　　　C. quick　　　　D. natural

Unit **8**

段落填空 (二)

Focus II 兩段落以上的短文

在 Unit 7 中所說的段落填空短文只有一段，受試者只要注意主題句與其相關的支持句之間是如何組織起來。是舉例？是比較？是因果關係？是定義？是過程描述？是分類？是描寫？是記述？抑或論述？但文章更常見的是兩或三段以上。這時還要注意**兩段之間如何轉折**，這也是段落填空的重點之一。又在讀兩或三段以上的文章時，還要注意針對某一主題作者**可能談及哪些相關層面**。依此練習以下的測驗。

練習九

請從下面四個選項中選出最適合題意的字或詞。

A rich businessman had an extramarital affair with a woman, and in order to win her heart, he gave her $1 million. __**1**__, when their romance fell apart, the businessman demanded that the woman return the money to him. He filed suit against her, and miraculously he won the case. The businessman said that after the __**2**__ the woman and her relatives gathered in front of his house and his office where they shouted and swore at him. The businessman argued that the woman's act had constituted __**3**__ to his personality. Under civil law, he had the right to __**4**__ his offering. The judge took the man's side and decided that the woman was guilty of slander. She had to pay back the $1 million.

This is the __**5**__ that a mistress will run into. She covets a man's wealth and destroys a family. In the end, she herself loses both love and money. But the man who is __**6**__ to his wife also has to pay a high price. He ends up with a broken family and his reputation is damaged. The most __**7**__ victims are the man's wife and children. The law cannot pick up those pieces.

1. A. Therefore   B. However   C. Similarly   D. Additionally

2. A. sell-out   B. get-together   C. breakaway   D. break-up

3.　A. an insult　　B. an obstacle　　C. a boost　　D. a dilemma

4.　A. make　　B. accept　　C. withdraw　　D. keep

5.　A. debt　　B. criticism　　C. opposition　　D. trouble

6.　A. unfriendly　　B. unfaithful　　C. obedient　　D. grateful

7.　A. ignorant　　B. tolerant　　C. miserable　　D. sensible

練習十

請從下面四個選項中選出最適合題意的字或詞。

The regulation of student hairstyles has often been criticized for several reasons. Liberals dismiss it as a relic of the late president Chiang's authoritarianism. The military crew cut, __1__ a very short hairstyle, has been used to foster a sense of obedience and __2__. During Chiang's rule, short-haired school children, in khaki uniforms, had to stand up straight when his name was mentioned. On his birthday, students, with their hair cut short, stood in line __3__ in praise of the Great Leader. On the other hand, students nowadays have become more __4__ and they question the legitimacy of the regulations. Twenty years ago, questioning the regulations would have landed them in big trouble. But with the rapid political change in Taiwan, such regulations seem to be something of an anachronism.

__5__, Mr. Du, the Minister of Education, declared recently that the regulations would be abolished. Students will be given the right to determine their own hairstyle. Though he has since gained widespread support for his decision, a number of __6__ principals and education officials put up stiff resistance. Some of them suspect that the decision is politically motivated. They are vowing to maintain the regulations for __7__ they call "hygiene and health reasons."

1.　A. and　　B. or　　C. but　　D. though

2.　A. shame　　B. belonging　　C. loyalty　　D. security

3.   A. singing   B. to sing   C. sang   D. sung

4.   A. aggressive   B. creative   C. active   D. assertive

5.   A. Even so   B. By contrast   C. Moreover   D. Therefore

6.   A. senior   B. conservative   C. ambitious   D. devoted

7.   A. which   B. as   C. what   D. that

✎ 練習十一

請從下面四個選項中選出最適合題意的字或詞。

    July in the Chinese lunar year is the ghost month, and there are quite a few superstitions associated with it. People who travel during this month are advised to do the following __1__ they might encounter a ghost.

● Avoid rooms whose windows are close to tall trees. It is said that spirits tend to attach themselves to __2__ trees.

● Avoid rooms in which there is a mirror directly in front of the bed. A mirror can reflect the image of a person or a thing, and should you rise from the bed at midnight, you might be __3__ by your own image in the mirror.

● Before entering a hotel room, knock on the door three times. This is meant to tell the spirit in the room, should it be haunting it, that you will only stay there one or two nights, never __4__ to occupy the room for a long time.

● Don't open a window at midnight if you hear any sound outside it. With a sudden gust of __5__, a spirit might come into the room through the window.

● If there are two beds in a room, don't scatter your belongings on the bed that you won't be sleeping in. It is an insult to the spirit that is haunting the room, and it might take __6__ you at midnight.

● Before you fall asleep, remember to leave __7__ on all night. An evil spirit likes to appear in complete darkness.

1. A. so that   B. in that   C. suppose that   D. for fear that

2. A. shady   B. leafless   C. hollow   D. blossoming

3. A. amused   B. frightened   C. angered   D. excited

4. A. intended   B. to intend   C. intending   D. intend

5. A. light   B. wind   C. sound   D. smell

6. A. revenge on   B. pity on   C. notice of   D. advantage of

7. A. gas   B. fire   C. a radio   D. a light

練習十二

請從下面四個選項中選出最適合題意的字或詞。

Retinal detachment is a serious eye disorder that might lead to vision loss. The retina, the innermost layer of the wall of the eyeball, is about as __1__ as a piece of wet tissue paper. When it detaches, it separates from the back wall of the eye and is cut off from its blood supply and source of nutrition.

The symptoms of retinal detachment include floating spots, flashing lights, and a veil in the eye. The condition is painless, but __2__. When the center of the retina is affected, vision is distorted, becoming wavy and indistinct, and there will be sudden decrease in vision. __3__ surgical repair, total blindness of the eye will result.

With old age or nearsightedness, the retina gradually becomes thinner and more fragile. __4__, retinal detachment usually develops in middle-aged or older people. It is more likely to occur in people who are very nearsighted. Furthermore, a hard blow to the eye can also cause the retina to detach, so people should avoid being hit directly in the eye, __5__, when catching a baseball. Some other diseases can contribute to retinal detachment. Patients with diabetes or tumors are highly likely to suffer from this eye disease. High-__6__ groups are advised to get an eye examination at least once a year. Early discovery and treatment of the disease can greatly improve the chances of restoring one's ___7___.

1. A. fragile
   B. sticky
   C. greasy
   D. transparent

2. A. pleasing
   B. amazing
   C. annoying
   D. piercing

3. A. Despite
   B. Without
   C. Besides
   D. Like

4. A. However
   B. Similarly
   C. Finally
   D. Therefore

5. A. at any rate
   B. by the way
   C. in fact
   D. for example

6. A. ranking
   B. spirited
   C. risk
   D. income

7. A. sight
   B. confidence
   C. health
   D. balance

練習十三

請從下面四個選項中選出最適合題意的字或詞。

2360 people in Taiwan were reported to have committed suicide in 2004. Suicide has become the ninth leading cause of death in Taiwan. To promote respect for life, the John Tung Foundation has a website called "Save Life", which tells people how to reduce ___1___ and how to prevent attempting suicide.

With the economic downturn, the unemployment rate has hit an all-time high. Many middle-aged people have lost their ___2___ and have found it difficult to support their families. Hardly a day goes by without a report of suicide. Very often innocent children are also killed as part of the ___3___. Last year a man, together with his wife and four children, drove his car off a cliff and they all plunged to their deaths in the sea. The man earned his living by serving breakfast in front of a temple in Kaohsiung. He was strapped for cash and borrowed money from a loan shark. The ___4___ sealed his whole family's fate.

The well-___5___ John Tung Foundation might be helpful to those who are suffering from some affective disorder—a teenager who feels that life is meaningless, a woman who has lost her love, a man who cannot get ahead at his job. But for those who are in a ___**6**___ crisis, a sum of money is the only lifeline. Unfortunately, the foundation doesn't offer this. A loan shark does, but contacting one is tantamount to receiving the kiss of death.

1. A. debt   B. stress   C. costs   D. risks

2. A. hope   B. interest   C. opportunities   D. jobs

3. A. tragedy   B. accident   C. adventure   D. murder

4. A. accident   B. deal   C. loan   D. poverty

5. A. meaning   B. behaved   C. disciplined   D. known

6. A. housing   B. financial   C. energy   D. identity

練習十四

請從下面四個選項中選出最適合題意的字或詞。

Recently oil prices have shot up to $67 a barrel. Some economists fear that high oil prices might lead to inflation, recession, or ___**1**___. However, consumers continue spending; they do not seem to be ___**2**___ by the oil price increase. Even taxi drivers have not strongly demanded a taxi fare increase. The consumer price index for July did show inflation edging up, but it hasn't alarmed government officials. The world economy is improving, and even Japan has been crawling out of its 15-year economic ___**3**___.

There are several reasons why the current oil price hike doesn't seem to hurt. Firstly, consumers seem accustomed to fluctuations in oil prices and have developed an immunity ___**4**___ being affected by sharp oil price rises. It might be partly because people are richer. Secondly, oil-importing countries have been boosting fuel-efficiency. The best example of this is the popularity of ___**5**___ cars. Thirdly, China's demand for oil has somewhat declined. Over the past ten years, China has imported a large quantity of oil to sustain its rapid economic growth, ___**6**___ oil prices even higher. But China now is attempting to engineer an economic soft landing, as witnessed by its recent revaluation of the Chinese Ren Min Bi.

1. A. either　　　B. both　　　C. neither　　　D. all

2. A. excited　　　B. surprised　　　C. amused　　　D. bothered

3. A. downturn　　　B. growth　　　C. miracle　　　D. upturn

4. A. in　　　B. with　　　C. to　　　D. for

5. A. luxury　　　B. sports　　　C. diesel　　　D. compact

6. A. to push　　　B. pushing　　　C. push　　　D. and pushes

✎ 練習十五

請從下面四個選項中選出最適合題意的字或詞。

　　Lately there has been a vinegar drinking trend. Vinegar is said to have __1__ properties. Some consumers claim that vinegar can be used to treat rashes and bites. Others even claim that it can __2__ arthritis. Japanese people believe that vinegar is good for improving circulation and reducing fatigue. It is even reported that rice vinegar will help one lose weight.

　　However, conventional vinegar cannot be drunk. __3__ soy sauce, vinegar is only used for improving the taste of food or for preserving food. Some people with a(n) __4__ flair have developed vinegar-based drinks. For example, fruits such as apples, grapes, or raspberries are fermented and their __5__ is made into fruit vinegar. Another example is vinegar water. Bottled vinegar water contains only about 1% vinegar. Since __6__ vinegar-based drinks were introduced into the market, their sales have jumped sharply. In fact, they have firmly established themselves __7__ heath drinks in the minds of many consumers.

1. A. medicinal　　　B. chemical　　　C. physical　　　D. mental

2. A. cause　　　B. intensify　　　C. cure　　　D. enhance

3.　A. Despite　　　B. Besides　　　C. Thanks to　　　D. Like

4.　A. artistic　　　B. business　　　C. scientific　　　D. linguistic

5.　A. skin　　　B. juice　　　C. seeds　　　D. flesh

6.　A. many　　　B. few　　　C. some　　　D. such

7.　A. for　　　B. with　　　C. as　　　D. in

課後作業

請從下面四個選項中選出最適合題意的字或詞。

Questions 1-5

A conservation institute in the USA has produced eight wildcat kittens through cloning. The eight kittens were born to two separate mothers, but they all have a __1__ father. The father himself is a clone of another wildcat. Up to now, they are all healthy and doing very well.

This achievement has great significance for wildlife conservation. The researchers say that better cloning procedures can help to save __2__ animals from extinction. If the cloned animals can survive, mate with each other, and give birth to offspring, then we can preserve threatened species.

However, some scientists are not so optimistic. One of the greatest threats to a species is the destruction of its habitat. A more urgent action would be to __3__ their natural home; not to clone several of them in an unnatural environment. __4__, for cloning to play a significant role in preserving endangered species, cloned animals must be able to breed normally once they are introduced to the __5__. So far no good examples of this have been found.

1. A. different   B. healthy   C. alien   D. common

2. A. domestic   B. wild   C. extinct   D. endangered

3. A. restore   B. find   C. move   D. flatten

4. A. Even so   B. In short   C. Moreover   D. Therefore

5. A. zoo   B. field   C. wild   D. farm

Questions 6-11

Last night more than 100 migrant workers, mostly Thais, ran amok in their dormitory at Kangshan in Kaohsiung. They set fire to houses, cars, and facilities and beat up some of the management staff. The __6__ did not stop until the police were called in. But a lot of damage had been done and it is estimated that the Kaohsiung MRT company suffered a great loss of about NT$10 million.

The incident occurred when several Thai workers returned to their dormitory with liquor and cigarettes, which are __7__ in the dormitory. They clashed with the management staff immediately after they were prevented from entering the dormitory. The police are now gathering evidence in order to bring the ones who led the rioting to __8__.

__9__, some officials are meeting with representatives of the foreign workers and listening to their demands. Among other things, they __10__ that mobile phones be allowed to be used in the dormitory, that their overtime pay be given them, and that a satellite dish be installed __11__ they can watch TV programs from Thailand.

6. A. carnival   B. parade   C. strike   D. riot

7. A. sold   B. produced   C. banned   D. bought

8. A. justice   B. hospital   C. heel   D. senses

9. A. Therefore   B. Meanwhile   C. Suddenly   D. Curiously

10. A. suggest   B. insist   C. prefer   D. demand

11. A. in case   B. so that   C. since   D. until

Questions 12-16

The Department of Health has drafted a law allowing surrogacy. A childless couple will now be allowed to enlist a surrogate mother to have a baby for them. It is really good news for a couple with __12__ problems. But the law has run into criticism.

Some women's rights activists denounce it as male chauvinism. In their view, a woman's traditional duty is to have babies so that her husband's family __13__ will not be discontinued. To allow surrogacy is to reinforce the notion of male chauvinism. Being paid for surrogate motherhood is no different than earning money by having sex with a man. In the former case, a woman rents her womb to ensure a man's family lineage, __14__ in the latter, she rents her vagina to satisfy a man's sexual desire. On the other hand, some critics argue that surrogacy might become a __15__ enterprise. They warn that brokers might recruit poor women or foreign migrant workers to act as surrogate mothers, and surrogacy will become a multi-million-dollar business. As it happens in the sex industry, the __16__ rate will rise along with this highly profitable business.

12. A. fertility   B. health   C. emotional   D. financial

13. A. business   B. reunions   C. line   D. ties

14. A. because   B. when   C. though   D. while

15. A. free   B. commercial   C. private   D. joint

16. A. crime   B. divorce   C. birth   D. employment

Questions 17-22

There has been a surge of illegal cash transfers through the Internet recently. Nine such thefts __17__ a total of 9.4 million Japanese yen have been reported from three banks since July. Online thieves infiltrate the computers of __18__ bank customers to steal their code numbers. Then they use the numbers to gain access to the customers' accounts. Another trick used by online thieves is to design a home page similar to __19__ of a bank. An unsuspecting customer enters the fake website and keys in his code number, and then suddenly the home page disappears from the __20__. The customer's code number has been appropriated by the thief. Cash from the customer's account will then be illegally transferred to the thief's account. This has happened in Taiwan as in the case of a bank customer who lost more than NT$2 million.

Countermeasures have now been taken against online thieves. Customers are advised to change their code numbers every time they make an online money transfer. The number of transactions made and the sum of money transferred are also __21__. The purpose of this is to reduce the loss should a customer's code number be stolen and an illegal money transfer made. In addition, online customers are advised to install anti-theft software. This is the best way to __22__ online theft.

17. A. involve   B. involving   C. involved   D. to involve

18. A. electronic   B. commercial   C. investment   D. savings

19. A. one   B. this   C. that   D. those

20. A. bank   B. account   C. customer   D. screen

21. A. limited   B. recorded   C. increased   D. changed

22. A. look into   B. engage in   C. ward off   D. cover up

Unit 9

閱讀理解 (一)

✪ Focus I 主題

✪ Focus II 主旨

✪ Focus III 重要細節

✪ 課後作業

閱讀能力的強弱取決於字彙量的多寡和文法理解程度。另外對文章組織的瞭解也是關鍵性的因素。本單元就專注在文章的組織及依其組織如何做有效率的閱讀。

通常完整的一個段落都有一**主題句(topic sentence)**，這個主題句濃縮了作者對某一**主題(topic)**的看法。這個主題句往往出現在該段落的第一句。有時也會出現在第二或三句，此時它前面的句子是用來提供主題句的背景知識，在兩者交會處通常會有一轉折語做連接。另外有些段落的主題句出現在最後一句，具有總結的功用。當然也會有文章第一句或句中出現一主題句，而在文章末又有一結語。更有些段落並沒有主題句，但結構依然完整，這時讀者要自己去推論。

主題句是作者對某一主題的看法，是段落的**主旨(main idea)**。它的特質是概括性、抽象的陳述。作者接著會個別、具體的詳述他的主旨。他或許會舉例說明，或說明因果關係，或做比較，或條列各步驟，或做主客觀定義，或細部描寫，或記述始末，或做說服性論述。這些叫作**支持性細節(supporting details)**，用來支持主題句概括性、抽象性的陳述。如此才能取信讀者。

支持性細節又分兩類：一為**主要細節(major supporting details)**，一為**次要細節(minor supporting details)**。主要細節用來具體化主旨，而次要細節用來使主要細節更周詳。

譬如說某一個段落的主題是「學生的英文程度」，作者的看法是「學生的英文程度明顯下降」，這是他的主旨。在此主題句之前他也許會用一兩句話說明目前英文已成為全民運動，而且學英文的時期也提早到小學三年級，這幾句就是主題句的背景知識。讀者讀到「明顯下降」這一陳述時，一定會問「明顯下降」的證據何在？作者必須提出具體事實。他可能會舉大學入學考試、托福考試、多益考試，和全民英檢等客觀成績作為實證。這些考試就是主要細節。接著他會分別詳細說明這些成績的統計數字，這些統計數字就是次要細節。他或許會做個小結論：雖然學習英文已成全民運動，但贏在起跑點並不保證英文程度會跟著提高。

「閱讀理解」題就是來測驗受試者能否知道某一段落的主題是什麼、主旨為何、有哪些重要細節，以及能否從段落的上下文猜測不認識的字，較難的是能否讀出作者的弦外之音，也就是做合理推論。上一段「學生的英文程度明顯下降」就是暗示「小時了了，大未必佳」。

Focus I 主題

決定段落的主題基本原則是這個主題必須含蓋所有該段落的重要細節。如果未全部含蓋則太窄 (too narrow)。但也不能包括該段落未提及的事，也就是不能含蓋太大，否則就太寬 (too broad)。此一般稱作雨傘原則。

譬如筷子、湯匙、飯碗、盤子等，我們統稱「食具」。如果用「工具」稱之則太寬，因為鐵鎚、鐮刀也是工具。如果用「容器」稱之則太窄，因為飯碗、盤子是容器可裝東西，但筷子很明顯就不屬於容器了。

在「閱讀理解」題中，考主題的題幹會用以下兩種陳述法：

例　The topic of this passage is _____.

The best title for this passage is _____.

✎ 練習一

請細讀以下兩個段落並選出適當的答案。

Question 1

Taiwan's supermodel Lin Chih-ling was flown by a special medical evacuation plane back to Taiwan after two weeks of medical treatment in China for a serious chest injury. She was thrown violently from a horse and trampled underfoot while she was shooting a commercial for Olay, an international cosmetics brand. In the accident six of her ribs were fractured. Upon her arrival, Lin was rushed to National Taiwan University Hospital for further treatment.

1.　The topic of this passage is _____.
   A. Taiwan's supermodel
   B. medical treatment
   C. Lin's return to Taiwan
   D. a medical evacuation plane

Question 2

Bird flu has killed hundreds of millions of ducks and chickens since 2003. It can also be transmitted to humans and spread among them. Until now 57 people, most of them in Vietnam and Thailand, have died because they had close physical contact with their infected fowl. There have even been a few cases in which people have come down with the disease when looking after their infected relatives.

2. The best title for this passage is "_____".
   A. Bird Flu
   B. The Death of Fowl
   C. Physical Contact with Fowl
   D. The Transmission of Bird Flu to Humans

Focus II 主旨

找出段落的主題句是回答「閱讀理解」主旨題目的祕訣。如果段落沒有主題句，則必須從重要細節去歸納。在「閱讀理解」題中，考主旨的題幹會用以下陳述法：

例 The main idea of this passage is _____.

The purpose of this passage is to _____.

✎ 練習二

請細讀以下兩個段落並選出適當的答案。

Questions 1-2

The world witnessed three bomb attacks in July. On July 7th three bombs exploded in the London subway, killing 56 people and injuring more than 700 people. Two weeks later, London experienced another bomb attack. Fortunately no one was inured. On July 24th a quick series of car bombs ripped through a luxury hotel and a coffee shop at the Egyptian Red Sea resort of Sharm el-Sheik, killing at least 83. As in other terrorist attacks, the finger was pointed at Muslim extremists.

1. The topic of this passage is_____.
    A. bomb attacks
    B. Muslim extremists
    C. the explosions in the London subway
    D. the bombing at an Egyptian Red Sea resort

2. The main idea of this passage is:
    A. Muslim extremists launched attacks again.
    B. There were three bomb attacks this July.
    C. A lot of people died in the three bomb attacks.
    D. Britain and Egypt are under attack because they ally themselves with America.

Questions 3-4

Six people living in the vicinity of Song Jiang Road in Taipei were diagnosed with cancer recently. The residents put the blame on the Taiwan Fixed Network Company which was reported to have put its equipment in an apartment in this residential area. The residents say electromagnetic radiation emitted from the equipment is the root cause of the cancer that the six people are now suffering from.

But experts are divided over the issue. No conclusion has been reached yet that electromagnetic radiation poses a threat to our health. Even so, people are advised to avoid exposure to it. The next time if you use a microwave oven, an hairdryer, or a mobile phone, be sure to keep a reasonable distance from them.

3. The topic of this passage is _____.

A. electromagnetic radiation

B. the effects of electromagnetic radiation on humans

C. the causes of cancer

D. the main sources of electromagnetic radiation

4. The main idea of this passage is:

A. The residents' accusation against Taiwan Fixed Network Company is groundless.

B. Electromagnetic radiation is harmful to our health.

C. Electromagnetic radiation will not harm our health.

D. Though the effects of electromagnetic radiation on humans are still unknown, we had better avoid it.

Questions 5-6

Quite a few highly-educated women in Taiwan are not willing to get married. Even if they do eventually get married, they are not willing to have children. They are independent—both financially and intellectually. On the other hand, a large number of poorly-educated men have trouble finding local women to marry, and they are induced to pay a certain sum of money for foreign brides, especially ones from Vietnam or Indonesia. There is estimated to be nearly 300,000 foreign wives in Taiwan. In addition, the forgeign wives tend to have more children who may have problems adapting to the local culture.

There is growing alarm at the consequences. Some people have expressed their concerns in terms of of eugenics, while others are concerned about ensuing social problems.

5. The best title for this passage is "_____".
   A. Local Women vs. Foreign Women
   B. Interracial Marriage
   C. The Imbalance of Baby Births
   D. The Failure of Birth Control

6. The purpose of this passage is to _____.
   A. tell why well-educated women don't get married
   B. tell why foreign women are willing to have babies
   C. indicate the fact that more babies are born of foreign women than of well-educated local women
   D. indicate the fact that many social problems have arisen from interracial marriage

Focus III 重要細節

　　首先要瞭解作者如何詳述他的主旨。到底是舉例說明，或說明因果關係，或做比較，或條列各步驟，或做主客觀定義，或細部描寫，或記述始末，或做說服性論述，而辨識所使用的轉折語則可很迅速地得知作者是用何種方式詳述他的主旨。

　　譬如看到 for example，就可知作者是用舉例來說明主旨。此外，還有其他常見的轉折語如下：

意　涵	關鍵字
列舉	first, second, besides, moreover, also
因果關係	therefore, so, because
比較	by contrast, similarly

　　另外把主旨句變成恰當的 WH 問句，也可預期要找的重要細節。譬如：The world has witnessed three bomb attacks this July. 這句主題句變成恰當的 WH 問句是：What are the three bomb attacks that the world has witnessed this July? 在看本文

時只要去找這三個炸彈攻擊事件就可以了。然後再找相關資料如：在世界何處、何時發生？死亡多少？何人所為？為何發生？等等。

 練習三

請細讀以下段落並做題目，做答時請在文章中圈出關鍵的轉折語。

Questions 1-2

  Nearly 38,000 people a year get lung cancer in the UK, of whom 33,000 die within six months because their illness was diagnosed too late. In Taiwan lung cancer is one of the ten major causes of death. What worries doctors most is that the number of people who contract lung cancer is increasing every year. Doctors say that, if you lose weight suddenly for no reason, continue coughing for more than three months, or find it difficult to breathe, go to the doctor for the checkup right away.

1. Why will most of the people who get lung cancer die within six months?
  A. Because their illness is not serious at the beginning.
  B. Because their illness is hard to diagnose.
  C. Because their illness was not diagnosed soon enough.
  D. Because they live either in the UK or in Taiwan.

2. Which is NOT one of the signs of lung cancer?
  A. Being overweight
  B. Continuous coughing
  C. Breathlessness
  D. Losing weight suddenly

Questions 3-7

The Central Bank of Taiwan raised interest rates by 0.125% again. Two reasons were given for the hike. For one thing, interest rates in the USA have been rising recently. For another, if Taiwan keeps interest rates down, it will speed up the outflow of foreign capital from the country. It is apparent that there is a trend towards higher interest rates. Savers will be happier because they will earn more interest. But those who borrowed money to buy their houses in previous years will be running up huge debts.

3.   What is the topic of this passage?
    A. The winners of the interest rate hikes
    B. The losers of the interest rate hikes
    C. Interest rate hikes
    D. The causes of interest rate hikes

4.   How much did interest rates go up in Taiwan?
    A. By 0.125%
    B. By 1.025%
    C. By 0.215%
    D. By 1.25%

5.   What is one of the reasons why interest rates were raised?
    A. Bankers have lost a lot of money for the past several years.
    B. The government wants foreign capital to remain.
    C. People find it difficult to get bank loans.
    D. Inflation is going up.

6.   Who will feel unhappy about the news?
    A. Savers
    B. The government
    C. Borrowers
    D. Foreigners

7. The author expands on his main idea by _____.

    A. making a comparison

    B. giving reasons

    C. defining a term

    D. narrating an event

Questions 8-11

Last month US Secretary of State Condoleezza Rice visited Asia and her message was clear. She stressed the Bush Administration's view that freedom and democracy are the essential underpinnings to keep peace and maintain economic well-being. In China she hoped Chinese leaders could persuade North Korea to give up its nuclear weapons, and she expressed her disapproval of China's anti-secession law against Taiwan. She said that it was an unnecessary threat to cross-strait peace.

8. The topic of this passage is _____.

    A. Rice's visit to Asia

    B. America's relations with China

    C. cross-strait peace

    D. Rice's diplomatic mission to Asia

9. Why did China make Miss Rice unhappy?

    A. Because China helped North Korea to produce nuclear weapons

    B. Because China passed an anti-secession law.

    C. Because people in China cannot enjoy freedom

    D. Because China did not welcome her heartily

10. What are the two most important ideas held by Mr. Bush?

    A. Freedom and democracy

    B. Law and order

    C. Nuclear weapons and law

    D. Law and democracy

11. The author expands on his main idea by _____.
    A. describing something
    B. demonstrating a process
    C. giving examples
    D. defining a term

Questions 12-15

The 2004 tsunamis took tens of thousands of people's lives and the tragedy remains etched in our memory. But by December 2006, the Indian Ocean will have a hi-tech tsunami early warning system in place. The warning system will go off at once should another tidal wave begin. There is no doubt that if the warning system had been in place, a lot of lives would have been saved from the 2004 tsunamis. However, some people don't think that is enough to defend people there against the assault of another tsunami. Fishermen living along the coasts next to the Indian Ocean are often too poor to live decent lives, let alone buy mobile phones. That means that a warning message might not be able to get to them in case of an emergency.

12. The main idea of this passage is :
    A. The 2004 tsunamis caused a lot of damage and took a lot of lives.
    B. The early warning system will go off before a tsunami hits.
    C. An early warning system will not be enough to guard fishermen against a tsunami.
    D. Fishermen along the coasts of India are mostly poor.

13. By when will the Indian Ocean be equipped with a hi-tech tsunami early warning system?
    A. October, 2006
    B. December, 2006
    C. November, 2006
    D. September, 2006

14. Why is the warning system not enough to save the people along the coasts of the Indian Ocean?

    A. Because the warning system will not go off on the beach.

    B. Because mobile phones are not available in poor countries.

    C. Because the coasts stretch to the horizon.

    D. Because the people are too poor to have access to the warning system.

15. The author expands on his main idea by _____.

    A. giving reasons

    B. offering arguments

    C. making a contrast

    D. giving examples

課後作業

每段短文後有 2-3 個相關問題，請從四個選項中選出最適合的答案。

Questions 1-2

English is one of the Indo-European languages. Although there is no proof of its existence, there seem to be strong indications that all European languages came from what is called Proto-Indo-European. The Indo-European languages include seven main branches; Latin and the romance languages (French, Spanish, etc), the Germanic languages, Sanskrit and other Indo-Iranian languages, the Slavic languages, the Baltic languages, the Celtic languages, and Greek. If you take the English word *father*, you will find that it is spoken as *vater* in German, *pater* in Latin, and *pitr* in Sanskrit. We can actually see the connections between these language groups from the similarities of words in different Indo-European languages.

1. This passage is about _____.

    A. Indo-European languages.

    B. English

    C. European languages

    D. Latin and its relation with European languages

2. English is one of the Indo-European languages because _____.

    A. the English were once ruled by the Roman empire

    B. the English look like Indo-European people

    C. many English words are similar to those in the other Indo-European
       languages

    D. English sounds like the other Indo-European languages

Questions 3-5

A huge military exercise was conducted at Chin Chuan Kang Airbase in Taichung county. The exercise was designed to demonstrate Taiwan's ability to repel enemies should they launch a surprise airborne attack on a major airbase. The exercise involved more than 2,000 servicemen. The most highly sophisticated weapons were employed in this exercise, including F-16 fighters, CH-47 Chinook transport helicopters, CM-11 tanks, V150 armored personnel carriers, and Avenger surface-to-air missiles. The drill came at a time when China's military buildup has begun to cause alarm all over the world. Seven hundred missiles have been aimed at Taiwan so far, and one senior Chinese general even threatened to destroy hundreds of American cities with nuclear missiles if America should dare come to Taiwan's rescue.

3. The military exercise was conducted _____.

    A. when a lot of people in Taiwan were still not awake to China's threat

    B. after Taiwan had acquired a lot of sophisticated weapons

    C. at the urging of an alarmed America

    D. with the rise of an aggressive China

4. The enemy soldiers were supposed to _____ during this exercise.

   A. wade onto the beach

   B. drop from their planes

   C. hide in the mountains

   D. cross the border

5. The exercise was unique for several reasons. Which of the following is NOT one of them?

   A. A lot of soldiers were involved.

   B. Several advanced weapons were used.

   C. American soldiers also took part.

   D. Taiwan is under threat.

Unit 10

閱讀理解 (二)

⭐ Focus IV 推論

⭐ Focus V　修辭

⭐ 課後作業

Focus IV　推論

推論有兩種。一種是根據邏輯的演繹，這種推論一定是對的。另一種是根據證據及你自己的知識或經驗做暫時合理的推測，這種推論則可能是正確的。譬如說你看到海倫把車停在路邊，那麼我們根據邏輯推論她一定會開車；而如果看見她抱著肚子衝進醫院，那麼我們可以依據我們的知識或經驗猜測她是肚子痛要去掛急診，但也許她只是要到醫院借廁所。

以下的練習就在訓練讀者以合理推論的方式理解題意，找出答案。

✎ 練習四

請細讀以下描述後找出合理的答案。

Questions 1-5

1. Mary is beaming with happiness these days, and she likes to show off the ring on her finger.

   It can be inferred that Mary _____.

   A. has bought a fake ring

   B. has lost her ring

   C. has gotten engaged

   D. has gotten divorced

2. A monk walked down a path that led to a cabin. In the moonlight he pushed open the door and entered the cabin.

   It can be inferred that _____.

   A. the monk knew there was someone in the cabin

   B. the monk knew there was no one in the cabin

   C. the door was locked

   D. the door was open

3. Mike saw that the ceiling was wet with water. He picked up the telephone and dialed a number.

It can be inferred that _____.

A. Mike called the person upstairs, telling him that his bathtub was leaking

B. Mike called the police, complaining to them about the noise made by his neighbor

C. Mike called a construction worker, telling him that the roof was going to cave in

D. Mike called 119, saying there was a fire

4. No valuables were stolen, and the furniture was all in place. But the police officer found that the skin on the body had turned pink .

It can be inferred that _____.

A. the person might have died of carbon monoxide poisoning

B. the person might have died of food poisoning

C. the person might have died of lead poisoning

D. the person might have been murdered

5. Lulu jumped out of the bed when she smelt something burning. She rushed to the kitchen.

It can be inferred that _____.

A. something was cooking in the kitchen

B. there was a gas leak in the kitchen

C. the sink in the kitchen was leaking

D. something exploded in the kitchen

Questions 6-8

Lulu, a 23-year-old girl, reported to the police that she was raped by a man whom she had become acquainted with over the Internet. She said that she agreed to meet him because he lavished praise on her and that he showed love for her. However, on their first date, he forced her to go to a motel with him and he raped her. She showed the police the bruises and injuries on her body, and she told them that the man called himself Hsiao Chiang. He had a scar on his cheek and had long dark curly hair. Like many other women who have similar experiences Lulu is single and very shy. She has no particular hobbies except for work, and worse still, she has few chances to meet members of the opposite sex.

6. This passage suggests that, when Hsiao Chiang was attempting to rape Lulu, she _____.
   A. put up resistance
   B. managed to escape
   C. made love with him
   D. drove him out

7. It can be inferred that quite a few women _____.
   A. form lasting friendships through the Internet
   B. have never checked into a motel
   C. hate to make love in a motel
   D. are lonely and need love

8. The best title for this passage is "_____".
   A. Online Dating
   B. Date Rape
   C. Crime
   D. Rape Victims

Questions 9-11

Much to the relief of the astronauts' families and people all over the world, the Space Shuttle Discovery returned home safely on August 9, 2005. NASA immediately celebrated the first successful space shuttle landing since the crash of the Space Shuttle Columbia. But after Discovery blasted off on its successful mission, experts discovered small pieces of debris had fallen from its external fuel tank during lift-off. Fortunately, the debris did not hit the frame of the shuttle and didn't put the crew at risk. A similar accident happened in 2003 when the Space Shuttle Columbia blasted off. A suitcase-sized piece of debris broke off it and punched a big hole in the space shuttle's wing. Super-heated gases escaped into its frame, and then the shuttle blew up. All seven astronauts on board were killed. But this time the experts didn't take any chances. They postponed the blast-off until everything was OK.

9. The passage suggests that _____.
   A. debris is very explosive, as witnessed by the 2003 accident
   B. since the 2003 accident, scientists have become more alert to the danger of falling debris
   C. debris should not be kept in the fuel tank
   D. debris must be prevented from escaping into the frame of a space shuttle

10. It can be inferred that the frame of a space shuttle is _____.
   A. combustible
   B. fragile
   C. airtight
   D. airless

11. The Space Shuttle Discovery _____ as a result of small pieces of debris found falling from its external fuel tank.

    A. blasted off as scheduled

    B. landed on Mars

    C. was destroyed immediately

    D. was not allowed to leave the ground

Questions 12-14

A mystery illness has killed 27 farmers so far in Sichuan province, China. The number of people infected with the disease has gone up to 131. The infection is spread by contact with dead pigs. The death rate is more than 20 percent higher than that of SARS, which also originated in China. The symptoms of the current disease include high fever, nausea and vomiting. Health officials say the disease could be a variant of the streptococcus bacteria, often found in pigs. The variant might be more deadly than average. Tourists are advised not to go to Sichuan and its neighboring areas. Pork from Sichuan should be banned.

12. The main idea of this passage is:

    A. A new disease has broken out again in China.

    B. Dead pigs are the cause of all diseases.

    C. Diseases that spread from China are always deadly.

    D. Deadly diseases are always difficult to understand.

13. If someone contracts this disease, _____.

    A. he will have a headache and feel tired

    B. his body temperature will go up and his face will turn pale

    C. he will throw up and his body temperature will rise sharply

    D. he will feel dizzy and pass out

14. This passage suggests that _____.

A. we had better not eat pork

B. several mystery diseases first appeared in China

C. those who have come down with the disease will die as a result.

D. tourists who go to Sichuan must be banned from returning home.

Focus V　修辭

為了使文章更生動，作者會用一些修辭技巧。以下列舉最常用的修辭技巧：

1. 明喻 (simile)	用 like (像) 或 as (正如) 等轉折語連接兩人或事物。以具體比喻抽象，以已知比喻未知。 a. 芙蓉如面柳如眉，對此如何不淚垂。 b. Love is **like** a cigar. If it goes out, you can light it again, but it never tastes quite the same. c. Information technology is to the 20th century **as** steam was to the 19th century.
2. 隱喻 (metaphor)	將明喻句裡的 like (像) 或 as (正如) 去掉，即形成隱喻。 a. 山是眉峰聚，水是眼波橫。 b. Out, out, brief candle! **Life's but a walking shadow, a poor player** That struts and frets his hour upon the stage, And then is heard no more. It is a tale Told by an idiot, full of sound and fury, signifying nothing.　− Shakespeare
3. 擬人化 (personification)	把沒有人性的事物賦與人性化的特質。 a. 青天有月來幾時，我今持杯一問之。 b. And this same flower that smiles today, Tomorrow will be dying.　− Shakespeare

4. 修辭問句 (rhetorical question)	表面是問句，事實是陳述句。 a. 十年來，深恩負盡，死生師友，**問人生到此淒涼否**？ 　　(言下之意是人生很淒涼) b. Can the leopard change his spots? 　　(言下之意是花豹不可能改其斑點)
5. 重復 (repetition)	重複某個字詞，用來表示重複的行為或強調某一字詞。 a. 庭院**深深**幾許。 b. **Work! Work! Work!** Till the stars shine through the roof. c. A **desperate** man's **desperate** measures will make his country only more **desperate**.
6. 押韻 (rhyme)	兩字的字尾發音相同。 a. 抽刀斷水水更**流**，舉杯消愁愁更**愁**。 b. I'll win Jane's heart and mind by **hook** or by **crook**.
7. 頭韻 (alliteration)	兩字的字首發音相同。 a. 明月松間照，**清泉**石上流。 b. They think with their **hearts** not with their **heads**.
8. 擬聲 (onomatopoeia)	摹擬某一動作的聲音。 a. 帝城春欲暮，**喧喧**車馬度。 b. In the Royal City, spring is almost over, 　　**Tinkle, tinkle** – the coaches and horsemen pass.
9. 對照 (antithesis)	意義相反的字放在一起做對比。 a. 人有**悲歡離合**，月有**陰晴圓缺**。 b. He that has never **hoped** can never **despair**.
10. 平行句 (parallelism)	句型結構相同的兩句放在一起。 a. **儒以文亂法，俠以武犯禁**。 b. **Not that I love Caesar less, but that I love Rome more**.

11. 遞增 (climactic sentence order)	由較不重要逐漸至較重要，最後高潮結束。 a. 父兮生我，母兮鞠我。拊我畜我，長我育我。顧我復我。出入腹我。欲報之德，昊天罔極。 b. He dares to **think**, dares to **speak**, and dares to **act**.
12. 遞減 (anticlimactic sentence order)	與遞增相反，由較重要逐漸至較不重要。 a. 父之族，無不乘車者；母之族，無不足於衣食者。妻之族，無凍餒者。 b. He lost his **wife**, his **child**, his **household goods**, at one fell swoop.

瞭解這些修辭技巧，平時可增進對文章的欣賞與理解能力，而在面臨考試時，則可以迅速抓到重點，不被旁枝末節的修飾詞藻所混淆。

✎ 練習五

請細讀以下段落並做題目。

Questions 1-3

Bee farmer Luo Hsin-li from Lungtan Township in Taoyuan County succeeded in getting 500,000 bees to crawl all over him by placing 12 queen bees on his body to attract them. It looked as if he was wearing a "bee dress". The "bee dress" was as thick as five centimeters and weighed more than 30 kilos. Luo said that the bees were like electric fans when they fluttered their wings on his body. However, he could not shout, yawn, or sneeze because the bees might launch a massive attack.

1. The best title for this passage is "_____".
   A. Queen Bees
   B. Electric Fans
   C. A Bee Dress
   D. A Massive Attack

2. What rhetorical device is used in this passage?

   A. Simile

   B. Hyperbole

   C. Metaphor

   D. Irony

3. This passage suggests that _____.

   A. the farmer used queen bees to guard him against the other bees

   B. the farmer stood motionless and speechless

   C. queen bees are under the influence of ordinary bees.

   D. the farmer used electric fans to help the bees flutter their wings

Questions 4-8

Japanese scientists have developed a female android, the most human-looking robot developed so far. Repliee Q1, as the android is dubbed, has 41 degrees of movement in her upper body. Her skin is made of silicone rather than hard plastic, so her appearance and touch are humanlike. With highly sensitive skin sensors attached to 11 places on her body, she can react in various ways depending on how she is touched. She can flutter her eyelids, or turn around and wave her hands. She even appears to breathe. Professor Ishiguro, the android's designer, has found that people tend to forget she is an android while interacting with her. They communicate with her as if she were a real woman.

4. What rhetorical device is used in this passage?

   A. Pun

   B. Symbol

   C. Allusion

   D. Personification

5. What makes the new robot unique is that _____.
    A. it looks like a real human
    B. it can talk as a human does
    C. it makes people become forgetful
    D. it can be touched

6. The robot looks the way it is because it is made of ____.
    A. hard plastic
    B. silicone
    C. artificial skin
    D. sensors

7. The robot responds with the aid of _____.
    A. silicone
    B. hard plastic
    C. skin sensors
    D. people

8. The purpose of this passage is to _____.
    A. show how people can interact with the new robot
    B. explain why the new robot can look and act like a woman
    C. introduce the person who developed the new robot
    D. explain why people tend to forget

課後作業

每段短文後有 3-4 個相關問題。請從四個選項中選出最適合的答案。

Questions 1-3

A new law, if passed, will require people aged 14 and above to be fingerprinted when applying for national identification cards. The fingerprinting policy has triggered a heated debate. Human rights activists have expressed concern that the fingerprint files might be leaked if the government fails to provide proper protection for the data. On the other hand, government officials argue that the new policy will help track down criminals and curb crime. One senior official says that an efficient monitoring system will be established to prevent the fingerprint files from being leaked. Opinion polls show that nearly 80% of the people in Taiwan support the fingerprinting policy. They seem to care more about crime than their right to privacy.

1. The best title for this passage is "_____".
   A. Fingerprinting—a controversial policy
   B. Fingerprinting—the best way to fight crime
   C. Fingerprinting—an invasion of privacy
   D. Fingerprinting—a lost cause

2. A _____ system can provide proper protection for the fingerprint files.
   A. legal
   B. computer
   C. criminal justice
   D. monitoring

3. It can be inferred that _____.

    A. common people are not aware of the danger of leaking fingerprint files

    B. human rights activists do not seem to understand common people's concerns

    C. people aged 14 and above tend to commit crimes

    D. human rights activists want national identification cards abolished

Questions 4-7

A historic bridge in Nantou's Guoxin Township drew the premier's attention recently. The Glutinous Rice Bridge took its name from the fact that it was built from glutinous rice, lime and sugar rather than from steel and concrete. It was completed in 1940 and has gone through all kinds of natural disasters. The bridge is not only a scenic attraction but also a historic site in Nantou. It remained intact even after the 921 earthquake, the strongest one in Taiwan for a hundred years, which wreaked great havoc in Nantou. But the bridge has been severely damaged because of last summer's Tropical Storm Mindulle which washed parts of it away. Premier Xie promised to help the township preserve the famous bridge when he paid a visit to the site. The premier said, "We must try our best to recover it, renovate it and restore it."

4. The Glutinous Rice Bridge is special for several reasons. Which of the following is NOT one of them?

    A. Its building materials are quite different from the ones commonly used now.

    B. It has a long history.

    C. It has withstood many natural disasters.

    D. It is the first bridge that Premier Xie has ever visited.

5. What is the building material that was NOT used to build the bridge?

   A. Lime

   B. Metal

   C. Sugar

   D. Rice

6. The bridge was damaged by _____.

   A. an earthquake

   B. a bomb

   C. a storm

   D. a fire

7. The premier was quoted as saying, "We must try our best to recover it, renovate it and restore it." In the quotation, the rhetorical devices he used are _____.

   A. alliteration and climactic sentence order

   B. rhyme and anticlimactic sentence order

   C. repetition and climactic sentence order

   D. onomatopoeia and anticlimactic sentence order

Questions 8-11

[1]A recent survey found that online teens are increasingly tech-savvy. [2]Nearly nine out of ten Taiwanese teenagers say they use the Internet. [3]Eighty-nine percent of them use the Internet to send or read e-mail. Eighty-one percent play online games. [4]Eighty percent visit websites about TV, music or sports stars. [5]Seventy-six percent get news online. [6]And 43 percent make purchases online. [7]Another finding is that teenagers very much like to send text messages to each other. [8]Generally speaking, they use the Internet for fun and chatting rather than for academic study. [9]It comes as no surprise that many teenagers fail in school. [10]The reason is that they spend a lot of time online.

8. The author uses _____ to elaborate his main idea.
   A. experiments
   B. statistics
   C. personal experiences
   D. arguments

9. The passage suggests that teenagers use the Internet primarily for _____.
   A. recreation and communication
   B. studying and chatting
   C. shopping and getting news
   D. crime and transactions

10. The topic sentence of this passage is sentence :
    A. 8
    B. 9
    C. 2
    D. 1

11. The word "savvy" may mean "_____".
    A. very much afraid
    B. very much stupid
    C. knowing a lot
    D. talking a lot

Questions 12-14

A sports scandal erupted again recently. Ten people—including Chen Chao-ying, a catcher for the La New Bears, and Tsai Sheng-feng, coach of the Macoto Cobras' farm team—have been nabbed so far for involvement in a multi million-dollar professional baseball game-fixing scandal. A criminal group paid bribes, provided sexual services, and even threatened players to rig the games. In fact, illegal gambling on baseball games is not new in Taiwan. Eight years ago, the same kind of game-fixing landed several baseball players in jail. This kind of scandal has tarnished the image of professional baseball, and the latest scandal has further undermined its credibility.

12. It can be inferred that illegal gambling based on the results of baseball games is _____ in Taiwan.
    A. rare
    B. profitable
    C. not serious
    D. hard to stop

13. The criminal group used several ways to persuade baseball players to cheat. Which of the following is NOT one of them?
    A. Women
    B. Payoffs
    C. Bullying
    D. Promotion

14. As a result of the rigging, spectators might _____.
    A. lose interest in baseball
    B. be forced to pay higher prices for tickets to professional baseball games
    C. doubt the outcome of any professional baseball game
    D. be put at risk

Part

寫作能力測驗篇 Writing

2

Unit **11**

中譯英 (一)—基本句型

中譯英主要是要瞭解受試者掌握英文基本句型的能力如何。因此 Unit 11 和 Unit 12 的重點就是介紹英文句子的形成。 Unit 11 練習七大句型，而 Unit 12 練習複雜句與複合句。

Pattern I　S + (Aux) + Be + SC

上面的句型裡， S 代表主詞， Aux 代表助動詞， SC 代表主詞補語，主詞補語可以是以下幾種形式：

(1) 名詞

(2) 形容詞

(3) that 子句

(4) WH 子句

(5) WH- + to + V

(6) 不定詞

(7) 動名詞

(8) 地方副詞

此外，有少數不及物動詞，如： die, turn, play, become, make ，其後也可接一名詞當作主詞補語。

✏️ **練習一**

請翻譯下列句子。

1. 葡萄是酸的。

_____

2. 美的東西是永恆的喜悅。

_____

3. 事實是抽煙為肺癌的主因。

_____

4.　吳先生成為英雄。

Pattern II　S + (Aux) + Vi

　　Vi 代表不及物動詞，不用接受詞，但可有副詞來修飾它，常見副詞如下表所列：

副　詞	舉　例
頻率副詞	always, usually, often, sometimes, seldom, never, once a week
狀態副詞	quickly, happily, carefully, with difficulty, in surprise
時間副詞	yesterday, already, yet, just, three days ago
地方副詞	here, there, in the living room, at home

✎ 練習二

請翻譯下列句子。

1.　我每天總是走路上學。

2.　珍能唱歌唱得很美。

3.　這部電腦二萬元。

4.　這個箱子重三公斤，長寬各四十和三十公分。

5.　你穿什麼沒關係。

Patter III S + (Aux) + Vi + Adj

在上述句型中的 Vi 是一個連綴動詞，常見的連綴動詞如下：

動　詞	舉　例
感官動詞	look, taste, smell, sound, feel, ring, appear, seem
表「變成」	become, turn, get, go, come, fall, grow, wear
表「依然」	remain, stay, stand, keep
其他	die, prove, return

✎ 練習三

請翻譯下列句子。

1. 很多動物可能已經絕種了。

   _____

2. 山姆保持沉默。

   _____

3. 咖啡嚐起來是苦的。

   _____

4. 懷特年紀輕輕就死了。

   _____

5. 我們的產品證實獲利很高。

   _____

Pattern IV S + (Aux) + (Adv₁) + Vt + O + (Adv₂)

上述句型中的 Vt 為及物動詞， O 指動詞的受詞，受詞必須是個名詞片語。
Adv_1 表示頻率副詞。 Adv_2 表示狀態副詞、地方副詞或時間副詞。

這種句型中的主詞和受詞須爲名詞片語(NP)。名詞片語(NP)有以下幾種：

名　詞　片　語	舉　　　　　　例
1. (定詞) + 名詞	children, Tom, water, a book
2. (定詞) + 形容詞 + 名詞	my new bicycle, that young lady, a dancing girl
3. 代名詞	you, I, me, he, him, she, her, they, them, it, all, both, most, either, neither
4. (for sb) + to + V	to get up early, for you to eat
5. (所有格) + V-ing	playing in the street, my singing
6. that 子句	that the earth is round
7. WH-子句	when he will come, whether you like it or not
8. WH- + to + V	what to do, where to go
9. the + 名詞 + that 子句	the fact that the earth moves around the sun
10.(代) 名詞 + 關係子句	the man who is standing there
11. 名詞 + 介系詞片語	the book on the desk

註　定詞指的是 a/an, the, this/that, these/those ；所有格如： his, my, Tom's 。

✎ 練習四

請翻譯下列句子。

1.　我還沒決定去哪裡。

_____

2.　看到那個人踢我的狗讓我生氣。

_____

3.　老鼠會吃人不願吃的東西。

_____

4.　傑克否認考試作弊。

_____

5.　山姆保證盡力而為。

_____

6. 老牛從不承認自己曾經是小牛笨。

_____

7. 我忘記把燈關掉。

_____

8. 我不知道誰拿走桌上的筆。

_____

Pattern V S + (Aux) + Vt + O_1 + O_2

句型 S + (Aux) + Vt + O_1 + O_2 = S + (Aux) + Vt + O_2 + to/for + O_1 。這類句型中及物動詞有兩個受詞。一個為直接受詞 (O_2)，通常為事物；一個為間接受詞 (O_1)，通常為人。這類動詞有： give, send, lend, write, bring, offer, earn, wish, make, choose, promise, deny, refuse, assign, sell 。

練習五

請翻譯下列句子。

1. 她向我飛吻。

_____

2. 你可以找些吃的給我嗎？

_____

3. 我給自己訂購了火腿三明治。

_____

4. 茱莉亞為自己做了一件毛衣。

_____

5. 我祝他們快樂。

_____

Pattern VI　S + (Aux) + V + O + OC

上述句型中，OC 代表受詞補語，可以是以下幾種形式：

(1) 形容詞

(2) 名詞

(3) that 子句

(4) WH 子句

(5) WH- + to + V

(6) 不定詞

(7) 省略 to 的不定詞

(8) 現在分詞

(9) 過去分詞

 練習六

請翻譯下列句子。

1. 珍把頭髮染成紅色。

   _____

2. 我媽媽把我的頭髮剪短。

   _____

3. 裁判宣佈傑克是勝利者。

   _____

4. 她告訴我她很快就要離開。

   _____

5. 我將告訴她如何操作洗衣機。

   _____

6. 他要求我和他去爬山。

_____

7. 他的勇氣使我們尊敬他。

_____

8. 我看著果實掛在樹上。

_____

9. 喬治在打架中打斷鼻子了。

_____

10. 抱歉讓妳久等了。

_____

Pattern VII S + (Aux) + Vt + O + Prep + NP

　　有些及物動詞在它的受詞之後還要附一個介系詞片語，例如光說 I put the book 語意不夠完整，其後還需要一個表示地方的副詞片語，如：I put the book there. 或 I put the book on the desk. 這樣的句子才能表達一個完整的意思。

✐ 練習七

請翻譯下列句子。

1. 他的朋友把他視為笨蛋。

_____

2. 運動能預防我們罹患心臟病。

_____

3. 我把她誤認為是她妹妹。

_____

課後作業

請將下列的中文段落翻譯成通順、達意且前後連貫的英文。

1. 我喜歡搭公車上班。搭公車省下我很多錢，我一天只花六十元台幣。相對照下，一部車子至少要價五十萬台幣，還不括每年一萬台幣的稅金和保險費。除此之外，修理維護的費用非常高、油價又一直漲；更糟的，有時還必須繳超速或違規停車的罰金。

2. 飛機使我們能環球旅行。它們既快速又安全。即使如此，仍然有些人害怕坐飛機旅行。其中一個理由是他們怕在撞機中喪命。而且，撞機時極少人能倖存；最糟的是，受害者都是橫死。

Unit **12**

中譯英 (二)
一複雜句和複合句

- ✪ **Type I** 因果關係

- ✪ **Type II** 目的

- ✪ **Type III** 比較相同

- ✪ **Type IV** 對比和讓步

- ✪ **Type V** 增加

- ✪ **Type VI** 選擇

- ✪ **Type VII** 條件

- ✪ **Type VIII** 時間

- ✪ **Type IX** 地方

- ✪ 課後作業

　　為文造句時不可能全都用簡單句，有時情況需要必須用到連接詞來連接兩個簡單句。這些連接詞各司不同語意功能。而在文法功用上有些是附屬連接詞 (如：when, if, though, because, whenever, wherever, however, whoever, whatever)，連接一副詞子句修飾主要子句，或者是一關係詞 (如：who, whom, which, that, whose, when, where, why, whoever, whatever)所引領的形容詞子句用以修飾一名詞片語，或者是像 that 及疑問代名詞所引領的名詞子句在句子中當主詞、受詞、主詞補語、或受詞補語。這些句子叫作「複雜句」。

　　另外有些連接詞(如：and, or, but)所連接的兩個簡單句具有平等地位，這種連接詞叫「對等連接詞」。它們所形成的句子稱為「複合句」。形容詞子句和名詞子句分別在 Unit 6 和 Unit 11 談過，本單元專注於包含副詞子句的複雜句和複合句，並以其語意功能做分類。

Type I 因果關係

　　兩個句子之間的關係，第一種稱為「因果關係」，表「因果關係」的連接詞包括下表中所列：

類　型	連接詞
類 1	because (因為), as (因為), since (既然), now that (既然), seeing that (既然)
類 2	so (所以), so + adj/adv + that (如此...以至於), such...that (如此...以至於)

✎ **練習一**

請翻譯下列句子。

1. 大部分的哈雷慧星很難見得到，因為它們又遠又模糊不清。

   _____

2. 既然我們無法得到我們喜歡的，就讓我們喜歡我們所能得到的。

   _____

3. 島嶼國家像台灣和日本缺石油，所以它們必須從國外進口石油。

   _____

4. 我對他如此生氣，以至於我發現很難控制我的脾氣。

_____

5. 那女人是這樣一個騙子，以至於妳不能相信她所說的。

_____

Type II　目的

第二種句與句間的關係是為了表達「目的」的語意，表「目的」的連接詞包括：

語　意	連接詞
1. 為了...目的	so that, in order that
2. 惟恐、以免	lest, in case, for fear that

✏️ 練習二

請翻譯下列句子。

1. 我穿上外套以免感冒。

_____

2. 他努力工作，為了讓他家人能過得舒服。

_____

Type III　比較相同

第三種型態，是為了比較兩句之間相同的狀況，表「比較相同」的連接詞包括下列兩類：

類　型	連接詞
類 1	(just) as (正如), as...as (和...一樣), as...so... (正如...也), A is to B as C is to D (A 之於 B 正如 C 之於 D)
類 2	as if/though (好像)

✎ **練習三**

請翻譯下列句子。

1. 他窮得跟教堂的老鼠一樣。

_____

2. 正如人會活，他也會死。

_____

3. 在羅馬就要跟羅馬人一樣做事 (入境隨俗)。

_____

4. 這件毛衣看起來像是從對街的商店買來的。

_____

5. 閱讀之於心靈，正如運動之於身體。

_____

6. 正如大家所料，約翰贏了賽跑。

_____

Type IV　對比和讓步

第四種句意間的關係，我們稱作「對比和讓步」的關係，表「對比和讓步」的連接詞有以下四種：

語　意	連接詞
1. 但是、而	but, while, whereas
2. 雖然	though
3. 即使	even if, even though
4. 無論	whoever (無論是誰), whatever (無論是什麼), whenever (無論何時), wherever (無論何處), however (無論如何)

✏️ 練習四

請翻譯下列句子。

1. 這房子雖小，卻溫暖舒適。

_____

2. 即使我已經節食一段時間了，我看起來還是胖胖的。

_____

3. 最近幾年「意圖自殺」的情況維持在一定水平，但自殺死亡的案例卻急速上升。

_____

4. 無論代價多少，她都會買下那件衣服。

_____

Type V 增加

在此所謂的增加是表示「除...之外還有」的意思，表達這類語意的連接詞有：not only/just...but (also), and 。

✏️ 練習五

請翻譯下列句子。

1. 菲律賓人不僅推翻馬可仕，他們也舉行了該國最公平的一次總統選舉。

_____

2. 設法吃少一點，運動多一點。

_____

Type VI 選擇

第六種句意的表達是指在兩者中間做選擇，表「選擇」的連接詞有： or, either...or。

✎ 練習六

請翻譯下列句子。

1. 你要麼跟我一起去看電影，要麼就待在家裡。

   _____

2. 給我自由，否則讓我死。

   _____

Type VII 條件

第七種要說的是表示「條件」的句意，也就是說在某種情況之下，或者具備了某種條件之後，作者所說的事情才成立。表「條件」的連接詞有： if (假如), as long as (只要), unless (除非)。

✎ 練習七

請翻譯下列句子。

1. 要是喝太多茶或咖啡，我會難以入睡。

   _____

2. 除非找到一些額外的錢，否則這個圖書館將會關閉。

   _____

3. 只要你做完家庭作業，就可以出去外面玩。

   _____

Type VIII 時間

第八種我們在文句中可能需要表達的是時間上的先後與頻率，這時就需要表示「時間」的連接詞，包括以下三類：

類　型	連接詞
類 1	before (之前), until (直到)
類 2	when (當...時候), while (同時、在...期間), as (當...時候), once (一旦), whenever (無論何時), no matter when (無論何時), every/each time (每次), as soon as (一...就), no sooner...than (一...就), scarcely...when/before (一...就), hardly...when/before (一...就)
類 3	since (自從), after (在之後), and (然後)

✎ 練習八

請翻譯下列句子。

1. 小雞孵出來之前不要計算它們。

   _____

2. 繼續朝這個方向走，直到看到一家 Seven-Eleven.

   _____

3. 過馬路時，我遇見一個老朋友。

   _____

4. 一旦被剝奪自由，你才能體會它的價值。

   _____

5. 無論何時我聽到那首曲子，就想起學生時代。

   _____

6. 王先生一開始講話就再次被觀眾打斷。

   _____

7. 山姆睡著時，我闖進屋子拍照。

   _____

8. 結婚不久之後瑪麗就懷孕了。

_____

9. 自從在大學認識之後，我們就一直是朋友。

_____

Type IX 地方

最後一種在句意上常會出現的是表達事件發生的地方或物品所在之處，表「地方」的連接詞有： where, wherever, no matter where 。

 練習九

請翻譯下列句子。

1. 把藥放在小孩子拿不到的地方。

_____

2. 無論你到哪裡，都要好好對待別人。

_____

課後作業

請將下列三段中文翻譯成通順、達意且前後連貫的英文。

1.　雖然學習英文的年齡已經降至九歲，我國學生的英文能力似乎沒有改善。大學入學考試的平均分數最近幾年已經下降。十六萬即將進入大學的學生中有一半得不到四十分。而且，根據最近的托福成績報告，我們在亞洲排行十四。這顯示較早學英文不保證英文能力水準會較高。

2.　大量的金錢花在教育上，但是卻找不到什麼令人滿意的結果，其中主要原因之一是大部分的錢浪費在不必要的設備上。現在幾乎每間教室都備有電腦，老師一下課學生就衝到電腦前打電玩而不是收集資料。同樣的，一間語言實驗室花費納稅人一百多萬元。不幸的是，昂貴的冷氣實驗室卻成為學生睡覺最舒適的房間。

3.　九月一日一超級颱風襲擊台灣，強烈的風和雨造成嚴重損害，電線被切斷而樹木被連根拔起。有幾個鄉鎮淹水，桃園居民再次遭受缺水之苦。更糟的是，有五十九人受傷，三人死亡。就像今年稍早的颱風一樣，泰林 (Talim) 摧毀了蔬菜水果。結果，蔬菜價格暴漲，一公斤蔥 (chives) 要價台幣三百塊錢。

Unit **13**

英文作文 (一)—段落

- ✪ Focus I 段落的形成
- ✪ Focus II 寫作注意事項
- ✪ 課後作業

Focus I 段落的形成

文章是由段落形成的，因此我們在寫作時，首先必須知道一個段落包含了哪些要項。

在 Unit 9 談到完整的一個段落都有一**主題句**(topic sentence)，這個主題句濃縮了作者對某一**主題**(topic)的看法。這個主題句往往出現在該段落的第一句。有時也會出現在第二或三句，此時它前面的句子是用來提供主題句的背景知識，在兩者交會處通常會有一轉折語作連接。主題句是作者對某一主題的看法，是段落的**主旨**(main idea)。它的特質是概括性、抽象的陳述。

作者接著會個別、具體地詳述他的主旨。他或許會舉例說明，或說明因果關係，或做比較，或條列各步驟，或做主客觀定義，或細部描寫，或記述始末，或做說服性的論述。這些叫作**支持性的細節**(supporting details)，用來支持作者概括性、抽象的陳述。如此才能取信讀者。支持性的細節又分兩類：

1. **主要細節 (major supporting details)** ——用來具體化主旨。

2. **次要細節 (minor supporting details)** ——用來使主要細節更周詳。

Focus II 寫作注意事項

以下是在寫作一個段落時應注意的事項：

1. 主題句的陳述必須是概括性的，但又不可涵蓋太廣，否則小小一段落的份量無法盡述。另一方面也不能過於狹隘，否則會淪為說明性的細節。同時主題句的陳述最好能吸引人。

2. 段落中的每個句子一定都要和主題句宣示的主旨有關，無關的句子再怎麼漂亮也須刪除。

3. 在主題句之後必須提出合理有說服力的細節證詞。這些細節證詞可為個人經驗、事實、統計、實驗、引言，或邏輯說理。

4. 善用語言，使句句通順相連。這些語言技巧包括：替換、指涉、省略和轉折語。

5. 一段落的結束可有一結論句。這個結論句可用不同的語句來呼應主題句所宣示的主旨，或者用一句話歸納各主要細節。千萬不可節外生枝，寫些與主旨無關的話。寫不出好的結論句，寧可不要寫。

✎ 練習一

請細讀以下段落，之後回答文章下面的題目。

The Internet has become indispensable to our lives. We can book rooms or seats via the Internet. We can also shop online. And it is cheap and fast to transmit messages by e-mail. Most importantly, we can get information we need at the click of a mouse. In short, the dot.com industry has become a multi-billion-dollar business.

1. Underline the topic sentence of this passage.

2. Circle the transitional words or phrases.

3. Which transitional word or phrase suggests that the sentence after it is a concluding sentence?

4. How does the author support his main idea? By giving examples, making a comparison/contrast, explaining a cause-and-effect relationship, defining a term, describing a process, or narrating an event?

5. Do you think the concluding sentence is appropriate? If not, rewrite it.

✎ 練習二

請細讀以下段落，之後回答文章下面的題目。

There are several advantages to having men and women working together. First, a man will become more interested in his work and will stay in the office longer to attract the attention of his female colleagues. After all, hard work is always regarded as a virtue. Few women like a man who is lazy and irresponsible. Besides, good feelings will develop. It is believed that sexual desire between animals helps to create a warm and friendly atmosphere. Men become eager to please women and women appear to be kinder to men. Also both men and women will pay more attention to their own looks. Men want women to think of them as gentlemen, so men will shave regularly, have their hair cut and will wear their best clothes. Likewise, women believe that the best way to win a man's heart is to have good looks. Thus, they are always beautifully dressed and wear makeup. This can show that they are well-heeled and well-behaved. Moreover, men and women will help each other more. While men may be slow to come to the aid of their male colleagues, they jump at the chance to help their female colleagues. They follow nature's law that members of the opposite sex attract each other. Finally, men and women may fall in love with each other and get married. This brings happiness not only to the newly-weds but also to the company. The couple will work together in harmony.

1. Find the topic sentence of the passage and underline it.

2. Circle any transitional words or phrases that indicate an important supporting detail will follow.

3. Write down the important details.

4. How does the author expand on each of his important details? Does he use statistics, does he conduct an experiment, or does he do anything else?

5. There is a sentence that is irrelevant to the point at hand. Find it and delete it.

✏️ **練習三**

請細讀以下的段落，然後從段落後的選項挑出適合本段落的主題句。挑選時要考慮它是否恰當——會不會太概括性、太狹隘？或是恰到好處？

_____ First of all, you should consider the publishing company and look at the publishing date. Is the company an expert in producing dictionaries? Has the dictionary been regularly updated? Then, read its introduction. Are there any specific features in this dictionary? How many entries are there in this dictionary? Moreover, you should thumb through the dictionary. Does it contain a lot of example sentences? Does it give usage notes? Last but not least, you should consider whether the dictionary meets your needs. If you want to use it to read, say, *The Economist*, then you should have a collegiate dictionary which contains more than one hundred and sixty thousand entries. On the other hand, if you need a dictionary to help you write, then you should select an advanced learners' dictionary for non-native speakers.

A.   Analyzing one's needs is the most effective way to select a good dictionary.

B.   Selecting a good dictionary demands keen judgment.

C.   There are several ways to distinguish a good reference book from a bad one.

✏ **練習四**

請細讀以下主題句，你認為哪些句子較能吸引你？為什麼？

a.   People have become slaves to the mass media.

b.   I find it frustrating to get along with women.

c.   As Dickens once said, "It was the age of wisdom, it was the age of foolishness."

d.   In some ways nature trails are like freeways.

e.   An octopus appears to be just a huge head with eight long, fearful arms.

✎ **練習五**

以下兩個段落都缺了主題句，請在細讀之後替它們補上主題句。

1. Since traffic conditions are worsening, _____. Some people suggest that the government discourage people from driving cars by imposing a heavy tax on car owners. Others ask that more parking lots be built. Still others think it is important that public transportation be promoted.

2. According to a recent study, women live about eight years longer than men. _____ The stereotype of men is that they are daring, adventurous and macho, while that of women is that they are prudent, quiet and attractive. Therefore, men take risks to assert their masculinity. In contrast, women tend to remain weak to win attention and love. Ever since childhood, men have been trained to bear hardship, which has caused them to be exposed to danger and uncertainty. No wonder that men are destined to suffer from more physical and mental stress. To make matters worse, they have been indoctrinated with altruism—they should make sacrifices for the sake of their family's welfare.

練習六

下面有一未完成的段落，它有主題句，但漏了敘述主題句的主要細節。請按所提示的主題句寫出三個主要細節使成一完整段落。注意要善用轉折語。

A Public-Spirited Neighbor

　　Mr. Lee, who is a doctor and very interested in law, lives next door to me. He is really a public-spirited neighbor. _____

_____

_____

_____

_____

_____

_____

_____

課後作業

　　下面有一未完成的段落，它有主題句，也有主要細節，但漏了敘述主要細節的次要細節。請按所提示的主題句和主要細節寫出一完整段落。注意要用個人經驗、事實、統計、實驗、引言或邏輯說理來擴充主要細節。

　　Advertisers use several methods to persuade us into buying their products. The most popular way is to play on our fear of being unhealthy or unattractive. _____

_____

_____

_____

_____

Another method is to employ well-known movie stars or athletes to promote their products. _____

_____

_____

_____

They also use pseudoscience to mislead consumers. _____

_____

_____

_____

_____

Unit 14

英文作文 (二)－文章

Focus I 文章的結構

在 Unit 13 談論到段落結構，其型式如下：

主題句 ─ 宣示一個段落的主旨。

　主要細節句 ₁ ─次要細節句

　主要細節句 ₂ ─次要細節句

　主要細節句 ₃ ─次要細節句

(結論句─回應主題句或綜合各個主要細節)

然而文章通常不只一段。雖然如此，它的結構還是相似的：第一段是介紹段落 (introductory paragraph)，說明整篇文章的主旨或目的。此相當於段落的主題句。之後每一段落說明一個主要細節 (supporting paragraph)。如有三個主要細節，則有三個段落，這三段就是文章的主體。最後可有一結論段落，相當段落的結論句 (concluding paragraph)。

練習一

請細讀以下一篇文章，然後依照提示寫出這篇文章每個段落的主旨。

　　Success in life doesn't come easy. Of course, it takes hard work. We have to put a lot of effort into improving our work skills, and great talent is also needed. We also have to depend on luck to have a chance to fulfill our talents. But to get ahead, it is no less important to enjoy friendly relations with others. We should make friends with others and get along well with them. They may be very helpful to us in finding opportunities to fulfill our talents and dreams. A famous person may feel lonely on his way up, but a successful person is happy and popular.

　　But how can we improve personal relations? First, it is advantageous to us to have good looks. If we were not born pretty, then we should dress up and use makeup so that we can attract other people's attention.

Second, we should be eager to share with others. Sometimes we can treat people to a big meal, and at other times we can give them gifts. Above all, we should make sure that every one of them feels that they have gotten the lion's share.

Thirdly, we should sit on the fence instead of taking sides. When two sides are arguing, it is dangerous to get involved in the argument. A wise person will make each of the two sides believe that he is on their side.

Finally, we should say words that are music to the ears of others. It will do us good to often say things like, "You look really nice" or "You did a fine job." Even if we hate listening to a particular person, we should put on our best faces and say "What a good idea!" after he finishes talking. Telling the plain truth sometimes only makes us enemies.

Improving interpersonal relations may not help us win fame, but it will lead us to success in life—we may be able to get a better job, earn extra money, or mingle with VIPs. These four methods help us win other people's hearts and help us climb the ladder of success.

Outline

The Introductory Paragraph : _____

　Supporting Paragraph$_1$: _____

　Supporting Paragraph$_2$: _____

　Supporting Paragraph$_3$: _____

　Supporting Paragraph$_4$: _____

The Concluding Paragraph : _____

Focus II 構思的方法

構思作文的方法，包括以下幾種：

1. 自由暇想：針對某一主題，將能想到的有關想法寫下來。這時不要管文法對不對，只專注 ideas。

2. 提出問題：針對某一主題提出各種問題，用疑問詞 why, when, where, how, who, whom 等列出很多問題。

3. 集思廣益，自由討論：可找同伴，共同針對某一主題交換意見，然後一一列出重點。

4. 串聯：將所想到的想法，利用線條、箭頭、圓圈等標示之間的關係。

5. 大綱：將所想到的想法做成有條理的大綱。

✎ 練習二

幾乎每個人都有打工的經驗。現在針對你某一次打工的經驗，寫一篇作文。文章分兩段。第一段描述那次打工的狀況。第二段寫你從那次打工中得到什麼教訓。在正式寫時，先構思。可利用以上五種方法中的任何一項做準備工作。

Focus III 寫作過程

構思完成，真正進入寫作過程後，可運用以下方式組織完成一篇文章。

1. 縮小：視文章長度將主題涵蓋的範圍縮小。

2. 剪裁：將與主題涵蓋範圍之外的想法去除，並加入臨時想到有關的資料。

3. 陳述主旨：切記一個段落只能有一個主旨。初學者可把主題句放在一個段落的第一句。

4. 決定寫作模式：視主題句決定要舉例說明，或說明因果關係，或做比較，或條列各步驟，或做主客觀定義，或細部描寫，或記述始末，或做說服性的論述。

5. 加入支持性的細節：支持性的細節要具體、生動、有說服力。

6. 善用轉折語：各種轉折語請參閱 Unit 1 和 Unit 2。

7. 檢查文法、拼字、標點符號：文法請參閱 Unit 5 和 Unit 6。

8. 修訂改寫句子：簡單句、複雜句、複合句交替並用會有加分效果。請參閱 Unit 11 和 Unit 12。

 練習三

請利用你的構思草搞，組織成一完整文章。

課後作業

1. 人事行政局宣布公務人員如果通過英檢考試可以加積分。你認為這個政策好嗎？請明示你的立場並提出你的理由。

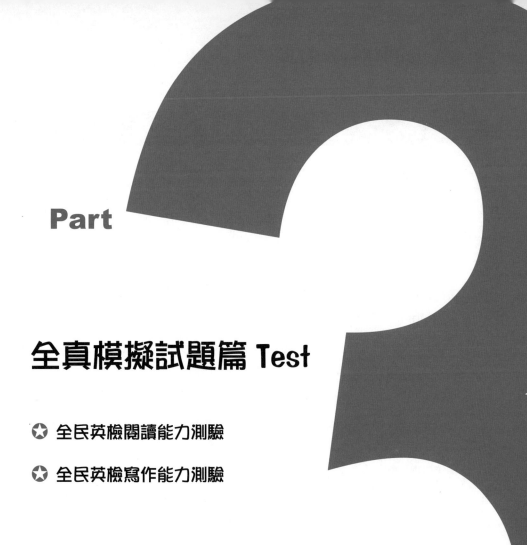

Part

全真模擬試題篇 Test

⭐ 全民英檢閱讀能力測驗

⭐ 全民英檢寫作能力測驗

3

全民英檢閱讀能力測驗

第一部分　詞彙和結構

本部分共 15 題，每題含一個空格。請就試題上 A、B、C、D 四個選項中選出最適合題意的字或詞。

1. When you are invited for dinner, be sure to be _____. It is impolite to be late.
   A. truthful　　　B. faithful　　　C. realistic　　　D. punctual

2. What _____ me was that my students spent little time on their studies. That was the reason why I felt like retiring.
   A. thrilled　　　B. frustrated　　　C. terrified　　　D. embarrassed

3. There was a rock blocking the way. I got out of my car and removed the _____.
   A. container　　　B. cement　　　C. grave　　　D. obstacle

4. Where life began remains a _____. No one can give a definite answer to this question. That is, we are still in the dark about it.
   A. legend　　　B. mystery　　　C. tradition　　　D. rumor

5. The 50 states _____ the United States, and there is a federal government.
   A. constitute　　　B. represent　　　C. possess　　　D. govern

6. It is easier to _____ a friendship than to cultivate it. When you fall out with someone, it is hard to make up.
   A. strike up　　　B. bask in　　　C. break off　　　D. build up

7. Business is picking up, and factories have begun to _____ new workers _____ for their assembly lines.
   A. lay...off　　　B. pass...by　　　C. call...up　　　D. take...on

8. At 210 cm, Sam towers over his classmates; in fact, he even _____ in any crowd.
   A. draws back   B. cheers up   C. makes up   D. stands out

9. I am very busy these days. Visiting you on Wednesday is quite _____.
   A. out of season   B. out of fashion
   C. out of the ordinary   D. out of the question

10. I've been feeling a little _____ this week. I'm afraid I must go to see a doctor.
    A. under the weather   B. out of my element
    C. at a loss   D. behind the times

11. Can you imagine! At this time tomorrow I _____ home. In fact, even now I feel as if I were on a flight.
    A. have flown   B. am flying   C. will fly   D. will be flying

12. Fortunately, we found a temple and took shelter in it. Otherwise, we _____ wet in the sudden downpour.
    A. might get   B. might have gotten
    C. would rather get   D. should have gotten

13. She speaks perfect English. If you don't see her _____, you may well mistake her for an American.
    A. to speak   B. spoke   C. speaks   D. speaking

14. He is 70, but most expect him, health _____, to seek a second term of office in 2008.
    A. permitting   B. permitted   C. permits   D. to permit

15. When I am listening to music, I often wear a pair of earphones, which _____ plugged into my CD player.
    A. have   B. has   C. is   D. are

第二部分 段落填空

本部分共 10 題，包括二個段落，每個段落各含 5 個空格。請就試題上 A 、 B 、 C 、 D 四個選項中選出最適合題意的字或詞。

Questions 16-20

A student who carried his classmate on his back fell down the stairs accidentally. Unfortunately, the fall killed his classmate who was afflicted with ontogenesis imperfecta, a bone disorder. As for the student, he was accused of __16__ and had to pay more than NT$3 million in compensation.

The verdict set off a huge public outcry. Most people question the judge's __17__ judgment. They do not understand why a person who is willing to help a disabled person should be punished. Besides, they are worried that the sentence will have a(n) __17__ effect. From now on, people might have second thoughts when about to lend someone a hand.

In fact, the effect has already been felt. Recently, a 60-year-old schoolteacher demanded that one of his students' parents __19__ a document saying that they themselves would take responsibility if any accident should occur to their child. The child has amblyopia, an eye condition characterized by reduced vision which is not correctable through prescriptive eyewear. In another case, a man collapsed from a heart attack in a schoolyard while more than a hundred people at the scene looked __20__, with no one willing to assist him. Obviously, the judge has sentenced sympathy to death.

16. A. murder   B. neglect   C. cheating   D. gambling

17. A. political   B. clinical   C. artistic   D. moral

18. A. undesirable   B. beneficial   C. significant   D. possible

19. A. would submit   B. must submit   C. submit   D. submitted

20. A. up   B. down   C. on   D. in

Questions 21-25

It takes hard work to earn money, but spending it is not atall difficult. Of course, you need to spend money on certain things if you want at all to live a good life—paying the bill for dinner, for example. On the weekend you may have nothing to do and may feel __21__, so you decide to go to the movies. Sometimes, you reach for some __22__ when a poor child stretches out his hand for a handout. And a close relative of yours, say your cousin, may come to you saying he is short of money. You lend him some money __23__ you know he may not be able to pay you back. Then your wife argues with you over what you should buy your father for his birthday. You want to get him a shirt, but your wife thinks a necktie would be much better. __24__, you find that little hard-earned money is left over for car repairs. Then you realize you haven't __25__ your money well. Worse still, you haven't set aside any money each month for future use.

21. A. bored   B. surprised   C. ashamed   D. frustrated

22. A. bills   B. checks   C. toys   D. coins

23. A. if   B. though   C. because   D. after

24. A. Even so   B. In addition   C. In the end   D. Earlier on

25. A. earned   B. managed   C. saved   D. invested

第三部分　閱讀理解

本部分共 15 題，包括數段短文，每段短文後有 2~5 個相關問題。請就試題上 A、B、C、D 四個選項中選出最適合者。

Questions 26-29

Women's virginity has always been a contentious issue. Recently this issue became the focus of discussion again amongst women's groups when a 38-year-old woman asked Cathay General Hospital for NT$5 million in damages for rupturing her hymen during a medical check-up.

The hymen is a piece of skin that partly covers the opening of a woman's vagina (or the passage between a woman's outer sexual organs). An unbroken hymen shows that a woman has never had sex. Traditionally a woman's virginity is highly valued, so operations for replacing the hymen are common among some women. It is said that some female sex workers will have such operations to deceive their patrons. Further, with intermarriage between Taiwanese men and foreign women increasing, spouse introduction agencies guarantee the virginity of foreign brides by having their hymens replaced if necessary.

Women's rights activists lament that a woman's hymen is being commercialized. They also criticize men for their hypocrisy in that some of them have multiple partners but still demand that their brides be virgins. For the case at hand, the activists think that the doctor responsible should apologize to the woman for causing discomfort rather than for damaging the woman's hymen.

26. This passage suggests that, if female sex workers have their hymens replaced, _____.
    A. their patrons might be safe from sexually transmitted diseases
    B. their patrons are willing to pay a higher price
    C. police will not arrest them
    D. they will look more attractive

27. This passage suggests that _____.
    A. some foreign brides, in fact, are not virgins
    B. some foreign brides, in fact, are not single
    C. spouse introduction agencies earn a lot of money
    D. Taiwanese men cannot find virgin brides in their own country

28. From the _____ viewpoint, women's rights activists consider the doctor responsible to be wrong.
    A. educational
    B. commercial
    C. sexist
    D. medical

29. Women's rights activists criticize men for hypocrisy because _____.
    A. they are harsh on women
    B. they are sexually ignorant
    C. they have double standards
    D. they show strong sexual desire

Questions 30-33

When Mr. Lien, the former KMT party chairman, went on a trip to China, the Chinese leaders promised him a pair of pandas as a gift to Taiwan. Obviously, the furry creatures are being used by China as a propaganda tactic. More amusingly, they are also serving the KMT's political purposes. Mr. Lien made it known recently that he hoped the pair of pandas would be first kept in Taichung. The local media speculated that by doing so, the KMT was trying to help Mayor Jason Hu win a second term in office in the year-end mayoral election. But politics aside, should the Taiwanese government accept China's offer? Many people say "NO" for several reasons.

Firstly, environmentalists are concerned that a suitable living environment for the pandas might not be found. Pandas are facing extinction because they are not adaptable to a different environment and they only feed on arrow bamboo. Besides, they do not breed quickly—at most females may only have one or two cubs a year. And it is very difficult to raise the pandas, especially in a zoo. Environmentalists argue that the best place to raise pandas is in their natural environment.

Secondly, health officials pointed out possible epidemics which first appeared in China such as the outbreak associated with streptococcus suis in pigs in Sichuan Province and avian flu in Guangdong Province. A few years ago, the outbreak of SARS threw all of whole Asia into a panic. It killed human beings and it destroyed the economy as well. A sick panda may be no less dangerous than a sick bird or pig.

Finally, some critics are alarmed at the astronomical expenses needed to support the pair of pandas. Furthemore, Taiwan must pay US$300 million to China for the creatures each year. When people are struggling to survive during the recent economic downturn, it is anything but wise to spend so much money on these animals.

30. According to environmentalists, pandas are difficult to raise for several reasons. Which one of the following is NOT one of them?
    A. Pandas do not adjust very well.
    B. Pandas do not produce many babies.
    C. Pandas are very picky about food.
    D. Pandas get sick easily.

31. _____ in China is another worry for people in Taiwan.
    A. Infection
    B. Crime
    C. Safety
    D. Corruption

32. The passage suggests that _____.
    A. sending Taiwan the pandas is a goodwill gesture from China
    B. Taichung is the best place to keep the pandas
    C. raising the pandas will be a drain on the country's finances
    D. raising the pandas is dangerous

33. China's decision to send Taiwan the pandas and the discussion about where to keep the pandas are _____ motivated.
    A. economically
    B. politically
    C. racially
    D. environmentally

Questions 34-36

There are several good reasons to open casinos in Penghu, a group of outlying islands. One of the advantages is that doing so will produce income for the local government. For many years, the local government in Penghu has lacked money to improve its infrastructure. A casino can be a magnet—people from the rest of the country will flock to the islands to spend money, and entrepreneurs will invest heavily in hotels and leisure facilities, among other things. Thus, the local government's tax revenues will shoot up. Another advantage is that casinos will create a lot of jobs for local people. The unemployment rate in Penghu has risen by 2% recently, and young people have been forced to leave their hometowns and try to find jobs in Taiwan. If casinos can be opened in Penghu, thousands of jobs will be created for local people, as witnessed by Indian reservations in the United States.

34. From the _____ viewpoint, the author argues in favor of opening the casinos.
    A. political
    B. economic
    C. environmental
    D. recreational

35. The passage suggests that _____.
    A. the manufacturing industry will take off as a result of the opening of casinos
    B. Indians in the Untied States have become rich because they like to gamble
    C. the population of Penghu is steadily decreasing
    D. local businessmen will lose out to those from Taiwan

36. There are several good reasons for opening casinos. Which of the following is NOT one of them?

    A. Many jobs will be created.

    B. Roads and public buildings will be improved.

    C. The public purse will be increased.

    D. Local people will become better educated.

Questions 37-40

　　Some lawmakers propose that casinos be allowed to be opened in Penghu because it would provide extra income for the local government. However, there have been some serious reservations voiced by many local people. The most serious problem would be crime. With gambling comes organized crime, and it is not uncommon for gangs to try to control casinos. Gang violence would ensue. On top of that, the sex industry would thrive. People would come not only for gambling but also for womanizing. To meet the demand, gang members would abduct innocent women and force them to work as prostitutes. Then, AIDS would be rampant. Witness the sex industry in Thailand, where a lot of people, male and female alike, have contracted AIDS and a lot of children have been orphaned as a result. Last but not least, traditional values would be ruined. We tell our children that gambling is the root of all evil, but now we are embracing it and touting it as the only way to revitalize the economy. To sum up, allowing casinos to open in Penghu would be equivalent to striking a Faustian bargain.

37. Gang violence would break out because _____.

    A. gangs will surely compete with each other for control of casinos

    B. police are not allowed to crack down on casinos

    C. gangs are not well organized

    D. gamblers are ill disciplined

38. Which of the following is NOT mentioned in the passage?

    A. Gang members would engage in woman traffickingl.

    B. Many families would be destroyed.

    C. Many prostitutes would come from Thailand.

    D. Gambling and sex are closely connected.

39. The author is worried that children might be _____ about traditonal values.

    A. curious

    B. confused

    C. ignorant

    D. certain

40. A Faustian bargain might mean _____.

    A. doing two things in the wrong order

    B. depending completely on one thing in order to have success

    C. trying to do more than one is able to do

    D. exchanging one good thing for several bad things

全民英檢寫作能力測驗

一、中譯英

請將下列的一段中文翻譯成通順、達意且前後連貫的英文。

> 約翰一聽到電話響就衝下樓去接。不幸地,他跌倒且扭傷腳踝。要是他當時慢慢走,他就不會遭此意外。自從被送進醫院,已經有三天了。他喜歡打籃球。現在他就只能躺在床上看電視。

二、 英文作文

請依下面所提供的文字提示寫一篇英文作文,長度約 120 字(8 至 12 個句子)。評分重點包括內容、組織、文法、用字遣詞、標點符號、大小寫。

> 提示:人有生就有死。死是必須面對的。如果你還有三天可以活,你將如何度過這三天?請以 If I had only three days to live 為題寫一短文。

Part

翻譯與解析
Translation and Answer Key

Unit 1 詞彙和結構─字彙 (一)

一、同義字、定義、或重述關係

例 這間房子是由一隻凶猛的狗所看守。那隻凶暴的狗會攻擊進入房子的陌生人。

A. 流浪的　　　　B. 抓狂的　　　　C. 野生的　　　　D. 兇猛的

例 在過去，中國皇帝擁有絕對的權力。他們被稱為天子。

A. 知識分子　　　B. 修侶　　　　　C. 平民　　　　　D. 皇帝

例 莎士比亞是位著名的劇作家。連六歲大的小孩都知道他的大名，也讀過他的劇本。

A. 聰明的　　　　B. 卑鄙的　　　　C. 著名的　　　　D. 神秘的

練習一

《Answers》 --

| 1. B | 2. D | 3. B | 4. A | 5. C | 6. C | 7. C | 8. A | 9. A | 10. B |

1. It takes time and effort to learn a foreign language, and it is still more difficult to <u>be good at</u> it. And only a few native speakers can _____ it.

   學習一種外語需要時間與努力，即便如此，要精通該語言也是難上加難。只有少數說母語的人能專精於該語言。

   A. 濫用　　　　　B. 專精　　　　　C. 詮釋　　　　　D. 精鍊

2. I like to <u>put my cards on the table</u> so that no misunderstandings will arise. Similarly, I expect _____ answers when I put questions to you.

   我喜歡開誠佈公，這樣就不會有誤會產生。同樣地，我期望當我向你提出問題時，也能獲得直接的回答。

   A. 聰明的　　　　B. 簡短的　　　　C. 立即的　　　　D. 直接的

3. I work as a(n) _____. I find it great fun to <u>show people around</u>.

我的工作是導遊。我喜歡帶領大家四處參觀。

A. 運動員   B. 導遊   C. 機長   D. 導演

4. We <u>all agree that</u> we need to boost our sales. It is this _____ goal that helps us to put aside our differences.

我們一致認為需要增加我們的銷售。就是這個共同的目標，讓彼此的歧見擱置一旁。

A. 共同的   B. 遙遠的   C. 立即的   D. 最終的

5. We have agreed to have a college class reunion, but the date has not yet been _____. Once the date <u>is set</u>, we will begin to prepare for it.

我們已經贊同要舉辦一個同學會，但是日期還沒有決定。一旦日期決定之後，我們就會開始籌備。

A. 取消   B. 延長   C. 決定   D. 改變

6. <u>Share prices fell sharply, and many factories were shut down. Unemployment shot up to a previously unheard-of 5%.</u> The prime minister's popularity was hit by the economic _____.

股價突然跌落，許多工廠關閉。失業率衝上前所未聞的 5% 高比例。首相的支持度也因為經濟危機而下降。

A. 奇蹟   B. 狀況   C. 危機   D. 成長

7. Some countries in the world are still very _____. For example, they still <u>do not have running water</u>, and they <u>live on handouts from developed countries</u>.

世界上的有些國家仍然非常落後。舉例而言，他們仍然沒有自來水，依賴已發展國家的施捨生存。

A. 侵略的   B. 繁榮的   C. 落後的   D. 民主的

8. Professor Lee _____ that I become his assistant. But I rejected his <u>offer</u>.

李教授提議讓我當他的助理。但是我拒絕他的提議。

A. 提議   B. 堅持   C. 命令   D. 要求

9.　Illness and age had changed her beyond _____.　Had she <u>not noticed</u> me first, I would have mistaken her for a total stranger and passed her by.

由於疾病與歲月的緣故，她的容貌已經改變，讓人無法辨識。若不是她先注意到我，我會誤以為她是完全的陌生人，就直接走過去。

A. 辨識　　　　　B. 批評　　　　　C. 控制　　　　　D. 比較

10.　Mr. Church has had a heart attack and his doctor is <u>operating on him</u>. The _____ will take six hours.

喬奇先生有心臟病，他的醫生正在為他開刀。這個手術將進行六小時。

A. 健康檢查　　　B. 手術　　　　　C. 痙攣　　　　　D. 治療

二、對比關係和反義字

例　鮑博曾經坐牢，但是不久之後就被釋放，因為警察誤認他是搶劫銀行的人。

　　A. 拘留　　　　　B. 釋放　　　　　C. 起訴　　　　　D. 赦免

例　我的母語是台語，但是另一方面，我可以說兩種外國語言。一個是英語，一個是法語。

　　A. 人工的　　　　B. 正式的　　　　C. 外國的　　　　D. 官方的

練習二

《Answers》

1. B	2. B	3. B	4. B	5. D	6. D	7. A	8. A	9. C	10. C

1.　Work <u>began</u> on the temple in 1858, and was _____ in 1862. Since then, it has become a tourist attraction.

這座廟宇於 1858 年動工，1862 年完成。自此之後，已經變為一個觀光景點。

A. 設計　　　　　B. 完成　　　　　C. 摧毀　　　　　D. 修復

2. An increase in the crime rate comes as a shock to _____ people. Unlike high-ranking officials, they go around without bodyguards to protect them.

犯罪率的增加對一般民眾造成衝擊。不像一些高層的政府官員，民眾的日常生活並沒有保鑣來保護。

A. 幸運的　　　　B. 一般的　　　　C. 固執的　　　　D. 無知的

3. Clothes made of _____ fibers such as wool and cotton are more expensive than those made of synthetic fibers such as nylon.

天然纖維的衣服，如毛料與棉質衣物，比一些合成纖維的衣服如尼龍等，還要貴。

A. 人工的　　　　B. 天然的　　　　C. 粗糙的　　　　D. 優良的

4. No one can prove that ghosts do _____, but some people believe in ghosts all the same.

沒有人可以證明鬼真的存在，但是有些人依然相信鬼神。

A. 存活　　　　B. 存在　　　　C. 消失　　　　D. 交配

5. I had an intense desire to own that beautiful dress; however, I had to _____ the desire because I was low on cash.

我有強烈的慾望想要擁有那件漂亮的衣服；但是我必須克制那個慾望，因為我沒錢。

A. 表達　　　　B. 理解　　　　C. 屈服　　　　D. 抑制

6. Mr. Rush is thought of as a born orator now, but when he was a student, he was _____ of giving even a casual talk in public.

羅斯先生被認為是天生的演說家，但是當他還是學生時，他連一般的公開演說都會害怕。

A. 厭倦的　　　　B. 有能力的　　　　C. 自信的　　　　D. 害怕的

7. Your report is too lengthy; you should _____ it. A condensed report is more readable.

你的報告太長，你應該把它縮減。一個精簡的報告比較具有可閱讀性。

A. 縮減　　　　B. 確認　　　　C. 提出　　　　D. 發表

8. The bill seems, on the _____, to be genuine, but on closer inspection, it is clear that it is counterfeit money. At first glance, you may be tricked into believing it is real.

    這張鈔票表面上看起來像真的，但是近一點觀察之後，就很清楚知道是張假鈔。剛看到時，你可能會被騙相信它是真的。

    A. 表面   B. 全部   C. 平均   D. 相反

9. Anita arrived just as I was leaving, but whether this was by accident or by _____, I'm not sure. But I feel that she is unwilling to come into contact with me.

    我要離開時，安妮塔正好到達，我不確定這是巧合還是故意。但是我感覺她不願意和我有接觸。

    A. 猜測   B. 直覺   C. 設計   D. 錯誤

10. The USA is a wealthy nation, but some people are still living in _____. The homeless are often seen sleeping on street corners.

    美國是個富有的國家，不過仍然有些人生活在困苦當中。常常可見到遊民睡在街角。

    A. 恐懼   B. 舒適   C. 窮困   D. 和平

三、舉證

例 像美國、日本、法國這樣富有的國家都被要求取消他們對非洲貧困國家的債權。

A. 公司   B. 國家   C. 組織   D. 家庭

練習三

1. I find a bicycle is a(n) _____ way to get around town. For one thing, a cyclist doesn't get stuck in traffic jams. For another, it is easy to park a bicycle, even in small spaces.

   我發現腳踏車是一種非常方便大家在市區活動的方法。一方面而言,騎士不會被困在塞車當中。另一方面而言,只要小小的空間就可以停車,非常簡單。

   A. 合法的　　　　B. 愉快的　　　　C. 昂貴的　　　　D. 方便的

2. I am not interested in _____ affairs such as who goes to bed with whom.

   我對像誰跟誰上床這種私人的事情沒有興趣。

   A. 外國的　　　　B. 國內的　　　　C. 私人的　　　　D. 公眾的

3. The appeal for _____ supplies to help the refugees met with a positive response. People from all over the world hurried to donate food, clothing and money.

   提供救濟物資來幫助難民的請求獲得正面回應。來自世界各地的人們火速捐獻食物、衣服與金錢。

   A. 救濟的　　　　B. 軍事的　　　　C. 醫療的　　　　D. 燃料

4. There was _____ evidence that the car had been in an accident. The headlight was broken, and there were scratches on the finish.

   有具體的證據顯示那輛車發生了車禍:大燈損毀,烤漆上還有刮痕。

   A. 具體的　　　　B. 不足的　　　　C. 統計的　　　　D. 不確定的

5. He is a man of great _____. The young and old, and males and females are all attracted to him.

   他是個非常有魅力的人。老的、少的、男的、女的,全部都被他吸引。

   A. 遠見　　　　B. 財富　　　　C. 魅力　　　　D. 潛力

6. When the fireworks went off, they presented/created a _____ sight. They produced loud noises, colorful sparks and beautiful designs.

   當煙火點燃時，會呈現出一種壯觀的景象。煙火會產生巨大的聲響、五彩繽紛的火花和漂亮的圖案。

   A. 可憐的　　　　B. 恐怖的　　　　C. 令人不安的　　D. 壯觀的

7. The decision to offer English classes in elementary schools raised some _____, one of which was that few of the classes would be taught by qualified teachers. Even teaching materials were called into question.

   在小學教授英語課的決定引起了部分質疑。其中一個疑慮就是只有極少數的班級可以接受合格的老師教導。甚至是教材都被懷疑。

   A. 希望　　　　　B. 質疑　　　　　C. 抗議　　　　　D. 恐懼

8. Her three sons have pursued different _____: the eldest son is a jeweler, the second one a butcher, and the youngest one a college professor.

   他的三個兒子分別追求不同的職業生涯：最大的兒子是個珠寶商，二兒子是個肉販，最小的兒子是大學教授。

   A. 時尚　　　　　B. 職業　　　　　C. 風俗　　　　　D. 政策

9. While reading, you should be able to _____ opinions from facts. For example, "Mr. X was born in 1951" is a fact whereas "Mr. X is handsome" is an opinion.

   在閱讀時，你應該要能夠區分事實與意見的不同。舉例而言，「X 先生出生於 1951 年」是個事實，然而「X 先生很帥」是個意見。

   A. 擷取　　　　　B. 選擇　　　　　C. 隔離　　　　　D. 區分

10. The best way to help teenagers develop a sense of responsibility is to involve them in decision making. They should be encouraged to _____ their ideas.

    幫助青少年建立責任感的最佳方式是讓他們參與決策。這樣可以鼓勵他們貢獻他們的意見。

    A. 修正　　　　　B. 貢獻　　　　　C. 釐清　　　　　D. 蒐集

四、因果關係

例 過去學校的生活對她而言是那樣生動，猶如昨天的記憶。

  A. 無價的   B. 苦樂參半的 C. 乏味的   D. 生動的

練習四

《Answers》--

| 1. A | 2. B | 3. C | 4. A | 5. C | 6. C | 7. C | 8. A | 9. B | 10. D |

1. I am _____ of snakes because I was once bitten by a snake when I was a child.

  我很怕蛇，因為在我小時候曾經被蛇咬過。

  A. 害怕的   B. 喜歡的   C. 厭倦的   D. 忌妒的

2. The children made such a _____ in the living room that I had to spend a lot of time clearing it up.

  孩子們把客廳弄得這樣亂，以至於我必須花很多時間清理它。

  A. 大驚小怪 B. 混亂   C. 大吵大鬧 D. 展示

3. Their arrival was delayed because of heavy _____. They were caught in a long line of cars for three hours.

  因為塞車，他們晚到。他們被困在排著長隊的車陣中三個小時。

  A. 反諷   B. 香水   C. 交通   D. 消費

4. Jean lives beyond her means; no wonder she has gotten into _____.

  珍入不敷出，難怪她已欠下債務。

  A. 債   B. 政治   C. 恐慌   D. 狂怒

5. Helen <u>has a good figure</u>. She is also <u>nice-looking, athletic, and outgoing</u>. She is expected to win the beauty contest and be _____ the Queen of Beauty.

   海倫有付好容貌。她長得漂亮、強健,而且個性外向。大家都期待她能贏得選美比賽,成為選美皇后。

   A. 任命   B. 綽號   C. 加冕   D. 指定

6. The air in the desert is very <u>dry</u>; it contains hardly any _____.

   在沙漠中的空氣非常乾燥,幾乎不含水分。

   A. 氧氣   B. 氫   C. 水分   D. 灰塵

7. (With) the outbreak of SARS, people are advised to <u>take their temperature</u> twice a day to see if they have a(n) _____.

   因為爆發 SARS ,人們被建議一天量兩次體溫以確實是否發燒。

   A. 頭痛   B. 震驚   C. 發燒   D. 傷害

8. Before taking any medicine, you should be sure to read and follow all the directions. Some chemical _____ might (result from) the <u>misuse of medicine</u>.

   在吃任何藥之前,你應該確定看過說明並遵照指示。有些化學中毒可能是由於藥物誤用。

   A. 中毒   B. 成分   C. 物質   D. 元素

9. The workers <u>weren't satisfied with</u> their low wages and long work hours; (therefore,) they walked out and staged a(n) _____.

   這些工人不滿意他們的低工資和長時間工作;因此,他們罷工並發起示威運動。

   A. 捲土重來   B. 示威   C. 展覽   D. 歌劇

10. A bomb <u>exploded</u>, sending shockwaves throughout the building. In an instant, the building fell into _____.

   一枚炸彈爆炸了,其衝擊波動傳遍了整棟建築物。一瞬間,整棟建築物已毀滅。

   A. 腐朽   B. 廢棄   C. 年久失修   D. 廢墟

課後作業

1. Keep your camera _____ while you're taking a picture. Otherwise the photo might be blurred.

   A. afloat   B. steady   C. apart   D. aflame

   照相時把你的照相機保持固定；否則，照片會模糊不清。

   A. 漂浮   B. 固定   C. 分開   D. 燃燒

   《正確答案》 B
   《解題關鍵》 轉折語 otherwise（否則），表示不照指示做，會有某種後果，為因果關係。
   《補充說明》 keep + sb/sth + 形容詞（保持某人或物在某種狀態）。

2. I am in _____ with my wife over money management. I prefer saving money in a bank, but she likes to invest in the stock market.

   A. partnership   B. sympathy   C. conflict   D. contact

   我跟我老婆對於錢的管理方式有所衝突。我喜歡把錢存在銀行，但她喜歡投資在股票買賣。

   A. 合夥關係   B. 同情   C. 衝突   D. 接觸

   《正確答案》 C
   《解題關鍵》 一個要存錢，一個要投資股票，互為衝突的例證。因此答案為(C)。
   《補充說明》 in + sth. +with 的結構，除了四個選項外，還有 in agreement/harmony with（與……一致）, in league with（與……聯盟）, in cooperation with（與……合作）

3. People used to be _____ about sex, but now even women are more open about discussing it.

   A. mad   B. bitter   C. frank   D. shy

過去人們面對性總是害羞的，但現在女人能更公開討論它。

A. 發瘋的　　　　B. 痛苦的　　　　C. 坦白的　　　　D. 害羞的

《正確答案》　D

《解題關鍵》　轉折語 but 表示前後兩句成對比關係。 open 的反義字為 shy 。表示對
某事的態度的形容詞，其後介系詞用 about 。

《補充說明》　be skeptical about（對某事懷疑）, be curious about（對某事好
奇）, be optimistic/pessimistic about sth（對某事樂／悲觀）

4.　The crowd picked up sticks and bottles and threw them at the police. The
police used shields to guard themselves against the _____.

A. punishment　　B. reward　　　　C. attack　　　　D. signal

群眾撿起棍棒和瓶子然後向警察丟過去。警察拿著盾牌保衛自己免於攻擊。

A. 處罰　　　　　B. 獎勵　　　　　C. 攻擊　　　　　D. 信號

《正確答案》　C

《解題關鍵》　用棍棒和瓶子丟警察為惡意行為，是攻擊行動。

5.　Jack tripped over a chair and fell. His ankles were injured and started to
_____. His mother put an ice pack on them.

A. bleed　　　　　B. shake　　　　　C. bend　　　　　D. swell

傑克被椅子絆到而跌倒。他的腳踝受傷，開始腫大。他媽媽把冰袋放在腳踝上。

A. 流血　　　　　B. 搖動　　　　　C. 彎曲　　　　　D. 腫大

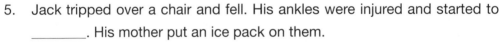

《正確答案》　D

《解題關鍵》　腳踝扭傷處理方式是冰敷，這題是因果關係。因為扭傷腫起來，所以冰
敷。

6. The twins look so much alike that I often _____ one with the other.

A. associate   B. compare   C. replace   D. confuse

雙胞胎看起來很像，我常會弄不清楚他們倆。

A. 聯想   B. 比較   C. 取代   D. 混淆

《正確答案》 D
《解題關鍵》 so...that（如此……以至於），為因果關係的轉折語。太相像以至於將他們搞混。

7. The balloons are available in _____ colors—red, white, green, and so on.

A. various   B. brilliant   C. natural   D. somber

氣球有各種顏色－紅色、白色、綠色等等。

A. 各種的   B. 光亮的   C. 自然的   D. 陰沈的

《正確答案》 A
《解題關鍵》 轉折語 and so on 表示舉例。顏色有紅、白、綠，表種類多。

8. It is impolite to _____ when someone is speaking. Instead, you should wait until he finishes.

A. nap   B. interrupt   C. sigh   D. shrug

當有人在說話時，打斷人家的話是不禮貌的。你應該等到他結束。

A. 打盹   B. 打斷   C. 嘆氣   D. 聳肩

《正確答案》 B
《解題關鍵》 轉折語 instead（代替）表示對比。instead 的句子裡 wait 和 interrupt 成對比。

9. Make sure the soil is _____ before planting the seeds. If it is dry, spray water on it.

   A. fertile   B. barren   C. moist   D. sandy

   在種種子前，確定土壤是潮濕的。如果它是乾的話，在上面灑一些水。

   A. 肥沃的   B. 貧瘠的   C. 潮濕的   D. 多沙的

   《正確答案》　C

   《解題關鍵》　此題考對比關係，dry（乾燥）的相對語是 moist（潮濕）。

10. The child put a coin in his mouth and almost _____ to death. His face was twisted in pain and he turned pale.

    A. starved   B. froze   C. choked   D. bled

    這個小孩把硬幣放進他的嘴裡，差點窒息而死。他的臉因痛苦而扭曲，變得蒼白。

    A. 餓死   B. 凍僵   C. 窒息   D. 流血

    《正確答案》　C

    《解題關鍵》　此題為因果關係。錢幣放在口裡，結果差點噎死。

    《補充說明》　與 to death 連用的動詞，除了選項四個外，還有 be bored/worried/ scared/stabbed to death 無聊死／擔心死／嚇死／被刺死

11. I was almost out of breath after walking up the _____ hillside. Because the path rose up so quickly, I sweated heavily all the way.

    A. steep   B. rocky   C. slippery   D. sloping

    在走上這陡峭的山坡後，我幾乎快喘不過氣來。因為這條路上升得很快，整條路我都猛流汗。

    A. 陡峭的   B. 岩石的   C. 滑的   D. 傾斜的

《正確答案》 A

《解題關鍵》 這題是定義。rose up so quietly 用來解釋空格的 steep。

12. I have poor _____, so I cannot see things clearly without glasses.

    A. hearing   B. judgment   C. records   D. vision

我的視力不好，所以沒有戴眼鏡的話，我無法看清楚。

    A. 聽力   B. 判斷   C. 紀錄   D. 視力

《正確答案》 D

《解題關鍵》 此題的轉折語 so（所以），說明前後是因果關係，沒戴眼鏡看不清，當然是視力差。

13. I finally climbed the_____, but it nearly wore me out. I was gasping for breath. It took me two hours to reach the summit.

    A. peak   B. valley   C. cliff   D. cave

我終於爬上山頂，但差不多累翻了。我上氣不接下氣地呼吸。我花了兩個小時到達峰頂。

    A. 山頂   B. 山谷   C. 懸崖   D. 洞穴

《正確答案》 A

《解題關鍵》 此題為同義字，句末的 summit 和空格中的 peak 為同義字，都是「山頂」的意思。

14. When water is cooled below 0 degrees, it freezes and becomes ice. If the temperature goes up again, the ice _____.

    A. melts   B. shines   C. vanishes   D. drifts

當水在零度以下時，它凝固且變成冰。如果溫度再上升，冰就融化了。

A. 融化　　　　　B. 發光　　　　　C. 消失　　　　　D. 漂流

《正確答案》　A

《解題關鍵》　此題考因果關係，也考對比關係。水溫度下降結冰，溫度上升冰則融化。

15. Male teachers are generally in the _____ at school. One in ten teachers is male. That could have a certain influence on students.

A. minority　　　　B. majority　　　　C. limelight　　　　D. dock

在學校，男老師普遍是少數。十個老師中只有一個是男的，那對學生有一定的影響。

A. 少數　　　　　B. 多數　　　　　C. 石灰光　　　　　D. 被告席

《正確答案》　A

《解題關鍵》　十個老師中只有一個是男性。意味男老師很少，因此答案為 minority（少數）。

Unit 2 詞彙和結構—字彙 (二)

五、上位詞關係

例 慢慢地用汁燉煮肉。我們必須煮到肉變嫩。

A. 煮　　　　B. 磨　　　　C. 溶解　　　　D. 冷凍

練習五

《Answers》

1. A	2. B	3. C	4. C	5. D	6. C	7. D	8. A	9. C	10. B

1. Mr. White has retired as <u>sales manager</u> and his _____ will be taken over by Mr. Church.

   懷特先生從營業經理退休了，他的職位將由邱池先生接管。

   A. 職位　　　　B. 事業　　　　C. 領導　　　　D. 公司

2. Jane gave up her _____ . She was <u>a nurse</u>. She felt she couldn't get ahead at the job.

   珍放棄了她的工作。她本來是一位護士，但她覺得無法在工作上獲得進展。

   A. 習慣　　　　B. 事業　　　　C. 財產　　　　D. 計畫

3. I bought <u>a flute</u> for my daughter. The _____ cost me $NT4,000.

   我買了一隻笛子給我女兒，花了四千元。

   A. 工具　　　　B. 武器　　　　C. 樂器　　　　D. 金屬

4. When the company got into financial trouble, the bank came to its rescue with <u>a huge loan</u>. The financial _____ prevented the company from going bankrupt.

   當公司遭遇財政困難時，銀行以巨大貸款舒困。由於財政上的援助，公司才免於破產。

   A. 危機　　　　B. 情況　　　　C. 支持　　　　D. 獨立

5. The age of _____ maturity varies from person to person. Some people attain <u>intellectuality</u> sooner than others.

   心理成熟的年齡是因人而異的。有些人會比其他人較早獲得智能。

   A. 性的　　　　　B. 感情的　　　　C. 心理的　　　　D. 身體的

6. The president had a(n) _____ with a pop singer. <u>The scandal</u> led to the fall of his government.

   總統跟流行歌手傳出緋聞，而這個醜聞導致他的政府垮臺。

   A. 聊天　　　　　B. 面談　　　　　C. 緋聞　　　　　D. 約會

7. A car speeding down the street at night created a(n) _____. Many people were aroused from sleep by <u>the noise</u>.

   夜裡，一輛在街上急駛的車子引起了騷擾。許多人在睡夢中被噪音吵醒。

   A. 危機　　　　　B. 幻念　　　　　C. 轟動　　　　　D. 擾亂

8. With _____ supplies running short, few people in this country can survive the harsh winter. Many factories will shut down for lack of <u>oil</u>.

   在這個國家，因為燃料補給品缺乏，很少人可以度過嚴酷的寒冬。許多工廠將因缺少石油而關閉。

   A. 燃料　　　　　B. 武器　　　　　C. 食物　　　　　D. 醫療的

9. A nutritious <u>meal</u> is important to children. It must contain numerous vitamins and minerals, and the _____ must be high in protein.

   營養餐對孩童來說是重要的。營養餐必須包含許多的維他命和礦物質，還有飲食必須含有高蛋白質。

   A. 藥物　　　　　B. 飲料　　　　　C. 飲食　　　　　D. 原料

10. Linda was <u>nibbling</u> a piece of bread. Her mother shouted at her, "_____your breakfast quickly, or you will be late for class."

    琳達正慢慢咬著一片麵包，她媽媽對她大叫著說：「快吃你的早餐，不然上學要遲到了。」

    A. 煮　　　　　　B. 吃　　　　　　C. 服務　　　　　D. 購買

六、類比

例 正如運動能增強精神，閱讀能敏銳心智。

A. 腐敗　　　　B. 使平和　　　　C. 分散　　　　D. 使敏銳

練習六

《Answers》---

| 1. A | 2. D | 3. B | 4. A | 5. C | 6. B | 7. D | 8. A | 9. C | 10. A |

1. Jack cannot _____ good music. If you play him a sonata, it is just like casting pearls before swine.

   傑克不懂得欣賞好音樂。如果你對他彈奏鳴曲，就好像是對牛彈琴。

   A. 欣賞　　　　B. 作曲　　　　C. 演奏　　　　D. 錄製

2. Having a low-salt and fat-free diet can _____ the risk of heart disease. Similarly, the possibility of getting heart disease can be lowered if we exercise regularly.

   吃低鹽無脂的飲食可以減少心臟病的風險；同樣地，如果我們有規律地運動，也能降低得到心臟病的可能性。

   A. 包含　　　　B. 增加　　　　C. 引起　　　　D. 減少

3. In a co-educational school, boy and girl students can _____ together freely just as they do in society.

   在男女同校的校園裡，男生和女生自由交往，就像在社會中一樣。

   A. 勞動　　　　B. 混合　　　　C. 遷移　　　　D. 結巴

4. The clams were delicious. Likewise, the smoked salmon was _____.

   這些蛤蜊很美味；同樣地，這些煙燻鮭魚也很棒。

   A. 優秀的　　　　B. 有營養的　　　　C. 有毒的　　　　D. 腐爛的

5. There were <u>no more than two hundred words</u> in her first composition and her second composition was similarly _____.

   她的第一篇作文不超過兩百個字;而同樣地,她的第二篇作文也很簡短。

   A. 完美的   B. 冗長的   C. 簡短的   D. 無聊的

6. Wine is best when it is preserved over a long time, and as with <u>fine wine</u>, France likes its politicians to _____ over time.

   好酒需要長時間釀造,而法國也希望它的政治家能像好酒一樣,隨著長時間而成熟。

   A. 變老   B. 變成熟   C. 消失   D. 枯萎

7. A ship is to the sea as _____ is to the desert.

   大海上的一艘船就像沙漠中的駱駝。

   A. 四輪馬車   B. 綠洲   C. 仙人掌   D. 駱駝

8. James is as busy as a _____, but he is still as poor as a church mouse.

   詹姆士就像蜜蜂一樣忙碌,但他仍然一貧如洗。

   A. 蜜蜂   B. 蜻蜓   C. 蝴蝶   D. 蚱蜢

9. Our life span is <u>short</u>, so life is often compared to _____.

   我們壽命是短暫的,所以生命常被比喻成蠟燭。

   A. 天堂   B. 深淵   C. 蠟燭   D. 舞臺

10. Japan's <u>economy</u> is dependent primarily on exports. Like Japan, Taiwan has also enjoyed _____ by exporting its products all over the world.

    日本的經濟主要是依賴輸出品;如同日本,台灣也靠著輸出到全世界的產品而繁榮。

    A. 繁榮   B. 安全   C. 穩定   D. 可信性

七、陳述句的名詞化

例 那個男孩常在辦公室製造噪音,我不能忍受這樣的行為。

     A. 痛苦   B. 熱   C. 反對   D. 行為

練習七

《Answers》 --

| 1. D | 2. C | 3. B | 4. A | 5. C | 6. B | 7. D | 8. C | 9. A | 10. B |

1. We have been told that <u>global warming might cause a lot of damage to the earth and the life on it</u>. These _____ sound reasonable but are actually overblown.

   據說，全球氣溫上升可能會對地球造成許多損害。這些警訊聽起來合理，但實際上是誇張的。

   A. 懷疑　　　　　B. 事件　　　　　C. 謠言　　　　　D. 警訊

2. <u>Two cars collided with each other</u> on the highway. The _____ resulted in a traffic jam. Fortunately, no one was injured.

   在公路上，有兩輛車相撞在一起。這場意外導致交通堵塞，幸好沒有人受傷。

   A. 排練　　　　　B. 功績　　　　　C. 意外事故　　　D. 悲劇

3. <u>The political party's chairman firmly believed that he could seize power by continuing the mass demonstration</u>, but some of its younger members didn't sympathize with his _____.

   這個政黨主席堅信他能藉著不斷的示威運動而奪權，但政黨中較年輕的成員不贊成他的看法。

   A. 假說　　　　　B. 看法　　　　　C. 威脅　　　　　D. 命令

4. <u>Three bombs exploded in the London subway</u>, killing 56 people. All political leaders condemned this barbaric _____.

   三枚炸彈在倫敦地鐵爆炸，奪走了五十六條人命。所有的政治領袖譴責這種野蠻的行為。

   A. 行為　　　　　B. 習俗　　　　　C. 對待　　　　　D. 懲罰

5. The tax burden is mostly on salary men while rich people enjoy tax cuts and street vendors do not need to pay any tax. This _____ must be corrected.

   稅的重擔大部分落在薪水階級身上,而有錢人享受減免稅負,街上的小販不必付任何稅。這樣的不公平必須修正。

   A. 印象　　　　B. 缺乏　　　　C. 不公正　　　　D. 發音

6. China exports a lot more to America than it imports from it. This trade _____ has strained relations between the two countries.

   中國輸出到美國比從美國進口的多,這樣的貿易順差使兩國關係緊張。

   A. 合同　　　　B. 多餘　　　　C. 障礙　　　　D. 政策

7. Two Palestinian gunmen opened fire on a car at Kissufim, a key entry point into Gaza's Israeli settlements, and killed an Israeli man and his wife. Israeli troops chased the two gunmen and killed them. This _____ has endangered a peace agreement between the two sides.

   奇蘇分是一個進入迦薩以色列屯墾區的重要據點。在這裡,有兩名巴勒斯坦人對著一部車子開槍,殺了一名以色列男子和他的妻子。以色列軍隊追擊這兩名槍手,並且殺了他們,這樣的衝突危及兩邊的和平協議。

   A. 談判　　　　B. 貿易　　　　C. 爭吵　　　　D. 衝突

8. Hundreds of gays marched down the street, demanding their civil rights, but their _____ was disrupted by anti-gay activists.

   數百名同志在街上遊行示威,要求他們的民權,但他們的示威運動被反同性戀的激進份子給中斷。

   A. 遊行　　　　B. 嘉年華會　　　　C. 示威　　　　D. 慶祝

9. Police ran after a suspect in the London subway. The _____ lasted for a few minutes, and then suddenly gunshots rang out in the subway. The man was killed on the spot.

   警察在倫敦地鐵追趕一個嫌疑犯,這場追逐持續了幾分鐘後,突然從地鐵傳出槍聲,那名男子當場死亡。

   A. 追逐　　　　B. 行軍　　　　C. 爭吵　　　　D. 戰鬥

10. <u>The mayor said that a new baseball stadium would be built in three years,</u>
    but his _____ was never fulfilled.

    市長說過在三年內要蓋棒球場，但他的承諾從未實現過。

    A. 角色　　　　　B. 承諾　　　　　C. 責任　　　　　D. 預言

八、語言外的生活經驗

例 一看到公牛向我們衝過來，我們朝不同方向散開。

　　　A. 集合　　　　　B. 散開　　　　　C. 抗議　　　　　D. 凝視

✎ 練習八

《Answers》--

| 1. A | 2. C | 3. A | 4. B | 5. A | 6. D | 7. B | 8. A | 9. B | 10. C |

1. 發生了森林大火，數百名消防員趕去山上救火，許多樹都燒毀了。

   A. 森林　　　　　B. 電的　　　　　C. 煤　　　　　D. 瓦斯

2. 喬吉先生的新書出版了，在每個書店都能買到。

   A. 可看見的　　　B. 貴重的　　　　C. 可買到的　　　D. 耐用的

3. 有一輛公車撞上樹，幸運地，司機跟乘客都沒受傷。

   A. 乘客　　　　　B. 工程師　　　　C. 全體船員　　　D. 職員

4. 已經很久沒下雨了，所以市長拿著香，跪著向上天祈禱。

   A. 回答　　　　　B. 祈禱　　　　　C. 服從　　　　　D. 反對

5. 我對於驚奇的瀑布景象感到驚訝，瀑布從懸崖流下並注入大水池。

   A. 驚奇　　　　　B. 憂鬱　　　　　C. 恐怖　　　　　D. 孤獨

6. 每當選手犯規，裁判就會吹哨子，希望能阻止不公平的比賽。

   A. 他的鼻子　　　B. 他的喇叭　　　C. 保險絲　　　　D. 哨子

7. 總統把花圈放在戰爭紀念碑上，紀念那些在戰爭中喪命的無名英雄。

   A. 磚塊　　　　　B. 花圈　　　　　C. 地毯　　　　　D. 礦坑

8. 水滾了，蒸氣從水壺的壺嘴散發出來。

   A. 蒸氣　　　　　B. 光線　　　　　C. 煙　　　　　D. 香味

9. 當我在發表演說時，一群笨蛋在教室角落不停地聊天。最後我的耐心用盡，痛罵他們。

   A. 力量　　　　　B. 耐心　　　　　C. 話題　　　　　D. 資源

10. 最近許多工人被解雇，在沒有經濟復甦跡象前，他們不能謀生，只能領救濟金過日。

    A. 罷工　　　　　B. 審判　　　　　C. 福利　　　　　D. 休假

課後作業

1. Cindy slammed the door in a(n) _____ and burst into tears. No one in the office knew why she was so angry.

A. hurry　　　　B. panic　　　　C. temper　　　　D. instant

仙蒂生氣地砰然關門，突然哭了起來。辦公室裡沒有人知道她為什麼這麼生氣。

A. 匆忙　　　　B. 恐慌　　　　C. 怒氣　　　　D. 立刻

《正確答案》　C
《解題關鍵》　第二句 she was so angry（她如此生氣），說明了第一句砰然關門是怒氣沖沖（in a temper），這題考同義字

2. The doctor examined Janet carefully and _____ her illness as a rare bone disease. To date, no cure for the disease has been found.

A. dismissed　　B. described　　C. diagnosed　　D. accepted

醫生仔細檢查珍妮後，診斷出她的疾病是罕見的骨骼疾病。至今，這個疾病還沒有治療的方法。

A. 貶視　　　　B. 描寫　　　　C. 診斷　　　　D. 接受

《正確答案》　C
《解題關鍵》　醫生幫病人做體檢之後，依生活經驗可知他就要診斷病情。

3. When you have a headache, take two aspirin. The pills will ease your

_____.

A. anxiety　　　B. pain　　　　C. crisis　　　　D. mind

當你頭痛時，就服兩顆阿斯匹靈，這些藥丸會減輕你的疼痛。

A. 焦慮　　　　B. 痛苦　　　　C. 危機　　　　D. 心靈

4. In English "envious" and "jealous" are synonyms. There are _____ differences in their meanings.

   A. significant　　B. considerable　C. subtle　　　　D. noticeable

   在英語中，"envious"和"jealous"是同義字，但他們在意義上還是有些微的不同。

   A. 重要的　　　　B. 相當的　　　　C. 微妙的　　　　D. 顯著的

《正確答案》 C
《解題關鍵》 既然 envious 與 jealous 為同義字，則其義意之區別一定是很細微
　　　　　　（subtle），這題考定義。

5. After 40 minutes of keen competition, the game ended in a _____. Neither team got the better of the other.

   A. tie　　　　　　B. victory　　　　C. fight　　　　　D. tragedy

   在四十分鐘的激烈競賽後，這場比賽結果不分勝負，每個隊伍不分上下。

   A. 平手　　　　　B. 勝利　　　　　C. 打架　　　　　D. 悲劇

《正確答案》 A
《解題關鍵》 第二句後說誰也沒站在誰的上方，即平手之義。

6. Fruit picking is _____ work; that is, certain fruit is picked during a particular time of the year.

   A. routine　　　　B. manual　　　　C. seasonal　　　D. intellectual

   採收水果是季節性的工作，也就是說某些水果在一年中特定的時間採收。

   A. 例行的　　　　B. 手工的　　　　C. 季節的　　　　D. 智力的

《正確答案》 C

《解題關鍵》 轉折語 that's ，預示以下的句子是來解釋前句，只有在一年某一特定時間採摘，所以當然是季節性的工作。

7. The custom of forcing a woman to marry is only _____ to some tribes. Not all aborigines have this kind of custom.

   A. harmful   B. peculiar   C. familiar   D. advantageous

   強婚習俗是某些種族特有的，不是所有的原住民都有這樣習俗。

   A. 有害的   B. 獨特的   C. 熟悉的   D. 有利的

《正確答案》 B

《解題關鍵》 第二句的 not all 是部分否定，因此強婚習俗只有一些部落才有。

8. To his teacher's surprise, John got all the answers right. Later on, he confessed to cheating on the test. He was quite _____-stricken.

   A. panic   B. conscience   C. poverty   D. terror

   讓約翰的老師感到驚訝的是他的答案都是對的，後來，約翰坦承他作弊，而良心不安。

   A. 恐慌   B. 良心   C. 貧窮   D. 恐怖

《正確答案》 B

《解題關鍵》 認錯告白，與良心不安有關。

9. On summer nights, we can see numerous stars _____ in the sky. The brightest one in the north is called the North Star.

   A. vanish   B. twinkle   C. dim   D. revolve

在夏天的夜裡，我們可以在天空中看見許多閃爍的星星。在北方最亮的那顆就是北極星。

A. 消失　　　　　B. 閃爍　　　　　C. 變陰暗　　　　D. 旋轉

《正確答案》 B

《解題關鍵》 第二句 brightest（最明亮）表示星星在閃爍（twinkle）。

10. Under the glare of the sun, the ice ___ until it turned into water.

A. drifted　　　　B. gleamed　　　C. melted　　　D. cracked

在刺眼的陽光下，冰塊融化成水。

A. 漂流　　　　　B. 閃爍　　　　　C. 融化　　　　　D. 破裂

《正確答案》 C

《解題關鍵》 依常識判斷冰遇熱會融化。

11. There was a flash of _____ a moment ago.　The sound of the thunder will come soon after.

A. pity　　　　　B. excitement　　　C. lightning　　　D. inspiration

剛才有一道閃電，之後馬上會有雷聲。

A. 憐憫　　　　　B. 興奮　　　　　C. 閃電　　　　　D. 靈感

《正確答案》 C

《解題關鍵》 依經驗打雷之前常會有閃電。

12. The general manager presented a _____ report, warning that the company might not be able to balance its budget.

A. technical　　　B. financial　　　C. environmental　D. medical

總經理提出一個財政報告，提醒公司也許不能平衡預算。

A. 技術的　　　　　B. 財政的　　　　　C. 環境的　　　　　D. 醫學的

《正確答案》 B

《解題關鍵》 句末 balance its budget（平衡預算）與 financial（財政）有關。

13. You'd better choose good comic books for your son to read. Some evil thoughts in bad ones may _____ his mind. He's still too young to tell right from wrong.

A. ease　　　　　B. broaden　　　　　C. sharpen　　　　　D. poison

你最好替你兒子選擇好的漫畫來閱讀。在不好的漫畫中，有些邪惡的思想可能會污染他的心智，他還年輕不會分辨是非。

A. 減輕　　　　　B. 擴大　　　　　C. 使敏銳　　　　　D. 毒害

《正確答案》 D

《解題關鍵》 句中的 evil（邪惡的），與 poison 有關。

14. His speech barely stimulated my interest. I was _____ to death.

A. worried　　　　　B. sentenced　　　　　C. bored　　　　　D. frightened

他的演說幾乎不能引起我的興趣，我無聊死了。

A. 擔心　　　　　B. 宣判　　　　　C. 厭煩　　　　　D. 害怕

《正確答案》 C

《解題關鍵》 演說了無興趣，當然令人無聊死，考因果關係。

15. Mr. White is very strict with his children. He demands total obedience and requires them to meet his _____.

A. obligations　　　　　B. deadline　　　　　C. expectations　　　D. expense

懷特先生對自己的小孩非常嚴厲。他要求完全服從並達到他的期待。

A. 義務　　　　　B. 截止期限　　　C. 期待　　　　　D. 費用

《正確答案》 C

《解題關鍵》 要求服從,也就是要孩子聽話,與此有關是符合他的期待。

16. I didn't go to the karaoke bar with them because I had to make some _____. I was running out of food, and the supermarket was about to close.

A. purchases　　B. choices　　　C. requests　　　D. decisions

我不想跟他們去卡啦 OK ,因為我必須去買些東西。我的食物快吃完了,而超市即將關門。

A. 購物　　　　　B. 選擇　　　　　C. 要求　　　　　D. 決定

《正確答案》 A

《解題關鍵》 第二句說到超級市場買食物,與此有關當然是去採購食品。

17. After the downfall of the Soviet Union, some of its republics separated from it and declared their _____.

A. loyalty　　　　B. independence C. intention　　　D. innocence

在蘇聯垮臺後,共和國中的一些國家都分離出來並宣布獨立。

A. 忠誠　　　　　B. 獨立　　　　　C. 意圖　　　　　D. 無罪

《正確答案》 B

《解題關鍵》 與 separated(分開)同義的是 independence(獨立)。

18. A cold front swept the whole island with pouring rain and freezing winds. Our plan to hold an outdoor party was completely _____.

    A. devised   B. spoiled   C. fulfilled   D. disclosed

冷鋒挾帶傾盆大雨和寒冷的風席捲了整座島嶼,讓我們舉行戶外派對的計畫完全被搞亂了。

    A. 設計   B. 搞糟   C. 履行   D. 透露

《正確答案》 B

《解題關鍵》 此題考因果關係,壞天氣為因,戶外派對開不成是果。

19. You should learn to _____ your rights. No one can stand up for your own rights.

    A. abuse   B. exercise   C. defend   D. surrender

你應該學會捍衛自己的權利,沒有人可以維護你自己的權利。

    A. 濫用   B. 使用   C. 保衛   D. 放棄

《正確答案》 C

《解題關鍵》 此題為同義字,第二句的 stand up for 同義的選項是 defend。

20. We pitched our camp by the lake and began to _____ some chicken over a fire. As we did, we added sauce for flavor.

    A. stir-fry   B. roast   C. steam   D. stew

我們在湖邊搭帳棚,接著開始在火上烤一些雞肉,為了增添風味,再加上醬汁。

    A. 炒   B. 烤   C. 蒸   D. 燉

《正確答案》 B

《解題關鍵》 空格後 chicken over a fire 把雞肉放在火上,就是烤(roast)。

21. I asked my mother if I could go to the movies, but she rejected my
_____. She wanted to punish me for my poor grades.

A. request　　　B. offer　　　　C. application　　　D. suggestion

我問我媽我可不可以出去看電影，我媽拒絕了我的要求，因為她想懲罰我考不好。

A. 請求　　　　B. 提供　　　　C. 申請　　　　D. 建議

《正確答案》 A
《解題關鍵》 此題考同義字，動詞 ask 與選項的 request 同義。

22. Two boy students put on girls' school uniforms and went dancing downtown. It is surprising that they should choose to adopt this _____ to
draw the public's attention.

A. custom　　　B. method　　　C. attitude　　　D. suggestion

有兩名男學生穿上了女制服，到市中心跳舞。他們會選擇用這樣的方式來吸引大眾
的注意力，真是令人驚訝。

A. 習俗　　　　B. 方法　　　　C. 態度　　　　D. 建議

《正確答案》 B
《解題關鍵》 此題為陳述句的名詞化。穿上女生制服到市區跳舞，是要引人注意的「方
法」。

23. Singapore's _____ achievements are extraordinary. Their standard of
living reflects their prosperity.

A. academic　　　B. economic　　　C. technological　　　D. diplomatic

新加坡經濟成就是驚人的，他們的生活水準反映著他們的繁榮。

A. 學術的　　　　B. 經濟的　　　　C. 科技的　　　　D. 外交的

《正確答案》 B
《解題關鍵》 第二句的 standard of living 是生活水準的意思，與此有關的是經濟。

24. The newly built 54-story skyscraper near the Taipei Train Station has formed a _____ in Taipei. It can be seen from many miles away.

    A. square   B. shelter   C. landmark   D. background

    在台北車站附近新建的五十四層摩天大樓已經成為台北的地標，從好幾哩外就能看見它。

    A. 廣場   B. 避難所   C. 地標   D. 背景

《正確答案》 C
《解題關鍵》 第二句說此大樓在好幾哩外就可看得見，表示是確定方向的指標，與此有關的字是 landmark（地標）。

25. We all _____ at the vastness of Lake Michigan. We could only see the horizon in the distance.

    A. blushed   B. marveled   C. grieved   D. trembled

    我們都驚訝於密西根湖的廣闊，只能看到遠處的水平線。

    A. 臉紅   B. 感到驚訝   C. 悲傷   D. 發抖

《正確答案》 B
《解題關鍵》 只能看到遠處的水平線，表示此湖很大。看到大的東西，依我們的自然反應是讚嘆驚奇。

26. Many Chinese people still live in the same house with their parents as well as their children; however, the _____ family is becoming more and more popular today, especially in the city.

    A. royal   B. adoptive   C. nuclear   D. extended

許多中國人仍然跟自己的父母和小孩住在一起；然而，核心家庭愈來愈普遍，尤其是在城市裡。

A. 王室的　　　B. 收養的　　　C. 核心的　　　D. 延伸的

《正確答案》 C

《解題關鍵》 此題考對比，轉折語 however（然而），說明前後兩句成相反。前句明顯是指大家庭，因此後句應是相反的核心家庭。

27. The city government has banned citizens from setting off _____ in residential areas. For one thing, it produces noise pollution. For another, it may start a fire.

A. firecrackers　　B. bombs　　　C. the alarm　　D. the fire bell

市政府禁止市民在住宅區放鞭炮，因為放鞭炮會產生噪音，也可能引起火災。

A. 鞭炮　　　　B. 炸彈　　　　C. 警報器　　　D. 失火警鈴

《正確答案》 A

《解題關鍵》 會製造很大噪音，又會引起火災，較適合的選項應是鞭炮。

28. Ancient Egyptians knew how to _____ dead bodies. They rubbed a dead body with salt and resin and then wrapped it in hundreds of yards of linen.

A. preserve　　　B. bury　　　C. expose　　　D. identify

古代的埃及人知道如何保存死者的屍體，他們用鹽巴跟樹脂擦在屍體上，然後用百碼長的亞麻布把屍體包裹起來。

A. 保存　　　　B. 埋葬　　　　C. 暴露　　　　D. 指認

《正確答案》 A

《解題關鍵》 第二句說擦鹽巴和樹脂很明顯是防腐，故答案為 preserve。

29. When driving, make sure to _____ your seat belt. By doing so you can avoid being seriously hurt if you have an accident.

    A. fasten   B. undo   C. loosen   D. design

開車時要繫好安全帶，以免發生意外時有嚴重的傷害。

    A. 繫緊   B. 打開   C. 鬆開   D. 設計

《正確答案》 A
《解題關鍵》 開車避免意外傷害，就得繫好安全帶，依生活經驗。

30. Whenever bus drivers stage a strike, the mayor yields to their demands. This soft stance has weakened the city government's _____.

    A. forces   B. confidence   C. economy   D. authority

每當公車司機罷工，市長總是屈服於他們的要求，這樣的柔軟態度削弱了市政府的權力。

    A. 軍力   B. 信心   C. 經濟   D. 權威

《正確答案》 D
《解題關鍵》 市長屈服罷工，表示沒魄力，則政府威信掃地，故答案為 authority。

31. Mind your _____ at the party. Don't devour the snacks as if you were starving to death.

    A. tongue   B. step   C. manners   D. business

注意你在派對上的禮貌。不要狼吞虎嚥地吃點心，那看起來好像你快餓死了。

    A. 舌頭   B. 腳步   C. 禮貌   D. 生意

《正確答案》 C
《解題關鍵》 大庭廣眾大吃點心，此乃禮節問題，故選 manners。

32. That black people are inferior to white people is a deep-rooted _____; it is hard to remove.

    A. suspicion　　　B. prejudice　　　C. dislike　　　D. faith

    黑人比白人差是根深蒂固的偏見，很難消除這偏見。

    A. 懷疑　　　　　B. 偏見　　　　　C. 不喜愛　　　D. 信念

    《正確答案》 B
    《解題關鍵》 黑人比白人差是種族偏見，此依據認知經驗。

33. In order to improve efficiency, many factory owners have _____ old machines with new ones. The new machines are computerized and user-friendly.

    A. identified　　　B. combined　　　C. integrated　　　D. replaced

    為了改善效率，許多工廠的老闆會以新的機器代替舊的機器。新的機器是電腦化和容易使用的機器。

    A. 認同　　　　　B. 結合　　　　　C. 合併　　　　D. 取代

    《正確答案》 D
    《解題關鍵》 第二句新機器電腦化又好用，而能提高效率，此暗示它們「取代」了舊機器。

34. Boys like toys such as guns, cars, and so on. By _____, most girls pre-fer dolls and stickers.

    A. contrast　　　B. profession　　　C. definition　　　D. tradition

    男生喜歡像槍、車子這類的玩具；相對的，大部分的女生較喜歡洋娃娃和貼紙。

    A. 對比　　　　　B. 職業　　　　　C. 定義　　　　D. 傳統

《正確答案》 A
《解題關鍵》 前後兩句說明男女所愛好之物不同，要用表「對比」的轉折語。

35. Mrs. Jones couldn't bear _____. So after her husband died, she got a dog to keep her company.

A. noise   B. pain   C. hardships   D. loneliness

瓊斯太太不能忍受孤獨，所以在她先生死後，她養了一隻狗來作伴。

A. 噪音   B. 痛苦   C. 艱苦   D. 孤獨

《正確答案》 D
《解題關鍵》 第二句句末 keep her company（陪伴她），與此有關的心境是孤獨。

36. Our boss is in a _____ mood today because he has just signed a new sales contract which will bring in record profits.

A. thoughtful   B. sorrowful   C. melancholy   D. cheerful

我們老闆今天心情很好，因為他剛簽下新的銷售契約，而這份契約將帶來空前的利潤。

A. 體貼的   B. 悲傷的   C. 憂鬱的   D. 興高采烈的

《正確答案》 D
《解題關鍵》 拿到賺錢的契約，正常心理反應是快樂。

37. The newlyweds are renting a house because they cannot _____ to buy a house of their own.

A. resolve   B. afford   C. promise   D. refuse

這對新婚夫婦通常租借房子，因為他們買不起自己的房子。

A. 決心   B. 負擔得起   C. 承諾   D. 拒絕

《正確答案》 B
《解題關鍵》 新婚經濟能力未穩定，只能租房子住，暗示買不起房子。

38. Whenever Jill goes out on a date, she likes to put on make-up so that her _____ will be enhanced.

    A. beauty　　　　B. tension　　　　C. value　　　　D. awareness

    每當吉兒出去約會，她喜歡化妝讓自己更美麗。

    A. 美麗　　　　　B. 緊張　　　　　C. 價值　　　　D. 認知

《正確答案》 A
《解題關鍵》 與化妝品（make-up）有關的是美麗（beauty）。

39. You must assert your _____; otherwise, people might think you are guilty of stealing the money.

    A. innocence　　B. independence　C. authority　　D. superiority

    你必須聲明自己的清白；否則人們可能以為你偷錢。

    A. 清白　　　　　B. 獨立　　　　　C. 權威　　　　D. 優越

《正確答案》 A
《解題關鍵》 與第二句的 guilty 成對比的字是 innocence。轉折語 otherwise 表示前後句相反意思。

40. The gap between the rich and the poor has become even wider. We should try hard to narrow the _____ gap.

    A. income　　　　B. trade　　　　C. generation　　　D. gender

    貧富之間的差距擴大了，我們應該努力試著縮小所得差距。

    A. 收入　　　　　B. 貿易　　　　　C. 世代　　　　D. 性別

《正確答案》 A

《解題關鍵》 與貧富有關的字是收入（income）。

41. Dick had a sense of _____ after realizing that he had made an error. He was ashamed of himself.

A. guilt B. justice C. security D. pride

在了解自己犯了一個錯誤後，迪克有罪惡感，他覺得很羞愧。

A. 罪惡 B. 公正 C. 安全 D. 驕傲

《正確答案》 A

《解題關鍵》 第二句的 shamed（羞恥）暗示人有犯錯。

42. You are always _____ with others but you lose your temper easily with your own brothers.

A. furious B. strict C. patient D. frank

你總是有耐心地對待別人，但對於自己的兄弟，你就容易發脾氣。

A. 狂怒的 B. 嚴格的 C. 有耐心的 D. 坦白的

《正確答案》 C

《解題關鍵》 轉折語 but 說明前後句成對比，後句是發脾氣，那麼前句應是有耐心。

43. Chris often acts on _____; she just follows her heart without thinking carefully.

A. impulse B. information C. advice D. orders

克莉絲常衝動地行動；她總是不加思索地想做什麼就做什麼。

A. 衝動 B. 消息 C. 勸告 D. 命令

《正確答案》 A
《解題關鍵》 分號（；）後句用具體說明來重述前句抽象的概念，隨心所欲，亦即衝動（impulse）。

44. Peter left the school in _____ because the train was about to leave in five minutes.

    A. despair　　　B. shock　　　C. joy　　　D. haste

    彼得匆忙離開學校，因為火車在五分鐘後就要開走了。

    A. 絕望　　　B. 衝擊　　　C. 歡樂　　　D. 急忙

《正確答案》 D
《解題關鍵》 火車即將離站，所以正常反應是急忙追去。

45. Mr. Hall has made no secret of his wish to dominate the fast-growing broadcasting industry. His _____ ambition poses a threat to his rivals.

    A. humble　　　B. sensible　　　C. political　　　D. intense

    霍爾先生毫不保留地表示想要支配急速發展的廣播業，他強烈的野心威脅了他的對手。

    A. 謙恭的　　　B. 明智的　　　C. 政治的　　　D. 強烈的

《正確答案》 D
《解題關鍵》 毫不掩飾想要掌控的欲望，此為強烈野心的表現。

46. Gary's _____ deepened when he heard the news that his son was lost in the mountains.

    A. crisis　　　B.anxiety　　　C. hatred　　　D. voice

當蓋瑞聽到他兒子在山中失蹤後，變得更焦慮不安。

A. 危機   B. 焦慮   C. 憎恨   D. 聲音

《正確答案》 B
《解題關鍵》 聽到兒子走失了，正常反應是焦慮。

47. There was an air of _____ at the meeting. The people in attendance observed a three-minute silence in honor of the dead.

    A. mystery   B. excitement   C. dignity   D. grief

會場上氣氛哀傷。參加的人默哀三分鐘向死者表示敬意。

    A. 神秘   B. 興奮   C. 尊嚴   D. 悲痛

《正確答案》 D
《解題關鍵》 第二句說明默哀以示敬意，明示氣氛哀傷。

48. In _____, the project sounds practicable. In practice, you'll find a lot of problems with it.

    A. reality   B. general   C. brief   D. theory

理論上這個計畫好像行得通；事實上你會發現它有許多問題。

    A. 事實   B. 一般   C. 簡短   D. 理論

《正確答案》 D
《解題關鍵》 聽起來可實行，做起來問題多多，表對比的句子，in theory（理論上）的相對詞是 in practice（實際上）。

49. Nowadays it is very common for women to have their hair _____.
    Blonde hair is their favorite.

    A. dyed   B. combed   C. trimmed   D. shampooed

    現在常見到女人把自己的頭髮染上顏色，金黃色就是她們最愛染的顏色。

    A. 染色   B. 梳理   C. 修剪   D. 洗髮

    《正確答案》 A

    《解題關鍵》 第二句 blonde hair（金髮）與此有關的是頭髮的顏色，故選 dyed。

50. I am staying here for only one month. I would like to rent a(n) _____
    house because I cannot afford to stay in a hotel for that long.

    A. imaginary   B. luxurious   C. furnished   D. deserted

    我只待在這裡一個月，我想要租一間附有家具的房子，因為我付不起長時間住旅館的費用。

    A. 想像中的   B. 奢侈的   C. 附有家具的   D. 荒廢的

    《正確答案》 C

    《解題關鍵》 居住要有床、桌、椅，即指有家具，故答案為 furnished。

Unit 3 詞彙和結構—片語 (一)

✏️ 練習一

《Answers》--

1. B　　2. D　　3. A　　4. C　　5. B

1. 所有的選手必須遵守比賽規則；否則，他們將不允許參加比賽。
   A. 譏笑　　　　　B. 遵守　　　　　C. 規避　　　　　D. 違反

2. 走在街上時，我碰巧遇見了一位老朋友。我從沒想到畢業十年後會再次碰到他。
   A. 通過　　　　　B. 看著　　　　　C. 像　　　　　D. 偶然遇見

3. 既然你已經答應要給你兒子禮物，就應該說到做到。
   A. 信守　　　　　B. 嘲笑　　　　　C. 驚奇　　　　　D. 因...臉紅

4. 保羅面臨財政危機，但是他的老婆仍然支持他，最後，他總算東山再起。
   A. 與...競爭　　　B. 問起某人健康　C. 支持　　　　　D. 拼命要抓住

5. 保羅在乎的是錢，為了錢，他甚至可以犧牲性命。
   A. 因...而感到好奇　B. 在乎　　　　C. 因...而蒼白　　D. 感到疑惑

✏️ 練習二

《Answers》--

1. A　　2. D　　3. B　　4. C　　5. C

1. 在海外旅遊二十天後，我們開始想念我們的家鄉。
   A. 渴望　　　　　B. 聽說　　　　　C. 尋找　　　　　D. 代表

2. 我知道被看不起是怎樣的感覺，所以當馬克被他的同學嘲笑時，我會同情他。
   A. 尋找　　　　　B. 不期而遇　　　C. 與...分手　　　D. 同情

3. 銀行被搶了，警察正在調查這起搶劫案。為了找出是誰搶了銀行，他們正看著錄影帶。

   A. 干涉　　　　　B. 調查　　　　　C. 發誓戒掉　　　　D. 不願做

4. 這本文法書的長處在於它的例句是直接從報紙和雜誌上引用而來。

   A. 發生　　　　　B. 結果　　　　　C. 在於　　　　　D. 不同

5. 小心那隻狗，牠會咬人。

   A. 以...為食物　　B. 處理掉　　　　C. 當心　　　　　D. 伸手拿

✎ 練習三

《Answers》---

　1. D　　2. A　　3. C　　4. B　　5. B

1. 為了尋找這起謀殺案子的線索，警察正在檢查受害者的公寓。

   A. 處理　　　　　B. 注意　　　　　C. 亂弄　　　　　D. 檢查

2. 彼得攻擊傑克，並尖叫著說：「我會狠狠打你一頓！」

   A. 攻擊　　　　　B. 要求　　　　　C. 告密　　　　　D. 依靠

3. 這個廣告利用了我們的恐懼，呈現出一個染上愛滋病的人，它的目的是要警告我們不要隨便發生性行為。

   A. 處理　　　　　B. 決定　　　　　C. 利用　　　　　D. 思索

4. 在你簽合約前，必須仔細讀裡面的細節。

   A. 略過　　　　　B. 細讀　　　　　C. 遵守　　　　　D. 適應

5. 當我們不知道要怎麼做時，約翰突然想出一個好主意。

   A. 忙於　　　　　B. 突然想出　　　　C. 堅持　　　　　D. 熱衷於

✎ 練習四

《Answers》 --

> 1. B　　2. D　　3. A　　4. C　　5. A

1. 鮑伯非常努力用功，但在學校裡，他似乎沒有進步，他的分數仍然不好。

   A. 鬼混　　　　　　B. 進步　　　　　　C. 回嘴　　　　　　D. 走開

2. 有人溺水時，有誰可以自在地袖手旁觀，不做任何事呢？

   A. 後退　　　　　　B. 不停地跳舞　　　C. 落後　　　　　　D. 袖手旁觀

3. 珍一個月只賺兩萬元，但她試著靠這些微薄的錢過活。她非常節儉。

   A. 過活　　　　　　B. 經過　　　　　　C. 逝去　　　　　　D. 繼續做

4. 珍因為太熱而暈倒，在我們把她放在大橡樹的樹陰下後，她才甦醒過來。

   A. 逐漸衰弱　　　　B. 遊手好閒　　　　C. 甦醒　　　　　　D. 袖手旁觀

5. 我住在緬因街，歡迎你隨時順道過來喝杯咖啡。

   A. 順道訪問　　　　B. 敷衍過去　　　　C. 走開　　　　　　D. 勉強餬口

✎ 練習五

《Answers》 --

> 1. D　　2. B　　3. C　　4. A　　5. C

1. 天氣太熱了，以至於我差點熱暈了。

   A. 振作　　　　　　B. 彎下　　　　　　C. 盛裝　　　　　　D. 昏倒

2. 和平會談失敗了，兩邊又再度拿起武器。

   A. 成功　　　　　　B. 失敗　　　　　　C. 拖延　　　　　　D. 得到的結果

3. 李先生的演講太無聊了，以至於有些學生開始打呵欠和打瞌睡。

   A. 冷靜　　　　　　B. 投降　　　　　　C. 打瞌睡　　　　　D. 相繼死亡

4. 為了考試，珍一定熬夜唸書到半夜之後，所以今天上課她睡著了。

   A. 熬夜   B. 化妝   C. 變冷淡   D. 簽到

5. 當有困難發生時，你必須學會如何處理。

   A. 爆發   B. 發射   C. 突然發生   D. 爆炸

課後作業

1. Comic books really <u>appeal to</u> young people.

    A. surprise   B. attract   C. disappoint   D. anger

    漫畫書很吸引年輕人。

    A. 驚訝   B. 吸引   C. 失望   D. 生氣

    《正確答案》 B

2. We must <u>awake to</u> the dangers facing our country.

    A. realize   B. ignore   C. avoid   D. create

    我們必須了解我們國家面對的危險。

    A. 了解   B. 忽視   C. 避免   D. 創造

    《正確答案》 A

3. It seems that my explanation only <u>adds to</u> your bewilderment.

    A. causes   B. eases   C. increases   D. highlights

    看來我的解釋只有增加你的困惑。

    A. 造成   B. 減輕   C. 增加   D. 突顯

    《正確答案》 C

4. Chris <u>blacked out</u> in the scorching sun. We used ice-water to bring her around.

    A. died   B. fainted   C. vomited   D. fell

克莉絲因為炎熱而昏倒了。我們用冰水使她甦醒。

A. 死   B. 昏倒   C. 嘔吐   D. 跌倒

《正確答案》 B

5. The judge <u>called on</u> both sides to settle their dispute out of court, but they persisted in bringing it to court.

A. forbade   B. challenged   C. expected   D. asked

法官要求兩造在法庭外解決他們的爭論，但他們堅持帶進法庭。

A. 禁止   B. 挑戰   C. 期待   D. 要求

《正確答案》 D

6. With entry to the WTO, farmers <u>call for</u> government subsidies. They claim that they can not eke out a decent living without subsidies.

A. refuse   B. demand   C. grant   D. provide

隨著加入 WTO（世界貿易組織），農民要求政府補助。他們宣稱沒有補助金，他們不能過像樣的生活。

A. 拒絕   B. 要求   C. 給予   D. 提供

《正確答案》 B

7. Nowadays, one of the major concerns is how to <u>dispose of</u> nuclear waste. It will not go away as time passes.

A. examine   B. conceal   C. store   D. discard

現今，主要關心的事務之一就是如何處理掉核廢料。它不會隨著時間而消失。

A. 檢查   B. 隱藏   C. 貯存   D. 丟棄

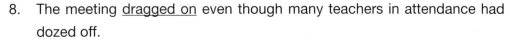

《正確答案》 D

8. The meeting <u>dragged on</u> even though many teachers in attendance had dozed off.

   A. continued   B. ended   C. began   D. occurred

即使許多參加的老師已經打瞌睡，會議仍繼續進行。

   A. 繼續   B. 結束   C. 開始   D. 發生

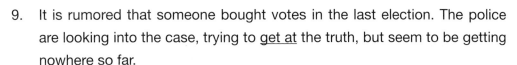

《正確答案》 A

9. It is rumored that someone bought votes in the last election. The police are looking into the case, trying to <u>get at</u> the truth, but seem to be getting nowhere so far.

   A. distort   B. tell   C. discover   D. reveal

謠傳在上次選舉有人買票。警察正在調查這件事，試著發現事實，但迄今似乎毫無結果。

   A. 扭曲   B. 告訴   C. 發現   D. 顯露

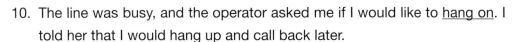

《正確答案》 C

10. The line was busy, and the operator asked me if I would like to <u>hang on</u>. I told her that I would hang up and call back later.

   A. leave   B. talk   C. sleep   D. wait

電話線很忙碌，接線生問我是否願意等候。我告訴她我會掛掉，等一下再打。

   A. 離開   B. 說話   C. 睡覺   D. 等候

《正確答案》 D

11. A bomb exploded at the railroad station, injuring several people. The police are <u>inquiring into</u> this case. They are determined to find out who is responsible for the explosion.

    A. hearing   B. investigating   C. solving   D. citing

    一枚炸彈在鐵路車站爆炸了，有幾個人受到傷害。警察正在調查這案件。他們決定找出該為這場爆炸負責的人。

    A. 審理   B. 調查   C. 解決   D. 引用

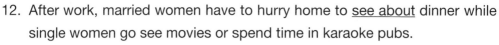

《正確答案》 B

12. After work, married women have to hurry home to <u>see about</u> dinner while single women go see movies or spend time in karaoke pubs.

    A. eat   B. prepare   C. buy   D. enjoy

    下班後，已婚的婦女必須急著準備晚餐，而單身女子則去看電影或去卡啦 OK 店。

    A. 吃   B. 準備   C. 買   D. 享受

《正確答案》 B

13. He only earns fifty thousand dollars a month; therefore, a donation of one hundred thousand dollars is not to be <u>sneezed at</u>.

    A. wasted   B. shared   C. ignored   D. exaggerated

    他一個月只賺五萬元；因此，捐獻十萬元是不可小覷的。

    A. 浪費   B. 分享   C. 忽視   D. 誇張

《正確答案》 C

14. The letter "V" <u>stands for</u> victory.

　　A. represents　　　B. causes　　　C. matches　　　D. prevents

　　字母「V」代表勝利。

　　A. 代表　　　　　B. 造成　　　　C. 配合　　　D. 阻止

《正確答案》 A

15. It is unfair of you to <u>trade on</u> Ted's generosity. You act like a parasite.

　　A. despise　　　B. praise　　　C. exploit　　　D. criticize

　　你利用泰德的慷慨是不公平的。你表現得像一隻寄生蟲。

　　A. 鄙視　　　　B. 讚美　　　C. 利用　　　D. 批評

《正確答案》 C

Unit 4　詞彙和結構─片語 (二)

✏️ 練習六

《Answers》--

> 1. C　　2. A　　3. D　　4. B　　5. B

1. 你不是我的上司，我不認為你有權利任意驅使我。

　　A. 嚇走　　　　　B. 使安靜下來　　C. 任意驅使　　D. 說服

2. 為了蓋奢華飯店，他們拆毀了在市中心的一些房子。

　　A. 拆毀　　　　　B. 關閉　　　　　C. 歸還　　　　　D. 藏起來

3. 搶劫犯仍逍遙法外，但警察決定追捕他們並將他們移送法辦。

　　A. 使冷靜下來　　B. 驅逐　　　　　C. 踢打　　　　　D. 追捕

4. 顧客們時常抱怨麵包的品質不好，但麵包師傅總是漠視他們的抱怨，說是顧客太挑剔了。

　　A. 記錄　　　　　B. 漠視　　　　　C. 區別　　　　　D. 削弱

5. 發生了一場暴動，警察被召集去鎮壓。兩個小時後，事情恢復了正常。

　　A. 輕描淡寫　　　B. 鎮壓　　　　　C. 一笑置之　　　D. 撇開

✏️ 練習七

《Answers》--

> 1. B　　2. D　　3. A　　4. C　　5. C

1. 我去機場送蒂娜，她要去法國。

　　A. 責備　　　　　B. 送行　　　　　C. 釋放　　　　　D. 收買

2. 珍炫耀她新買的一件洋裝，她說那件洋裝要一萬元，而且她熱切地期望她的同事能稱讚她。

　　A. 把...算入　　　B. 繳交　　　　　C. 脫掉　　　　　D. 炫耀

3. 因為有颱風，我們必須取消去野餐的計畫。

    A. 取消　　　　　　B. 提出　　　　　　C. 縮減　　　　　　D. 逐步實施

4. 工廠即將歇業，員工將被裁撤。

    A. 開釋　　　　　　B. 倒胃口　　　　　C. 裁員　　　　　　D. 打斷說話

5. 鮑伯欠債，必須靠著賣車付清債務。

    A. 註銷　　　　　　B. 對...充耳不聞　D. 付清　　　　　　D. 降價

✏️ 練習八

《Answers》 --

1. A	2. C	3. B	4. D	5. C

1. 在找到適合的鞋子前，我已經試穿許多雙鞋。

    A. 試穿　　　　　　B. 脫掉　　　　　　C. 挑選　　　　　　D. 分發

2. 當賽跑者跑最後一圈時，群眾越過他們，「加油」的喊叫聲催促著跑者。

    A. 擊昏　　　　　　B. 排除　　　　　　C. 給...加油　　　　D. 輾過

3. 我必須排除傑克，因為他有雙重國籍。依照法律，他不能競選這職位。

    A. 找出來　　　　　B. 排除　　　　　　C. 指出　　　　　　D. 爭取

4. 你在說什麼啊？我完全不了解你的意思，事實上，我一點頭緒也沒有。

    A. 仔細查看　　　　B. 拖延　　　　　　C. 忽略　　　　　　D. 了解

5. 在你接受她寬厚的提議前，你至少應該要花一天的時間考慮一下。你必須確定她沒有別的目的。

    A. 轉讓　　　　　　B. 拒絕　　　　　　C. 考慮　　　　　　D. 苦思而得出

練習九

1. A　　2. B　　3. D　　4. B　　5. C

1. 他們在橋上丟下一枚炸彈，然後炸燬橋。

   A. 炸毀　　　　　B. 清理　　　　　C. 分裂　　　　　D. 支持

2. 當蒂娜的父母死時，她才兩歲大，因此她的祖父母就養育她。

   A. 振作　　　　　B. 養育　　　　　C. 痛打　　　　　D. 挑選

3. 這個故事不是真的，是我捏造的。

   A. 溫習　　　　　B. 反覆考慮　　　　C. 接收到　　　　D. 捏造

4. 我將在這禮拜完成這個企劃，當我結束後，我會通知你。

   A. 推動...通過　　B. 完成　　　　　C. 大肆渲染　　　D. 提出

5. 我把答案寫在錯的格子裡，因此，我搞糟了考試，考不及格而被當。

   A. 草擬　　　　　B. 仔細查看　　　　C. 弄糟　　　　　D. 安全渡過

練習十

1. C　　2. A　　3. B　　4. D　　5. A

1. 琳達很隨和，所以她能跟大家和睦相處。

   A. 尊重　　　　　B. 區別　　　　　C. 與...和睦相處　　D. 輕視

2. 我一直在咳嗽，還有喉嚨痛，我擔心我已經感冒了。

   A. 罹患　　　　　B. 站起來反抗　　　C. 避免　　　　　D. 期望

3. 昨天我去台北拜訪一位老朋友，我們很高興在大學畢業三十年後，能再見到彼此。

   A. 逼近　　　　　B. 拜訪　　　　　C. 同意　　　　　D. 避開

4. 有人闖入辦公室偷走了筆記型電腦，我想知道誰是小偷。

    A. 彌補   B. 利用   C. 緊抓住   D. 竊走

5. 約翰並不有錢，他應該減少他的支出。

    A. 減少   B. 提出   C. 達到   D. 爭取

> 課後作業

1. You have to <u>account for</u> the sudden change in your thinking.

   A. make　　　　B. explain　　　C. oppose　　　D. experience

   你必須解釋你想法為何突然改變。

   A. 做　　　　　B. 解釋　　　　C. 反對　　　　D. 經歷

   《正確答案》 B

2. All players must <u>abide by</u> the rules of the game.

   A. pass　　　　B. break　　　　C. bend　　　　D. obey

   所有選手必須遵守比賽規則。

   A. 通過　　　　B. 破壞　　　　C. 彎曲　　　　D. 遵守

   《正確答案》 D

3. Sales <u>added up</u> to $2 million last year.

   A. totaled　　　B. exceeded　　C. included　　　D. excluded

   去年的銷售額總計兩百萬元。

   A. 總計　　　　B. 超過　　　　C. 包括　　　　D. 排除

   《正確答案》 A

4. Even when <u>allowing for</u> delays, we should finish the work early.

   A. making　　　B. avoiding　　C. considering　　D.causing

   即使有耽誤的考慮，我們還是應該及早結束這工作。

   A. 做　　　　　B. 避免　　　　C. 考慮　　　　D. 導致

《正確答案》 C

5. All attempts to <u>bring about</u> a change in Jack's condition have failed.

    A. cause   B. explain   C. avoid   D. understand

    所有試著改善傑克病症的嘗試都失敗了。

    A. 引起   B. 解釋   C. 避免   D. 了解

《正確答案》 A

6. Most members were against Bob, who would have lost his position if I hadn't <u>backed</u> him <u>up</u>.

    A. deserted   B.known   C. introduced   D.supported

    大部分的成員都反對鮑伯，如果我不支持他，他可能會失去他的職位。

    A. 拋棄   B. 知道   C. 介紹   D. 支持

《正確答案》 D

7. Sorry to <u>break in on</u> you, but someone is asking for you at the door.

    A. awaken   B.leave   C. interrupt   D. frighten

    很抱歉打斷你的話，但門口有人找你。

    A. 叫醒   B. 離開   C. 打斷   D. 驚嚇

《正確答案》 C

8. How did it <u>come about</u> that humans can speak so many languages?

    A. happen   B. continue   C. end   D. last

人類會說這麼多語言是如何發生的呢？

A. 發生　　　B. 繼續　　　C. 結束　　　D. 持續

《正確答案》 A

9. How on earth did you <u>come by</u> these tickets for the concert?

A. sell　　　B. lose　　　C. steal　　　D. obtain

你到底是如何獲得這些演唱會的票呢？

A. 賣　　　B. 失去　　　C. 偷　　　D. 獲得

《正確答案》 D

10. Since I have promised to take my daughter to the zoo, I must <u>carry</u> my promise <u>out</u>.

A. break　　　B. fulfill　　　C. make　　　D. ignore

因為我已經答應要帶我女兒去動物園，我必須實現我的承諾。

A. 違反　　　B. 實現　　　C. 做　　　D. 忽視

《正確答案》 B

11. The attempt to save the victims from the fire <u>came off</u>, and the fire fighters were hailed as heroes.

A. succeeded　　　　　　B. failed

C. was justified　　　　　D. was interrupted

消防員成功救出受害者，他們被呼為英雄。

A. 成功　　　B. 失敗　　　C. 合理的　　　D. 被打斷的

《正確答案》 A

13. He <u>popped up</u> on television in army fatigues and with an AK-47, calling himself a freedom fighter.

A. fainted   B. appeared   C. exclaimed   D. admitted

他穿著軍服並攜帶 AK-47 步槍出現在電視中宣稱他自己是自由鬥士。

A. 昏倒   B. 出現   C. 呼叫   D. 承認

《正確答案》 B

13. Old newspapers and magazines are piling up; I am afraid that you will have to <u>do away with</u> some of them.

A. collect   B. calculate   C. discard   D. study

舊的報紙和雜誌愈堆愈多，我想你必須要丟掉一些了。

A. 收集   B. 計算   C. 拋棄   D. 學習

《正確答案》 C

14. Tina <u>fell out</u> with her boyfriend yesterday, but now they have made up.

A. quarreled   B.consulted   C. agreed   D. competed

昨天蒂娜跟她男友吵架，但現在他們已經和好了。

A. 爭吵   B. 商量   C. 同意   D. 競爭

《正確答案》 A

15. Chris has been given a leave of absence to attend a computer course. Can you <u>fill in for</u> her for a few days?

A. contact B. replace C. teach D. leave

克麗絲請假去參加一個電腦課程，這幾天你可以代替她嗎？

A. 接觸 B. 取代 C. 教 D. 離開

《正確答案》 B

16. You promised to return my money today, but now you want to <u>go back on</u> your promise. How can I trust you?

A. make B. fulfill C. break D. honor

你答應今天還我錢的，但現在你想說話不算話。我要如何相信你呢？

A. 做 B. 實現 C. 違反 D. 遵守

《正確答案》 C

17. The pickpocket <u>broke away</u> from the crowd and ran off down the street.

A. separated B. disappeared C. came D. escaped

扒手從人群中逃脫，在街上逃走了。

A. 分離 B. 消失 C. 來 D. 逃脫

《正確答案》 D

18. Politicians tend to make more promises than they can deliver in order to be voted into office. Once they are in power, they find ways to <u>get around</u> their credibility problem.

A. solve B. avoid C. create D. understand

為了能當選，政客的承諾多於實踐。一旦他們有權力後，他們總是有辦法規避信用問題。

A. 解決　　　　　B. 規避　　　　　C. 創造　　　　　D. 了解

《正確答案》　B

19. You had better <u>hold off</u> making any decision until you talk it over with your wife. After all, it is you two that are going to live in the house.

A. deny　　　　　B. risk　　　　　C. delay　　　　　D. admit

在你跟你老婆商量前，你最好暫緩任何決定，畢竟，是你們兩個即將住進那房子裡。

A. 否認　　　　　B. 冒險　　　　　C. 延緩　　　　　D. 承認

《正確答案》　C

20. A man wearing a helmet tried to <u>hold up</u> a bank on Nan Hai Road, but he was subdued by a guard. The gun used in the robbery turned out to be a toy gun.

A. rob　　　　　B. surround　　　　　C. manage　　　　　D. establish

一個戴安全帽的男人試著搶劫在南海路上的一家銀行，但他被警衛制服了。搶劫用的手槍是一把玩具槍。

A. 搶劫　　　　　B. 包圍　　　　　C. 管理　　　　　D. 建立

《正確答案》　A

21. Before we use this computer, we have to <u>iron out</u> some operating problems first; otherwise, it might crash.

A. solve　　　　　B. identify　　　　　C. create　　　　　D. raise

在我們使用這台電腦前，我們必須先解決一些操作問題；否則，電腦會當機。

A. 解決　　　　　B. 指認　　　　　C. 創造　　　　　D. 提出

《正確答案》 A

22. I wish the rain would <u>let up</u> before I set out on my trip, but it seems that it will go on.

A. continue　　　B. fell　　　　　C. stop　　　　　D. pour

我希望在我開始旅行前，雨會停，但看起來好像會繼續下。

A. 繼續　　　　　B. 掉落　　　　　C. 停止　　　　　D. 注入

《正確答案》 C

23. It sounds like someone is <u>listening in</u> on our conversation. I suspect that my telephone has been bugged.

A. insisting　　　　　　　　B. eavesdropping

C. expanding　　　　　　　D. reflecting

好像有人竊聽我們的對話，我懷疑我的電話被安裝了竊聽器。

A. 堅持　　　　　B. 偷聽　　　　　C. 詳述　　　　　D. 沉思

《正確答案》 B

24. I managed to <u>set aside</u> some money each month from my salary and now it adds up to one million dollars. I have decided to use it as a down payment for a new apartment.

A. spend　　　　B. borrow　　　　C. save　　　　　D. withdraw

我試著每個月從薪水中存下一些錢，現在加起來有一百萬了。我已決定把它拿來當買新公寓的第一期款。

A. 花費　　　　　B. 借　　　　　C. 儲存　　　　　D. 取款

《正確答案》 C

25. That woman <u>owned up</u> to shoplifting after the shopkeeper found a lipstick in her purse.

A. objected　　　B. admitted　　　C. witnessed　　　D. stuck

店主在她的手提包中發現一隻口紅後，那女人承認在商店行竊。

A. 反對　　　　　B. 承認　　　　　C. 目擊　　　　　D. 堅持

《正確答案》 B

26. Mark has a keen interest in jigsaw puzzles. He must be able to <u>match up</u> all the pieces.

A. collect　　　　B. recognize　　　C. assemble　　　D. separate

馬克對拼圖很感興趣，他一定能把每一片配好。

A. 收集　　　　　B. 認出　　　　　C. 裝配　　　　　D. 分離

《正確答案》 C

27. Clear this mess up immediately; I can't <u>put up with</u> it anymore.

A. endure　　　　B. forget　　　　C. remember　　　D. understand

立刻把這亂七八糟的地方整理乾淨，我再也不能忍受了。

A. 忍耐　　　　　B. 忘記　　　　　C. 記得　　　　　D. 了解

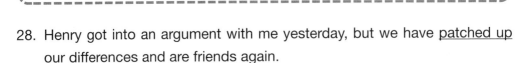

《正確答案》 A

28. Henry got into an argument with me yesterday, but we have <u>patched up</u> our differences and are friends again.

    A. stressed   B.resolved   C. ignored   D. told

    昨天亨利跟我吵了一架，但是我們平息了不和，現在又是朋友了。

    A. 強調   B. 解決   C. 忽視   D. 告訴

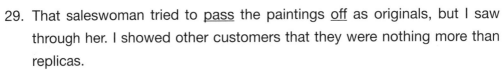

《正確答案》 B

29. That saleswoman tried to <u>pass</u> the paintings <u>off</u> as originals, but I saw through her. I showed other customers that they were nothing more than replicas.

    A. disguised   B.dismissed   C.hailed   D. described

    那位女售貨員試著將這些畫當成真品，但我看穿了她，我向其他顧客說明那些只不過是複製品。

    A. 偽裝   B. 貶視   C. 歡呼   D. 描述

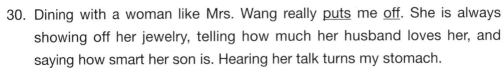

《正確答案》 A

30. Dining with a woman like Mrs. Wang really <u>puts</u> me <u>off</u>. She is always showing off her jewelry, telling how much her husband loves her, and saying how smart her son is. Hearing her talk turns my stomach.

    A. frightens   B. amuses   C. embarrasses   D. disgusts

    我真的無意跟王太太那樣的女人吃飯，她總是炫燿她的珠寶，談論著她老公有多愛她，或者她兒子有多聰明之類的話。聽她說話讓我倒盡胃口。

    A. 驚嚇   B. 歡樂   C. 發窘   D. 厭惡

《正確答案》 D

31. The house was an awful mess after the party. We <u>set about</u> cleaning up as soon as the guests left.

A. began   B. continued   C. finished   D. avoided

這房子在派對過後是一團亂，當客人離開後，我們就開始清理。

A. 開始   B. 繼續   C. 結束   D. 避免

《正確答案》 A

32. After he retired from the school, Tim <u>set up</u> his own business. He ran a publishing company. Many of his colleagues wished him well in his new career.

A. quitted   B. increased   C. started   D. restricted

提姆從學校退休後，他建立了他自己的事業。他經營一家出版公司，許多他的同事都祝福他新事業能有所發展。

A. 結束   B. 增加   C. 創辦   D. 限制

《正確答案》 C

33. I hung around the hotel lobby for half an hour, but Tina didn't <u>show up</u>. Finally, I left. I hate those who are never on time.

A. leave   B. wait   C. apologize   D. appear

我在飯店大廳徘徊了半小時，但蒂娜就是沒出現。最後我離開了，我討厭那些不準時的人。

A. 離開   B. 等待   C. 道歉   D. 出現

《正確答案》 D

34. The owner wants $8 million for his house and won't <u>settle for</u> anything less.

    A. pay　　　　　B. return　　　　C. raise　　　　D. accept

    屋主要八百萬才賣房子，低於這個價錢他可不接受。

    A. 付　　　　　B. 返回　　　　C. 舉起　　　　D. 接受

《正確答案》 D

35. Bob tried to <u>strike up</u> a conversation with the girl sitting opposite him. He cleared his throat and said, "Hi. Do you also like to travel by train?"

    A. end　　　　　B. continue　　　C. start　　　　D. change

    鮑伯試著開始跟坐在他對面的女孩聊天，他清了一下喉嚨說：「嗨！你也喜歡搭火車旅行嗎？」

    A. 結束　　　　B. 繼續　　　　C. 開始　　　　D. 改變

《正確答案》 C

36. We usually <u>sum up</u> our main points in the last paragraph.

    A. present　　　B. discuss　　　C. omit　　　　D. summarize

    我們通常在最後一段總結我們的重點。

    A. 提出　　　　B. 討論　　　　C. 刪去　　　　D. 總結

《正確答案》 D

37. Jack is seriously ill, so I will <u>stand in for</u> him in tonight's performance of the play.

A. comfort   B. replace   C. defend   D. accompany

傑克病得很嚴重，所以我代替他演出今晚的戲劇。

A. 安慰   B. 取代   C. 防禦   D. 陪伴

《正確答案》 B

38. Rick <u>takes after</u> his father not only in appearance but also in personality. His father is very proud that Rick's behavior mirrors his own.

A. imitates   B. remembers   C. disappoints   D. resembles

瑞克不僅在容貌上長得像他爸爸，連個性也很像。他爸爸非常得意瑞克的舉止反映出他自己的。

A. 模仿   B. 想起   C.使失望   D. 像

《正確答案》 D

39. Rick's boss tends to overwork his staff mercilessly. He often forces Rick to <u>take on</u> several tasks at the same time. Worse still, the tasks Rick is entrusted with are quite challenging.

A. complicate   B.shirk   C. glorify   D. undertake

瑞克的老闆總是殘忍地讓職員過度工作，他時常強迫瑞克在同一時間承擔許多工作，更糟的是，委託給瑞克的工作都是相當有挑戰性的。

A. 使複雜化   B. 逃避   C. 讚美   D. 承擔

《正確答案》 D

40. I was <u>tied up</u> all morning. I did not even have time to go to the bathroom.

   A. busy   B. tired   C. sick   D. sad

   我整個早上都忙碌，甚至沒有時間去廁所。

   A. 忙碌的   B. 疲累的   C. 生病的   D. 難過的

   《正確答案》 A

Unit 5 詞彙和結構－文法結構 (一)

✏ 練習一

《Answers》--

> 1. B   2. C   3. A   4. D   5. A

1.　媽，有東西聞起來好香，你正在煮什麼呢？

2.　一位老人正要過馬路，我及時煞車。

3.　只要我有足夠的錢，就會買新車。

4.　自從我一出生，就一直住在台北。

5.　在我上大學前，已經學了六年的英文。

✏ 練習二

《Answers》--

> 1. C   2. B   3. C   4. D   5. B   6. A

1.　珍打網球打得很好，我不是她的對手。

　　A. 將　　　　　　　B. 應該　　　　　　C. 能　　　　　　　D. 必須

2.　你原本可以救起溺水的男孩，但你卻站在一旁。

　　A. 能救　　　　　　B. 原本可以救起　　C. 一定救　　　　　D. 一定早就是

3.　蘇：電話響了。

　　海倫：那一定是山姆，他說過這個時候要打來的。

　　A. 也許是　　　　　B. 早就可能是　　　C. 一定是　　　　　D. 一定早就是

4.　麥克：我昨晚看到瑞絲跟湯尼在酒吧喝酒。

　　艾咪：你看到的那女孩不可能是瑞絲，她昨晚一直待在我家。

　　A. 也許現在不是　　B. 也許過去不是　　C. 現在不可能是　　D. 過去不可能是

5. 先生：昨晚我被鎖在門外。

   老婆：當你出門時，應該帶鑰匙的。

   A. 應該帶　　　　　B. 早該帶　　　　　C. 必須帶　　　　　D. 一定帶

6. 令人驚訝的是，昨天你竟然拒絕她的邀請。

   A. 過去竟然　　　　B. 過去一定　　　　C. 現在竟然　　　　D. 現在一定

 練習三

《Answers》--

| 1. C | 2. A | 3. D | 4. B | 5. B | 6. C | 7. A | 8. D |

1. 正如玉石必須雕刻或琢磨，心智也應該被培養。培養心智最好的方法就是閱讀好書。

   A. 跟...一樣　　　B. 同樣地　　　　C. 正如　　　　　D. 同樣地

2. 一張鐵製的桌子比木製的桌子更耐用。它可以用上好幾十年，但木製的桌子十年內就會磨損。

   A. 比...更耐用　　B. 比...還不耐用　　C. 一樣耐用　　　D. 一樣不耐用

3. 客觀來說，自從十六世紀以來，波蘭比任何時候更來得富裕。然而，當前卻見愁雲慘霧。

   A. 一樣貧困　　　　B. 一樣富裕　　　　C. 比...更貧困　　D. 比...更富裕

4. 對鋼鐵的需求不可能更高了；因此，它的價格已經達到空前的高峰。

   A. 高　　　　　　　B. 更高　　　　　　C. 最高　　　　　　D. 最不高

5. 昨天有一輛汽車被炸，死了兩名以色列士兵。在最前線負責安全的官員中，心情是難過多於憤怒。他們對於巴勒斯坦人，不會感到許多憤怒；相反的，他們對於死亡的士兵表達了最深層的傷心。

6. 珍是兩個姊妹中較高的一個。她 160 公分高，而她的妹妹只有 155 公分高。

7. 在台灣，個人電腦的銷售達到了三十億元，是前兩年的兩倍。

8. 九二一地震的死亡人數持續增加，成為自 1900 年來最慘重的災害。

✎ **練習四**

《Answers》 ---

| 1. C | 2. A | 3. B | 4. D | 5. D | 6. A |

1. 假使我再活一次，我仍然會愛上薇薇安。

2. 如果海倫上星期來開會，她就會遇到大衛。不幸地，她生病了。

3. 天上聚集了許多烏雲，看起來好像要下雨了。

4. 我的衣服濕了，也許看起來就像我曾坐在蒸汽浴缸裡。

5. 我希望再度年輕。

6. 若非你的幫忙，我去年就破產了。

課後作業

1. The bill amounts to $550, including a 10% tip. If the 5% tax is also added, the bill _____ $575.

    A. was   B. will be   C. is going to be   D. is about to be

    帳單總計 550 元，包括 10% 的小費。如果 5% 的稅也加入的話，那帳單將是 575 元。

    《正確答案》 B
    《解題關鍵》 if 副詞子句中用簡單式，但主要子句還是要用 will + V 表未來。

2. I was relieved when I learned that all the children _____ back safe and sound.

    A. had come   B. has come   C. came   D. come

    當我知道孩子們早就安然無恙回來後，我鬆了一口氣。

    《正確答案》 A
    《解題關鍵》 回來在先，知道在後，在先的動作用過去完成。

3. The wind was so strong that, when Peter _____ the wall, he lost his balance and fell off the ladder.

    A. was painting   B. painted   C. had painted   D. would paint

    當彼得正在油漆牆壁時，風吹得很強，以至於他失去平衡，從梯子上摔下來。

    《正確答案》 A
    《解題關鍵》 過去某個動作在進行，而另一動作穿插進來，進行的動作用過去進行式。
              油漆在進行，而失去平衡摔下來是其中穿插的行為。

4. Look at the way the couple _____ to each other. They must have been in love for a long time.

A. are talking   B. talked   C. will talk   D. have talked

看著那對情侶說話的樣子，他們一定已經戀愛很久了。

《正確答案》 A
《解題關鍵》 祈使句暗示有一動作正在進行，故用現在進行式。

5. You have always had poor digestion. I am afraid that there _____ something wrong with your stomach.

A. must be   B. shall be

C. must have been   D. might have been

你總是消化不良。我擔心你的胃腸一定有問題。

《正確答案》 A
《解題關鍵》 從消化不良斷定胃腸有問題，對現在的推測用 must + V。

6. Paul: _____ you _____ go for a drink after work?

Billy: Well, yes, I guess that would be okay.

A. Do...have to   B. Are...to   C. Ought...to   D. Would...like to

保羅：下班後，你想跟我去喝酒嗎？

比利：好啊，我想沒問題。

《正確答案》 D
《解題關鍵》 表示邀請用 would you like...?。

7. Jane: Oops. I spilled my juice.

   Paul: Don't worry. I _____ go get a paper towel.

   A. am going to   B. am to   C. should   D. will

   珍：哎喲！果汁溢出來了。

   保羅：別擔心！我會去拿紙巾。

   《正確答案》 D
   《解題關鍵》 立即的決定用 will + V。

8. Chris: Let's go for a walk after dinner, _____?

   Sam: O.K.

   A. will you   B. shall we   C. will we   D. shall you

   克里斯：晚飯後一起去散步，好嗎？

   山姆：好的。

   《正確答案》 B
   《解題關鍵》 Let's 後的附加問句用 shall we?

9. He spoke with an air of importance as if he _____ the president of the company.

   A. were   B. is   C. had been   D. has been

   他帶著了不起的樣子說話，就好像他是公司的總裁一樣。

   《正確答案》 A
   《解題關鍵》 as if 後的句子與現在事實相反，用過去式動詞，如為 be 動詞，則用 were。

10. It irritates me to have to listen to those women's idle gossip. I wish my boss _____ in the office every day so that they would shut their big mouths.

    A. will be   B. will have been

    C. would be   D. would have been

必須聽那些女人愚蠢的談話令我煩躁。我希望我的老闆可以每天在辦公室裡，以至於那些女人會閉上他們的大嘴巴。

《正確答案》 C

《解題關鍵》 wish 後面的子句用假設法。與未來事實相反用 would + V。

11. If the sun _____ in the west, I would lend money to you.

    A.had risen   B. should rise

    C.were to rise   D. should have risen

如果太陽從西邊升起，我就借錢給你。

《正確答案》 C

《解題關鍵》 與未來事實相反的假設句中用 were to + V。

12. When driving, make sure to fasten your seat belt. By doing so, you can avoid being seriously hurt if a car crash _____.

    A. should happen   B. would happen

    C. happened   D. has happened

開車時，確定繫緊你的安全帶。這樣做，如果車子發生衝撞，你可以避免受到嚴重傷害。

《正確答案》 A

《解題關鍵》 if 句中如果表示機率很低，用 should + V（萬一）。

13. If I _____ in the stock market last year, I _____ spare cash for new furniture now.

    A. didn't invest; will have
    B. hadn't invested; would have

    C. should invest; will have
    D. hadn't invested; would have had

    如果去年我不投資股票，現在我就有多餘的現金來買新家具。

    《正確答案》 B

    《解題關鍵》 if 句中指去年，與過去事實相反用過去完成式，而主要子句時間是現在，因此與現在事實相反用 would + V。

14. Cindy is thirty years old, but if she wears makeup, she will look _____ she really is.

    A. as young as
    B. less young than

    C. as old as
    D. younger than

    仙蒂三十歲了，但如果她化妝的話，她看起來比她實際年齡年輕。

    《正確答案》 D

    《解題關鍵》 but 表示對比，年齡三十歲，但化妝會看起來較年輕，用比較級。

15. Taipei is Taiwan's capital, so it is _____ in Taiwan.

    A. most prosperous

    B. as prosperous as

    C. more prosperous than any other city

    D. more prosperous than any city

    台北市是台灣首都，所以它比起任何其他城市都較繁榮。

    《正確答案》 C

    《解題關鍵》 台北與台灣其他都市相比，而台北也是台灣的一部分，因此 any 後要加 other。如把 other 去掉，則表示台北非台灣一部分。

Unit 6 詞彙和結構─文法結構 (二)

✎ 練習五

《Answers》--

　　1. D　　2. B　　3. C

1. 這本書很值得閱讀。

2. 昨晚發生奇怪的事。

3. 人們認為這男子是被落石砸死的。

✎ 練習六

《Answers》--

　　1. C　　2. A　　3. D　　4. B　　5. B　　6. D

1. 哥倫布在 1492 年發現美洲,他以為那裡的人是印第安人。

2. 這些年輕人,大多是貧窮又沒受過什麼教育,總看不出他們人生有何希望。

3. 傑克跟一位大他二十歲的女人結婚,這件事讓我們全部的人都很驚訝。

4. 警察試著去避免發生的事就是暴力。

5. 你一定能打倒那傢伙,我不認為他很強。

6. 他不夠強硬,無法去做必要的改革,而這些改革又是每個人所認同的。

✎ 練習七

《Answers》--

　　1. A　　2. C　　3. B　　4. D　　5. B　　6. D　　7. D　　8. C　　9. B　　10. D

1. 據說,莉莉看到那男的死在街上。他慘遭橫禍。

2. 我感覺房子正在搖動,衝動地跑出來。

3. 在醫生檢查前，我得等一個小時。

4. 別忘了繳交你的報告。最後期限是三月一日。

5. 我仍然記得當房子猛烈搖晃時，我哭著求救。

6. 他把手放進口袋，這樣看起來好像伸手在找某個東西。

7. 在鄉下長大，麥克很擅長砍木材。他能砍一次把木頭一分為二。

8. 歐尼斯‧海明威寫的《老人與海》中，主要的主角是一位老人航行在大海上，獵捕鯊魚。

9. 違反罷工的工人冒著遭受攻擊的危險離開工廠。

10. 聽到狗被踢死的消息，蓋瑞跳起來，氣到臉發抖。

 練習八

《Answers》

1. are	2. is	3. is	4. come	5. were
6. are	7. is	8. makes	9. were	10. live, swim
11. is	12. indicate			

1. 有很大比例的女人決定不結婚。

2. 我薪水中的一小部分被拿來償還我的貸款。

3. 在台灣，今年嬰兒出生數目預料會減少。

4. 少部分的學生來自這城市。

5. 當琳達跳迪斯可時，其他的女孩都以欽佩的眼光注視著。

6. 人們發現失業的人很容易沮喪。

7. 除了他的親戚外，沒有人願意幫他。

8. 只工作不玩耍，聰明孩子也變傻。

9. 幾十哩的鐵路軌道被 1999 年的地震震裂開了。

10. 鮭魚住在海裡，但要產卵時，會往上游。

11. 煙燻鮭魚是美味的。

12. 官方統計資料指出房價已經減少百分之十。

課後作業

1. A huge wind rose for a moment, whipping the four palm trees that
_____ near his house.

   A. was standing
   B. stood
   C. had been standing
   D. has been standing

   強大的風吹了一陣，抽打著他房子旁邊的四棵棕櫚樹。

   《正確答案》 B
   《解題關鍵》 此題不可用進行式，因為樹屹立在房子附近，是永久的，如用進行式表示
   它目前在那裡，等一下就不在那裡了。

2. Don't interrupt me when I _____ on the telephone. Can't you wait until
I _____?

   A. talk, finish
   B. talk, will finish
   C. am talking, finish
   D. am talking, will finish

   當我正在講電話時，不要打斷我的話。難道你不能等到我講完嗎？

   《正確答案》 C
   《解題關鍵》 正在講電話才會被打擾，因此第一個空格用進行式。 until 為一時間連接
   詞，其引領的子句中，用現在式動詞代替未來式。

3. A large amount of money _____ into the state-owned companies, but
they still cannot thrive.

   A. is injected
   B. was injected
   C. has been injected
   D. will have been injected

   大部分的錢已經投入國營公司，但他們仍然不能成功。

4. Jane took the first train, so she _____ there now. I will get there to pick her up. She is eager to be home.

   A. might have been　　　　　B. might be

   C. should have been　　　　D. should be

   珍搭第一班火車，所以她現在應該到那裡了。我將去那裡接她，她急著回家。

《正確答案》 D
《解題關鍵》 對現在的預測，助動詞後用原形。所以(A)和(C)不對。 might 表可能性一半， should 表可能性 90% 。

5. I waited for more than one hour. You _____ me you were going to be late, but you didn't give me a ring at all.

   A. should tell　　　　　　　B. must have told

   C. could tell　　　　　　　D. could have told

   我等了快一個小時。你原本可以告訴我你會遲到，但是你卻連一通電話也不打給我。

《正確答案》 D
《解題關鍵》 表示過去有能力做但卻沒做，用 could have + V-ed 。

6. The streets are humming with life even during the night. You _____ used to the hustle and bustle as soon as possible. This is the only advice that I can give you.

   A. had better get　　　　　B. can get

   C. might get　　　　　　　D. will get

即使在夜晚，街上還是很忙碌。你最好盡可能地習慣忙碌跟喧鬧。這是我給你的唯一忠告。

《正確答案》 A

《解題關鍵》 最後一句 advice（建議），表示建議的助動詞用 had better。

---

7. Sales of PCs amounted to $3 billion in Taiwan, _____ what they were two years earlier.

A. twice as much as　　　　　B. twice as many as

C. twice more than　　　　　D. twice less than

在台灣，個人電腦的銷售量達到三十億元，是前兩年的兩倍多。

《正確答案》 A

《解題關鍵》 兩倍多句型為 twice as.....as。指錢為不可數用 much。

---

8. This is a war. AIDS has killed _____ the case in all previous wars. We must not continue to be debating or arguing when people are dying.

A. fewer people than have been　　　B. fewer people than they have been

C. more people than has been　　　　D. more people than it has been

這是一場戰爭。比起之前的戰爭，AIDS 已經殺死更多的人。當人們快死亡時，我們不能繼續爭論或爭吵。

《正確答案》 C

《解題關鍵》 較多用 more，連接詞 than 之後名詞主詞與動詞倒裝，原來為 than the case has been 倒裝句 than has been the case。

---

9. Our eyebrows serve a useful purpose. Without eyebrows, drops of sweat _____ down into our eyes. We _____ very well.

    A. would run, could not see
    B. will run, will not see
    C. run, do not see
    D. ran, did not see

    我們的眉毛有個好功用。沒有眉毛的話，一滴滴的汗水會跑進我們的眼睛裡，我們就看不清楚了。

    《正確答案》 A
    《解題關鍵》 without（若非）如果句子是與事實相反則用假設語氣。

10. Sometimes I feel life is not worth living and wish I _____ born.

    A. were never
    B. had never been
    C. was never
    D. have never been

    有時候我覺得生命沒有意義，希望我從來沒有出生。

    《正確答案》 B
    《解題關鍵》 wish 後的句子用假設法，出生是過去，與過去事實相反，用過去完成式。

11. Mr. Smith garnered 51 percent of the vote, so _____.

    A. the winner was declared him
    B. the winner declared him
    C. he was declared the winner
    D. he declared the winner

    史密斯先生獲得百分之五十一的投票數，所以他被宣布為優勝者。

    《正確答案》 C
    《解題關鍵》 受詞補語不可移作被動式的主詞位置，此句 the winner 為受詞補語，因此(A)及(B)不對。又 declare 要接受詞和受詞補語，因此(D)不對。

12. The door _____ all the day. No wonder the burglar could sneak in and out at will.

A. was opened

B. was open

C. had opened

D. had been opened

這個門一整天都是打開的，難怪竊賊可以隨意地偷偷進出。

《正確答案》 B

《解題關鍵》 open 如當動詞，則不可與一段時間如 all the day（整天）等連用，只能把它當形容詞。答案為(B)。

13. On the way up to the peak of the mountain, I found a stone _____ someone had carved the Chinese character "忍", meaning "perseverance."

A. that   B. where   C. on which   D. on which

在往山頂的路上，我發現一顆石頭，上面刻著中國字「忍」。「忍」是堅忍不拔的意思。

《正確答案》 C

《解題關鍵》 a stone 為非特定，故關係子句用限定型，即其前不加逗點，(B)和(D) 錯誤，文意上將「忍」字刻在石頭上，要加一介系詞 on ，故選(C)。

14. If you say someone has a round face, people can understand. Anything _____ is round looks like a circle. But if you say someone is beautiful, it will be difficult to imagine _____ she looks like. Beauty itself is abstract.

A. that; what   B. which; what   C. that; how   D. which; how

如果你說某人有個圓臉，人們可以理解。任何圓的事物看起像圓圈。但如果你說某人是漂亮的，那將很難去想像她長得怎樣。美麗本身就是抽象的。

《正確答案》 A

《解題關鍵》 先行詞是不定代名詞如 anything ，關係代名詞用 that 。第三句的字末 like 是介系詞，要接受詞， how 是副詞不可當受詞，故選 what 。

15. After all the votes had been counted, the judge announced the outcome of the election. The winner was David _____ would become the next chairman of the Amateur Athletic Association.

A. who   B. that   C. , who   D. , he

在全部的票都已經算完後，裁判宣布選舉結果。當選的是大衛，他將是下一屆業餘運動協會的主席。

《正確答案》 C

《解題關鍵》 David 是特定人，故其關係子句用非限定型，即關係代名詞前要加逗號，選(C)。又(D)不對，連接兩句要有連接詞。

16. Susan emerged from the pool, _____.

A. and blue with cold   B. blue with cold.

C. she was blue with cold   D. which was blue with cold

蘇珊從水池出來，冷得全身發青。

《正確答案》 B

《解題關鍵》 (A)不對，因為缺動詞。(C)不對，缺連接詞。(D)不對， which 修飾 pool ，意思不對，游泳池為非生命不可能冷得發青。

17. Human waste, like nuclear waste, can cause serious damage to the environment _____.

A. if not disposing of properly   B. it not to dispose of properly

C. if not disposed of properly   D. if we are not disposed of properly

如果沒有適當處理，人類的廢料，像核廢料，就可能對環境造成傷害。

《正確答案》 C

《解題關鍵》 分詞構句修飾 waste（廢物）時，廢物是被處理，應用過去分詞。因此 (A)及(B)錯誤。(D)不對，因處理對象是廢物不是人。

18. Sherry blushed with embarrassment when she was found _____ her nose.

A. to pick B. picking C. pick D. picked

當雪莉被人發現在挖鼻孔時，她因為尷尬而臉紅。

《正確答案》 B

《解題關鍵》 find 的受詞補語如與受詞是主動關係，用現在分詞表無意中被發現。

19. There is a girl _____ leaflets to passers-by at the gate.

A. who distributes B. to distribute
C. distributing D. distributed

有個女孩正在發傳單給過路的人。

《正確答案》 C

《解題關鍵》 (A) 不對，distributes 現在簡單式，表習慣，應該改為進行式。(C)不對，因人發傳單是主動，宜用現在分詞。

20. Mary stroked the young man's cheek tenderly with her delicate hands. The soft touch made him _____ with happiness.

A. drink B. drunk C. drinking D. to drink

瑪莉用她纖細的手溫柔地愛撫年輕男子的臉頰。這溫柔的碰觸讓他因幸福而陶醉。

21. I need _____ me of some of the administrative work.

    A. to hire someone to relieve   B. to hire someone relieving

    C. hiring someone to relieve   D. hiring someone relieving

    我需要雇用人來減輕我的一些行政工作。

《正確答案》 A

《解題關鍵》 need 的受詞補語用不定詞表主動關係。

22. Thirty percent of well-educated women _____ to marry. The high percentage _____ the government very much.

    A. refuse, alarms   B. refuse, alarm

    C. refuses, alarms   D. refuses, alarm

    百分之三十的高學歷女人不願意結婚。這樣高比例讓政府非常驚慌。

《正確答案》 A

《解題關鍵》 percent 後如為複數可數名詞，其後動詞用複數形。但 percentage 後動詞用單數形動詞。

23. Statistics _____ too difficult a subject to study. Moreover, the figures are often open to dispute. Among them, government economic statistics _____ the most confusing.

    A. are, is   B. are, are   C. is, is   D. is, are

    統計學是一門很難研讀的科目。而且，數字常引起爭論。其中，尤以政府的經濟統計資料最令人困惑。

《正確答案》 D

《解題關鍵》 statistics 當學科時，用單數形動詞，但當統計數字時，用複數形動詞。

24. If all _____ smoothly, we will arrive at the lake as scheduled. Then all except the driver _____ going to have a picnic by the lake.

A. goes, is   B. goes, are   C. go, is   D. go, are

如果所有的事都進行順利的話，我們將按照預定時間抵達湖邊。然後，除了司機外，所有人將在湖邊野餐。

《正確答案》 B

《解題關鍵》 all 如指事物為單數，如指人為複數。

25. Thirty years _____ passed since I began to teach. Thirty years _____ really a long time.

A. have, is   B. have are   C. has, is   D. has, are

自從我開始教書，已經三十年了。三十年真的是一段很長的時間。

《正確答案》 A

《解題關鍵》 三十年過去，是時間一分一分地過去，表示時間的移動為複數，但如指一段時間為一單位，則視為單數。

Unit 7 段落填空 (一)

✏️ **練習一**

《Answers》---

1. A	2. C	3. D	4. B	5. B	6. D

　　最近，蜂蜜純度的測試引起了蜂農間一場叫囂憤怒。根據消基會的說法，在台灣大部分銷售的蜂蜜都不純。消基會指出蜂農在蜂蜜中加入了蔗糖，他們從較差的混合物中獲得巨額的利潤。如果消基會不願意承認不恰當測試蜂蜜純度的話，蜂農們揚言要告消基會。蜂農們要求賠償他們巨大的損失。蜂蜜的銷售下跌，因為訂單變少了，一位蜂農估計每天的損失大概在十萬元到二十萬元間。更令蜂農生氣的是，消基會用牙籤來測試蜂蜜純度。他們宣稱那樣的方法是錯的，測試純度最好的方法是將水加入蜂蜜中，然後搖晃它。如果蜂蜜是純的，液體會是髒且混濁的，還有許多泡泡。他們懷疑那些坐在冷氣房裡的蛋頭學者可能從未做過蜂蜜，只吃過蜂蜜，怎麼有能力判斷純蜂蜜或假蜂蜜呢？

1. A. 純的　　　　B. 便宜的　　　C. 甜的　　　　D. 黏的

2. A. 奇怪的　　　B. 複雜的　　　C. 次等的　　　D. 獨特的

3. A. 股份　　　　B. 進口　　　　C. 價格　　　　D. 銷售

4. A. 驚訝　　　　B. 怒氣　　　　C. 鬆口氣　　　D. 高興

5. A. 雖然　　　　B. 如果　　　　C. 因為　　　　D. 除非

6. （選項無法翻譯。）

✎ **練習二**

《Answers》--

1. A	2. C	3. B	4. D	5. A	6. D

　　自從兩岸旅行禁令取消後，年老的台灣男子跟年輕的大陸女子通婚的情形愈來愈多，而且已經產生一些社會問題。有一名年老的老兵用他的退休金娶了一位大陸農村女子當老婆。大陸女子願意跟一位大她兩倍歲數的老男人結婚，就是期待先生死後，她可以領到一半的退休金，對一位大陸農村女人來說，一個月有三萬元可是一大筆數目。一旦結婚，大陸農村女子就開始虐待她的台灣丈夫。另有些時候她拿著先生的存款逃走，回到家鄉享受生活。一位老兵向社工員展示他身上多種傷害。他說自從他們結婚，他的大陸妻子從未跟他睡在一起。她時常打他，使他生活在恐懼中。至少有十五萬大陸女子嫁來台灣。像這樣的家庭暴力只是冰山一角。現在政府提議在公務員退休前兩年或退休後結婚的話，公務員的退休金不能轉移給他的配偶。

1. 　A. 願意的　　　　B. 幸運的　　　　C. 強迫的　　　　D. 羞愧的

2. 　A. 那　　　　　　B. 它　　　　　　C. 那個　　　　　D. 這

3. 　A. 貯存　　　　　B. 帶...逃走　　　C. 輸光　　　　　D. 用盡

4. 　A. 皺紋　　　　　B. 刺青　　　　　C. 刺傷　　　　　D. 傷害

5. 　A. 恐懼　　　　　B. 貧窮　　　　　C. 和平　　　　　D. 安靜

6. 　A. 種族的　　　　B. 性別的　　　　C. 政治的　　　　D. 家庭的

✎ **練習三**

《Answers》--

1. A	2. C	3. B	4. D	5. A	6. C

　　台灣第一名模，林志玲，在中國從馬背上摔下來，遭受到嚴重的傷害。這個意外馬上成為頭條新聞，但它也揭露了不公平的全民健保制度。根據地方新聞報導，儘管林志玲每年收入超過四千三百萬元，但每個月健保，她只需要付六百零四元。同樣荒謬的

是，在台灣惡名昭彰的綁架犯張錫銘，因槍傷急忙送到醫院。醫院發現他根本從未取得任何保險，但健保局代表他申請了全民健保。可笑的是，在現今的全民健保制度下，他不需要付任何健保費用。也就是說，無辜的人民必須替他付醫療帳單，估計超過二十萬元。高收入的藝人比低收入的人們付較少的保險費，而凶暴的逃命犯享受免費的健保。這讓我們懷疑原先設計這制度的人的智商。

1. A. 不公平的　　　B. 複雜的　　　C. 彈性的　　　D. 完美的

2. A. 不像　　　　　B. 除...之外　　C. 儘管　　　　D. 除...之外

3. A. 謠言　　　　　B. 荒謬　　　　C. 理論　　　　D. 醜聞

4. A. 支持　　　　　B. 看見　　　　C. 承蒙好意　　D. 代表

5. A. 無辜的　　　　B. 有錢的　　　C. 貧窮的　　　D. 生意

6. A. 道德　　　　　B. 健康　　　　C. 智力　　　　D. 力氣

練習四

《Answers》

1. B	2. A	3. D	4. C	5. A	6. D

　　有一些習俗是相當有趣的，但沒有任何習俗比在一個人還活著時，就蓋他的墳墓來得有趣。在花蓮玉里鎮，有不少人這樣做。有些人甚至把自己的墳墓蓋在院子裡。他們要蓋自己的墳墓是有幾個原因的。首先，有些人認為在他死後，他不能看到自己墳墓的樣子，所以在死前就先蓋好自己的墳墓。當他們的墳墓蓋好時，他們邀請親朋好友來參加典禮。他們甚至會在清明節時在自己的墓前哭泣。此外，還有一些人因為沒有子孫，他們擔心當他們死後沒有人埋葬他們，那他們的來世將會不幸。第三個原因是，有些人有浪漫的想法。一個有錢人有一個老婆和兩個小老婆，他蓋了輝煌的墳墓，希望死後仍然可以跟三個女人在另一個世界生活。他現在八十六歲，仍然非常健康。他豪華的墳墓已經蓋了三十年了。

1. A. 醒著的　　　　B. 活著的　　　C. 年輕的　　　D. 有錢的

2. A. 首先　　　　　B. 總結　　　　C. 此外　　　　D. 結果

3.　A. 笑　　　　　　B. 私語　　　　　C.說　　　　　　D.哭泣

4.　A. 孤獨的　　　　B. 忙碌的　　　　C. 不幸的　　　　D.普通的

5.　A. 浪漫的　　　　B. 奇特的　　　　C. 荒謬的　　　　D. 有價值的

6.　A. 舒適的　　　　B. 寬敞的　　　　C. 現代的　　　　D. 輝煌的

 練習五

《Answers》--

> 1. C　　2. B　　3. D　　4. A　　5. D

　　布希政府拒絕 1997 年的京都協定書。這個協議書是打算在 2012 年前，靠減低工業化國家溫體氣體的排放量來保護地球免於全球氣溫上升。跟美國一樣，澳洲也拒絕簽署這個協定。首先他們抱怨有些開發中國家，像印度和中國，就免於簽署。然而，隨著他們快速的經濟發展，印度跟中國溫體氣體的排放量卻極高。此外，這個協定嚴重損害了美國跟澳洲的經濟，毀了他們的工作。許多工廠可能會關閉，美國和澳洲工業將輸給新興國家，像印度和中國。

1.　A. 除...以外　　B. 由於　　　　C. 像　　　　　　D. 儘管

2.　A. 已開發　　　B. 開發中　　　C. 國外的　　　　D. 共產主義的

3.　（選項無法翻譯。）

4.　A. 工作　　　　B. 制度　　　　C. 信念　　　　　D. 土地

5.　A. 政府　　　　B. 武器　　　　C. 人口　　　　　D. 工業

 練習六

《Answers》--

> 1. D　　2. B　　3. A　　4. C　　5. B

　　對日本來說，補鯨是它文化的一部分。但是商業補鯨活動的中止已經使得日本補鯨業衰落了，日本一直努力試著保存這行業。藉著科學的名義日本一直在增加補鯨數量。

如果沒有阻止，日本探究船每年將在南極海域捕捉超過一千隻鯨魚。雖然日本科學家是在做實驗，但鯨魚肉卻賣給批發商，並在餐廳供應給顧客。此外，日本時常被控告賄賂一些小國家要他們投票贊成恢復捕鯨業。日本政府一直嚴正地否認這樣的控訴。然而，多米尼加，一個加勒比海的小國家，在 2000 年失去了環境大臣，因為有消息指出日本靠援助買了它的政府投票權。

1. A. 貿易　　　　B. 文化　　　　C. 自然　　　　D. 科學

2. A. 如同　　　　B. 雖然　　　　C. 除非　　　　D. 當

3. A. 回復　　　　B. 結束　　　　C. 線索　　　　D. 障礙

4. A. 消息　　　　B. 謠言　　　　C. 控告　　　　D. 承諾

5. （選項無法翻譯。）

✏️ 練習七

《Answers》 --

> 1. C　　2. A　　3. B　　4. D　　5. B　　6. C

　　熱浪席捲了歐洲，溫度持續上升。歐洲人一直在尋找涼爽的方法，沒有比裸體走動且同時觀賞色情畫還要舒服的。有沒有任何地方可以提供這樣輕鬆的氣氛？有的，維也納有名的利奧波德博物館現在正展示 1990 年代早期的色情藝術「裸體的事實。」為了吸引更多人來看展覽，博物館提供免費的入場卷給任何願意只穿泳裝或者裸體的人入館參觀。許多裸體或穿著很少的人們，有男有女，徘徊在博物館內的電視攝影機前。許多從海外來的旅客感到有趣的離開博物館，但對於羅馬天主教神職人員來說，這不是一件好玩的事。然而，博物館職員對於他們的抗議只是輕描淡寫的說，他們只想要給人們一個涼爽的機會，並且公開展示裸體。至於裸體的訪客對於天主教會的憤怒叫囂也只是聳肩不理會。他們當中的一個人表示：「這有什麼大不了的？我們一出生就是裸體，為什麼我們不能有時候裸體在世界上走著？」

1. A. 可恥的　　　B. 適當的　　　C. 舒服的　　　D. 悲傷嚴肅的

2. A. 引誘　　　　B. 驅趕　　　　C. 引進　　　　D. 拉

3.	A. 離開	B. 穿上	C. 在...裡	D. 越過
4.	A. 不能相信的	B. 可能的	C. 驚奇的	D. 有趣的
5.	A. 清理	B. 冷卻	C. 打瞌睡	D. 炫耀
6.	A. 在乎	B. 努力	C. 衣服	D. 面具

 練習八

《Answers》---

| 1. A | 2. C | 3. B | 4. D | 5. A |

　　比爾菲斯特，上議院領導者指出政府應該鼓勵幹細胞的研究，並提供政府的錢當基金。如同其他支持者，他認為幹細胞為治療癌症和老人癡呆症帶來希望。他的看法跟布希總統的看法相牴觸，布希總統強烈反對這樣的研究。如同其他反墮胎活動者一樣，布希總統認為提取幹細胞的過程破壞了胚胎，中止了性命。據說，當布希總統第二任期滿後，菲斯特先生有意爭取共和黨的總統候選人。結果，菲斯特先生支持幹細胞的決定可能毀損他被提名進入白宮的機會。然而，身為外科醫生的菲斯特先生堅持他仍然反對墮胎，而幹細胞研究則是科學事件，不是信念事件。

1.	（選項無法翻譯。）			
2.	A. 提供資金	B. 贊成	C. 反對	D. 做
3.	A. 維持	B. 終止	C. 重新創造	D. 削弱
4.	A. 即使如此	B. 相對照之下	C. 最後	D. 結果
5.	A. 信念	B. 生意	C. 教育	D. 藝術

課後作業

Question 1-5

According to a recent report, the birth rate in Taiwan has fallen to a new low. Having fewer babies means that fewer young people will work in the future and that elderly people will not be well looked after. __1__, the country's economy will be weakened, and the government will have to spend an astronomical sum of money to take care of the __2__. Another effect is that a low birth rate will cause some people to lose their __3__. Recently, many schools have become overstaffed because there are fewer pupils now. The __4__ of teachers has posed a big problem for education officials. Finally, to make up for the labor shortage, a lot of foreign workers have to be hired to build houses or bridges, to work as nannies, and so on. Many __5__ have arisen, as witnessed by the recent Thai workers' riot in Kaohsiung.

根據最近的報導,在台灣的出生率已經下降到新的低點。有較少的嬰兒意味著將來較少年輕人會工作,而老人將無法受到很好的照顧。因此,國家經濟將衰弱,政府必須花龐大數額的資金來照顧老人。另一個影響是低出生率將造成有些人失去他們的工作。最近,許多學校變得超額,因為現在學生較少。對教育官員來說,師資過多已經產生大問題。最後,為了補充勞工短缺,雇用了許多的外籍勞工來蓋房子或橋樑,或者當保姆等等。許多衝突已經產生,最近泰勞在高雄的騷動就是一個例證。

1. A. At any rate　　B. As a result　　C. On the whole　　D. In other words
　　無論如何　　　　因此　　　　　　一般說來　　　　　換言之

《正確答案》 B
《解題關鍵》 上下句呈因果關係,人口降低,未來勞力減少,老人乏人照顧,結果是經濟力削弱等。

2.　A. babies　　　　　B. young　　　　　C. disabled　　　　D. aged
　　　嬰兒　　　　　　　年輕的　　　　　　廢殘的　　　　　　年老的

《正確答案》　D
《解題關鍵》　前句指 elderly people，與此同義字的是 the aged。

3.　A. jobs　　　　　　B. chances　　　　C. temper　　　　　D. balance
　　　工作　　　　　　　機會　　　　　　　脾氣　　　　　　　平衡

《正確答案》　A
《解題關鍵》　空格後面句子，說明出生率低，造成老師供應過多與工作有關。

4.　A. qualification　　B. health　　　　　C. oversupply　　　D. overwork
　　　資格　　　　　　　健康　　　　　　　供應過多　　　　　過勞

《正確答案》　C
《解題關鍵》　與前句 overstaffed 同義的為 oversupply。

5.　A. opportunities　B. conflicts　　　　C. obligations　　　D. needs
　　　機會　　　　　　　衝突　　　　　　　義務　　　　　　　需求

《正確答案》　B
《解題關鍵》　後半句舉例高雄外勞暴動，此乃 conflict 之例子。

Question 6-11

Though the death penalty cannot completely curb crime (as human rights activists claim), it should not be abolished, at least until a more effective way can be devised to replace it. First of all, the death penalty saves hundreds of millions of tax dollars that would normally be spent to keep criminals in prison for life. ___6___ a rough estimate, meals and lodging alone cost taxpayers at least NT$12,000 for each convict per month. Compared with a homeless person, a convicted criminal lives ___7___ he were a king. In addition, imprisonment doesn't act as a deterrent to other criminals. If a criminal need not worry about being put to death, he will be ___8___ to kill. Under these circumstances, can innocent people expect to feel safe from harm? Most importantly, death is an appropriate punishment for someone who commits a terrible crime. A victim's family is desperate to see ___9___ being done. For a killer, death is not only the best way to redeem himself but also the most honorable way to ___10___ his conscience. For example, a notorious death-row inmate in America constantly appealed to the courts to execute him immediately after he had been in jail for twenty years. He preferred to die a ___11___ death rather than languish in prison.

雖然人權激進份子宣稱死刑不能完全遏止犯罪，但死刑不應該廢止，至少在設計更有效的方法取代它之前不能廢止。首先，死刑省下了數百萬稅金，這些錢是花在把罪犯關在牢裡的生活。粗步估計，納稅人每個月至少花了一萬二千元在每個罪犯的用餐和住宿上。跟游民比較起來，一個罪犯的生活像國王般享受。此外，監禁並不能威嚇其他罪犯。如果一個罪犯不需要擔心被處死，那他將放手殺人。在這種情況下，無辜的人們可以期待免於傷害嗎？更重要的是，當某人犯了可怕的罪行時，死亡是適當的處罰。受害者的家庭渴望見到正義伸張。對一位兇手來說，死亡不僅是償還的最好方法，也是減輕良心不安的最光榮方法。舉例來說，在美國一個惡名昭彰的死刑囚犯被關了二十年之後，他經常懇求法庭，馬上將他處死。他想立即快速地死亡，而不願在牢裡長期受苦。

6.　A. In　　　　　　　B. By　　　　　　C. With　　　　　D. For
　　在……裡面　　　　　根據　　　　　　和……一起　　　　為了

《正確答案》　B
《解題關鍵》　estimate 前介系詞用 by。

7.　A. just as 正如同　　　　　　　　B. simply because 只因為
　　C. even if 即使　　　　　　　　　D. as if 猶如

《正確答案》　D
《解題關鍵》　空格後為 he were，很明顯是與事實相反的假設。可用的連接的是 even if 和 as if。此句是在做比較，過國王般的生活，因此選 as if。

8.　A. free　　　　　　B. careful　　　　C. reluctant　　　D. afraid
　　不受約束的　　　　仔細的　　　　　　不情願的　　　　害怕的

《正確答案》　A
《解題關鍵》　依上文罪犯不需擔心處死，當然就能放手殺人。

9.　A. wonders　　　　B. tricks　　　　　C. justice　　　　D. harm
　　驚奇　　　　　　　詭計　　　　　　　正義　　　　　　傷害

《正確答案》　C
《解題關鍵》　受害家庭要求正義。

10. A. ease   B. examine   C. trouble   D. arouse
    減輕   檢查   麻煩   喚起

《正確答案》 A
《解題關鍵》 前半句 redeem himself 是懺悔贖罪，因此是為了心安。

11. A. violent   B. accidental   C. quick   D. natural
    激烈的   意外的   快速的   自然的

《正確答案》 C
《解題關鍵》 與 languish 相對的形容詞為 quick。

Unit 8 段落填空 (二)

✎ 練習九

《Answers》--

| 1. B | 2. D | 3. A | 4. C | 5. D | 6. B | 7. C |

　　一個有錢的生意人跟一位女人有婚外情，為了贏得她的心，他給她一百萬元。然而，當他們的羅曼史結束後，那個生意人卻要求女人把錢歸還給他。他對她提出訴訟，出乎意料地，他贏了這案件。那個生意人說在分手後，那女人跟她的親戚聚集在他的房子和辦公室前，大聲喊叫並且咒罵他。生意人認為那女人的行為已經對他的人格構成侮辱。依據民法，他有權利要回他的禮物。法官接受了他的論點，判決那女人犯了誹謗罪。她必須付還給他一百萬元。

　　這是情婦會遇上的麻煩。她貪圖他的財富，破壞了一個家庭。最後她自己賠上愛情跟金錢。但是對自己老婆不忠的男人也必須付出高代價。最後他得到破碎的家庭和損毀的名聲。最不幸的受害者是那男人的妻子跟小孩，法律不能收拾這殘局。

1.　A. 因此　　　　　B. 然而　　　　　C. 同樣地　　　　D. 而且

2.　A. 出賣　　　　　B. 聚會　　　　　C. 逃開　　　　　D. 分手

3.　A. 侮辱　　　　　B. 障礙　　　　　C. 推動　　　　　D. 困境

4.　A. 做　　　　　　B. 接受　　　　　C. 撤回　　　　　D. 保留

5.　A. 債　　　　　　B. 批評　　　　　C. 反對　　　　　D. 麻煩

6.　A. 不友善的　　　B. 不忠實的　　　C. 服從的　　　　D. 感謝的

7.　A. 無知的　　　　B. 容忍的　　　　C. 不幸的　　　　D. 明智的

練習十

《Answers》 --

| 1. B | 2. C | 3. A | 4. D | 5. D | 6. B | 7. C |

　　學生髮型的規定時常因許多理由而受批評。自由主義者認為那是蔣家威權的遺毒。軍人的平頭，也就是說很短的髮型一向是用來培養服從和忠誠的手段。在蔣家統治下，短頭髮的學生，穿著卡其色的制服，當名字被提及時，就要站得直挺挺的。在偉大領導者生日時，剪著短頭髮的學生，站著歌誦偉大的領導者。相反的，現在的學生變得很有自信，質疑這樣規定的合理性。在二十年前，質疑這樣規定的人很可能惹上大麻煩。但隨著台灣政治的急速改變，這樣的規定似乎是落伍了。

　　因此，教育部長杜先生最近宣稱這樣的規定將被廢止。學生有權利去決定他們自己的髮型。雖然他的決定得到普遍的支持，但許多保守的校長跟教育官員仍強硬反抗。他們之中有人懷疑這樣的決定有政治動機。為了他們所謂的衛生與健康，他們發誓維持這樣的規定。

1. A. 和　　　　　B. 或　　　　　C. 但是　　　　D. 雖然

2. A. 羞愧　　　　B. 歸屬　　　　C. 忠誠　　　　D. 安全

3. A 唱　　　　　B. 唱　　　　　C. 唱　　　　　D. 唱

4. A. 侵略的　　　B. 創造的　　　C. 活躍的　　　D. 自信的

5. A. 即使如此　　B. 相比之下　　C. 此外　　　　D. 因此

6. A. 年長的　　　B. 保守的　　　C. 有野心的　　D. 奉獻的

7. （選項無法翻譯。）

✏️ 練習十一

《Answers》

1. D	2. A	3. B	4. C	5. B	6. A	7. D

農曆七月是中國的鬼月,有許多迷信跟它有關。人們若在農曆七月旅行的話,要做以下的事情以免見到鬼。

● 避免窗戶靠近高大樹木的房間。據說鬼魂容易依入附在多樹蔭的樹上。

● 避免鏡子直接面對床的房間。鏡子可以反射一個人或一個東西的影像,萬一你半夜起床的話,可能會被自己的身影嚇到。

● 在進入飯店房間前,先在門上敲三下。這是在告訴房裡的鬼魂(萬一它縈繞著房間)你將只待在那裡一、兩個晚上,不打算長期佔據那房間。

● 假如你在半夜聽到外面有任何聲音,絕不要打開窗戶。隨著突然的一陣風,鬼魂可能就會透過窗戶進來房間。

● 如果在房間裡有兩張床,不要把你的所有物散放在你沒睡的那張床上。這對縈繞房間的鬼魂來說,是一種侮辱,它可能會在半夜報復你。

● 在你睡前,記得在夜裡留一盞燈。邪惡的鬼魂喜歡出現在全黑的夜裡。

1. A. 為了...目的　　B. 因為　　　　C. 假如　　　　D. 唯恐

2. A. 多樹蔭的　　　B. 無葉的　　　C. 中空的　　　D. 開花的

3. A. 娛樂　　　　　B. 害怕　　　　C. 生氣　　　　D. 興奮

4. A. 打算　　　　　B. 打算　　　　C. 打算　　　　D. 打算

5. A. 燈火　　　　　B. 風　　　　　C. 聲音　　　　D. 氣味

6. A. 報復　　　　　B. 同情　　　　C. 注意　　　　D. 利用

7. A. 瓦斯　　　　　B. 火　　　　　C. 收音機　　　D. 燈

✏️ **練習十二**

《Answers》 ---

| 1. A | 2. C | 3. B | 4. D | 5. D | 6. C | 7. A |

　　視網膜剝離是嚴重的眼睛疾病，有可能導致失明。視網膜是眼球內壁最裡面的那一層，它就像濕的衛生紙一樣容易碎。當它分開時，會使眼睛後壁分離，切斷血液的供給和營養的來源。

　　視網膜剝離的症狀包括見到漂浮的斑點、閃爍的光線、眼睛裡有遮蔽物。這樣的情況是不會痛的，只是令人困擾。當視網膜中央受到影響時，視力已經扭曲了，變得波動且不清楚，還有視力可能突然減低。沒有外科手術修復的話，可能會導致眼睛失明。

　　因為年紀大了或近視，視網膜逐漸變薄且更容易碎。因此，視網膜剝離通常發生在中年或年紀較大的人身上。更有可能發生在有近視的人身上。甚至，給眼睛一個重擊也有可能導致視網膜剝離，所以人們必須小心避免直接撞到眼睛，舉個例來說，當打棒球時。其他疾病也有可能導致視網膜剝離，罹患糖尿病或腫瘤的病人很有可能得到眼睛疾病。高度危險群應該每年至少檢查一次眼睛，早期發現及治療可以改善視力恢復的機會。

1. A. 易碎的　　　　B. 黏的　　　　　C. 油膩的　　　　D. 透明的

2. A. 令人愉快的　　B. 令人驚奇的　　C. 惱人的　　　　D. 刺痛的

3. A. 儘管　　　　　B. 沒有　　　　　C. 此外　　　　　D. 像

4. A. 然而　　　　　B. 同樣地　　　　C. 最後　　　　　D. 因此

5. A. 無論如何　　　B. 順便一提　　　C. 事實上　　　　D. 舉例來說

6. A. 等級　　　　　B. 有精力的　　　C. 危險　　　　　D. 收入

7. A. 視力　　　　　B. 自信　　　　　C. 健康　　　　　D. 平衡

練習十三

《Answers》

1. B	2. D	3. A	4. C	5. A	6. B

2004 年，台灣報導指出有兩千三百六十人自殺。在台灣，自殺已經成為死亡率的第九名。為了促進尊重生命，董氏基金會有個「拯救生命」的網站，告訴人們如何減輕壓力，避免企圖自殺。因為經濟蕭條，失業的比率創下空前的紀錄。許多中年男子失去了他們的工作，發現很難去養他們的家庭。一天中很難沒有自殺事件的報導，很多無辜的小孩也被殺死，成為悲劇的一部分。去年，有一個男人帶著他的妻子和四個小孩，開車衝出懸崖，掉入海裡死掉。這個男人在高雄一間寺廟前賣早餐過活，他急需要錢，向高利貸借了錢。這個貸款決定了他們全家的命運。

好心的董氏基金會熱心於幫助那些遭受感情困擾的人──覺得生命無意義的年輕人、失戀的女人、事業沒進展的男人。但是對那些經濟困難的人來說，錢就是唯一的生命線。不幸地，這個基金會不提供這些，高利貸款者卻提供，但是接觸他們就等於接受死亡之吻。

1.	A. 債	B. 壓力	C. 花費	D. 危險
2.	A. 希望	B. 興趣	C. 機會	D. 工作
3.	A. 悲劇	B. 意外	C. 冒險	D. 謀殺
4.	A. 意外	B. 交易	C. 貸款	D. 貧窮
5.	A. 心意	B. 行為	C. 紀律	D. 聞名的
6.	A. 住宅	B. 財政的	C. 精力	D. 認同

練習十四

《Answers》 --

| 1. B | 2. D | 3. A | 4. C | 5. D | 6. B |

　　最近，石油價格上升到一桶六十七元。有些經濟學家害怕高油價可能導致通貨膨脹，經濟衰退，或者兩者都有。然而，顧客繼續花費；他們似乎不擔心油價上漲，甚至計程車司機也不強烈要求提高計程車費用。七月份的消費者物價指數呈現通貨膨脹緩慢上升的現象，但這並未讓政府官員恐慌。世界經濟正在改善，甚至日本也已經從十五年來的經濟衰退爬出來。

　　有幾個原因可解釋為什麼現今油價上漲似乎不造成傷害。首先，顧客似乎習慣油價的波動，發展出對高油價的免疫力。有部分可能是因為人們更有錢了。第二點，進口石油的國家已經增加燃料效能，最好的例子就是小型車的普遍率。第三點，中國對石油的需求稍微衰退。在過去十年中，中國進口了大量的石油來維持急速的經濟發展，使得油價更高。但是現在中國想要製造經濟軟著落，這由最近人民幣貶值可以為證。

1.	A. 任一的	B. 兩者	C. 兩者都不	D.全部
2.	A. 興奮的	B. 驚訝的	C. 好玩的	D. 擔心的
3.	A. 衰退	B. 成長	C. 奇蹟	D. 好轉
4.	（選項無法翻譯。）			
5.	A. 豪華	B. 運動	C. 柴油引擎	D. 小型的
6.	A. 推	B. 推	C. 推	D. 推

✎ 練習十五

　　最近，喝醋已經成為一種趨勢。據說，喝醋有醫療的功效。有一些顧客宣稱醋可以用來治療疹子和咬傷。其他人甚至宣稱醋可以治療關節炎。日本人相信醋可以改善循環和減低疲勞。甚至，據說米醋可以減肥。

　　然而，傳統的醋不能喝。像醬油一樣，醋是用來改善食物的味道或保存食物的。有生意頭腦的人研發出以醋為底的飲料。舉例來說，像蘋果、葡萄或覆盆子這樣的水果被發酵成汁，做成水果醋。另一個例子是醋水，瓶裝的水包含了百分之一的醋。這樣以醋為底的飲料引入市場後，銷售量急速上升。事實上，他們已成功地成為顧客心中的健康飲料。

1.　A. 醫療的　　　　B. 化學的　　　　C. 身體的　　　　D. 心理的

2.　A. 導致　　　　　B. 增強　　　　　C. 治療　　　　　D. 提升

3.　A. 儘管　　　　　B. 此外　　　　　C. 由於　　　　　D. 像

4.　A. 藝術的　　　　B. 生意的　　　　C. 科學的　　　　D. 語言的

5.　A. 皮膚　　　　　B. 果汁　　　　　C. 種子　　　　　D. 肉

6.　A. 許多　　　　　B. 少　　　　　　C. 一些　　　　　D. 這樣的

7.　（選項無法翻譯。）

課後作業

Question 1-5

A conservation institute in the USA has produced eight wildcat kittens through cloning. The eight kittens were born to two separate mothers, but they all have a __1__ father. The father himself is a clone of another wildcat. Up to now, they are all healthy and doing very well.

This achievement has great significance for wildlife conservation. The researchers say that better cloning procedures can help to save __2__ animals from extinction. If the cloned animals can survive, mate with each other, and give birth to offspring, then we can preserve threatened species.

However, some scientists are not so optimistic. One of the greatest threats to a species is the destruction of its habitat. A more urgent action would be to __3__ their natural home; not to clone several of them in an unnatural environment. __4__, for cloning to play a significant role in preserving endangered species, cloned animals must be able to breed normally once they are introduced to the __5__. So far no good examples of this have been found.

在美國，一個自然保護的研究協會透過複製繁衍了八隻小山貓。這八隻小山貓分別來自兩位媽媽，但他們都有一位共同的爸爸。爸爸本身也是從另一隻山貓複製繁衍來的。至今，他們都很健康，而且表現都很好。

這項成就對野生生物的保護有很大的意義。研究者說更好的複製法可以幫助瀕臨絕種的動物免於絕種。如果複製出來的動物能夠生存，彼此交配，產出下一代，那我們就可以保存飽受威脅的物種。

然而，有些科學家並不這麼樂觀。對物種來說，最大的威脅之一就是棲息地被破壞，更迫切的行動是恢復他們自然的家。此外，複製要在保存瀕臨絕種動物中扮演重要角色的話，被複製的動物必須能投入荒野，自然繁殖。迄今，這樣成功的例子尚未見到。

1.　A. different　　　B. healthy　　　C. alien　　　D. common
　　　不同的　　　　　健康的　　　　　外國的　　　　共同的

《正確答案》　D
《解題關鍵》　轉折語 but 表示對比，因此其前說不同的媽媽，那麼 but 後的貓爸爸應是相同一隻。故選 common。

2.　A. domestic　　　B. wild　　　　C. extinct　　　D. endangered
　　　家庭的　　　　　野生的　　　　　絕種的　　　　快要絕種的

《正確答案》　D
《解題關鍵》　本段最後一行 threatened species 就是指 endangered animals。

3.　A. restore　　　　B. find　　　　C. move　　　　D. flatten
　　　恢復　　　　　　找到　　　　　　移動　　　　　弄平

《正確答案》　A
《解題關鍵》　前句提到自然棲息地遭破壞是野生動物最大的威脅，因此可推測當務之急是恢復（restore）棲息地。

4.　A. Even so　　　　B. In short　　　C. Moreover　　　D. Therefore
　　　即使如此　　　　簡言之　　　　　此外　　　　　因此

《正確答案》　C
《解題關鍵》　空格前後看不出對比關係，也看不出因果關係，因此(A)及(D)不對。應該是在說另一問題，答案為(C)。

5.　A. zoo　　　　　B. field　　　　C. wild　　　　D. farm
　　　動物園　　　　　　田野　　　　　　荒野　　　　　　農場

《正確答案》　C
《解題關鍵》　本段前半部談論當務之急是恢復自然棲息地，接著可想是複製的動物能回
　　　　　　　到自然棲息地生活，即 the wild 。

Question 6-11

　　Last night more than 100 migrant workers, mostly Thais, ran amok in their dormitory at Kangshan in Kaohsiung. They set fire to houses, cars, and facilities and beat up some of the management staff. The __6__ did not stop until the police were called in. But a lot of damage had been done and it is estimated that the Kaohsiung MRT company suffered a great loss of about NT$10 million.

　　The incident occurred when several Thai workers returned to their dormitory with liquor and cigarettes, which are __7__ in the dormitory. They clashed with the management staff immediately after they were prevented from entering the dormitory. The police are now gathering evidence in order to bring the ones who led the rioting to __8__.

　　__9__, some officials are meeting with representatives of the foreign workers and listening to their demands. Among other things, they __10__ that mobile phones be allowed to be used in the dormitory, that their overtime pay be given them, and that a satellite dish be installed __11__ they can watch TV programs from Thailand.

　　昨晚，超過一百名的外籍勞工－大部分是泰勞，在高雄岡山的宿舍裡發狂。他們放火燒房子、車子和設備，而且還毆打了一些管理員。這場暴動一直到警察來了才停止。但已經造成許多傷害，估計高雄捷運公司損失大約一千萬元。

發生這事件是因為有幾名泰勞帶著酒跟香菸回到宿舍，但在宿舍是禁止菸酒。當他們被阻止進入宿舍時，他們馬上跟管理員起了衝突。警察正在收集證據，好把引起騷動的人移送法辦。

同時，有些官員正跟泰勞代表們開會，聽聽他們的要求。譬如說他們要求在宿舍可以使用行動電話，要還給他們加班費，安裝天線接受器讓他們可以觀賞泰國的電視節目。

6.　A. carnival　　　B. parade　　　C. strike　　　D. riot
　　　狂歡　　　　　　遊行　　　　　　罷工　　　　　暴動

《正確答案》　D
《解題關鍵》　放火燒房子、車子，痛打管理人員此乃暴動之行為。

7.　A. sold　　　　　B. produced　　C. banned　　　D. bought
　　　賣　　　　　　　生產　　　　　　禁止　　　　　買

《正確答案》　C
《解題關鍵》　不准許進入，因此帶酒和煙進宿舍是不容許，故答案為(C)。

8.　A. justice　　　　B. hospital　　　C. heel　　　　D. senses
　　　司法　　　　　　醫院　　　　　　腳後跟　　　　感覺

《正確答案》　A
《解題關鍵》　警方搜證當然是要將為首份子移送法辦。答案為 (A)。
《補充說明》　bring sb to hospital（帶進醫院就醫）、bring sb to heel（使某人屈服）、bring sb to his senses（使某人思考及行為合理）

9.　A. Therefore　　　B. Meanwhile　　C. Suddenly　　D. Curiously
　　　因此　　　　　　　同時　　　　　　突然地　　　　　好奇地

《正確答案》　B
《解題關鍵》　兩車同時進行用 meanwhile，一邊調查，一邊協商。

10.　A. suggest　　　　B. insist　　　　C. prefer　　　　D. demand
　　　建議　　　　　　　堅持　　　　　　更喜歡　　　　　要求

《正確答案》　D
《解題關鍵》　前句是說官員傾聽外勞的要求，因此空格要填 demand。

11.　A. in case　　　　B. so that　　　　C. since　　　　D. until
　　　惟恐　　　　　　　為了　　　　　　因為　　　　　　直到

《正確答案》　B
《解題關鍵》　架設衛星碟，目的是看電視，表目的的連接詞為 so that。

Question 12-16

　　The Department of Health has drafted a law allowing surrogacy. A childless couple will now be allowed to enlist a surrogate mother to have a baby for them. It is really good news for a couple with __12__ problems. But the law has run into criticism.

　　Some women's rights activists denounce it as male chauvinism. In their view, a woman's traditional duty is to have babies so that her husband's family __13__ will not be discontinued. To allow surrogacy is to reinforce the notion of male chauvinism. Being paid for surrogate motherhood is no different than earning money by having sex with a man. In the former case, a woman rents her womb to ensure a man's family lineage, __14__ in the latter, she rents her vagina to satisfy a man's sexual desire. On the other hand, some critics argue that surrogacy might become a __15__ enterprise. They warn that brokers might recruit poor women or foreign migrant workers to act as surrogate mothers, and surrogacy will become a multi-million-dollar business. As it happens in the sex industry, the __16__ rate will rise along with this highly profitable business.

衛生署草擬通過代理孕母法案。沒有小孩的夫婦將可以獲得代理孕母的幫助而擁有一個孩子。對有生殖問題的父母來說，這真是一個好消息。但這樣的法案卻飽受批評。

有些女權主義者譴責這是男人沙文主義。在他們的觀點中，傳統女人的責任就是生小孩，以免夫家斷了香火。允許代理孕母就是增強男性沙文主義的觀點。當代理孕母賺錢與靠著發生性關係賺錢的女人沒有什麼不同。前者女人出租她的子宮，而後者出租她的陰道來滿足男人的性渴望。另一方面，有些批評是認為代理孕母可能會商業化。他們警告中間人可能雇用貧窮的女人或外籍女工來當代理孕母，代理孕母可能變成數百萬元的生意。正如發生在性產業一樣，犯罪率可能隨著高利潤的商業行為而上升。

12. A. fertility   B. health   C. emotional   D. financial
    繁殖力   健康   感情的   財政的

《正確答案》 A
《解題關鍵》 生孩子是繁殖力問題。

13. A. business   B. reunions   C. line   D. ties
    商業   團聚   家系   關係

《正確答案》 C
《解題關鍵》 生孩子是傳宗接代的事，故與此有關的選項是 (C)。

14. A. because   B. when   C. though   D. while
      因為   當   雖然   而

《正確答案》 D
《解題關鍵》 成對比的轉折語用 while。

15. A. free   B. commercial   C. private   D. joint
      自由的   商業的   私人的   聯合的

《正確答案》 B
《解題關鍵》 後面一句說代理孕母將成數百萬的生意，與生意有關的字是 commercial。

16. A. crime   B. divorce   C. birth   D. employment
      犯罪   離婚   出生   職業

《正確答案》 A
《解題關鍵》 色情行業因有利可圖，常與犯罪有關。

Question 17-22

There has been a surge of illegal cash transfers through the Internet recently. Nine such thefts __17__ a total of 9.4 million Japanese yen have been reported from three banks since July. Online thieves infiltrate the computers of __18__ bank customers to steal their code numbers. Then they use the numbers to gain access to the customers' accounts. Another trick used by online thieves is to design a home page similar to __19__ of a bank. An unsuspecting customer enters the fake website and keys in his code number, and then suddenly the home page disappears from the __20__. The customer's code number has been appropriated by the thief. Cash from the customer's account will then be illegally transferred to the thief's account. This has happened in Taiwan as in the case of a bank customer who lost more than NT$2 million.

Countermeasures have now been taken against online thieves. Customers are advised to change their code numbers every time they make an online money transfer. The number of transactions made and the sum of money transferred are also __21__. The purpose of this is to reduce the loss should a customer's code number be stolen and an illegal money transfer made. In addition, online customers are advised to install anti-theft software. This is the best way to __22__ online theft.

最近，透過網路的不法現金移轉忽然增加。報導指出，從七月後有九起偷竊案發生在三家銀行，共損失九千四百萬日圓。線上的竊賊滲透電子銀行偷取顧客的密碼，然後使用密碼進入顧客帳戶。另一種線上竊賊使用的方法是，設計跟銀行相似的首頁。不經心的顧客進入假網址，輸入自己的密碼，然後網頁突然從螢幕消失。顧客的密碼已經被盜竊用了，現金將會從顧客帳戶中不合法地轉移到竊賊的帳戶。這樣的情況也發生在台灣，一位銀行顧客損失了兩百萬元。

現在已經採取對抗網路竊賊的對策了。每次顧客在網路上轉移錢時，會被建議改變密碼。交易的數目和總金額也受限制。這樣做的目的是萬一顧客密碼被偷，不法金錢轉移時，能減少損失。此外，也建議線上顧客灌反竊賊軟體。這是避開線上竊賊最好的方法。

17. A. involve   B. involving   C. involved   D. to involve
（選項無法翻譯。）

《正確答案》　B

《解題關鍵》　這句已經有動詞 have been reported，很明顯 involve 要改成現在分詞來修飾 thefts。

18. A. electronic   B. commercial   C. investment   D. savings

     電子的   商業的   投資   存款

《正確答案》 A

《解題關鍵》 網路交易當然是電子銀行。

19. A. one   B. this   C. that   D. those

    （選項無法翻譯。）

《正確答案》 C

《解題關鍵》 代表特定名詞用 that，這裡 that = the home page。

20. A. bank   B. account   C. customer   D. screen

     銀行   帳戶   顧客   螢幕

《正確答案》 D

《解題關鍵》 首頁是在電腦螢幕，故答案為(D)。

21. A. limited   B. recorded   C. increased   D. changed

     限制   紀錄   增加   改變

《正確答案》 A

《解題關鍵》 空格後面句子說此目的是萬一顧客錢被竊取，可減少損失，因此可推測是「限制」金額的轉出。

22. A. look into   B. engage in   C. ward off   D. cover up
     調查   從事於   防止   掩飾

《正確答案》 C

《解題關鍵》 這一段都是在討論防止存款被竊。因此答案為 (C)。

Unit 9　閱讀理解 (一)

練習一

《Answers》

1. C　　2. D

Question 1

台灣第一名模，林志玲，在大陸兩個禮拜治療嚴重胸腔傷害後，搭特別的醫療飛機返回台灣。當她為國際化妝品牌——歐蕾，拍攝廣告時，重重地從馬背上摔下來，被馬腳踐踏。這場意外造成她六根肋骨斷裂。當她一抵達國門，馬上被送去台大醫院，接受更進一步的治療。

1. 這段的主旨是 _____ 。
   A. 台灣超級名模
   B. 醫療
   C. 林志玲返回台灣
   D. 醫療飛機

Question 2

自從 2003 年來，禽流感已經殺死了數百萬的鴨和雞。禽流感也有可能傳染給人類，且在人類中擴散。迄今，有五十七人，大部分是越南或泰國人，已經因為接觸了感染的雞鴨而死亡了。甚至也有少數的例子是照顧感染病人的親戚們也被感染。

2. 這段最好的標題是 _____ 。
   A. 禽流感
   B. 家禽死亡
   C. 與家禽的身體接觸
   D. 禽流感傳染給人類

練習二

Questions 1-2

在七月，世界目睹了三起炸彈攻擊。七月七日，有三起炸彈在倫敦地鐵爆炸，奪走了五十六條人命，造成超過七百人受傷。兩個禮拜後，倫敦經歷了另一場炸彈攻擊。幸運地，沒有任何人受到傷害。七月二十四日，在埃及紅海旅遊聖地沙姆沙伊赫，一連串汽車爆炸迅速攻擊了一間豪華的飯店和一家咖啡廳，至少有八十三人死亡。正如其他的恐怖攻擊事件，伊斯蘭教的極端份子都被認為是肇事者。

1. 這段的主旨是 ＿＿＿＿＿＿＿＿＿ 。
   A. 炸彈攻擊
   B. 伊斯蘭教激進份子
   C. 倫敦地鐵的爆炸案
   D. 埃及紅海度假勝地的爆炸案

2. 這段主要的意思是 ＿＿＿＿＿＿＿＿＿ 。
   A. 伊斯蘭教激進份子再次發射攻擊
   B. 在七月有三起爆炸案
   C. 許多人在三起爆炸案中喪生
   D. 英國跟埃及被攻擊是因為他們跟美國同盟

Questions 3-4

在台北松江路，最近有六個人被診斷出癌症。這些居民責罵台灣固網公司，據說公司把它的設備放在住宅區的公寓裡。居民說電磁波的輻射從設備中散發出來，造成那六個人得到癌症。

但是專家對這個議題意見分歧。沒有任何結論證實電磁波的輻射會威脅我們的健康。即使如此，人們還是要避免曝露在電磁波下。下次當你使用微波爐、吹風機，或者手機時，一定要保持合理的距離。

3. 這段的主旨是 _____ 。

   A. 電磁波輻射

   B. 電磁波輻射對人類的影響

   C. 造成癌症的原因

   D. 電磁波的主要來源

4. 這段的主旨是 _____ 。

   A. 居民對台灣固網的控告是沒有根據的

   B. 電磁波輻射對我們的健康有害

   C. 電磁波輻射對我們的健康無害

   D. 雖然電磁波對人體是否有傷害仍然未知，但我們最好避免它

Questions 5-6

　　在台灣，有些高學歷的女人不願意結婚。即使他們最後真的結婚，他們也不願意生小孩。他們在經濟上和智能上都是獨立的。相反的，許多低學歷的男人很難找到當地女子結婚，他們通常以一定的價錢娶國外的新娘，特別是越南或印尼的女子。估計在台灣有接近三十萬的外籍新娘。此外，外籍新娘容易養育出難以適應當地文化的小孩。

　　對此結果有愈來愈多的警訊。有些人以優生學的觀點提出他們的關心，也有其他人關心接踵而來的社會問題。

5. 這段最好的標題是_____ 。

   A. 本土女人對外國女人

   B. 異族通婚

   C. 嬰兒出生的不平衡狀態

   D. 節育失敗

6. 這段的目的是 _____ 。

   A. 說明為什麼高學歷女人不結婚

   B. 說明為什麼外籍女人願意有小孩

   C. 指出外國女人生的小孩比受過良好教育的本國女人生的小孩還多

   D. 指出異族通婚已經造成很多社會問題

✏️ **練習三**

Questions 1-2

在英國，一年中差不多有三萬八千人得到肺癌，而有三萬三千人會在六個月內死亡，因為他們太晚發現肺癌。在台灣，肺癌是造成死亡的十大排名之一。最讓醫生擔心的是得到肺癌的人數每年都一直在增加。醫生說如果你突然沒有原因的變瘦，持續咳嗽超過三個月，或者發現呼吸困難，就要馬上去讓醫生做檢查。

1. 為什麼大部分得到肺癌的人會在六個月內死亡？

   A. 因為他們的病一開始並不嚴重

   B. 因為他們的病很難診斷

   C. 因為他們的病並沒有及早被診斷出來

   D. 因為他們住在英國或台灣

2. 哪一個不是肺癌的症狀？

   A. 變胖

   B. 持續咳嗽

   C. 喘不過氣

   D. 突然變瘦

Questions 3-7

台灣中央銀行再度調高 0.125% 利率。上升的原因有兩個，首先最近美國的利率一直在上漲。第二，如果台灣人保持低利率，將會使國外資金從撤離台灣。很明顯的，提高利率是一種趨勢。存錢的人將因賺到更多利息而開心，但之前那些借錢買房子的人將增加巨大的債務。

3. 這段的主旨是什麼？

    A. 利率上升的贏家

    B. 利率上升的輸家

    C. 利率上升

    D. 利率上升的原因

4. 在台灣，利率上升多少呢？

    A. 0.125%

    B. 1.025%

    C. 0.215%

    D. 1.25%

5. 哪個是利率上升的原因呢？

    A. 銀行家在過去幾年虧損了很多錢

    B. 政府想要留住外資

    C. 人們發現很難向銀行貸款

    D. 通貨膨脹提高

6. 誰會對這消息感到不開心呢？

    A. 存錢的人

    B. 政府

    C. 借錢的人

    D. 外國人

7. 作者用何種方式來詳述他的論點呢？

    A. 做比較

    B. 給原因

    C. 定義專有名詞

    D. 敘述事件

Questions 8-11

　　上個月美國國務卿萊斯走訪了亞洲，她表達了清楚的訊息。她強調布希政府的論點，自由和民主是維持和平和經濟福祉的主要支柱。在中國，她希望中國領導者能說服北韓放棄核子武器，此外，她表示反對中國以反分裂法對抗台灣，她說這對兩岸和平是一種不必要的威脅。

8.　這段的主旨是 _____ 。

　　A. 萊斯走訪亞洲

　　B. 美國跟中國的關係

　　C. 兩岸和平

　　D. 萊斯訪問亞洲的外交任務

9.　為什麼中國讓萊斯小姐不高興呢？

　　A. 因為中國幫助北韓生產核子武器

　　B. 因為中國通過反分裂法

　　C. 因為在中國的人民不能享受自由

　　D. 因為中國並不熱烈歡迎她

10.　哪些是布希先生最重要的兩個論點呢？

　　A. 自由跟民主

　　B. 法律跟秩序

　　C. 核子武器跟法律

　　D. 法律跟民主

11.　作者靠著什麼來詳述他的論點呢？

　　A. 描寫某事

　　B. 示範過程

　　C. 舉例子

　　D. 定義專有名詞

Questions 12-15

2004 年的海嘯奪走了好幾萬人的生命,而悲劇仍深刻留在我們的記憶裡。在 2006 年 12 月前,印度洋將會裝設高科技的海嘯警報器。萬一再有海嘯,這個海嘯警報器將馬上響起。若是這個警報器能及早裝設的話,2004 年的海嘯就能挽救許多生命。然而,有些人不認為這足夠保護人們免於海嘯的襲擊。住在印度洋附近海岸的漁夫,因為太窮了而過得不好,更不用說買手機。也就是說,若有警急事件,警告訊息可能無法及時通知他們。

12. 這段的主旨是 _____ 。
    A. 2004 年的海嘯造成許多傷害並奪走了許多人命
    B. 在海嘯攻擊前,警報器將會響起
    C. 光有警報器不足以保護漁夫免於受海嘯攻擊
    D. 住在印度洋海岸的漁夫大部分都很窮

13. 在何時前,印度洋將裝備高科技海嘯警報器呢?
    A. 2006 年 10 月
    B. 2006 年 12 月
    C. 2006 年 11 月
    D. 2006 年 9 月

14. 為什麼警報器不足以保護住在印度洋海岸旁的人呢?
    A. 因為警報器不能在海邊發聲響
    B. 因為在貧窮國家買不到手機
    C. 因為海岸延伸到地平線
    D. 因為人們太窮了無法接收到警報訊息

15. 作者用什麼方法詳述他的論點呢?
    A. 給理由
    B. 提供論點
    C. 做比較
    D. 舉例子

課後作業

Questions 1-2

English is one of the Indo-European languages. Although there is no proof of its existence, there seem to be strong indications that all European languages came from what is called Proto-Indo-European. The Indo-European languages include seven main branches; Latin and the romance languages (French, Spanish, etc), the Germanic languages, Sanskrit and other Indo-Iranian languages, the Slavic languages, the Baltic languages, the Celtic languages, and Greek. If you take the English word father, you will find that it is spoken as vater in German, pater in Latin, and pitr in Sanskrit. We can actually see the connections between these language groups from the similarities of words in different Indo-European languages.

英語是印歐語系的一種。雖然它的存在沒有證據，但似乎有強烈跡象指出所有歐洲語言都來自所謂的原始印歐語系。印歐語系包括七個主要的分支；拉丁語和羅馬尼亞語（法語、西班牙語等等）、日耳曼語、梵語，還有其他印度伊朗語，和希臘語。如果你以英語的「father」為例，會發現在日耳曼語是「vater」，拉丁語是「pater」，還有梵語是「pitr」。事實上我們可以從不同印歐語系中的相同字詞看到這些語言族群間的關聯。

1. This passage is about _____.

   這段是有關 _____ 。

   A. Indo-European languages. 印歐語系

   B. English 英語

   C. European languages 歐洲語言

   D. Latin and its relation with European languages 拉丁語跟歐洲語言的關係

《正確答案》 A

《解題關鍵》 第二行指出所有歐洲語言都來自印歐語系。接著說印歐語系包括哪些語言，很明顯主旨是印歐語。

2. English is one of the Indo-European languages because _____.

英語是印歐語系的一種是因為 _____ 。

A. the English were once ruled by the Roman empire

英國人曾被羅馬帝國統治過

B. the English look like Indo-European people

英國人長得像印歐語系的人

C. Many English words are similar to those in the other Indo-European languages

許多英文字詞跟印歐語系的字詞相似

D. English sounds like the other Indo-European languages

英語聽起來像其他的印歐語系

《正確答案》 C

《解題關鍵》 文中提到英文 father 與其他印歐語系的字很像，因此答案為 (C)。

Questions 3-5

A huge military exercise was conducted at Chin Chuan Kang Airbase in Taichung county. The exercise was designed to demonstrate Taiwan's ability to repel enemies should they launch a surprise airborne attack on a major airbase. The exercise involved more than 2,000 servicemen. The most highly sophisticated weapons were employed in this exercise, including F-16 fighters, CH-47 Chinook transport helicopters, CM-11 tanks, V150 armored personnel carriers, and Avenger surface-to-air missiles. The drill came at a time when China's military buildup has begun to cause alarm all over the world. Seven hundred missiles have been aimed at Taiwan so far, and one senior Chinese general even threatened to destroy hundreds of American cities with nuclear missiles if America should dare come to Taiwan's rescue.

　　一場大規模的軍事演習，在台中縣清泉崗空軍基地舉行。這場演習是展示萬一敵人對主要空軍基地做空中的突擊，台灣有擊退敵人的能力。這場演習包含了兩千多名軍人，使用了最尖端的武器，包括 F-16 戰鬥機、CH-47 契努克運輸直升機、CM-11 坦克車、V150 裝甲人員運兵車，還有復仇者地對空飛彈。這次演習選在中國軍力增加、開始造成世界緊張時操演。至今已經有七百顆飛彈瞄準台灣，一名中國高階將領甚至威脅如果美國敢來營救台灣的話，中國將用核子武器摧毀美國數百個城市。

3. The military exercise was conducted _____.

　這個軍事演習在何種情況下操演？

A. when a lot of people in Taiwan were still not awake to China's threat
台灣的許多人還沒有意識到中國威脅的時候。

B. after Taiwan had acquired a lot of sophisticated weapons
在台灣獲得許多尖端武器後。

C. at the urging of an alarmed America
在美國的鼓勵下。

D. with the rise of an aggressive China
富有侵略性的中國崛起時。

《正確答案》 D
《解題關鍵》 本文倒數第四行，說明這次演習是因中國軍事的擴充。

4. The enemy soldiers were supposed to _____ during this exercise.

　在這場演習中，假想敵人 _____。

A. wade onto the beach 涉過海邊
B. drop from their planes 從飛機空投
C. hide in the mountains 躲在山區
D. cross the border 越過邊界

《正確答案》 B
《解題關鍵》 第三行的 airborne 指著就是由空中攻擊。

5.　The exercise was unique for several reasons. Which of the following is
　　NOT one of them?

　　有幾種原因顯示這場演習是獨特的。下列哪一個不是其中之一？

　　A. A lot of soldiers were involved.　包含許多士兵

　　B. Several advanced weapons were used.　使用尖端武器

　　C. American soldiers also took part.　美國士兵也參加

　　D. Taiwan is under threat.　台灣被威脅

《正確答案》　C

《解題關鍵》　文中沒有提到美國大兵也參加。

Unit 10　閱讀測驗 (二)

✏️ 練習四

Questions 1-5

1.　這幾天瑪莉都帶著幸福的笑臉，她喜歡炫燿她手上的戒指。可以推想瑪莉已經

　　＿＿＿＿＿＿＿＿＿＿。

　　A. 買了假戒指

　　B. 弄丟了戒指

　　C. 已經訂婚

　　D. 已經離婚

2.　一位僧侶走在通往一間小屋的小路上。在月光下，他推開門，走進小屋。可以推測

　　＿＿＿＿＿＿＿＿＿＿。

　　A. 僧侶知道小屋裡有人

　　B. 僧侶知道小屋裡沒有人

　　C. 門鎖著

　　D. 門開著

3.　麥克看見天花板漏水，他拿起電話，撥了號碼。可以推想 ＿＿＿＿＿＿＿＿＿＿。

　　A. 麥克打電話給住在樓上的人，告訴他他的浴缸漏水了。

　　B. 麥克打電話給警察，抱怨他的鄰居製造噪音。

　　C. 麥克打電話給建築工人，告訴他他的屋頂快要坍塌了。

　　D. 麥克打給１１９，說他家著火了。

4. 沒有貴重的物品被偷，家具都在原先的地方，但警官發現屍體的皮膚已經變成粉紅色了。可以推想 ＿＿＿＿＿＿＿＿ 。

   A. 那個人死於一氧化碳中毒
   B. 那個人死於食物中毒
   C. 那個人死於鉛中毒
   D. 那個人已經被謀殺了

5. 當露露聞到燒焦味時，她從床上跳下來。她急忙跑到廚房。可以推想 ＿＿＿＿＿＿ 。

   A. 廚房正在煮東西
   B. 廚房瓦斯漏氣
   C. 廚房的水槽漏水
   D. 廚房有東西爆炸

Questions 6-8

露露，二十三歲的女生，向警察報案說她被網路上認識的網友強暴了。她說因為他一直讚美她，還說他很愛她，所以她答應跟他見面。然而，第一次約會，他就強迫她跟他到汽車旅館，強暴了她。她向警察展示她身上的淤青和受傷處，她告訴警察說那男的自稱名叫小強。在他的臉頰上有一道疤痕，留著又長又黑的捲髮。就像其他有相同經歷的女人一樣，露露單身且害羞。除了工作外，她沒有別的嗜好；更糟的是，她很少有機會認識異性。

6. 這段指出當小強企圖強暴露露時，她 ＿＿＿＿＿＿＿＿ 。

   A. 反抗
   B. 試著逃走
   C. 跟他發生關係
   D. 趕走他

7. 從這篇文章可推測很多女人 ＿＿＿＿＿＿＿＿ 。

   A. 透過網路建立永久的友情
   B. 從未進過汽車旅館
   C. 討厭在汽車旅館裡發生性關係
   D. 孤單且需要愛情

8. 這段最好的標題是 ＿＿＿＿＿＿＿＿＿ 。

A. 線上約會

B. 約會強暴

C. 犯罪

D. 強暴受害者

Questions 9-11

讓太空人的家人和世界各地的人們鬆了一口氣的是，2005 年 8 月 9 日，發現號太空梭安全返回地球。美國國家航空太空總署立即慶祝。自從上次哥倫比亞號撞毀後，這是第一次成功著陸的太空梭。但在發現號成功發射後，專家發現在離地升空時，有些小碎片從外部的燃料槽掉下來。幸運地，這些碎片並沒有撞到太空梭的骨架，沒有危害到全體機員。在 2003 年哥倫比亞太空梭發射時，也發生相同的意外。一塊像箱子大小的碎片擊中了太空梭機翼，形成了大洞。超高溫氣體跑進太空梭機體，然後太空梭爆炸，所有在太空梭上的七名太空人都喪生了。但這次專家不再冒險，他們延期發射時間，直到確定每件事情都做好了才發射。

9. 這篇文章暗示了 ＿＿＿＿＿＿＿＿＿ 。

A. 從 2003 年的意外事件可知碎片是非常有爆炸力的

B. 在 2003 年的意外後，專家更小心掉落碎片的危險性

C. 碎片不應該被留在燃料槽裡

D. 碎片應該避免跑進太空梭的主體中

10. 可以推測太空梭的結構是 ＿＿＿＿＿＿＿＿＿ 。

A. 可燃的

B. 易碎的

C. 密閉的

D. 無空氣的

11. 發現號太空梭 ＿＿＿＿＿＿＿＿＿ ，雖然發現一些碎片從外部的燃料槽掉下來。

A. 照預期發射

B. 在火星降落

C. 馬上被破壞

D. 不被允許離開地面

Questions 12-14

在中國四川省，神祕的疾病至今已經造成二十七位農夫死亡。感染這疾病的人數已經到達一百三十一人。這種感染是透過接觸死豬而傳播的。這疾病的死亡率比起同樣來自中國的 SARS 還要高百分之二十。這種疾病的特徵包括發高燒、噁心跟嘔吐。衛生官員說這種疾病可能是來自一種變形的鏈球菌，常在豬身上發現。這種變形菌很容易造成死亡，旅客最好不要去四川省跟它附近的區域，從四川來的豬肉應該被禁止。

12. 這段的主旨是 _____ 。

    A. 一種新的疾病再次在中國爆發

    B. 死豬造成所有疾病

    C. 從中國散播的疾病總是致命的

    D. 很難了解致命的疾病

13. 如果有人感染這種疾病，_____ 。

    A. 他將會頭痛且感到疲累

    B. 他的體溫會升高，而他的臉會變蒼白

    C. 他會嘔吐且體溫會突然升高

    D. 他會感到暈眩而昏倒

14. 這段暗示 _____ 。

    A. 我們最好不要吃豬肉

    B. 許多神祕的疾病都先在中國發生

    C. 那些感染疾病的人，最後都會死掉

    D. 去四川省旅行的旅客一定要禁止回國

✏️ **練習五**

Questions 1-3

　　桃園龍潭鎮的蜂農羅信力藉著在身上放十二隻女王蜂，來吸引蜜蜂，成功聚集了五十萬隻蜜蜂在他身上爬行，這讓他看起來好像穿了一件蜂衣。這件蜂衣有五公分厚，重量超過三十公斤。羅先生說當蜜蜂拍動他們的翅膀時，就好像電風扇一樣。然而，他不能喊叫、打呵欠或者打噴嚏，因為蜜蜂可能發動大規模攻擊。

1.　這段最好的標題是 _____ 。
　　A. 女王蜂
　　B. 電風扇
　　C. 一件蜂衣
　　D. 大進擊

2.　這段使用了什麼修辭技巧呢？
　　A. 明喻
　　B. 誇張
　　C. 隱喻
　　D. 反諷

3.　這段暗示 _____ 。
　　A. 農夫使用女王蜂保護自己免於其他蜜蜂攻擊
　　B. 農夫站著不動也不說話
　　C. 女王蜂受到普通蜜蜂的影響
　　D. 農夫使用電風扇幫助蜜蜂揮動翅膀

Questions 4-8

日本科學家已經發展出女性機器人，是至今發展最像人類長相的機器人。機器人取名為 Repliee Q1，她的上身裝了四十一部促動器。她的皮膚是以富彈性的矽樹脂取代堅硬的塑膠物料，所以她的外表跟觸感都很像真人。因為在她的身上十一處裝了高敏感皮膚感應器，她能夠對不同碰觸做不同反應。她可以眨眼，轉動和揮手。她甚至看起來會呼吸的樣子。設計 Repliee Q1 的石黑浩教授，發現人們與她共處時，會忘記她是機器人。他們跟她相處就好像她是真的女人一樣。

4. 這段使用了什麼修辭技巧呢？

    A. 雙關語

    B. 象徵

    C. 暗示

    D. 擬人化

5. 這個新機器人獨特的地方是，＿＿＿＿＿＿＿＿＿＿＿。

    A. 他看起來像真人

    B. 他可以像人類一樣說話

    C. 它使得人們變健忘

    D. 可以摸它

6. 這個機器人看起來像真的，是因為用 ＿＿＿＿＿＿＿＿＿ 做成的。

    A. 堅硬的塑膠

    B. 矽樹脂

    C. 人工皮膚

    D. 感應器

7. 這個機器人靠著 ＿＿＿＿＿＿＿＿＿ 來回應。

    A. 矽樹脂

    B. 堅硬的塑膠

    C. 皮膚感應器

    D. 人

8. 這段的目的是 _____ 。

    A. 顯示人們如何跟新機器人互動

    B. 解釋新機器人為什麼看起來跟動作都像女人

    C. 介紹發明新機器人的人

    D. 解釋為什麼人容易健忘

課後作業

Questions 1-3

A new law, if passed, will require people aged 14 and above to be finger-printed when applying for national identification cards. The fingerprinting poli-cy has triggered a heated debate. Human rights activists have expressed concern that the fingerprint files might be leaked if the government fails to provide proper protection for the data. On the other hand, government offi-cials argue that the new policy will help track down criminals and curb crime. One senior official says that an efficient monitoring system will be established to prevent the fingerprint files from being leaked. Opinion polls show that nearly 80% of the people in Taiwan support the fingerprinting policy. They seem to care more about crime than their right to privacy.

若新的法律通過，所有年滿十四歲以上的國民在申請國民身分證時，規定要印指紋。印指紋的政策已經激起熱烈的爭論。人權激進份子表示關心，如果政府沒有對資料提供適當的保護，那指紋檔案將被洩露。另一方面，政府官員認為新政策有助於追捕罪犯、抑制犯罪。一位高階官員說：將建立一套有效的監控系統以避免指紋檔案外洩。民調顯示在台灣差不多有百分之八十的人支持指紋政策。比起自己的隱私權，他們似乎更在乎犯罪。

1. The best title for this passage is "_____".

   這段最好的標題是 _____ 。

   A. Fingerprinting—a controversial policy 指紋——一個有爭議的政策
   B. Fingerprinting—the best way to fight crime 指紋——打擊罪犯最好的方法
   C. Fingerprinting—an invasion of privacy 指紋——侵略隱私權
   D. Fingerprinting—a lost cause 指紋——敗局已定的事

《正確答案》　A
《解題關鍵》　本文敘述對按指紋政策正反的議論，因此較適當答案為(A)。

2. A _____ system can provide proper protection for the fingerprint files.

一套 _____ 系統能保護指紋檔案。

A. legal 合法的

B. computer 電腦

C. criminal justice 犯罪的司法

D. monitoring 監控

《正確答案》 D

《解題關鍵》 倒數第四行 monitoring system。

3. It can be inferred that _____.

此篇文章可以推測 _____。

A. common people are not aware of the danger of leaking fingerprint files
一般人沒有意識到洩露指紋的危險

B. human rights activists do not seem to understand common people's concerns
人權激進份子似乎不了解一般民眾所關心的事

C. people aged 14 and above tend to commit crimes
滿十四歲的人容易犯罪

D. human rights activists want national identification cards abolished
人權激進份子想要廢除國民身分證

《正確答案》 B

《解題關鍵》 本文最後提到一個民調，有百分之八十的人支持按指紋政策，他們關心犯罪超過隱私。由此可知人權激進份子不知人民需要。

Questions 4-7

A historic bridge in Nantou's Guoxin Township drew the premier's attention recently. The Glutinous Rice Bridge took its name from the fact that it was built from glutinous rice, lime and sugar rather than from steel and concrete. It was completed in 1940 and has gone through all kinds of natural disasters. The bridge is not only a scenic attraction but also a historic site in Nantou. It remained intact even after the 921 earthquake, the strongest one in Taiwan for a hundred years, which wreaked great havoc in Nantou. But the bridge has been severely damaged because of last summer's Tropical Storm Mindulle which washed parts of it away. Premier Xie promised to help the township preserve the famous bridge when he paid a visit to the site. The premier said, "we must try our best to recover it, renovate it and restore it."

在南投國姓鄉，最近一座歷史悠久的橋吸引了行政院長的注意。糯米橋名字的由來是因為當時使用了糯米、石灰、糖來建造，而不是用鋼鐵和水泥。它在 1940 年完成，經歷各種自然災害，它不僅是風景名勝而且還是南投歷史古蹟。在台灣百年來，最強烈的九二一地震對南投造成大浩劫後，這座橋仍然毫無損傷。但是去年夏天敏督利颱風已經嚴重毀損它，沖走部分的橋面。當行政院長謝長廷視察糯米橋時，他承諾要幫助鄉鎮保存這有名的橋。他說我們要盡力恢復、修補、保存這座橋。

4. The Glutinous Rice Bridge is special for several reasons. Which of the following is NOT one of them?

    下列哪一個不是糯米橋獨特的原因？

    A. Its building materials are quite different from the ones commonly used now.

    它的建構材料相當不同於現在普遍使用的。

    B. It has a long history.

    它的歷史悠久。

    C. It has withstood many natural disasters.

    它抵擋過許多自然災害。

    D. It is the first bridge that Premier Xie has ever visited.

    它是行政院長謝長廷第一座拜訪的橋。

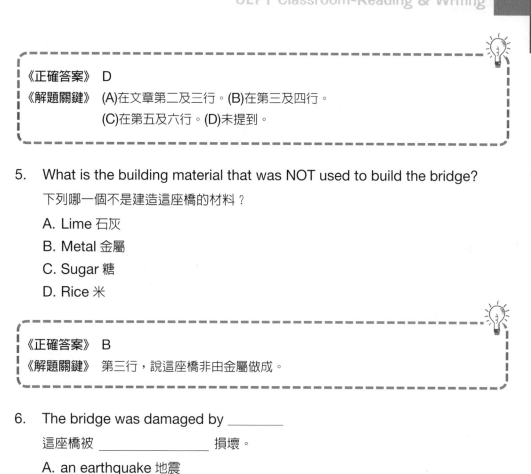

《正確答案》 D

《解題關鍵》 (A)在文章第二及三行。(B)在第三及四行。
(C)在第五及六行。(D)未提到。

5. What is the building material that was NOT used to build the bridge?

下列哪一個不是建造這座橋的材料？

A. Lime 石灰

B. Metal 金屬

C. Sugar 糖

D. Rice 米

《正確答案》 B

《解題關鍵》 第三行，說這座橋非由金屬做成。

6. The bridge was damaged by _____

這座橋被 _____ 損壞。

A. an earthquake 地震

B. a bomb 炸彈

C. a storm 暴風雨

D. a fire 火災

《正確答案》 C

《解題關鍵》 第七行說到這座橋是被熱帶暴風雨摧毀。

7. The premier was quoted as saying, "We must try our best to recover it, renovate it and restore it." In the quotation, the rhetorical devices he used are _____.

引用行政院長說的：「我們要盡力恢復、修補、保存這座橋。」這句話運用了什麼修辭技巧呢？

A. alliteration and climactic sentence order 頭韻跟漸進法
B. rhyme and anticlimactic sentence order 押韻跟漸降法
C. repetition and climactic sentence order 重複跟漸進法
D. onomatopoeia and anticlimactic sentence order 擬聲跟漸降法

《正確答案》　A
《解題關鍵》　recover, renovate 和 restore 都是 re-開頭，所以是頭韻(alliteration)，
　　　　　　　recover, renovate 及 restore 為漸進式。

Questions 8-11

[1]A recent survey found that online teens are increasingly tech-savvy. [2]Nearly nine out of ten Taiwan teenagers say they use the Internet. [3]Eighty-nine percent of them use the Internet to send or read e-mail. Eighty-one percent play online games. [4]Eighty percent visit websites about TV, music or sports stars. [5]Seventy-six percent get news online. [6]And 43 percent make purchases online. [7]Another finding is that teenagers very much like to send text messages to each other. [8]Generally speaking, they use the Internet for fun and chatting rather than for academic study. 9It comes as no surprise that many teenagers fail in school. 10The reason is that they spend a lot of time online.

　　最近的調查發現線上的青少年逐漸變成科技通。在台灣，十個中差不多有九個青少年說他們使用網路。他們之中的百分之八十九會使用網路寄信或看信，百分之八十一的人會玩網路遊戲，百分之八十的人會看電視、音樂或運動明星的網站，百分之七十六的人從網路上看新聞，還有百分之四十三的人會上網購物。另外還發現青少年很喜歡彼此傳簡訊。一般來說，他們使用電腦是為了樂趣跟聊天，而不是學術研究。許多青少年在學校成績表現不好，也不令人吃驚。因為他們花了許多時間在網路上。

8. The author uses _____ to elaborate his main idea.

這個作者用了 _____ 說明他主旨。

A. experiments 試驗

B. statistics 統計

C. personal experiences 個人經驗

D. arguments 爭論

《正確答案》 B

《解題關鍵》 整篇都是統計數字，故答案為 (B)。

9. The passage suggests that teenagers use the Internet primarily for _____.

這段指出青少年使用網路主要是為了 _____ 。

A. recreation and communication 休閒跟溝通

B. studying and chatting 研究跟聊天

C. shopping and getting news 買東西跟得到消息

D. crime and transactions 犯罪跟交易

《正確答案》 A

《解題關鍵》 本文倒數第三行，說青少年用網路主要是在 fun and chatting。

10. The topic sentence of this passage is sentence _____ :

這段的主題句是在第 _____ 句。

A. 8

B. 9

C. 2

D. 1

《正確答案》　D

《解題關鍵》　第一句說青少年是科技通，接著用不同的統計數字支持他們很通網路，這些統計數字是來支持第一句的，故第一句為主題句。

11. The word "savvy" may mean "＿＿＿＿".

"Savvy"可能意思是 ＿＿＿＿＿＿＿＿ 。

A. very much afraid 非常害怕

B. very much stupid. 非常愚蠢

C. knowing a lot 知道很多

D. talking a lot 說很多

《正確答案》　C

《解題關鍵》　第二句提到有很多青少年在使用網路，所以可以推知 savvy 的意思是指青少年對科技非常了解，故答案為 (C)。

Questions 12-14

A sports scandal erupted again recently. Ten people-including Chen Chao-ying, a catcher for the La New Bears, and Tsai Sheng-feng, coach of the Macoto Cobras' farm team—have been nabbed so far for involvement in a multi million-dollar professional baseball game-fixing scandal. A criminal group paid bribes, provided sexual services, and even threatened players to rig the games. In fact, illegal gambling on baseball games is not new in Taiwan. Eight years ago, the same kind of game-fixing landed several base-ball players in jail. This kind of scandal has tarnished the image of professional baseball, and the latest scandal has further undermined its credibility.

最近運動醜聞再度爆發。包括 La New 熊隊捕手陳昭穎和誠泰 Cobras 二軍教練蔡生豐在內的十人，因牽扯幾百萬元職業棒球簽賭案，已經被逮捕。犯罪集團收買賄賂，提供性服務甚至威脅球員，來操縱比賽。事實上，在台灣不法的職棒簽賭已不是第一次。八年前，同樣的操作比賽使得許多棒球選手坐牢。這樣的醜聞已經玷污了職棒形象，最近的醜聞更進一步破壞了職棒的信譽。

12. It can be inferred that illegal gambling based on the results of baseball games is _____ in Taiwan.

可以推測出在台灣不法的職棒賭博是 _____。

A. rare 很少的

B. profitable 可賺錢的

C. not serious 不嚴重的

D. hard to stop 難以阻止

《正確答案》 B

《解題關鍵》 第三行 multi-million-dollar 與 profitable 有關。

13. The criminal group used several ways to persuade baseball players to cheat. Which of the following is NOT one of them?

犯罪集團使用了許多方法來說服球員做假，下列哪一個不是其中之一的方法？

A. Women 女人

B. Payoffs 賄賂

C. Bullying 恃強欺弱

D. Promotion 推銷

《正確答案》 D

《解題關鍵》 女色、賄賂、恃強欺弱，在文章第四及五行提到。

14. As a result of the rigging, spectators might _____.

    操縱比賽可能導致觀眾 _____ 。

    A. lose interest in baseball

       對棒球失去興趣

    B. be forced to pay higher prices for tickets to professional baseball Games

       被迫以更高的價格來買職棒比賽的票

    C. doubt the outcome of any professional baseball game

       懷疑任何職棒比賽的結果

    D. be put at risk

       冒險

《正確答案》 C

《解題關鍵》 倒數第二行，說職業棒球運動的醜聞使它的公信力受影響，即 (C) 的意思。

Unit 11 中譯英 (一)－基本句型

練習一

1. Grapes are sour.
2. A thing of beauty is a joy forever.
3. The fact is that smoking is the leading cause of lung caner.
4. Mr. Wu became a hero.

練習二

1. I always walk to school every day.
2. Jane can sing beautifully.
3. This computer costs twenty thousand dollars.
4. The box weighs 3 kilograms and measures 40cm x 30 cm.
5. It doesn't matter what you wear.

練習三

1. Many animals may have become extinct.
2. Sam remained silent.
3. Coffee tastes bitter.
4. Mr. White died young.
5. Our products are proving highly profitable.

練習四

1. I haven't decided where to go.
2. Seeing that man kick my dog angered me.
3. A mouse will eat things that people won't eat.
4. Jack denied cheating on the test.

5. Sam promised to do his best.

6. The old cow will never admit that she was once a stupid calf.

7. I forgot to turn off the lights.

8. I don't know who took the pen on the desk.

✎ 練習五

1. She blew me a kiss.

2. Can you get me something to eat?

3. I ordered myself a ham sandwich.

4. Julia made herself a sweater.

5. I wished them happiness.

✎ 練習六

1. Jane dyed her hair red.

2. My mother cut my hair short.

3. The judge declared Jack the winner.

4. She told me that she would leave soon.

5. I will show her how to operate the washing machine.

   I will show her how she should operate the washing machine.

6. He asked me to go mountain climbing with him.

7. His courage makes us respect him.

8. I looked at the fruit hanging from the trees.

9. George had his nose broken in a fight.

10. I am sorry to have kept you waiting so long.

✎ 練習七

1. His friends regard him as a fool.

2. Exercise can protect us from heart disease.

3. I mistook her for her sister.

課後作業

1. 我喜歡搭公車上班。搭公車省下我很多錢，我一天只花六十元台幣。相對照下，一部車子至少要價五十萬台幣，還不括每年一萬台幣的稅金和保險費。除此之外，修理維護的費用非常高、油價又一直漲。更糟的；有時還必須繳超速或違規停車的罰金。

《參考答案》 I like to go to my office by bus. It saves me a lot of money to take the bus. I spend only NT$60 a day. By contrast, a car costs at least half a million dollars, not including NT$10,000 in taxes and insurance per year. Besides, the cost of repairs and maintenance is very high. Oil prices are rising. To make matters worse, fines for speeding or illegal parking must be paid.

2. 飛機使我們能環球旅行。它們既快速又安全。即使如此，仍然有些人害怕坐飛機旅行。其中一個理由是他們怕在撞機中喪命。而且，撞機時極少人能倖存；最糟的是，受害者都是橫死。

《參考答案》 Airplanes enable us to travel all over the world. They are both fast and safe. Even so, there are still some people who are afraid to travel by plane. One of the reasons for this is that they are afraid they might die in a plane crash. Besides, few people would be able to survive a plane crash. Worst of all, the victims would die a violent death.

Unit 12 中譯英 (二)－複雜句和複合句

✎ 練習一

1. Most comets are difficult to see because they are far away and faint.
2. Since we cannot get what we like, let's enjoy what we can get.
3. Island countries like Taiwan and Japan lack oil, so they have to import oil from abroad.
4. I was so annoyed with him that I found it hard to control my temper.
5. That woman is such a liar that you can't believe what she says.

✎ 練習二

1. I wore a coat lest I should catch a cold.
2. He worked hard so that his family could live in comfort.

✎ 練習三

1. He is as poor as a church mouse.
2. As man lives, so will he die.
3. When in Rome do as the Romans do.
4. The sweater looks as if (或 as though) it came from the store across the street.
5. Reading is to the mind what/as exercise is to the body.
6. As expected, John won the race.

✎ 練習四

1. Though the house is small, it is warm and cozy.
2. I still look fat, even though I've been on a diet for some time.

3. Attempted suicides have stayed flat in recent years, whereas deaths from suicides have soared.

4. She will buy that dress however much it costs.

✎ 練習五

1. Not only did the Filipinos bring down Marcos, they also held the fairest presidential election in their country.

2. Try to eat less and get more exercise

✎ 練習六

1. Either you go to the movies with me, or you stay at home.

2. Give me liberty or give me death.

✎ 練習七

1. If I drink too much tea or coffee, I will have trouble getting to sleep.

2. Unless some extra money is found, the library will close.

3. You can go out to play so long as you finish your homework.

✎ 練習八

1. Don't count your chickens before they are hatched.

2. Continue in this direction until you see a Seven-Eleven.

3. When I was crossing the street, I met an old friend of mine.

4. Once you are deprived of freedom, you will realize its value.

5. Whenever I hear that tune, it makes me think of my school days.

6. No sooner had Mr. Wang begun speaking than he was again interrupted by someone in the audience.

   Scarcely had Mr. Wang begun speaking when he was again interrupted by someone in the audience.

7. While Sam was asleep on the sofa, I snuck in and took a picture of him.

8. Mary got pregnant shortly after she got married.

9. We have been friends (ever) since we were at university together.

✎ **練習九**

1. Put the medicine where children cannot reach them.

2. Wherever you go, you should treat people well.

課後作業

1. 雖然學習英文的年齡已經降至九歲，我國學生的英文能力似乎沒有改善。大學入學考試的平均分數最近幾年已經下降。十六萬即將進入大學的學生中有一半得不到四十分。而且，根據最近的托福成績報告，我們在亞洲排行十四。這顯示較早學英文不保證英文能力水準會較高。

《參考答案》 Even though the age for learning English has been lowered to nine, English proficiency among our country's students does not seem to have improved. Average English test scores on university entrance examinations have fallen in recent years. Half of the 160,000 college-bound students got less than 40 points. Moreover, according to the latest reports on TOFEL scores, we are ranked the fourteenth in Asia. This shows that learning English earlier does not guarantee a higher level of proficiency in English.

2. 大量的金錢花在教育上，但是卻找不到什麼令人滿意的結果，其中主要原因之一是大部分的錢浪費在不必要的設備上。現在幾乎每間教室都備有電腦，老師一下課學生就衝到電腦前打電玩而不是收集資料。同樣的，一間語言實驗室花費納稅人一百多萬元。不幸的是，昂貴的冷氣實驗室卻成為學生睡覺最舒適的房間。

《參考答案》 A large amount of money has been spent on education, but there have been few satisfactory results. One of the main reasons for this is that most of the money has been wasted on unnecessary equipment. Now nearly every classroom has been equipped with computers. No sooner does the teacher dismiss class than students rush to the computers to play video games instead of gathering information. Similarly, a language lab can cost taxpayers more than one million dollars. Unfortunately, these expensive air-conditioned labs have become comfortable rooms for students to sleep in.

3. 九月一日一超級颱風襲擊台灣，強烈的風和雨造成嚴重損害，電線被切斷而樹木被連根拔起。有幾個鄉鎮淹水，桃園居民再次遭受缺水之苦。更糟的是，有五十九人受傷，三人死亡。就像今年稍早的颱風一樣，泰林（Talim）摧毀了蔬菜水果。結果，蔬菜價格暴漲。一公斤蔥（chives）台幣要價三百塊錢。

《參考答案》 A super typhoon hit Taiwan on September 1. Its strong winds and heavy rain caused severe damage. Power lines were cut and trees were uprooted. Several towns were flooded. Residents in Taoyuan suffered another water shortage. Worse still, fifty-nine people were injured and three were killed. Like earlier typhoons this year, Talim destroyed vegetables and fruits. As a result, vegetable prices went up sharply. Chives cost NT$300 per kilogram.

Unit 13 英文作文 (一)─段落

✏️ 練習一

《Answers》--

1. The Internet has become indispensable to our lives.
2. also, most importantly, in short
3. in short
4. by giving examples
5. The concluding sentence is inappropriate because it deviates from the main idea. The main idea is concerned with the indispensability of the Internet, not with its profitability. It should be rewritten as "In short, the Internet has ushered in a new era in which communication barriers have crumbled and news circulates as it is happening."

　　網路已經變成生活中不可少的了。我們可以透過網路預約房間或座位。我們也可以線上購物。藉著電子郵件來傳送訊息，既便宜又快速。更重要的是，我們可以按一下滑鼠，就得到我們需要的資訊。簡言之，dot.com 事業已經變成數十億元的生意。

1. 在這段的主題句下畫線。

2. 把轉折詞和片語圈起來。

3. 哪一個轉折詞或片語暗示在它之後的句子是結論句？

4. 作者如何支持他的主旨？藉著舉例子、做比較、解釋因果關係、定義專有名詞，描述過程，或者敘述事件呢？

5. 你覺得結語是適當的嗎？如果不是，重寫它。

✏️ 練習二

《Answers》---

1. Men and women working together can have several advantages.
2. first, besides, also, moreover, finally
3. (1) People become more interested in work.　(2) A good feeling will develop.
   (3) People will pay more attention to their looks. (4) They will help each other.
   (5)　They may fall in love and get married.
4. He provides a logical explanation for each of his supporting details.
5. This can show that they are well-heeled and well behaved.

　　讓男人跟女人一起工作有好幾個好處。首先，男人將變得對工作更有興趣，為了吸引女同事的注意，男人將在辦公室待更久的時間。畢竟，努力工作總被認為是一種美德。很少女人喜歡懶惰和不負責任的男人。此外，男女將發展好感。據說，動物之間的性渴望有助於創造溫暖和友善的氣氛，男人急著取悅女人，而女人似乎對男人更和藹。還有，男人跟女人也會更注意自己的外貌。男人想要女人認為他們是紳士，所以會定期刮鬍子、剪頭髮，還有穿上他們最棒的衣服。同樣地，女人相信贏得男人心的最好方法是擁有好看的外表。因此，他們總是穿得很漂亮，而且化妝。這可以顯示他們是富有的，且行為端莊的。此外，男人跟女人更會彼此幫助。男人也許會吝於提供幫助給男同事，但他們會立即跑去幫助女同事。他們遵循著異性相吸的自然法則。最後，男人跟女人可能會談戀愛而結婚。這不僅帶給新婚夫婦幸福，也帶給公司快樂。夫婦將一起和諧地工作。

1. 找出主題句，並在下面畫線。

2. 圈出任何指出重要支持細節的轉折語或片語。

3. 寫下重要的細節。

4. 作者如何闡明每一個重要細節？他使用統計資料嗎？他做實驗嗎？或者他使用任何其他事物呢？

5. 上面文章有個句子是文不對題的。找出來並刪掉它。

✏️ **練習三**

《Answer》 --

> B

　　選擇一本好的字典需要敏銳的判斷。首先，你應該考慮出版公司，看看出版日期。這間公司在出版字典方面是不是很專門？字典是不是定期更新？然後，閱讀它的說明。這本字典是不是有獨特的特點呢？這本字典有多少詞語呢？此外，你應該翻一下字典。它是不是包含例句呢？有沒有用法註解呢？最後但並非最不重要的是，你應該考慮這本字典是否符合你的需求？如果你想用來閱讀《經濟學人》，那你應該擁有一本大學程度的字典，裡面包含了超過十六萬的詞語。另一方面，如果你需要一本幫助你寫作的字典，那你應該選擇給非母語人士使用的進階學習字典。

A. 分析一個人的需求是選擇字典最有效的方法

B. 挑選一本好字典需要準確的判斷

C. 有好幾種方法能分辨好的或壞的參考書

✏️ **練習四**

a. 人們已經變成大眾傳播媒體的奴隸。

b. 我發現跟女人相處是令人沮喪的。

c. 狄更斯曾說過：「這是一個智慧的年代，也是一個愚蠢的年代。」

d. 在某些方面，自然的小路就像高速公路。

e. 一隻章魚就像一顆大頭帶著八隻可怕的長手臂。

✏️ **練習五**

《Answers》 --

> 1. it is essential that the government take drastic steps to improve the traffic situation.
> 2. The researcher attributes the gap to upbringing.

1. 因為交通狀況正在惡化，政府必須採取嚴厲手段來改善交通情況。有些人建議政府向車主課稅，以嚇阻人們開車，其他人要求蓋更多停車場，還有些人認為促進大眾交通工具更重要。

2. 根據最近的資料，女人大概比男人多活八年。研究者把這個差距歸因於教養。男人的刻板印象是，大膽、具有冒險心、有男子氣概；而女人是小心的、安靜的、吸引人的。因此，男人冒險去維護他們的男子氣概。相反地，女人容易保持脆弱來贏得照顧和情愛。從小孩開始，男人已經被訓練要忍受困苦，導致他們曝露在危險和不確定的因素中。難怪，男人註定要遭受身心上的壓力。更糟的是，他們已經被灌輸利他主義，為了他們的家庭福利，他們應該做些犧牲。

✎ **練習六**

《Answer》---

> For one thing, he often volunteers to clean up the neighborhood. Also, as a doctor, he has set up an emergency center to help those who have accidents. Finally, he likes to read books about law, so his neighbors often seek his advice.

一位熱心公益的鄰居

　　李先生，是一位對法律很感興趣的醫生，住在我的隔壁。他真的是一位熱心公益的鄰居。首先，他時常自願打掃社區。還有，身為醫生，他設立了緊急中心來幫助發生意外的人。最後，他喜歡閱讀法律，所以他的鄰居常常尋求他的忠告。

課後作業

《參考答案》 Advertisers use several methods to persuade us into buying their products. The most popular way is to play on our fear of being unhealthy or unattractive. A drug advertiser continually reminds us that a large proportion of the population in Taiwan has contracted hepatitis and that hepatitis can develop into liver cancer, which is one of the leading causes of death in Taiwan. Similarly, a cosmetics advertiser will bombard us with the fact that people who do not have good looks might find it difficult to find romantic partners. Another method is to employ well-known stars or athletes to promote their products. Lin Chih-lin, Taiwan's top supermodel, makes a lot of money by promoting products. Advertisers want to tell us that, if we buy and use their products, we will become as beautiful as Miss Lin. They also use pseudoscience to mislead consumers. A water filter advertiser will conduct a seemingly scientific experiment to show us that the tap water we drink every day is dirty. In fact, the way they conduct their experiment is questionable.

廣告商用了許多方法來說服我們買他們的產品。最常見的方法就是利用我們會擔心不健康或沒吸引力的心理。一名藥品廣告商不停地提醒我們在台灣有很大比例的人已經感染了肝炎，而肝炎可能發展成肝癌，肝癌是台灣最主要死亡的原因之一。同樣地，化妝品廣告商會不斷告訴我們長得不好看可能很難找到情侶。另一個方法是雇用知名的明星或運動家來促銷他們的產品。林志玲，台灣第一名模，靠著促銷產品賺了不少錢。廣告商想要告訴我們，如果我們買他們的產品，使用後我們將變得跟林小姐一樣美麗。他們也會使用假科學來誤導顧客。濾水器的廣告商做一個表面上像是科學的實驗，顯示我們每天喝的自來水是骯髒的。事實上，他們做實驗的方法是可疑的。

Unit 14 英文作文 (二)─文章

✎ 練習一

《Answers》 --

The Introductory Paragraph ：Enjoying good personal relations guarantees us success in life.

Supporting Paragraph₁ ：The first way to have good personal relations is to have good looks.

Supporting Paragraph₂ ：The second way is to be eager to share with others.

Supporting Paragraph₃ ：The third way is to never get involved in a conflict and just sit on the fence.

Supporting Paragraph₄ ：The fourth way is to say words that are music to the ears of others.

The Concluding Paragraph ：These four methods will help us succeed in life.

在生活中，成功不是那麼容易的。當然，它需要努力工作。我們必須付出努力來改善我們的工作技能，還有需要優秀的才能。我們也需要依靠運氣來擁有機會，實現我們的才能。但為了獲得成功，與別人有友善的關係也是很重要的。我們應該跟別人做朋友，好好地跟他們相處。他們可能有助於我們找到機會，來實現我們的才能跟夢想。一個著名的人在他人生往上爬時，也許會感到孤獨，但一個成功的人是快樂的，很受歡迎的。

但是我們要如何改善人際關係呢？首先，有個好看的外貌是有利的。如果我們不是一出生就漂亮的話，那我們應該要打扮，還有化妝，讓我們可以吸引他人的注意。

第二點，我們應該要熱切地跟別人分享。有時候我們可以請別人吃大餐，其他時候我們可以送他們禮物。最重要的是，我們要確定他們之中的每個人都覺得自己已經得到最好的那份。

第三點，我們應該持抱中性的態度，不偏袒某一邊。當兩邊爭論時，牽扯在爭論內是危險的。聰明的人應該讓兩邊中的任何一邊都相信自己是站在他們那邊的。

最後，我們應該要說悅耳的話。常說「你看起來很好」或「你做得很棒」對我們是有好處的。即使我們討厭聽特定的人說話，也應該擺出最好的面孔，在他結束說話後，說「這真是好主意！」。有時說出坦白的事實只會增加我們的敵人。

改善人與人之間的關係，也許不能幫助我們贏得名聲，但它將領導我們在生活中獲得成功——也許能得到更好的工作、賺額外的錢，或者和大人物交往。這四種方法幫助我們贏得別人的心，爬上成功的梯子。

大綱

開始段落：享受良好的人際關係保證我們在生活中成功。

發展段落 1：擁有好的人際關係的第一個方法是有好的外貌。

發展段落 2：第二個方法是熱切地跟別人分享。

發展段落 3：第三個方法是從不牽扯衝突，保持中立。

發展段落 4：第四個方法是說好聽的話。

總結段落：這四個方法將幫助我們在生活中成功。

✎ 練習三

《Answer》

Last summer after I graduated from junior high school, I went into a bakery and asked the shopkeeper whether she needed a sales clerk. To my delight, she was willing to offer me a job. I was required to work eight hours a day, from 7 am to 3 pm. I was very excited the first time I was behind the counter. But then I felt embarrassed and discouraged. For example, I rang up a bill to $78 by mistake when the bill should have been only $58. For this I was scolded by the customer. Then I was at a loss what to say when another customer asked me what ingredients were used to make the bread. One day a foreigner asked me how much a sandwich cost, and I was dumbfounded. I couldn't get myself to utter one word of English at all.

I have learned a lot from this working experience. First, I have to be very familiar with every product if I want to sell it to my customers successfully. Second, I have to improve my English. Third, I have learned the value of money and that it is hard to earn. But most importantly, I must learn how to deal with embarrassing situations.

　　去年夏天我從國中畢業後，就去一家麵包店，問老闆是否需要一個銷售員。令我開心的是，她願意給我工作。我一天要做八小時，從早上七點到下午三點。我非常興奮第一次能在櫃檯後面，但接著我感到尷尬和沮喪。舉例來說，當帳單只有五十八元時，我誤把帳單記錄成七十八元。因為這樣，我被顧客責罵。還有，顧客問我這個麵包是用什麼材料做成的，我常不知道要說什麼。有一天一個外國人問我一個三明治多少錢，我嚇呆了，連一句英文都說不出來。

　　從這次的工作經驗，我學到許多。首先，如果我想要成功地賣東西給顧客，我必須非常熟悉每種產品。第二點，我必須改善我的英語。第三，我已經了解錢的重要，賺錢是辛苦的。但最重要的是，我必須學習如何處理尷尬的情況。

全真模擬試題篇

全民英檢閱讀能力測驗

《Answers》

第一部分

1. D	2. B	3. D	4. B	5. A	6. C	7. D	8. D	9. D	10. A
11. D	12. B	13. D	14. A	15. D					

第二部分

16. B	17. D	18. A	19. C	20. C	21. A	22. D	23. B	24. C	25. B

第三部分

26. B	27. A	28. D	29. C	30. D	31. A	32. C	33. B	34. B	35. C
36. D	37. A	38. C	39. B	40. D					

第一部分 詞彙和結構

1. 當你接受邀請吃飯，務必準時，遲到是不禮貌的。

   A. 誠實的　　　　　B. 忠實的　　　　　C. 務實的　　　　　D. 準時的

2. 讓我挫折的是，我的學生花了很少時間唸書。這就是我想要退休的原因。

   A. 興奮　　　　　　B. 挫折　　　　　　C. 害怕　　　　　　D. 尷尬

3. 有一塊岩石擋在路中央，我下車把那個障礙物除掉。

   A. 容器　　　　　　B. 水泥　　　　　　C. 墳墓　　　　　　D. 障礙物

4. 生命是從哪裡開始的仍是一個謎。對於這個問題，沒有人可以給一個明確的答案。那也就是說，我們對它仍是不了解。

   A 傳說　　　　　　B. 謎　　　　　　　C. 傳統　　　　　　D. 謠言

5. 這五十州構成了美國，而共有一個聯邦政府。

   A. 構成　　　　　　B. 代表　　　　　　C. 擁有　　　　　　D. 統治

6. 中斷一份友誼比培養它要來得容易。當你跟某人吵架後,很難去修補它。

   A. 開始　　　　　　B. 沉浸　　　　　　C. 中斷　　　　　　D. 增進

7. 生意正在好轉,工廠已經開始雇用新的工人來生產。

   A. 解雇　　　　　　B. 忽視　　　　　　C. 打電話　　　　　D. 雇用

8. 山姆 210 公分高,在他同學的頭上,事實他在任何群眾中都是很突出的。

   A. 撤退　　　　　　B. 高興起來　　　　C. 化妝　　　　　　D. 突出

9. 我這幾天非常忙碌,要在禮拜三拜訪你是不可能的。

   A. 不合季節　　　　B. 不合流行　　　　C. 不平常的　　　　D. 不可能的

10. 這禮拜我已經感到有些不舒服,我恐怕必須去看醫生了。

    A. 不舒服　　　　　　　　　　　　　B. 不能發揮我的本領
    C. 困惑　　　　　　　　　　　　　　D. 落伍的

11. 你能想像嗎!明天的這個時候,我正飛回家。事實上,我甚至覺得現在就在飛機上了。

    A. 已經飛　　　　　B. 正在飛　　　　　C. 將飛　　　　　　D. 將正在飛

12. 幸運地,我們發現了一間寺廟,在那裡躲避。否則,我們早就因為突然的豪雨而淋濕了。

    A. 可能變得　　　　B. 可能早就變得　　C. 寧願變得　　　　D. 早該變得

13. 她的英語說得很好。如果你沒看著她說話,很可能會誤以為是美國人。

    A. 說話　　　　　　B. 說話　　　　　　C. 說話　　　　　　D. 說話

14. 他七十歲了,但大部分人猜想他如果健康允許,也會在 2008 年尋求連任。

    A. 允許　　　　　　B. 允許　　　　　　C. 允許　　　　　　D. 允許

15. 當我聽音樂時,我常戴著耳機,連接到我的 CD 唱機。

    (選項無法翻譯。)

第二部分 段落填空

Questions 16-20

　　一位背著同學的學生不小心從樓梯摔倒。不幸地，這個跌倒害死了他的同學——一位罹患先天性成骨不全症的同學。至於這個學生，他因疏忽而被控告，必須付超過三百萬元的賠償金。

　　這個判決引起巨大的民眾抗議。大部分的人質疑法官的道德判斷力。他們不了解為何一個願意幫助殘障人士的人要受處罰。此外，他們擔心這樣的判決會有不好的影響。從現在開始，當人們提供某人幫助時，他們可能會三思。

　　事實上，這個影響已經產生了。最近，一名六十歲的老師要求一名學生的父母接受一份文件，上面說明若有任何意外發生在他們的小孩身上，他們自己將負起責任。這名小孩有弱視，眼睛的特徵是視力減低，即使戴上眼鏡也不能矯正。另一個例子，是在運動場上有一個人因心臟病而倒下，當時有超過一百人旁觀，沒有人願意去協助他。明顯地，這個判決已經讓同情心死亡了。

16. A. 謀殺　　　　　B. 忽視　　　　　C. 欺騙　　　　　D. 賭博

17. A. 政治的　　　　B. 臨床的　　　　C. 藝術的　　　　D. 道德的

18. A. 不好的　　　　B. 有益的　　　　C. 重要的　　　　D. 可能的

19. A. 可能接受　　　B. 必須接受　　　C. 接受　　　　　D. 接受過

20. A. 向上來　　　　B. 俯視　　　　　C. 旁觀　　　　　D. 往內看

Questions 21-25

　　賺錢要努力工作，但花錢卻一點也不困難。當然，如果你想要過好的生活，你需要花錢在特定的事物上，例如付錢吃晚餐。在週末，你也許沒事做，可能感到無聊，所以你決定去看個電影。有時候，當窮小孩伸出他的手要求施捨時，你會伸手去給一些硬幣。跟你親密的親戚，譬如說你的表兄弟之類的，可能會跑來找你，說他正欠錢用。雖然你知道他可能不會還你，你還是借他一些錢。接著，你的老婆會跟你爭論在你父親生日時，你應該買什麼送他。你想要給他一件襯衫，但你老婆認為領帶可能比較適合。最後，你發現沒剩什麼錢來修理車子。然後你了解到你沒有好好管理你的錢。更糟的是，你沒有每個月留下任何錢給將來使用。

21. A. 無聊的   B. 驚訝的   C. 羞愧的   D. 挫折的

22. A. 帳單   B. 支票   C. 玩具   D. 硬幣

23. A. 如果   B. 雖然   C. 因為   D. 在...之後

24. A. 即使如此   B. 此外   C. 最後   D. 早先

25. A. 賺   B. 管理   C. 存   D. 投資

第三部分 閱讀理解

Questions 26-29

　　女人的童貞一直是爭議的目題。最近這個話題在女人中再度成為討論的焦點，有一名 38 歲的女人在醫療檢查時，處女膜被破壞了，她要求國泰綜合醫院賠償五百萬元。

　　處女膜是一片薄膜，部分地遮蓋住陰道的入口（或者說是在女人外部性器官間的通路）。處女膜未破表示女人尚未有性經驗。傳統上，一個女人的童貞是高度重要的，所以在一些女人之中處女膜手術很常見。據說，有些妓女會動這樣的手術來欺騙客人。再者，隨著台灣男子和外國女人的異國通婚愈來愈多，配偶仲介機構為保證外籍新娘的童真，如果需要的話，會重建他們的處女膜。

　　女權激進份子悲痛女人的處女膜被商業化。他們也批評男人很虛偽，他們有很多伴侶，卻要求他們的新娘是處女。對於這件案例，女權激進份子認為醫生該負責向那女人道歉，為了造成她不舒服，而不是為了弄破那處女膜。

26. 這段指出如果妓女重建他們的處女膜，_____。

     A. 他們的顧客將免於性病傳染

     B. 他們的顧客將願意付更高的價錢

     C. 警察不會逮捕他們

     D. 他們將看起來更有吸引力

27. 這段暗示 _____。

     A. 事實上有些外籍新娘不是處女

     B. 事實上有些外籍新娘不是單身

     C. 配偶仲介機構賺很多錢

     D. 台灣男子在自己國家找不到處女

28. 從 ＿＿＿＿＿＿＿＿＿ 觀點來看，女性主義者認為醫生有錯。

　　A. 教育的

　　B. 商業的

　　C. 性別主義者

　　D. 醫學的

29. 女權主義者批評男人虛偽是因為 ＿＿＿＿＿＿＿＿＿ 。

　　A. 他們對女人嚴厲

　　B. 他們是性無知

　　C. 他們有雙重標準

　　D. 他們表示強烈的性渴望

Questions 30-33

　　前國民黨主席連戰去中國旅行時，中國領導者答應要送一對熊貓給台灣當禮物。明顯地，這種有毛的生物被中國用來當宣傳策略。更有趣的是，他們也符合了國民黨的政治目的。連戰最近明確表示他希望這一對熊貓送來時能先在台中居住。當地媒體猜測這樣做是為了幫助胡志強在年底選舉贏得第二任期。但先把政治放在一邊，台灣政府應該接受中國的提供嗎？有幾個原因，讓許多人說「不」。

　　首先，環保人士擔心找不到適合熊貓居住的地方。熊貓正面臨絕種，因為牠們並不適合不同的環境，牠們只吃箭竹。此外，他們不會很快速地生產，大部分的雌熊貓一年只生一或兩隻小熊貓。飼養熊貓是困難的，尤其是在動物園裡。環境學家認為飼養熊貓最好的地方就是在牠們原生的環境。

　　第二點是，衛生官員指出可能會有傳染疾病，在中國常爆發流行病，像四川省豬隻的鏈球菌和廣東省的禽流感。幾年前，SARS 的爆發也令整個亞洲陷入恐慌。它害死了人類，也破壞了經濟。一隻生病熊貓的危險性並不少於一隻生病的鳥或豬。

　　最後，有些批評者警告要養一對熊貓需要花上龐大的費用。而且台灣每年為了動物要付給中國三十億美元。當人們正為經濟蕭條生活難過時，花大錢養這些動物是不智的。

30. 根據環境學家的說法，有幾個原因顯示熊貓很難飼養。下列哪一個不是其中之一？

 A. 熊貓適應不好

 B. 熊貓不會生很多小孩

 C. 熊貓很挑食物

 D. 熊貓容易生病

31. 中國的 ＿＿＿＿＿＿＿＿ 是台灣人的另一個擔憂。

 A. 傳染病

 B. 犯罪

 C. 安全

 D. 腐化

32. 這段暗示 ＿＿＿＿＿＿＿＿ 。

 A. 中國送台灣熊貓是一種友好的表示

 B. 台中是熊貓最好的居住地

 C. 飼養熊貓對國家財政可能是一種負擔

 D. 飼養熊貓是危險的

33. 這段暗示，中國送給台灣熊貓，以及討論哪裡適合熊貓居住是有 ＿＿＿＿＿＿＿＿

 動機的。

 A. 經濟

 B. 政治

 C. 種族

 D. 環境

Questions 34-36

　　在澎湖外島開設賭場有幾個好的理由。好處之一就是將產生的收入留給地方政府。許多年來，澎湖的地方政府一直缺乏錢去改善公共建設。一間賭場像一塊磁鐵──從這個國家其餘地區來的人會聚集在這島上花費，企業家會大大地投資飯店和休閒設施。因此，地方政府稅收將快速增加。其他的好處是，賭場將製造許多工作給當地人。澎湖的失業比率最近已經上升了 2%，年輕人都被迫離開家鄉，試著在台灣找工作。如果賭場能在澎湖開設，將產生數千個工作給當地人，美國的印地安保留區就是一個見證。

34. 作者是以 _____ 觀點贊成開設賭場。

　　A. 政治的

　　B. 經濟的

　　C. 環境的

　　D. 娛樂的

35. 這段暗示 _____ 。

　　A. 因為開設賭場製造業將起飛

　　B. 在美國的印地安人變富有是因為他們喜歡賭博

　　C. 澎湖的人口逐漸減少

　　D. 當地生意人會輸給台灣來的生意人

36. 開設賭場有許多好的理由，下列哪一個不是其中之一呢？

　　A. 會產生許多工作

　　B. 道路跟公共建設將改善

　　C. 公共財庫將增加

　　D. 當地人將變得更有教養

Questions 37-40

　　有些立法者建議允許在澎湖設立賭場，因為它將提供額外的收入給當地政府。然而，許多當地人已經表達嚴重的異議。最嚴重的問題就是犯罪。隨著賭博，有組織的犯罪也會到來，幫派想控制賭場是常見的。成群的暴力將接踵而來。更重要的是，性產業將興盛。人們來到這裡，不只是為了賭博，還要玩女人。為了達到需求，幫派份子將綁架無辜的女人，強迫他們當娼妓。接著，愛滋病將會猖獗。看看泰國的性產業，在那裡許多人，不論男女都感染愛滋病，結果許多小孩變成孤兒。最後但並非最不重要的是，傳統的價值觀將被毀壞。我們告訴我們的小孩，賭博是萬惡根源，但現在我們正要擁抱它、招徠它，好像這是唯一恢復經濟的方法。總結來說，允許在澎湖設立賭場就等於是做浮士德的交易。

37. 成群的暴力將爆發是因為 _____ 。

    A. 幫派一定會彼此競爭賭場控制權

    B. 警察不被允許取締賭場

    C. 幫派組織不良

    D. 賭徒紀律不好

38. 對這段的描述，下列哪一個是不對的？

    A. 幫派份子將從事非法買賣婦女

    B. 許多家庭會被破壞

    C. 許多娼妓會從泰國來

    D. 賭博跟性是密切的

39. 作者擔心小孩將對傳統價值觀感到 _____ 。

    A. 好奇的

    B. 困惑的

    C. 無知的

    D. 確定的

40. 浮士德的交易是指 _____ 。

    A. 將兩件事情顛倒做

    B. 為了成功，完全依賴一件事

    C. 企圖做超過自己能力所能負擔的

    D. 為了一件好的事，交換許多不好的事

全民英檢寫作能力測驗

一、中譯英（參考）

《Answer》

No sooner had John heard the telephone ringing, he rushed to answer it. Sadly, he fell down the stairs and sprained his ankle. If he had walked slowly, he would not have had the accident. It has been three days since he was taken to the hospital. He likes playing basketball, but now he can only lie in bed and watch TV.

二、英文作文

《參考答案》

If I Had Only Three Days To Live

If I had only three days to live and if I were fortunate enough to remain conscious and able to go around, I would go to work as usual. Just as a soldier dies a glorious death in the battle field, so a worker is proud to work until the last day of his life. I would contribute as many of my ideas as possible within the three days. On the last day, I would bid farewell to each of my colleagues, friends or foes alike.

I like to read, so I have bought a lot of books, many of which are great works. They are of great value to learners. Lest they should be reduced to ashes, I would send my books to the local library. Then I would make a list of my property. I would gather my family members and tell them to make the best use of the money.

Finally I would spend the three days revisiting my home town and the schools that I have ever attended. I would call on my brothers and sisters individually. I would arrange a family reunion. After that, I would hold an incense stick in front of my ancestors' memorial tablet. I would worship and pray, waiting for my death.

假如我還有三天可活

　　假如我還有三天可活而如果我還很清醒而且又能走動，我將跟往常一樣去工作。軍人光榮戰死殺場，工人以工作至死為榮。我將盡我所能在這三天獻出我所能。最後一天我將向每個同事一一告別，不管他們以前是我的好友或是冤家。

　　我喜歡讀書，因此買了很多書，其中很多是偉大的名著。對學習者有很大的價值。惟恐這些書付之一炬，我將把它們送給當地圖書館。然後我將把我的財產列表。我將召集家人要他們善用這些錢。

　　最後我將花這三天時間重訪家鄉和以前就讀的學校。我將一一拜訪我兄弟姊妹。我將安排家庭團聚。之後我將拿柱香在我祖先紀念牌位，膜拜禱告，等待死神。

附錄 **A** ：全民英檢中級答案紙範本

【聽力 & 閱讀能力測驗】

03-25-00555
准考證號碼

考生姓名：＿＿＿＿＿＿＿＿

注意事項：

1. 限用 2B 鉛筆作答，否則不予計分。

2. 劃記要粗黑、清晰、不可出格，擦拭要清潔，若劃記過輕或污損不清，不爲機器所接受，考生自行負責。

3. 劃記範例：

| 正確● | 錯誤⊘⊗●◐◑⦿ |

聽 力 測 驗		閱 讀 能 力 測 驗	
1 Ⓐ Ⓑ Ⓒ Ⓓ	26 Ⓐ Ⓑ Ⓒ Ⓓ	1 Ⓐ Ⓑ Ⓒ Ⓓ	26 Ⓐ Ⓑ Ⓒ Ⓓ
2 Ⓐ Ⓑ Ⓒ Ⓓ	27 Ⓐ Ⓑ Ⓒ Ⓓ	2 Ⓐ Ⓑ Ⓒ Ⓓ	27 Ⓐ Ⓑ Ⓒ Ⓓ
3 Ⓐ Ⓑ Ⓒ Ⓓ	28 Ⓐ Ⓑ Ⓒ Ⓓ	3 Ⓐ Ⓑ Ⓒ Ⓓ	28 Ⓐ Ⓑ Ⓒ Ⓓ
4 Ⓐ Ⓑ Ⓒ Ⓓ	29 Ⓐ Ⓑ Ⓒ Ⓓ	4 Ⓐ Ⓑ Ⓒ Ⓓ	29 Ⓐ Ⓑ Ⓒ Ⓓ
5 Ⓐ Ⓑ Ⓒ Ⓓ	30 Ⓐ Ⓑ Ⓒ Ⓓ	5 Ⓐ Ⓑ Ⓒ Ⓓ	30 Ⓐ Ⓑ Ⓒ Ⓓ
6 Ⓐ Ⓑ Ⓒ Ⓓ	31 Ⓐ Ⓑ Ⓒ Ⓓ	6 Ⓐ Ⓑ Ⓒ Ⓓ	31 Ⓐ Ⓑ Ⓒ Ⓓ
7 Ⓐ Ⓑ Ⓒ Ⓓ	32 Ⓐ Ⓑ Ⓒ Ⓓ	7 Ⓐ Ⓑ Ⓒ Ⓓ	32 Ⓐ Ⓑ Ⓒ Ⓓ
8 Ⓐ Ⓑ Ⓒ Ⓓ	33 Ⓐ Ⓑ Ⓒ Ⓓ	8 Ⓐ Ⓑ Ⓒ Ⓓ	33 Ⓐ Ⓑ Ⓒ Ⓓ
9 Ⓐ Ⓑ Ⓒ Ⓓ	34 Ⓐ Ⓑ Ⓒ Ⓓ	9 Ⓐ Ⓑ Ⓒ Ⓓ	34 Ⓐ Ⓑ Ⓒ Ⓓ
10 Ⓐ Ⓑ Ⓒ Ⓓ	35 Ⓐ Ⓑ Ⓒ Ⓓ	10 Ⓐ Ⓑ Ⓒ Ⓓ	35 Ⓐ Ⓑ Ⓒ Ⓓ
11 Ⓐ Ⓑ Ⓒ Ⓓ	36 Ⓐ Ⓑ Ⓒ Ⓓ	11 Ⓐ Ⓑ Ⓒ Ⓓ	36 Ⓐ Ⓑ Ⓒ Ⓓ
12 Ⓐ Ⓑ Ⓒ Ⓓ	37 Ⓐ Ⓑ Ⓒ Ⓓ	12 Ⓐ Ⓑ Ⓒ Ⓓ	37 Ⓐ Ⓑ Ⓒ Ⓓ
13 Ⓐ Ⓑ Ⓒ Ⓓ	38 Ⓐ Ⓑ Ⓒ Ⓓ	13 Ⓐ Ⓑ Ⓒ Ⓓ	38 Ⓐ Ⓑ Ⓒ Ⓓ
14 Ⓐ Ⓑ Ⓒ Ⓓ	39 Ⓐ Ⓑ Ⓒ Ⓓ	14 Ⓐ Ⓑ Ⓒ Ⓓ	39 Ⓐ Ⓑ Ⓒ Ⓓ
15 Ⓐ Ⓑ Ⓒ Ⓓ	40 Ⓐ Ⓑ Ⓒ Ⓓ	15 Ⓐ Ⓑ Ⓒ Ⓓ	40 Ⓐ Ⓑ Ⓒ Ⓓ
16 Ⓐ Ⓑ Ⓒ Ⓓ	41 Ⓐ Ⓑ Ⓒ Ⓓ	16 Ⓐ Ⓑ Ⓒ Ⓓ	
17 Ⓐ Ⓑ Ⓒ Ⓓ	42 Ⓐ Ⓑ Ⓒ Ⓓ	17 Ⓐ Ⓑ Ⓒ Ⓓ	
18 Ⓐ Ⓑ Ⓒ Ⓓ	43 Ⓐ Ⓑ Ⓒ Ⓓ	18 Ⓐ Ⓑ Ⓒ Ⓓ	
19 Ⓐ Ⓑ Ⓒ Ⓓ	44 Ⓐ Ⓑ Ⓒ Ⓓ	19 Ⓐ Ⓑ Ⓒ Ⓓ	
20 Ⓐ Ⓑ Ⓒ Ⓓ	45 Ⓐ Ⓑ Ⓒ Ⓓ	20 Ⓐ Ⓑ Ⓒ Ⓓ	
21 Ⓐ Ⓑ Ⓒ Ⓓ		21 Ⓐ Ⓑ Ⓒ Ⓓ	
22 Ⓐ Ⓑ Ⓒ Ⓓ		22 Ⓐ Ⓑ Ⓒ Ⓓ	
23 Ⓐ Ⓑ Ⓒ Ⓓ		23 Ⓐ Ⓑ Ⓒ Ⓓ	
24 Ⓐ Ⓑ Ⓒ Ⓓ		24 Ⓐ Ⓑ Ⓒ Ⓓ	
25 Ⓐ Ⓑ Ⓒ Ⓓ		25 Ⓐ Ⓑ Ⓒ Ⓓ	

註：請影印使用。

【寫作能力測驗】

座位號碼：＿＿＿＿＿＿

第一部分請由本頁第 1 行開始作答，請勿隔行書寫。第二部分請翻至第 2 頁作答。

5

10

15

20

第二部分請由本頁第 1 行開始作答，請勿隔行書寫。

5

10

15

20

25

30

35

40

45

50

55

60

65

70

75

國家圖書館出版品預行編目資料

全民英檢中級教室：閱讀&寫作 ＝ GEPT Classroom–
Reading & Writing (Intermediate) / 陳明華著. --初
版. -- 臺北市：臺灣培生教育, 2005〔民 94〕
　　面 ； 公分

ISBN 986-154-208-6 (平裝).

1. 英國語言 – 問題集

805.189　　　　　　　　　　　94017817

全民英檢中級教室—閱讀**&**寫作
GEPT Classroom—Reading & Writing (Intermediate)

編　　　　著	陳明華
發　行　人	洪欽鎮
主　　　編	李佩玲
責 任 編 輯	陳慧莉
協 力 編 輯	沈映伶
封 面 設 計	黃聖文
版 型 設 計	李青滿
美 編 印 務	楊雯如
行 銷 企 畫	朱世昌、劉珈利
發行所／出版者	台灣培生教育出版股份有限公司
	劃撥帳號／19645981　　戶名／台灣培生教育出版股份有限公司
	地址／台北市重慶南路一段 147 號 5 樓
	電話／02-2370-8168　　傳真／02-2370-8169
	網址／http://www.PearsonEd.com.tw
	E-mail／reader@PearsonEd.com.tw
香 港 總 經 銷	培生教育出版亞洲股份有限公司
	地址／香港鰂魚涌英皇道 979 號(太古坊康和大廈 2 樓)
	電話／(852)3181-0000　　傳真／(852)2564-0955
	E-mail／msip@PearsonEd.com.hk
台 灣 總 經 銷	創智文化有限公司
	地址／台北縣 235 中和市橋和路 110 號 2 樓
	電話／02-2242-1566　　傳真／02-2242-2922
學 校 訂 書 專 線	02-2370-8168 轉 695
版　　　次	2005 年 11 月初版一刷
書　　　號	TT029
I　S　B　N	986-154-208-6
定　　　價	新台幣 400 元

版權所有・翻印必究

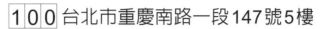

100 台北市重慶南路一段147號5樓

台灣培生教育出版股份有限公司　收
Pearson Education Taiwan Ltd.

書號：TT029

書名： 全民英檢中級教室─閱讀&寫作

回函參加抽獎喔！
（詳情請見下頁！）

台灣培生教育出版股份有限公司

★資料請填寫完整，才可參加抽獎哦！

讀者資料

姓名：＿＿＿＿＿＿＿＿＿＿＿＿ 性別：＿＿＿＿ 出生年月日：＿＿＿＿＿＿＿＿＿．

電話：(O)＿＿＿＿＿＿＿ (H)＿＿＿＿＿＿＿ (Mo)＿＿＿＿＿＿＿＿．

傳真：(O)＿＿＿＿＿＿＿ (H)＿＿＿＿＿＿＿．

E-mail：＿＿＿＿＿＿＿＿＿＿＿＿＿＿＿＿＿＿＿＿＿＿＿＿＿．

地址：＿＿＿＿＿＿＿＿＿＿＿＿＿＿＿＿＿＿＿＿＿＿＿＿＿＿．

教育程度：

□國小 □國中 □高中 □大專 □大學以上

職業：

1.學生 □

2.教職 □教師 □教務人員 □班主任 □經營者 □其他：＿＿＿＿＿＿

　任職單位：□學校 □補教機構 □其他：＿＿＿＿＿＿

　教學經歷：□幼兒英語 □兒童英語 □國小英語 □國中英語 □高中英語
　　　　　　□成人英語

3.社會人士 □工 □商 □資訊 □服務 □軍警公職 □出版媒體 □其他＿＿＿＿．

從何處得知本書：

□逛書店 □報章雜誌 □廣播電視 □親友介紹 □書訊 □廣告函 □其他＿＿＿＿．

對我們的建議：

＿＿＿＿＿＿＿＿＿＿＿＿＿＿＿＿＿＿＿＿＿＿＿＿＿＿＿＿＿＿＿＿＿

＿＿＿＿＿＿＿＿＿＿＿＿＿＿＿＿＿＿＿＿＿＿＿＿＿＿＿＿＿＿＿＿＿

＿＿＿＿＿＿＿＿＿＿＿＿＿＿＿＿＿＿＿＿＿＿＿＿＿＿＿＿＿＿＿＿＿

＿＿＿＿＿＿＿＿＿＿＿＿＿＿＿＿＿＿＿＿＿＿＿＿＿＿＿＿＿＿＿＿＿

感謝您的回函，我們每個月將抽出幸運讀者，致贈精美禮物，得獎名單可至本公司網站查詢。

讀者服務專線：02-2370-8168#695

http://www.PearsonEd.com.tw　　E-mail:reader@PearsonEd.com.tw